pepper
in the
BLOOD

pepper
in the
BLOOD

By Brian G. Dyson

Chatham International Corporation
Atlanta, Georgia 30305

Cover Design: House Design and Graphics, Beverly Hills, CA
Cover Photograph: House Design and Graphics, Beverly Hills, CA
Digital Prepress and Layout: Penstroke Graphics, Atlanta, GA
Project Consultant: R. Bemis Publishing, Ltd., Atlanta, GA
Copyediting: Phyllis Mueller, Atlanta, GA

ISBN: 0-9652958-3-4
Library of Congress Catalogue: CIP

Printed in the United States of America
By TechniGraphics, Atlanta, GA

Chatham International Corporation
3060 Peachtree Road, NW
Atlanta, Georgia 30305

To Susana, Tania and Penny:
we were all in the race together.

Chapter One

This part of the day was hers and hers alone, and she reveled in having the afternoon to herself. Karie Johnson ran up the lone rise on the road out of Goodland that went west, like a shot arrow, across the wheatfields of Kansas to the Colorado border. She often wondered what it would be like to just keep running, to follow that road west as far as it went. *Someday. It was just a matter of time.*

She came up to The Peak, and from here her course cut right and down along the fence, through the Badlands, where clumps of sagebrush lurked in ambush. Then she skirted Big Smoky Lake, fringed with willows, where the mist hung like puffs of breath in the cold. Karie couldn't remember when she'd come to give each section of the course the names she did. They just came to her as she ran. At the top she did an easy circle to take in the farmland resting under a quilt of fresh snow: a patchwork of farms and trees, held together by the stitching of fence lines.

It's a smudgy day, she thought as she was chased down a gully by an icy blast of wind. The day was sullen and undecided, not sure whether it had done enough to remind everyone that it was still February. Karie wore her baby blue ski mask with a hole cut in it for her ponytail because Coach Gertz said the cold air would zap your bronchial tubes. Tiny icicles formed on the rough wool as her breath came out in small, rhythmic puffs. Beads of sweat trickled from her training bra and she took off the socks that covered her mittens. Coming up on mile two, she felt the smooth flow of motion take over, as if her body were a big wheel rolling down the path of its own accord.

It had snowed again this morning. Over to the left her dog Bo, his black tail stiff as a periscope, scurried through a deep drift that muffled the jingle of his tags. Shortening her stride, she crunched through the deep snow of the Meadowlands. It felt like running over a field of meringues. The sound, captured by the frozen silence, was as if her feet were stirring up all the old, sleepy secrets the snow had hidden, in a language only she could understand.

Karie wondered if the reverberating crunch would continue if she stopped running.

She climbed the fence into the Black Forest and found the path that snaked through the woods to old Mrs. Kratohvil's place off from the main road. At Mrs. K's mailbox, she picked up the Sunday paper and ran up the lane to drop it on the porch—it added a half mile at least. Today, she had smelled the woodsmoke from afar, and she dodged back around the house and brought an armload of birch logs to the front steps. There she picked up the large cookie—in summer it was a cup of lemonade—just as Mrs. K opened the door. Karie shouted, "Hi," and waved over her shoulder as she raced Bo back to the road.

Karie checked her watch. She was making good time. She kept running, but dropped her arms by her sides to loosen up her shoulders. "Get the monkey off your back," Coach Gertz always said as he came up beside her on the track at school. She felt strong and relaxed by now, and the giddiness she had felt at the beginning of her run was giving way to a state that Karie called the zone. Her body took over and her mind was set free. It was the best thing in the world.

Before she started running, a typical Sunday meant charging upstairs to change into an old blue workshirt of Dad's and then heading out back to the workshop to help him paint or hammer or whatever until Mom called them in for supper. Dad would explain exactly how he did things and why. He was fond of saying, "Never do anything halfway. If you're going to do it—do it right." She felt a twinge of guilt at the thought of Dad in the workshop by himself.

As Karie watched her shadow traveling alongside her in the glassy winter light, she caught sight of a flash of purple in the mondo grass by the stream, and she ran down to have a look. Bo circled back toward her, big doggy breaths coming out his snout in white clouds. In summer he would leap into the stream to cool off, but today he just snuffled along its edges while Karie bent down to get a better look at the patch of purple crocuses pushing through the snow. *Say goodbye to winter*, she thought.

Now she shifted to cruise control and settled into the long stretch back from the north. Maybe this is what the coach meant by perpetual motion. With each new stride, she pulled her trailing leg forward. Her thighs flexed as her feet seemed to bounce off the ground. If she closed her eyes, she could just make out strains of the classical music her oldest sister Bonnie listened to late at night with the lights out. Flutes. Piano. Violins. Karie cruised on high, her rhythm fluid and rounded, as the telephone poles flowed toward her and clicked by.

She spread her arms to the wind that had come all the way from Canada to waft her home. *How can I make Mom and Dad see that I know what I'm doing?* She had always figured her parents would understand, but now she wasn't quite sure. She turned 13 last week, and there were things stirring inside her that made her want to cut loose. Springtime meant new beginnings, and she was ready. She felt herself slowing, then circling, and now racing back along the road with Bo chasing after.

Karie came back to the patch of mondo grass and got down on her knees to inspect the crocus blossoms. *They're not afraid of snow either*, she thought. Karie dug out a bit of snow surrounding the plants and, taking off her mittens to get a better grasp, plucked a few of the flowers. She took Mrs. K's cookie out of her front pocket and carefully placed the blossoms there. Then she took off running fast, back towards town. She felt her heart pumping as the speed built inside her...no one was in front...she was in the lead...she could feel nothing but the speed. Her shadow, long and stretched out, flew over the snowy ground. *There I go*, she thought. *I'm on my way.*

On the outskirts of town she bounded around the Jimenezes' trailer doing Indian war whoops and calling, "Rafael, time to wake up."

The trailer door squeaked open and Rafael Jimenez stepped out. Sundays were the only days Karie ever saw him in jeans. Every day except Sunday he wore dress pants, neatly creased all the way down the front. Karie's sister Annie always said he was the best dresser in the whole school. He was tall and skinny, with dark watchful eyes. Though he was in the same grade as Annie, Rafael was more Karie's friend. Karie used to think that Rafael was shy, but when she said so to Dad, he said, "No, Rafael is just focused. It's a good thing to be. Most people aren't." Karie wanted to be focused too, and now every time she saw Rafael, she studied his quiet ways.

Rafael squinted and shielded his eyes from the glare of the low winter sun on the snow. He smiled as he watched Karie prance in place.

"How many miles, Karie?"

"Mucho, mucho," she said pushing the ski mask up and off her face.

"You're not too cold? My mother made soup."

"Thanks, but I told Mom I'd get back before supper."

"Okay, see you around," he called after her.

She ran to a patch of ice that had frozen over a pothole and slid. Stumbling back onto the road, she yelled, "Adios, amigo."

Karie detoured to the track at Goodland High. She climbed the fence, then pulled it loose at the bottom so Bo could scrape under. She stepped out onto the track. It was too slippery for sprints, but she could still summon her vision of high kicking down the final straight at the Olympics, the crowd going wild as she ran right into a huge, billowing Stars and Stripes.

Three more blocks and Karie turned onto Chester Lane. As she eased into a light jog, she felt a warm expanding, almost a floating sensation, as if she were about to lift off. She ran to the front of her house and let out a whoop. As she ran to the back, she could hear Mom call her from the front door.

"Karie, come in out of the cold. Supper's almost on."

"Coming," Karie yelled back.

Karie dropped to the ground on her back and made a snow angel. Taking off her ski mask, she shook the snow from her pony-tail, gave half of Mrs. K's cookie to Bo and ran inside.

"Hey, Mom, I brought you something. Look!"

Karie's mother came into the kitchen from the dining room.

"I was wondering if you'd ever get back."

"I did the Big Loop today." Karie didn't mention stopping by Rafael's. "Here, look what I found by the stream."

Karie carefully pulled the crocuses from her jacket pocket and set them on the kitchen counter. They had fared well, with only tiny bruises on a few petals.

"I thought they'd look good on the table." Karie grabbed the small vase from the end cabinet and began to fill it with water. "I saw two jayhawks when I was heading past Big Smoky Lake..."

"You ran all the way to the pond?"

"Yeah, then I did the track." Karie set the vase on the kitchen table and began to fill it with the flowers.

"Here, honey, let me. I can't believe that you ran so far."

In the bathroom, Karie turned on the shower and undressed while the water warmed up. Using her T-shirt to wipe the fog off the glass, she examined her reflection in the clear patch of mirror. With the ponytail out, her blond hair fell lightly over her face and reached the middle of her back. Karie felt the soft rush of blood coursing through her body. Her red cheeks intensified the clear blue of her eyes. She was glad she'd brought the flowers.

Karie thought again of crossing the finish line. She imagined her parents and her sisters watching and cheering as the tape broke across her chest. Coach Gertz would be there too. Maybe Rafael. As she slowed her winning stride to a walk, she could hear the announcer state her time and name as the U.S. gold medalist. Now as she watched the steam curl off her body, she arched her back and threw up her arms.

Chapter Two

Andy Nagy parked his rented Chevy in the field behind the low-rise bleachers and, hunched over against the cold prairie wind, turned toward the track. He looked over the battered collection of pickups, vans and wagons—welcome to the Sunflower State—and wished he were driving his Porsche 911 Cabriolet so he could park it there with the top down. He rubbed his nose, feeling a pollen allergy coming on, and picked his way through the short grass as if wary of an occasional cow chip. There was a row of school buses with a bunch of kids milling around. That was a sure sign of no locker rooms. There might be some near the gym on the other side of the track, but Andy wouldn't have bet on it. Normally he wouldn't be anywhere near the Wichita Invitational Track Meet or even in Kansas. Mostly he found his talent in the western states, with an occasional side trip to Texas. But he'd had a tip.

He climbed the bleachers to the point above the final curve where he had a diagonal view of the oval. This was where the talent would show. Or chicken out. Andy checked the time schedule. It was past noon. They'd started at 10 o'clock and were now 40 minutes behind. They would never make it on TV. Unzipping a pocket of his Gucci shoulder bag, he took out the hoagie he'd picked up at Alfredo's on the way to LAX. *Bring your own or you'll end up eating prairie dogs.* Andy really wasn't in the market for anything special today, although the Pace Track Club could always use new bodies. *Just cut the weak and injured and bring on the new.* He liked the idea of keeping hopefuls waiting in the wings. The constant threat of a younger, better runner taking their places kept his girls on their toes. Still, Andy's roster was pretty full and if he were looking, it was for something more long-term than a pretty little thing who could scratch his itch and burn the straight in fewer than 11 seconds. Today he was prospecting for something close to natural perfection—raw and untrained maybe—but nothing less than flawless.

The PA system announced the results of the men's 110 meter hurdles and the start of the high jump. Andy chuckled as he picked

7

up his binoculars. Maybe they were trying to make up time, but it was tough on the guys still doing long jump if they were doing the high as well. When you've seen a real meet with the pink tartan track and the white sidings that made it look like a birthday cake and the bright green Bermuda grass and all the teams in their sleek race uniforms, been privy to the flags, music, TV cameras and coaches trying to look calm, heard the hush of the crowd as they see a staggered line drop to the set position—that moment of frozen motion—and the explosion of thrust before the sound of the starter's gun reaches across the field —well then, hey, it's real hard to come watch a bunch of farm kids in the boonies.

From his vantage point, he could see that they had set the last hurdle for the women's 100 meters on the men's mark. Not smart to have to add two meters to your stride. *Cockamamie*, he thought. Andy threw the crumpled up hoagie wrapper on the ground and walked down towards the official. Probably an English teacher or a parent, he thought, wondering why he bothered. Lucky for them he was in a good mood. Normally he'd say something about their entire set-up. The shot was in the infield and discus outside on a field that seemed to Andy freshly plowed under for the event. *Why not have javelin also?* he thought; *that would liven things up.* He grimaced in memory of an apparatchik who had been struck in the back and paralyzed by an errant hammer throw. That had been years back, in Hungary.

Andy Nagy had chosen athletics early in his life in Budapest. It was either that or the Party. He'd given himself entirely to the business of coaching because they expected you to have a more specialized athletic knowledge than medical doctors and chemists. He had delved into the musculoskeletal structure of the body and studied all the experiments in exercise metabolism. There he'd learned about fast-twitch muscle, strands of white angel-hair-like fiber that, depending on the ratio contained within the athlete's body, could send a runner down a track faster than a greyhound bitch in heat. He'd survived the formal classes in biochemistry and had gone on to the Institute for advanced courses in Biomechanics and Psychology. He had even studied with the Israelis on their techniques of Imaging and Target Point physics. There wasn't a coach anywhere at this meet, or any other, who could take an athlete to the limit and beyond the way he could.

Just give me the merchandise, Andy liked to say. Just give me a specimen with 80 percent plus fast-twitch muscle fibers that would fire like matchsticks for a burst of 10 seconds and then, after lift-off, maintain a fast pace for the duration. Andy often wondered why American athletes shouldn't be required to have muscle biopsies, like students took IQ tests and SATs.

Andy watched a tall, leggy brunette warming up. Looks great. Pity, she was jumping the hurdles, not running them. I *could fix it, but she's a slow-twitch princess*, he thought. Not a real sprinter. No way could he handle that.

Andy's girls—the Pace Girls—were real. Brilliant, all of them. Seven out of 10 were All-American or record holders. The Pace Girls had dominated the Outdoor Nationals, winning five times in six years, and when they didn't come in first, they placed third. Andy chuckled remembering how hard he'd been on them the year after they lost first place and how fiercely they attacked the competition the next year. After that win he gave them each a T-shirt with a large "5" and the legend "Your Pace or Mine?"

That's the way Andy coached. *With you and me, girl, the Outdoor Nationals are a piece of cake. But why stop there?* He trained some men, but they were too independent, too much testosterone, too many questions. Go with the girls, the earlier the better. Give them the treatment and then make them really stretch. Dominate. Don't let anyone else mindfuck or get under the tent. We're in this together, you and me. *You want to go all the way? Then trust me. There is no finish line, not until I say so.*

Last week he'd gone to the Playboy Mansion West with two of his Pace Girls. It was a sort of reward after the Oregon races. He told them to dress simple, not much makeup. It had been the usual scene. A few young Hollywood bucks in loafers and khakis, some silver haired suits, a couple of jocks and some women who were neither celebs nor Mrs. celebs—probably husband hunting—who overdressed like it was the Oscars. Everyone wanted to meet him and his girls. Kendra, the sprinter, had skin like burnt sienna. Donna, the All-American blue-eyed honey blond, would go the distance. The two of them—skin glowing, muscles looking so good, so ethereal—they had the whole room at their command. It was as if they were an entirely different species altogether. They could easily beat the crap out of any woman there and most of the men. *Wouldn't that be fun to see?* And all the time they stayed close to Andy. *Hef's got his Hutch, I've got mine.*

At the Institute, he had once been assigned to Professor Metz, who seemed to get off on human sweat. He studied sweat obsessively because he wanted to determine precisely what was being exuded from the body in order to better formulate what needed to be replenished. Perhaps to dignify the project, Professor Metz claimed that smelly sweat was secreted only from old glands that were an atavistic holdover from primitive times, whereas athletic sweat was part of the body's coolant system, a natural and odorless lubricant.

Andy thought the old fart was nuts. But his friend Milos, who was handling field research, considered it a case of serendipity.

"You should see the young beauties we're working with. They come in glistening off the track—ready to eat, like buns just out of the oven," Milos had paused as if savoring the experience. "I'm in charge of collecting the little beads. You should try it sometime. Tastes like absinthe."

Andy's thoughts drifted to his friend Carmen, whose phone call he still hadn't returned. She had been pestering him for help in shooting an exercise video in Spanish and thought that with all the Hollywood types hanging around his girls, he might know where to take such a product. Andy knew where he'd like to take Carmen all right. She was a real hot tamale who loved to dance salsa— maybe Milos had been onto something. Maybe he should take her to Cha Cha Cha. It would be his reward for coming to this cockamamie meet.

Andy watched the 400 meter prelims, but there was not much there. In the men's, the boys were ragged. Andy snorted in disgust. Don't any of these coaches teach the kids to breathe through their stomachs? By the time they hit the final straight, their shoulders were jerking like they were on horseback. In the women's, one girl had good style but she was much too slight for the 400—you need good bone structure to hang all that stuff on.

The Eastern Bloc coaches had been probing the limits of exhaustion for years, experimenting in the "red zone." They'd discovered it's the mind that orders the body to shut down—but if you blitz the mind with endorphins and hormones, the body will just keep going. The Russians had a problem with pole vaulters because the human body resists hanging upside down 20 feet in the air, so they concocted something in the lab. Now just pop this pill. Goodbye, fear of heights. Hello, world record. A Russian coach once told him, "Andrei, you throw a frog into a pan of boiling water...he jumps out. But you put the frog in nice warm water and then you slowly turn the heat up...hah, dinner is served." Andy had seen athletes crumple and fall on the track at the Institute, literally seizing up like an engine that ran out of oil. That's what he called hitting the wall, that's really body over mind. But never in America—not yet anyway.

He moved down from the bleachers to the black asphalt track with grass growing in the cracks. It took a couple of moments for the official to make sure all racers were accounted for, and Andy spotted the Mexican kid he'd heard about, shaking the nerves out of his arms. A stocky redheaded kid with a crew cut began way too fast and then tried to gut it out, but he was football squad material and the Mexican won easily. Even so, anyone could see track wasn't for him, 10K at least. He had a distance runner's stance and build, maybe with a little Tarahumara Indian in the genes. They began to set up the women's 800 meters. This was what Andy had come for.

Karie was in the infield with the others from Goodland High School when Coach Gertz told her to begin stretching. She had not done much in the long jump—a fourth place—but she'd been entered at the last minute. She was still in junior high, and the coach had agreed to let her run the 800 meters. Sometimes he let her be a rabbit in the 1500 meters if Jolene, his precious star, needed a pace-setter. While Karie was stretching, she could hear the starter talking with Coach Gertz.

The starter, an old guy with a beer belly said, "Talk about all hat and no cattle."

Coach Gertz turned to see Andy standing at the start of the final straight in boots, jeans and sports jacket, with dark glasses and a broad-brimmed hat. "Well, fancy that, it's Andy Nagy."

"Andy who?"

"Nagy. Big time coach from L.A. What brings the great Andy to Wichita?" But Coach Gertz thought he knew.

"Maybe he wants some pointers, you know," the starter rubbed his gut with the gun. "I hear they're all screwed up out there."

Karie bent to do her hamstring stretches. As she touched the ground with her palms, she looked through her legs in his direction. He did look kind of cool, really. Maybe they dressed like that in L.A. She was glad she'd ignored her mom and gone back to the bus to change into her silver uniform, which she wore under her warm-ups. Mom said it was too tight on her now.

"Start your warm-ups—no sprints." Coach Gertz sounded a little gruff, but the meet wasn't going well for them.

Karie knew that she would be running against older girls, but that was okay. If she couldn't handle seniors in the 800, then she wasn't going anywhere. Plus it was good to be the kid in the line-up and then to haul them in when they couldn't hang on. The coach was training her to focus, to get into the zone, then run the race they had planned. He had only started her in the 800 meters this season, but she liked the distance because in two-and-a-half minutes you have a lot of stuff going on. She always had enough steam in her to sprint at the end. Coach called it her kick. She had a strong kick, and they had made it part of her race plan. Whatever happened during the race, she would hit the last curve hard.

She took off her warm-ups as Coach Gertz came up. "Remember to keep a few paces off the lead," he said. "Don't get boxed in. Then as early as you can handle it, kick." He put his hands on her shoulders, "Karie, just blow it out, okay?" He had never said that before.

Karie leaned forward in the starting position of Lane 4, her arms hanging loosely at her sides. She felt a familiar expansive feeling, as if she were barely hovering over the track, not standing on it. Though her mind could barely acknowledge the significance of the moment, her body responded by drawing up every bit of strength, letting it build up like pressure in an air gun. The starter called, "Set..." The gun went off, and Karie shot out. Seconds barely passed before she was well into the turn. By the crossover she was already third.

The pace was faster than she expected but well within her range. Coach had told her to make sure the engine was running smoothly and to keep watching the lead. One girl was small and tight, like a fist. The other, on the outside, was rangy and ran with a bounding stride. By the sound of the bell for the final lap she was beginning to feel the urge to let it all out. With each stride, she could feel the power closing in. It was like a white, pulsing light that would grow in intensity until instinct and know-how told her it was time to kick.

After the 500 mark, she closed on the leaders and was watching to see if she might go between them—then, suddenly, the pack came up and she was caught up and being elbowed over to the infield line. Instinctively, she slowed and dropped back until she could jump outside, but now she was 20 meters off the lead. Karie felt the pulsing throb flicker. With a sob of anger, she swung wide and sprinted on the turn of the final 200, knowing she would be outside on both curves. Though frustrated, she knew she would hold the sprint until the light became a blinding flash...would not back off...would handle the pain...would keep her high-step style...would go, go, go!

As the rest of the pack crossed the finish line and slowed, Karie ran over to the long jump pit and then walked, hands on hips, head down. She knew she hadn't quite caught the lead girl. Her frustration turned to disappointment, and she began to cry. Coach Gertz had warned her and she'd let him down.

The coach came up and put his arm around her, "Great, Karie, great."

"I can't believe how mean they were." Tears ran down her cheeks and she sobbed silently as they walked together. "They played dirty. They kicked and pushed and elbowed..."

"But you showed them, didn't you?"

"Yeah." She looked up. "I beat them on the curve." Then she shook her head, "But I didn't win."

"You did for me," he said handing her his handkerchief.

She dried her eyes. At least she still had the relay to run.

Andy stood up, stretched and shouldered his bag. Only the 4 x 400 relays remained and even then he had time before his plane to kick some cowshit around. How big a move should he make on the girl? Maybe it was better to just sniff around. She was young yet, no telling how protective the parents were. Anyway he'd be in L.A. by evening and then it was dinner with the Hollywood man who wanted to do a movie about life on a track team. Very physical and very female, the man had said. *Find out what they want and let 'em have it.* The Olympics were headed for L.A., and all of America would be tuned in.

Andy sucked in his breath and thought for a moment about what *he* really wanted. Top class athletes in the best venues, complete with marquee events, big crowds, and power deals. Hell, it wasn't that much different from the scientists who had preceded him from Europe, dreaming of everything sybaritic America had to offer. But their grubby little accomplishments couldn't hold a candle to Andy and his girls. Talent such as his deserved to be rewarded. No holds barred. With five out of six nationals in his back pocket and Hollywood asking him for advice, Andy knew he nearly had it made. Nearly. Man, what a bitch it was to see the fruit and not taste it. Andy had never had a female athlete dominate her field worldwide. If Andrei Nagy could discover and train such an athlete, not only would he have realized his American dream but he would also cement his reputation as one of the world's finest coaches. Do that, and he could have all the Carmens he wanted.

Andy's dream was conceived when he finally decided to stop fighting a system in Hungary that continuously and officially reprimanded him for his "irregularities." A particular flash point had been his program to teach young hurdlers a new technique by shortening the hurdle distance to eight meters; then, once they were comfortable with his trailing leg innovation, he would gradually move the distance back to the regulation 10 meters. Dr. Littke, the director, had been livid.

"Who do you think you are, trying out unauthorized techniques behind my back? Are you trying to undo all my progress?" Littke had demanded.

Since then, Andy had seen the technique employed by many other coaches worldwide. Dr. Littke was no visionary, just a pedantic bureaucrat.

Littke had leaned forward, smelling of cheap cigarettes. "If you step out of line one more time, I'll crush you," he hissed.

Andy said not one word. He pretended to listen to Littke's tirade, but he knew it was time to get out.

It was a pity, really, that petty bureaucrats ran the show because the East Europeans were way ahead of the world in their physiological knowledge, if only because they experimented like young Frankensteins on their unwitting athletes. But even though the rigid and inflexible system had not allowed for any individualism, it was in this systematic mining of talent that Andy had come to realize his opportunity.

He would become the prophet. The shepherd among the naive but pragmatic Americans. He would use the best of the rigorous Eastern learning and harsh experimentation. He would cull, refine and add his own spin. He would prove his expertise on a fresh crop of young Americans. He would have the goods; they had the green.

Could a better match be made? As the new super coach, it would be his ultimate vindication—no, his duty—to create a world champion. Someone he could preen and prod into a real world-class athlete. But for that, he needed the right stuff.

The Wichita Invitational was definitely not his style. It was parochial and dusty, filled with Midwestern values. Small people with small ideas. But every now and then it wasn't such a waste of time after all. Like that Karie Johnson kid. She was a natural. The Eastern Bloc coaches would've grabbed her. She had that smooth cycling stride, the kind that pawed the ground rather than simply striking it, like the slow motion of big cats. "Grab time" was what he called it. You couldn't really teach it, though he'd tried. So she got boxed in. He shrugged as he thought about it. Technique would come with experience. It really shows guts when you hold a kick for 200 meters plus. And then in the relay he saw how her knees flexed easily, almost to the horizontal. Not really fast yet, but it was that staying power he wanted. Fast came with practice. Determination came from someplace so deep that only the devil, God and maybe Andy knew where.

Andy headed to where the girl's coach stood. Andy knew him. Or knew who he had been, at least. *Too bad talent comes connected with parents, friends, coaches and all their cockamamie ideas*, he thought.

"What brings the great Pace Track coach to Wichita, Andy?" said Coach Gertz.

"To see what you've been hiding, Lou." Andy stood, hands on his hips, smiling.

"She's in no way ready yet," said Gertz. Then he turned and motioned to Karie, who was standing six yards away, talking to her sister Annie.

Lou crossed over to her, calling, "Karie, could you come here a minute? There's someone here who wants to talk to you."

Out of the corner of her eye, Karie had seen the L.A. coach go and talk to Coach Gertz and then occasionally glance in her direction. Even though she was still warm from the 4 x 400 relay, she felt herself flush when the coach called her over.

"Karie, this is Coach Andy Nagy, from the Pace Track Club in L.A.," Coach Gertz said as he walked her to where Andy stood. Then, quietly, Gertz added, "Be careful."

Karie tossed her head as Andy came forward, tipping his hat and extending a hand. "You ran well, Karie." He made her name sound like "car-ree."

Karie felt a flush of pride. "I blew it," she said. Coach Gertz left them alone and was speaking to some parents, although he kept glancing in their direction.

"Everyone can make a mistake," Andy said gently. "That's how you learn."

"I can do better." Karie stood tall and straight. She would've run around the track in a split second if he were to ask.

"I know you can, Karie. That's why I'm here."

She found his voice soothing. He looked small, but wiry, more like a distance runner. When Coach Gertz spoke about Andy Nagy from L.A., he had always made it sound like Coach Nagy was a big, important man. Karie looked around for her sister, wondering if Annie would say he was cute. When she looked back at Coach Nagy she was surprised to see that he had his sunglasses off and was staring right at her.

Andy watched her fidget. *She recovers from a race fast,* he thought. "Karie," he asked, "do your parents take you to Disneyland?"

"In California?" The question threw her off balance.

Andy broke out into a grin. She made it sound like another country. "Yes, in California."

"I have two older sisters, and I think it would be kind of expensive for my Dad to take us all," she said.

"Do your sisters run also?" Maybe he'd struck gold.

Now Karie grinned. "No, Bonnie plays cello and Annie just kind of hangs out."

"Well, when you do make it out to L.A., I want to see you. You can see the club and the track where great talents such as yourself train. We have a lot of girls training in the team, and we're like a big family. You would have fun. Plus," Andy continued, "I could take you to Disneyland."

Karie liked the way he had said "when you come to L.A." and "great talents like yourself." She imagined racing on one of those huge pink tracks that she'd seen in running magazines with Coach Nagy on the sidelines yelling, "Way to go, Karie."

Karie heard Mom call her name and turned.

Andy looked up to see a woman walking towards them, but his gaze shifted back to Karie. Even now as she shifted from one foot to the other and turned away, Andy could see the flex of muscle under the smooth hairless skin. *There is such an exuberance to her*, he thought, *a promise of fulfillment and beauty*. Karie will grow to five-ten, he knew, and an inseam of 35 inches easy.

"And this must be your mother, yes?" He took Nancy's hand and bent to kiss it. Flustered, Nancy Johnson brought her other hand protectively to her chest.

"I must congratulate you, madam. Your daughter will be a great athlete." *The mother looks strong too, just out of condition*, he thought. *Clearly the dominant genes.*

Nancy bobbed her head and smiled uncertainly. "Yes, Coach Gertz said..."

"You must be very proud of her. One day," he continued, "she will be a big star."

"Yes, thank you," Nancy said in a small voice.

Andy stepped back and nodded to them both, "And now please, I must go for my plane." He waved a salute and walked briskly to the parked cars.

Nancy stood watching him walk into the distance, hoping that he would quite suddenly disappear.

"Mom, did you hear? That coach is all the way from L.A. He said I'll be a star someday, and he really knows."

"Dear," she said, "I just came to tell you to put some clothes on. I don't want you to catch cold."

"Mom, I'm fine."

"Karie, please. Just get your things. I'll be with Annie and your dad."

Karie grabbed her warm-ups and pulled on her jacket. She waved good-bye to Coach Gertz and ran over to her parents.

"Dad, that coach said I'm talented. He said we should go to Disneyland and when we're out in L.A., I could see where he trains his runners."

"He must be quite a coach if he can plan our vacations for us," Dad replied and started for the car.

Annie shot Karie a look. Best keep quiet, it seemed to say. Karie walked silently after her parents. All of sudden L.A. seemed very far away.

Chapter Three

Karie couldn't wait for her first day of high school to be over so she could go and talk to Coach Gertz. She was pretty sure she could talk him into letting her race the 400 meters as well as the 800 meters. Maybe he'd finally let her work out with free weights.

The first half of the day had gone by pretty fast. She spent lunch with Annie and her gang, and Rafael had come over to say hello. The bell rang and Karie jumped up from her seat. As she neared the coach's untidy office she could see through his open door that he was alone, sitting at his desk, reading, with his feet propped up against the football equipment he was stuck sharing the space with.

"Hey, Coach," Karie called out.

"Karie. How are you?"

"I'm in high school now," she said and returned his five.

Coach Gertz smiled. "I know. And how was your first day?"

"Kinda slow. There was a lot of roll taking and teachers explaining about the books and all that." Karie paused. She needed to talk quickly in case Jolene came by. "Coach, I know I'm only a freshman, but can I be on varsity?"

"Karie, we only have a varsity."

"But Jolene said you were splitting up the team and that freshmen and sophomores had to be junior varsity."

Lou made a mental note to speak to Jolene on the topic of hazing. "Listen, Karie, I wish I had enough people to coach two separate divisions, but I don't. You're doing 800 as always, in the same set-up, with pretty much the same team."

"Can I do 400?"

"Something wrong with 800?"

"I'll do both."

"No, I've got someone for the 400."

"Then I'll do the 1500."

"Karie, you know Jolene does the 1500."

"I can beat her." Jolene had big hips and ran like a cow.

"I need to have a full squad," said the coach. "Let's give everybody a chance." *And try and keep peace with the parents*, he thought. "Jolene has worked real hard."

Karie shrugged. "We want to win, don't we?" Goodland had not had a good season.

"There are different ways of winning, Karie."

Lou always wanted to laugh when Karie's stubborn streak showed, but luckily he knew better. Her face still had the childish rounding, a bit of a moon-face, but soon her cheekbones would be more pronounced, her features more defined. He had seen it happen before, and it always surprised him. With Karie, he guessed the results would be pretty dramatic. Who was he anyway, trying to preach teamwork to such an outstanding talent?

"Karie, I want the entire team to train hard and do well—then, if we win, that's icing on the cake."

Karie tossed her long blond hair and held his look. Maybe Coach Gertz couldn't take her where she wanted to go. But he knew a lot: she had seen photos of him at meets in Europe and watched him demonstrating the pole vault to the men's squad. She tried again, "I need to win big. I need to be state champ as a freshman; then I can go for the nationals." She tried to keep her voice steady. "Aren't they going to be in California?"

This was what he'd been afraid of.

"Nope, Florida. What did Coach Andy Nagy say to you?" he asked.

But perhaps he already knew the answer. All it took was for Andy to say, "I can make you a star," and the kids were hooked. Sure she had talent—maybe a great talent—but if she started too early, she'd peak early, and then what?

"He said I ran well, you know. That sort of thing."

"And that someday you should train with him, right?" What was he supposed to say? Big-time athletics could be a very nasty game, and Gertz figured she was probably too stubborn and naive to believe the rumors that swirled around Super Coach Andy Nagy. Now that the fire had been lit, Gertz felt that he should at least mind it. Karie was right about one thing; she could go a long way, national junior champion at least. Goodland High had never even had a state champ. Most coaches would go nuts at the chance.

He stood up and went to his files. "Listen, Karie, I'm your coach, you do as I say." He plopped two envelopes in front of her. "One of these is an insurance form and a physical exam sheet that has to be filled out by your parents and a doctor. New regulations. The other is some info on the Pace Track Club that Coach Nagy sent me to give to you. If your Dad has any questions about the physical, let me know and I'll talk to him."

Karie stood up and grabbed the envelopes eagerly. "Thanks, Coach."

"Don't mention it. And do me a favor and stay out of Jolene's way."

"Oh, I can handle her," she said and ran out.

After she was gone, he stood moodily in his office and stared into the hall at the cracked trophy case. He tried to remember back to his own early motivations. He had been on a fast track after graduating from Springfield College in Massachusetts with a phys. ed. degree and a minor in science education. He had immediately entered Officer Candidate School and received a temporary duty assignment to the Marine base at Camp Pendleton, California, to train for the decathlon. He had made the famous Kick Ass Team of '72 and won at the Quantico Relays in Virginia. Then he had represented the U.S. military at CISM—Conseil International du Sport Militaire—and spent two summers competing in Europe: he won in Paris, fell in love in Stockholm and was sidelined in Frankfurt by a recurring injury.

Eventually he had decided that all he really wanted to do was teach, and Goodland seemed as good as any place to start. He became a PE instructor at the high school. After a year, he took over as track and field coach and became Assistant Athletic Director. In that position, he worked with all the PE instructors in the county, helping them identify promising athletes early on. His competitive experience plus his formal training in physiology and chemistry all seemed the proper prelude to what could now be the main event—the opportunity to develop a Karie Johnson. With all this going for him, why was he so worried?

Coaching someone—especially someone as fresh and lively as Karie—meant treading a very thin line. Coaches on the wrong side of that line were manipulative and dominating parasites who used an athlete to accomplish dreams they could never fulfill on their own. Better coaches were nurturing and inspiring, encouraging their athletes to reach levels they could never have achieved. Lou sighed. Even if he were the best coach in the whole, wide world (and he knew he was not) and Karie the best athlete to come around in 20 years, the road one had to take to reach the dreams he saw shining in her eyes was the toughest road there was.

*   *   *

One evening after Dad left the dinner table Karie said, "Mom, can I have my allowance early? I need to buy a notebook and a calendar for my workouts." As she saw her mother turn questioningly to her, she added quickly, "And I need some more peds."

"More? But we've only just bought some."

"Look," said Karie, hoisting a threadbare foot up between the plates, glad she had shifted attention from her real purpose.

"Gross," shrieked Annie.

Bonnie stood up and moved away. "Give it to her, Mom. She'll only try and steal ours."

The next afternoon Karie lay on her bed, a spiral ring binder with light blue lines spread open to the first page. After some thought, she printed TRAINING AND STATISTICS on the top line and underlined the words in red. She took the family atlas and her school ruler and measured the distance in inches to Los Angeles; then to New York and Chicago; and, for fun, to Miami as well. She found the scale on the map and, using some scrap paper, figured the distances and wrote them into the notebook: Los Angeles was about 1,200 miles; New York a little farther, 1,350 miles; Chicago was closest at 600 miles; and Miami the farthest, some 1,500 miles.

Karie rolled over on her back, holding the notebook against her chest. She closed her eyes and dreamed about competing at a big meet with all the crowds and the cheering. She imagined the other girls looking back anxiously as she came up to pass. Then she pictured the empty track ahead as she ran the straight, ready to fling her arms up at the finish. Karie thought of Andy Nagy's words to her mother, "Your daughter will be a great athlete." Somehow they seemed less like a revelation than a reminder of what she must do.

Karie took her notebook to her parents' bathroom and, leaving the door ajar so she could listen for anyone returning early, undressed in front of the big mirror. Today Mom would be at church, planning the Thanksgiving social. Annie had a meeting at school. Unless Dad got off the job early, Karie had the house to herself.

She stood facing the mirror, her arms pressed flat against her sides. If there was any difference in her shape from last week, it was hard to tell. Karie looped the tape measure round her hips, nipped it tight, released it and recorded the number in her notebook on the clothes hamper. She measured her waist and both thighs and then, turning sideways, she checked the large dimples on her buttocks that appeared when she flexed. Bonnie and Annie were growing hippier. Bonnie was tall and slim, with silky long blonde hair like Karie's. Bonnie also had large breasts like their Mom. Karie thought about the girl, a senior from Kansas City High, who had carefully wrapped her bosom with an ace bandage before a meet. When the girl left the locker room to head out for the track, Jolene had made fun of her—that is, until she beat Jolene by 10 seconds.

Dad called Annie the fireball because her hair was slightly frizzy and light red like Mom's. But unlike Mom, Annie could hold her own in nearly any situation. *What about me*, Karie thought, *just a kid with no dates and not much social life?* Whenever there was a get-together at home, her sisters' friends always spent time with her. One of Annie's gang, a big redhead called Buzz, had wanted to kiss her. *If I were going to kiss anyone*, Karie thought, *I would rather kiss Rafael.* Though Annie had teased her about Rafael ever since he came up and said "Hi" at lunch, Karie didn't think of him like that.

Standing sideways in front of the mirror, Karie dropped to the on-your-mark position, and then tightened to the set. She traced the definition of her leg muscles up to the bunched power of her glutes. She always felt like there was a big cat inside her, ready to jump out. She could see herself exploding down the track so that even if she got the baton late, she would smear the competition by the finish. Now she stood and flexed her pectoral muscles and prodded the flesh around her nipples. Breasts, who needs them? She tried pressing her hands against her chest to flatten them out, but that only worked as long as she kept her hands there. Karie wished she'd missed, or could at least forget, the school nurse's sex education lecture.

"Women have a natural propensity towards weight gain," the nurse told them. "Each one of you will grow larger in the bust, buttocks and hip areas and will leave high school with a completely different body than the one you have now."

Though Karie knew her body was changing and would change even more, the thought of growing into a completely different person worried her. What if her body became like the bodies of some of the girls she'd seen, pear-shaped with a wide butt and stocky legs?

That day, Karie had gone straight to the Goodland Public Library after school and studied the photographs of Olympians Wilma Rudolph, Wyomia Tyus and Babe Didrikson. When she couldn't find a good picture of them in their early teens, she went to Coach Gertz's office and examined old photos of the women's track teams. Karie even began watching the older girls in the shower, and was becoming more and more convinced of her discovery, until there could be no doubt—it was all in the hips. To win, you had to have tight hips like the men. Hip power, that's where the thrust came from. There was no doubt about it. A Marilyn Monroe body couldn't do track.

Karie thought of the autographed photo the coach had of Bill Toomey, the decathlon champ, Mexico, 1968, and compared it to a photo of Dad, when he was a wrestler on his college team. Dad was a big man who had grown a little heavy. But he still had slim hips, and his pants tended to hang down so that you could see his crack when he worked in the yard. "Please, please," she said to the mirror, "can I have hips like Dad?" Every evening after her prayers, she would lie in bed with her hands held flat against her sides and whisper, "Hips, don't grow; hips, don't grow,"—until she fell asleep.

Karie kept her notebook under the lining of her sweater drawer because she didn't want her parents to find it. Not yet anyway. After Mom met Andy Nagy in Wichita, Karie saw her hurry over to talk with Dad and then noted how both fell silent as she approached. She could imagine Dad saying, "I don't want to hear any more about it, Nancy. Let this fool notion pass." She could see his face, the stern expression and the set jaw he wore when he'd made up his mind. Karie knew that it would take a lot to convince him and decided to concentrate even harder on winning.

*   *   , *

Karie stopped by the coach's office after school at least twice a week. She loved how the coach would sit back, feet propped up, pulling on his bottom lip when she came by to explain a new idea or tell him how classes were going. Sometimes she would go through his files of photographs and try to get him to talk about his competition days in Europe. He told her a few stories, but most of the time he would shake his head and say, "Karie, there's more to life than track."

A couple of times, Karie had been so annoyed that she almost snapped back, "Yeah, like what?" Because now track was her life. How could she live without it? It was like the page in her notebook where one day she'd written in big block letters: RUNNING IS WHAT I DO. Karie didn't want to play games. The sooner she opened the box and let it all spill out, the better.

After practice she pestered the coach to explain his training program and the reasons for a particular technique so that she could set up her own schedules. Because he would not let her do weights yet, she would go with Dad and work at his construction sites. Then whenever she could, mostly in the late afternoon, she would head for the trails with Bo racing ahead. She had worked out three separate cross country courses so that she could experiment with distance, sprints and recovery periods. After the first mile of her warm up, she felt a lubricity of motion that made her smile and cry out; at times she would bound forward, stutter-step, run backwards or leap from side to side, shouting, Yes! Yes! Yes!

In her notebook, Karie wrote:

5-23-83 Tuesday—clear, 75°
Track: 200 Intervals; Bleacher steps.
Park Trail: 43:22 (Easy)
Weight: 113.2 lbs.

Tuesdays she weighed in at the infirmary, before school started. She was happy with the way she was now gaining weight regularly. When she hit 120 pounds, she'd have new records all down the line. Next week she'd go for a PR—a personal record—on the Park Trail.

She ran through the fall, with leaves fluttering in her wake; then winter, with her sneakers crunching through the snow and her breath echoing in the silence. She knew the radiance of spring, when the turf was soft and resilient; and finally, the heavy air of summer, when her sweat would lubricate and cool her body. But always, at any time of year and in any weather, soon after she began her run, she could feel her body cruising smoothly with all the familiar dials and gauges checking in and telling her she was ready for action. Then she knew she could floor the pedal for a fast burn or settle back and let time click by until the final sprint. Karie could not imagine her life without motion and knew that she would follow happily wherever the road might lead.

Now that it was summer Karie went out as often as possible with Dad on his job sites. One day, as she watched how concrete was poured over the iron ribs that define the shape of the house, she came to another conviction about her body. As time passed and she grew in strength, she needed to define her own body's framework for greater speed and endurance. Through her training she could mold her body, just like the stays that Dad used to guide the young apple trees in the yard. Karie wrote this idea down in her notebook as soon as she got home that night.

Sometimes Karie headed to the double-wide trailer that Rafael lived in with his mother. She would drop by after her workout whenever she heard the music Rafael liked to play, which meant that his mother was working at the beauty salon or doing part-time at the catering service. Sometimes she talked about Lou Gertz's coaching, or what she wanted to do at an upcoming meet or how she had covered for one of her sisters if she had been out late. At other times, she would lie on the sofa just sifting through her thoughts— "marinating," Rafael called it.

Yesterday she realized she'd been rattling on about running while Rafael was sketching.

"You draw all the time, huh?" Karie asked.

Rafael looked up sheepishly. "I can't help it," he said. "It's like I forget my fingers are working, you know? I feel free."

"That's how I feel when I run. The guys at Dad's site tease me. They say it's weird for a girl to want to run all the time." Karie paused. "You don't think I'm weird do you?" she asked.

"Not weird, just...different."

Karie sat up. "Different?"

"No, no. Different is good. It means unique, special."

Karie thought this over for a while before saying, "I think you're different too, Rafael."

*   *   *

Lou Gertz sat in his office reading, feet up against the football equipment. He expected Karie to pop by any minute. When she appeared, she had that satisfied glow that meant she'd either aced a test or had unveiled the solution to one of the world's great mysteries.

"Coach, you know the new gym by the movie hall?"

He had wondered when Karie would find out. It had opened Labor Day weekend, the week before school started.

"They have this really cool Nautilus equipment. It keeps constant pressure—the guy was explaining it—I think it was iso-something."

"Iso-kinetic."

"Yeah, that's it. Well I was thinking it would be great for my training."

Coach Gertz smiled. It really would be good for her. Better than free weights at this stage anyway. But there was the small issue of the membership fee and the monthly dues...

"And you want me to help you get your parents to put up the money?"

"No, I have another idea."

Lou leaned back in his chair. He could tell this was going to get interesting.

"I was looking at this issue of *Muscle and Fitness.*" Karie showed him the magazine with color glossies of grotesque muscles, marbled with taut veins. "Now look at this woman here on the hip flexor—she doesn't even look natural."

He nodded and handed her the magazine. "And?"

"I could do that."

Lou looked at the photo again. "What, bench 140 pounds?"

"No," she knew he was kidding, "you know...demonstrate the equipment."

"So let me guess, you showed them the ad."

"Yup. There's a neat guy called Bob, and I told him that if he let me in for free, I would demo the equipment. And you know what?" She put a hand on his arm.

"He said, 'Yes,'" said the coach.

"Yes," said Karie, jumping up.

"You're not too young?"

"Not if my parents sign a release."

"That's great," he said. "What did your Mom say?"

"Well, I'd sort of planned it as a surprise."

He looked at her and sank back into his chair. "Maybe we should think about that."

Karie looked up at her coach. "This guy Bob told me how we need to shoot the photos with me in a leotard, and they have to do my hair, you know." She looked away. "And then I need to rub some oil on because it's supposed to make your skin look good—" Her voice trailed off.

He could see she was biting her lips now. "Why don't you let me go and talk to Bob?"

"Would you? Thanks, Coach." Then she left.

What's a coach for? Gertz said to himself.

Bob became very easy to deal with when Lou Gertz pointed out that Karie's parents would probably not sign the release unless they were sure their daughter would not be exploited. Bob agreed that Karie got the negatives, had to approve the print and could wear her hair in a ponytail. She would choose the leotard, and there would be no oil. Gertz also arranged for two other girls to be in the shoot to make it look like a contest, and they got free passes as well. When he was finally ready to break the news to Mrs. Johnson, Gertz took the release over to their home and found that Karie had already owned up to the whole idea.

* * *

Eigel Johnson decided that the summer of '83 was probably the happiest in his life. Everything seemed to have fallen into place. His residential building business had moved into the black despite the high mortgage rates. Nancy no longer pushed for them to take a vacation and was busy with her church socials. And their three daughters, while all quite different, were each happy. But he only realized this now, a year later.

He drove his Ford pickup to his current project and killed the engine. It was a little after dawn, and the crew would not be arriving for another half hour. He sat in the cab and opened his thermos of coffee. With a sadness that burrowed down inside him, he realized he always seemed to be looking back these days. He remembered how much he hated it when his own father would speak of the Old Days and things going-to-hell-in-a-handbasket, and how he had sworn to be different. Yet here he was, wondering why he had missed the opportunity to gather his family together and say he was taking them for a week's vacation to the Ozarks—or even Disneyland—and to say that he loved them more than anything he had ever loved. He wondered what their reactions would be if they could see him now, silent tears on his cheeks, banging his hands on the steering wheel in frustration. It suddenly hit him that maybe he would never be able to pour out his affection, and he wagged his head from side to side, trying to shake off the thought.

As he looked over the wood shoring of the new house through blurred eyes, he remembered how Karie had been a constant helper on the projects last summer. She had worn shorts, boots, a T-shirt and a hard-hat like all the men, with a pair of rough gloves tucked under her belt. He had watched her prepare stucco, lay brick, mix cement and pass timber up to the roofers and heard how the men talked easily with her, more easily than with him. He had watched her surreptitiously with a fierce pride, seeing her long legs and strong body and marveling at what she would grow into—and yet he had never ambled over to embrace her sweat-streaked body and thank her for not being the son he had hoped for.

But he did talk to her all the time about the business, about how to figure a bid and what sort of arrangements he made with suppliers. He showed her how he kept control of costs and how he made his deals with the two banks. Bonnie and Annie had never seemed interested. Karie was always hanging around asking things, until he was left with choosing between including her in the project or going crazy answering questions. He wasn't sure she'd last, but boy was she tough. And quick, too. Eigel began to notice that there were some jobs she could do better than the men.

He noticed other things as well. Like how he no longer recognized himself in the mirror when he shaved. Like how some of the pressure that had built up from years of waking at dawn, spending the day haggling with employees and suppliers, only to go home and pore over a contract, had begun to eat away at his insides, leaving him hollow and transparent. *I'm an idiot*, he thought, kicking at the clutch and brake pedals.

Two bricklayers drove up and he nodded to them, not wanting to move until he could ease his mind.

"Hey, Mr. J," said Hal, "it's a real neat poster Karie got herself into. Here," he passed a color glossy ad sheet through the window that had been an insert in the Sunday paper. "I'm telling Shorty here that she got that body working with us."

When Eigel first saw the ad that showed Karie in leotards doing weights at the gym, he had locked himself in his office for an hour and struggled with his thoughts. He examined every detail: how the rigid line of a ligament emphasized the smooth turn of her calf, where the flat stomach tunneled into her chest, the curve of her breasts beneath the patterned cloth and her serious look which gave a serenity to the pose despite the ponytail. It really was a great ad. But not so great that he could stand the thought that his 16-year-old was going to be leered at on the wall of every dive and repair shop in town. He had angrily accused Nancy of going behind his back, and then demanded just who was Coach Gertz to let his child be photographed like this.

He got out of the cab feeling like he had already put in a day's work. He wished he could turn the clock back to last summer. He'd be with Karie now, ready to go to work. Instead she was off with the coach, at the track or at that damn gym. The coach wanted her to compete in the state championship next weekend— well one thing for sure, he would drive Karie to Kansas City himself or she wouldn't be going. Nancy would have to stay behind to keep an eye on Bonnie and Annie, just so they didn't get any ideas.

It was quiet now in the old house as Nancy Johnson stood at her ironing board and watched Doris Day in *Pillow Talk* on the black and white TV. At dusk she had opened the windows and the front door to let the place breathe. Only now was she retrieving the thoughts which she had so dutifully suppressed over the past days. There had been a time when she spoke her mind quite freely and believed in taking people at their word until she learned, painfully, that she should make a practice of hiding her feelings. It simply worked better, in the end.

Eigel had driven off to Kansas City with Karie. It was good that they went together, although he was still cross about that silly advertising thing. Karie told him she'd done it on her own and she was responsible, but he'd still blamed the coach. Nancy tried to conjure up how she felt at Karie's age, back when she made the Debating Society and became Prom Queen. Still she couldn't quite identify with Karie. Karie seemed so determined. And then there was that dreadful Andy Nagy.

For more than two years now, as she watched Karie's training intensify, she had come to regard Andy Nagy as a symbol of temptation and a really nasty piece of work. Reluctantly she handed Karie the birthday cards that came each year from L.A., but the Christmas cards that man sent to the family were promptly ripped up and thrown in the trash before Karie came home from school. Coach Gertz had proved singularly obtuse, "He's supposed to be one of the best," was all he would say. *Professional courtesy*, she thought. Even the other week, when he'd come over with some papers for her to sign, he couldn't give her a straight answer. She'd asked him point blank, was Coach Andy Nagy the best thing for her daughter? Gertz just leaned against the kitchen counter, sipping the coffee Nancy made and said that if Karie did well in Kansas City, offers would be pouring in and Nagy would be a moot point. "Karie is working very hard; she really could do well at some of the big meets, like Chicago—" as if Eigel would stand still for that.

It was not that she wasn't proud of Karie. Nancy had been a strong swimmer in high school, but her team's coach had focused entirely on the men's team, so Nancy relived her own aspirations with every new medal and trophy that Karie brought home. And she had begun to realize what Coach Gertz, in his quiet methodical way, was trying to say—that from her union with Eigel had sprung an exceptional athlete. Yet she worried that this talent, together with the stubbornness that came from her father, would lead Karie down a road to Andy Nagy.

She was not worried about Melinda Anne. Annie, as they called her, was the busy sort. She organized groups of get-togethers rather than dating anyone in particular and showed an early bossiness with which Nancy could not identify. But there seemed to be safety in numbers, and she was always rushing here and there with her gang.

Nancy was more worried about her eldest. Bonnie was a music major and avidly studied the lives of the classical composers. Nancy once saw a movie about Chopin and had become convinced that these composers could stir grand passions. That worried Nancy. Bonnie was also the most feminine, and seemed somehow vulnerable. Despite that, Nancy had yielded to Bonnie's impassioned plea that afternoon to stay over at Susan's house, "Mom, why can't you trust me? Her folks are back in town." She didn't trust Susan's folks, but Nancy felt she had made her point by saying, "I don't know what your father would say."

More to the point was what Eigel would say if he knew Nancy had left pamphlets on birth control under her two older daughters' pillows for the past couple of years, and that when Lou Gertz had brought the model release over for Karie's "parent or guardian," to sign, Nancy did it without hesitation.

The phone rang. Eigel said they had been out to dinner with the team and were now back in the motel.

"Mom, we have these two humongous beds and a color TV and a neat shower that can give you a massage you know—" Nancy let Karie run on, sensing her excitement at being in a big city.

"Coach says it may rain tomorrow and you know how I love to

compete in bad weather." Karie paused. "Love you, Mom. Bye."
She passed the phone to her father.

Nancy said good-bye to Eigel and hung up, annoyed that she
had forgotten to wish Karie luck. She sighed as she pictured her
daughter in her race uniform, lining up for the 800 meters against
all the older girls. Slow down, Karie, she wanted to say, while hoping that she would win by a furlong.

She put away the ironing board and looked with annoyance at
Doris Day with her short skirt, tight sweater and that toothy, wist-
ful expression that was, presumably, emotion. Nancy had become
a little full-bodied, but she was still what people would call attractive.

*Why shouldn't I go away to Canyon Ranch like Susan's folks, and
come back tanned and slim? Maybe I should go over to the new gym—
I could probably get in free—and then Karie and I could do a mother
and daughter ad as a follow-up.* She smiled as she thought of Eigel's
reaction. What she really wanted was to spend a night, just one, in
a really nice hotel, so that she could order, just once, from room
service. For now, she folded the rest of the laundry and carefully
put away her thoughts for another day. Then she sat and watched
Doris Day. *With those ridiculous pointed breasts she could poke
somebody's eyes out.* To be in her robe, with the Sunday paper, and
order breakfast from room service was Nancy's secret yearning.
And when it happened, she would take a Polaroid of the table
setting, complete with flowers and finery.

*　*　*

Karie came in second in the state championships, and Coach
Gertz didn't stop hugging her and slapping her on the back until
he handed her off to her father. She had kept pace with the leaders,
even though she felt they were too slow, and then all three of them
had come to the line in a flying wedge. The photo finish apparatus
had not worked and the officials announced the results after a 20-
minute delay. Karie was satisfied. She knew that with another 10
meters she would have pulled ahead, and more importantly, she

learned that when the pace was slow she needed to pick it up and take the lead. She had also qualified for the junior nationals that would be in Indianapolis, five weeks ahead.

Coach Gertz said, "She's a sophomore, Mr. Johnson, did you see how big some of those women were? Maybe they have to burn the school down for them to graduate."

Eigel Johnson nodded and shook his head. He spent the rest of the afternoon in a daze as people came up to shake his hand. Karie thought it was good no one had asked him for the car keys or his wallet because he would probably just have dug into his pocket.

The next day, the sports page of the *Kansas Register* showed a photo of the three winners on the victory stand with the headline, "Shafted?" Perhaps, because Karie was a sophomore and the other two were seniors, the speculation went her way. It was reported that Karie, when asked if the result was fair, said, "Sure," which only added to the reporter's slant. The story was picked up by some out-of-state publications and the matter blossomed into a discussion on officiating in general.

By the time Karie returned to Goodland the next day, two newspapers had called, the Atlas Gym wanted to run another ad and Andy Nagy had left a message with Coach Gertz. Rafael had slipped a large purple envelope under her parents' door. Inside she found a clever re-cut of the news photo with her in the winner's position. It was neatly mounted on a cardboard backing with the inscription, The Girl from Goodland.

*   *   *

It was dark by the time Karie and her parents hit the road on the way back from the junior nationals in Indianapolis. She had taken third place in the 800 meters, beating her PR by almost two seconds, and she a ran a 400 meter split in the medley relay in 56 seconds. She had run hard and her muscles ached. Coach Gertz had been there at every finish line, yelling "Way to go, Karie." She had seen Andy Nagy from a distance, but he hadn't come over to speak with her. Karie massaged her calves and passed the time in the back of the car thinking ahead—the L.A. Olympics were in less than two months; Seoul, Korea, was next. Then it would be '92, wherever that would be, but she would probably have had enough after that.

Karie knew if she worked harder, she could do even better in her junior and senior years. She was satisfied with her performance in Indianapolis today. Karie lay down across the back seat. Her parents had been there to see it all. Well, not everything. In the bottom of her gym bag was a card from Andy Nagy. One of the Pace Girls at the meet had given it to Karie as she was leaving. On it was his new telephone number and an inscription, "We're waiting for you."

Chapter Four

Just as all lines meet at infinity, Karie could see her choices converging after graduation. June was less than four months away. Karie sat at her desk trying to decide if she should order graduation announcements in Script or Old English type. *Why are decisions so difficult?* she wondered.

Her parents wanted her to go to college while continuing to compete, but Dad wanted her to stay close. Denver or Kansas City was okay, he said. All colleges seemed to be the same to him. Of all the offers that had poured in over the summer of her junior year, Coach Gertz had recommended three colleges where she could get a full athletic scholarship. He favored Arizona University in Phoenix and hinted that he would be receiving an offer from them. And then there was L.A. She had received a birthday card from Andy Nagy that was a collage of scenes from the city, and inside he had enclosed a fold-out with the news article covering her win in the junior nationals last summer. As time passed, the differences between her options seemed to grow, and the choosing became more intense. No wonder she liked to hang out with Rafael.

When Rafael graduated two years ago, Dad had given him some simple drafting work for a home expansion. Rafael had since continued to work for Dad on occasional jobs. Karie watched him working in the trailer with the blueprints spread over the small dining table, from which he had removed the paper flower centerpiece.

"Are you going to become an architect, Rafael?"

"No," he said. "I would like to design clothes, not buildings."

Karie had laughed and asked, "So why don't you go to design school?"

He had paused for some time before replying, "You know what the man said when they asked him why he robbed banks, don't you—'because that's where the money is.' Karie, things don't always go in straight lines like the ones I draw on these plans."

One Sunday afternoon they went to the park. They walked

around a bit and then found a picnic table. Rafael sat on the table-top with his feet on the bench. He brushed off a section next to him and motioned for Karie to sit. Then he pulled out some apples and a canteen and his sketchbook out of an old army backpack. He cut the apples in sections and handed most of them to her. Karie sat next to him silently, wondering what they'd be doing a year from now.

"What are you thinking about?" she asked.

"*Mi padre*," he turned to her, "My father."

"You never mention him," she said.

It was as if Rafael had been holding back a long time. Staring intently out over the farmland, Rafael began to talk about his father as if his image were hovering just beyond the spring horizon.

"You know, Karie, it's not a case of abuse. He didn't beat my mother—it was nothing like that. When he was home, everything was just like it should be, except that it was life speeded up a little...and then he was gone. I never knew when he was going to come back. Or if he would. Or, in time, if he had even been home. I only knew I wanted him back."

Rafael began to sketch while he spoke. He told her he was born in El Paso, Texas, after his parents had come over from Ciudad Juarez. His father, Salvador, was a tall, austere figure who always wore dark suits. Rafael said that he looked like a real *padre*. Salvador would seem to want to make up for his absences by bringing gifts for Rafael and his mother, by taking him everywhere around town and then going over his school books as if examining his progress from the last visit. After a week or so, he would simply not be there any more. Sometimes this was presaged by an argument with his mother, but sometimes not.

One day his mother had told him to get everything together because they would be moving away. He never saw his father again, although his parents' wedding photograph in its ornate silvered frame was the first decoration unpacked after every move. Rafael said that it wasn't until much later that he had figured out that his father must have had another family, and that theirs was the *casa chica*, the little house. But memories of his father were good: "It was real quality time," he said.

Karie gulped and tried to remember the last time she hung out with Dad. Rafael put his pencil down and lightly blew his drawing clean.

"Look." He held it up.

It was a drawing of a heart, not the dime store card sort, but an actual biological human heart, with thorns wrapped around it, as if they were embracing it. The veins of the heart spread out all over the page and turned into ribbons that swirled into three loops. Inside each loop was a person. Karie recognized Rafael's mother and supposed the man with the hat was his father. In the upper right hand corner Karie saw one other person she recognized. Rafael had caught her in perfect profile.

"Rafael, it's beautiful."

"It's yours."

A couple of weeks later, Karie sat opposite Rafael in a drugstore booth. He had taken her to the matinee of *Superman* as a break from her preoccupation with college decisions. "That's it," she said. "That's how I want it to be—like Clark Kent."

Rafael squeezed her hand encouragingly.

"You know how he dashes into a phone booth and tears off his clothes, so that he can take off and fly?" she asked.

He nodded.

"Well, sometimes, I get this feeling that I want to rush onto a track and run as far and as fast as I can."

Rafael closed his eyes. He had a sudden vision of a gun sounding in a stadium, with Karie tearing out of the tunnel and taking off after the pack. He took out a pen and began to sketch her in a skin-tight Wonder Woman outfit. "I used to wish I was Superman," he said.

"It's what I really want to do. Finish one lap and then you have to do another. And another."

"The bigger boys would pick on me. It would have been nice to be Superman and knock their heads together." He smiled, "Even a Mexican Superman."

"Then when you really can't run any more, you give this one final sprint. That's it. You know you've just done the most important thing in your whole day." Karie sighed and shook her head. "I know I should go to college, but why can't Dad understand what I want?"

Rafael finished the sketch and pushed the place mat over to her. "You would have liked my dad."

She smiled at the sketch. "Can you make it spikes —not boots?"

"Dad had this expression, *hay que salir al ruedo*. It's a bull-fighting term, really. It means, go for it or face it. Whenever things were tough, that's what he'd say."

"Go for it," said Karie. "Okay."

"He would tell me, sometimes in life you need to take two tequilas, roll up your sleeves, step onto the street and go for it." He smiled, "So I did—but without the tequilas. There was this big boy who always used to taunt me."

"Why?"

Rafael shrugged. "Called me *hijo de la chingada*—you know, a bastard. So I went for him."

"You fought him?"

"He beat the crap out of me. But I got that one shot…I could hardly see by then…I can still feel my knuckles smacking into his nose and the blood spurting out."

Rafael wrote "Go for it" over the sketch and handed it to her. "I guess it worked. I went back to school a week later, and everybody left me alone after that."

* * *

By spring break, Karie still hadn't decided. On Friday she was sick, "from the stress," her Mom said. For two days Karie lay in bed, drifting in and out of sleep. Sunday morning she woke up sick and tired of the pressure from having to decide. Groggy, Karie walked downstairs. The house seemed awfully quiet. She found a note on the kitchen table.

Honey, we went to church. We'll be back later.
Please drink some juice. Love, Mom.

42

Karie got a glass of juice and went upstairs. She got on her bed and kicked the covers to the floor. She reached for her running notebook, and Rafael's drawings fell out. She put them aside and turned to a blank sheet of paper, writing on top, Arizona or Kansas City or Denver. She decided if she didn't come to a decision soon, she was going to flip a coin. When she laid out all her options, Arizona University seemed like the best choice. Not only was Lou Gertz scheduled to take over as the track and field coach, but Karie hoped AU's offer of a full athletic scholarship would appease Dad. Somehow he'd just have to accept that she was not a day's drive away. She didn't want to be in Kansas City or Denver. It seemed like the best choice. Good facilities and a good coach she knew. Besides, if things didn't work out at AU, then L.A. was not that far away. Karie felt as if the anvil that had been hanging over her head for months now finally vanished.

Karie got up and dressed. She wished someone was around to tell the news to. At least Bo was around.

"Hey Bo, you wanna go run?"

Bo lifted his head at the word *run*. Nobody could tell Karie he didn't know what that meant. Karie put on a pair of shorts, a T-shirt and her trail shoes. She leashed Bo, wrote her parents a note and ran to the Jimenezes' trailer.

The trailer seemed pretty quiet too. The curtains were drawn. Karie was beginning to feel as if she were in a *Twilight Zone* episode. *All of Goodland disappeared one Easter Sunday.* She considered heading back home but decided to knock anyway. Rafael opened the door, rubbing his eyes. His hair was rumpled, and he was wearing jeans and a tank top.

"Hey, Karie. You feeling better?"

"Yeah, thanks. Why is it so quiet? Is your Mom here?"

"No she's still at church. I was taking a nap."

"Oh, sorry, I'll go. I was just feeling better and I wanted to get out for a bit."

"No, don't go. Come in."

As soon as Karie stepped into the trailer, she realized why it had

43

seemed so strange. Not only were the curtains drawn, but there was a votive candle burning on the small dining table and a picture of a woman in a long red dress. Karie noticed a bouquet of roses where the paper flowers usually stood.

"Wow," Karie said.

"That's *La Virgen de Guadalupe*. She's the patron saint of Mexico. My mother always lights candles to her on Easter and on Christmas." Rafael went to open the curtains.

"No, don't," Karie said, "It looks cool with the curtains closed."

"Hey, I want to show you something," he said. "Last night I worked on my portfolio till 2 a.m. I think these are the best ones yet." Rafael spread the drawings out over the table.

Karie could never get over how the people in Rafael's drawings crackled with energy. It seemed as if they could step off the page any second. Maybe it was all that color.

"It's just so amazing, this used to be a blank sheet of paper. Now it's…it's practically alive," she said.

Rafael grinned. He loved showing Karie his work.

"How much more do you have to do till your portfolio's done?"

"It's due in July. I'm just gonna keep drawing till then."

"Hey, I finally decided where I'm going."

"Where?"

"Arizona. I figure it's best if I stick with Coach. I'll be farther away than Dad wants me to be, but I can't help that. It's what I gotta do."

"What about L.A.?"

"I'd rather stick with Coach."

"Well, congratulations, Karie." Rafael gave Karie a hug.

Karie squeezed back tightly. Suddenly it hit her how much she'd miss Rafael, and she didn't want to let go. Karie felt Rafael stroke her hair. Then his lips brushed against her neck very lightly. She tilted her head a bit and felt Rafael's lips brush up against her cheek. Then he kissed her ear. She turned her face to him and his lips found hers. Karie kissed back, thrilled when she felt Rafael's tongue dart into her mouth and search for hers. A slow, warm sensation traveled down her spine. She pressed up against him, put her hands underneath his shirt, and stroked his back. Rafael's hands had made their way underneath her bra. He brushed his fingertips ever so lightly against her nipples and Karie shivered, feeling as if the pleasure were already too much to bear.

Outside a car pulled up and Bo began to bark. Rafael and Karie jumped. They heard Rafael's mother call out, "Gracias, Anita, see you next Sunday," and the car door slam.

Rafael quickly tucked in his shirt and threw Karie a paperback. "Here, sit on the sofa!" He moved his drawings and sat down with his sketchbook just as his mother popped through the door.

"Hola," she called out, "Karie, how nice to see you again. Are you feeling better?"

"Yes. A lot better, thanks."

"Look at the light in here," she said as she opened the curtains. "You are going to ruin your eyes, both of you." Teresa surveyed the two of them. Rafael hunched over a drawing and Karie with her book. "Karie, did you get something to drink? Hijo, did you forget to offer Karie something?"

"Oh yeah, sorry, Karie," he said sheepishly and started to get up.

"No, no. I get it," his mother said. "You sit and draw."

Teresa smiled as she went to the back of the trailer to set down her purse. She began to hum to herself. *Those kids*, she thought. Karie's eyesight must be very good if she can read a book upside down.

* * *

At an afternoon workout that spring, Lou Gertz put down markers on the field for three interval periods: a nice, easy start, followed by a tempo build and then a final 150 meter blast. Karie completed her final lap, throwing up her arms at the finish and looping back to the coach for a high-five. "I hit it," she shouted.

She walked a few paces to catch her breath. "Coach, I never know when I'm going to hit that top speed, so I just keep coming round, and again, and then another time—until I nail it."

45

Coach Gertz said, "I've got the stopwatch. How d'you know—"

"You feel it, Coach. It's the rhythm." She danced round him. "There's a buzz in your head."

Lou tried to remember 10 years ago. Had he heard the buzz when he hit the curve on the 200?

"It's such a kick." She did a cartwheel and jumped back to him. "But then I think—there's always another level."

The level beyond, he thought. He'd lost the sheer joy of running—and jumping, and vaulting. Maybe he should get back to serious training. That's it. When they went to Arizona, they could train together. He could start preparing for the Masters.

"Coach." Karie stopped and turned to him; in spikes, she was already up to his chin. "When we go to Arizona—we need to keep pushing for the next level. Right?"

"They have an Exercise Lab," he said. "All sorts of tech stuff."

"I want to keep moving on."

He could just hug her. She'd be captain of the track team. "It's a deal," he said and they shook hands on the track. Now he really needed to follow up on his contract deal with Arizona University. His Marine buddy, John Faxon, the Athletic Director, kept telling him it was all set.

Karie picked up her warm-ups and headed home. If only Dad could understand that you have to keep moving on. Every week and month you have to go for that next level—all the time, you can't stop. She watched Dad now when they went to a job site together, or when he was dozing in his armchair in the evening. On those occasions, she would tiptoe in on bare feet and feel such a desire to put her arms around him that tears would come to her eyes.

Rafael kept telling her that Dad's obstinacy was perhaps the highest form of affection, and she should be proud of it. Rafael had a good perspective on Dad.

"So you want him to understand that you need to get on with your life, and you don't want to wake up five years from now to find out it's too late," Rafael told her one day when he and Karie

46

were speaking on the phone. "But then again, he has lived a lot more than us, Karie, and perhaps he can see things that we cannot."

Karie, thinking it over, was silent for a moment.

"No," he laughed on the other end, "You don't buy that, well, I didn't think so."

What she did buy was that she loved her parents deeply, especially Dad, and she didn't want him to be hurt. So she decided that sometime between graduation and when she went off to Arizona, she would talk to him in a way that he never talked to her—although in her mind, he had. She would tell him that she was a good person, that he and Mom had brought her up right, and that she would always be there for them. But the time came when you had to go out and make your own choices, and she had already made hers. And she would try and say all this without getting all choked up, as she was now.

*　　*　　*

After graduation, Karie needed to save money for college in Arizona. Her dad, who was softening a bit about her leaving the state, helped her get contacts for paint jobs. She used his blank forms to present estimates, and, if it were a big job, she would write up a contract. Whenever Rafael was not involved with drafting, he came along as her hired hand. They settled into an easy routine of being together through the long summer days, and she was almost as brown as he.

Karie felt proud of the deal she cut with Susan Trowbridge's father. Susan's parents had bought an old farmhouse five miles out of town and had it completely redone, including a swimming pool and croquet lawn. Mr. Trowbridge had taken over a large barn for his collection of Mercedes Benz cars, and he wanted the outside walls painted. It was her second job so far, but because it was such a big job, Karie charged $400, $230 more than her first job. She'd been giddy when she told Rafael the amount. "At this rate I won't even need the scholarship," she bragged. Karie agreed to do the job when the Trowbridge family was away for a long weekend in late June. The barn was locked, but Karie was given a key to the house because the paint and brushes were stored in the garage.

By early Saturday afternoon, the work had gone well and they only had one wall left—Karie felt they could relax a little.

"Wetback." She pushed Rafael into the pool and jumped in after him. They splashed and played around—then they were embracing in the shallows. Rafael was kissing her neck and she could feel his erection rubbing against her. She felt so rubbery-legged and excited that she pulled away.

Rafael stood breathing heavily. "Now I really need to cool off." He flopped back into the water.

Karie went in the pool house to put on her swimsuit. As she lay her clothes out to dry, she wondered why she hadn't let things go. Rafael looked a little bewildered as he sat in his shorts with his legs dangling in the water. She picked up their sandwiches and sat next to him.

"I think you have some paint spots from yesterday." She touched the green marks on his back.

"Yes, Boss," he smiled. "I didn't get them all off in the shower." He looked over at the barn. "Think we'll finish today?"

"Boss says, no hurry. We can come back tomorrow." Karie looked at the sweep of lawn that reached out to the windbreak of oaks, and the fence beyond. "Okay?"

"I like it here." He splashed the water.

She nudged his knee. "Have you done it?"

"Dad took me to a 'casa'—a house. Said I had to be educated."

"You mean they were prostitutes? You had to pay?"

"Dad's treat. I was 15—part of the Go for it program, I guess." He turned to her. "You rang the bell and they opened a grille and checked you out. Dad seemed to know the ropes."

Karie waited to see if he would go on.

"Dad bought me a beer and told me to look around. Some of the girls were very young. It was kind of weird. Then he found this woman he knew, Doña Marina, who seemed to be in charge. She called me 'Don Rafael' and took me upstairs."

"Did you—" she stopped. "I hope it's okay to ask?"

Rafael put his arm round her. "I was nervous. Sort of hot and cold. It was okay." He paused. "She gave me a sort of guided tour of the body. It was a bit like school—being told what to do all the time."

Suddenly she started laughing. "Did you get good grades?"

He said, "I had to go for tutorials every week."

Karie traced a pattern in the water with her foot. "I haven't yet. Can you tell?"

"It's okay. You have to be ready."

"Have you ever done it with anybody else?" she asked.

He rubbed her shoulder. "No. I think about it though. But I don't know…it's got to be right, you know?"

Later, she left Rafael painting and put in some interval training on the road from town. Then, in the early evening, when they had covered about half the wall, there was a rumble of thunder. They walked around the barn to see huge dark thunderheads rolling up in the distance. The tips of the trees were dead calm, as if holding their breath against the storm now massing over the wheatfields.

Karie said, "Every second between the flash of lightning and the thunder means you're seven miles from the heart of the storm."

"I think we should quit now, Boss." They took down the ladder and gathered their things. There would be no time to cycle back into town before the storm hit.

Inside, the house was still. "Wait, I've got an idea," said Karie. She walked through the kitchen to the dining room and on into the master bathroom. "Rafael, look at this." As she switched on the lights, the white and onyx-green motif jumped out at them: a huge tub with hydro-jets and a separate glassed-in enclosure with double shower heads.

"The boss wants you to take all your clothes off, so that she can scrub off all those paint spots." Karie put her arms round him and kissed his ear. "And if the hired hand finds any on me, he might do the same."

In the shower, Rafael bent down to lift her foot and scrub her toes. She balanced against him and rubbed the paint spots on his back with a cloth. His skin was smooth and warm, and she ran her fingers over an old scar on his shoulder. Streams of water from the twin heads drummed off their bodies and fogged the glass.

He had slowly soaped his way up her legs to her thighs. Now he rubbed gently between her legs as she arched her back. He took the shower spray and rinsed off the soap. The bubbly water pooled and slid down her inner thighs. She steadied herself on him as a tongue of warmth spread within her. He sponged her breasts in a slow, circular motion, until she reached out for him and they clung together. The silky feel of his body made her gasp for breath. He stepped between her legs and she felt him stroking her with the tip of his penis.

Flushed from the shower, they spread their towels on the bed. The lightning and thunder were closer now. She watched him grab his wallet from his shorts pocket and take out a condom.

Rafael smiled at her and kissed her breasts. "Any minute now," he said.

Then the storm was all around then, banging the windows shut and rattling the door. It was as if they had both been waiting for a signal. She knew a momentary discomfort and felt him entering her with a whispered, "Karie." She closed her eyes and saw a pinpoint of light inside her that steadily grew to a big, warm ball. It held preciously on the brink, then exploded into shuddering arcs as their bodies grew still. Rafael held her close. She could smell their mingled scents as she lay intoxicated in his arms, and she could not remember when she had ever known such deep, abiding warmth.

*   *   *

In July, when Karie was getting ready for a visit to Arizona, Coach Gertz asked her to come to his office. The coach started off telling her about the great athletic program at Arizona and how

50

her scholarship was in place, when she realized that something was seriously wrong.

"You'll have to go on ahead, Karie," he said. "And I'll have to catch up with you."

"What? I can't—" she struggled for the words. "I can't believe you're saying this."

"It may take another semester for me—a year at most."

"You promised me we were going together."

"I thought we were."

"I'm only going to Arizona because you were going. You lied to me. I could've stayed here like Dad wanted me to." *Or I could've gone to L.A.*, she thought.

"Karie—" This was worse than he expected.

"You just said it to keep me away from Andy."

"Karie. Sit down." He realized he was shouting. "They told me I had the job—now they're saying it will take a while for them to work out some of the details. It's not a big deal. Things like this happen all the time. So I stay—you go. Okay?"

"Why are you talking to me like I'm a kid?"

"Because you don't seem to understand what's..."

"I understand just fine. You lied to me." Karie was trying to choke back tears.

"Karie, I didn't lie to you."

"Well, I don't care. If you ever do get to Arizona, I'm not gonna be there."

Karie began to cry for real and ran out of the office.

Lou Gertz did not think he would ever forget her look. He had violated a trust—the one thing a coach should never do. Lou paced moodily round his desk. *Maybe Karie was right. Who cared about college anyway? Why not go for it all? Now.* He had never been that great an athlete, so who was he to judge? But Karie was different. She might go all the way. And all this, "There's more to life than track," stuff that he kept preaching—it didn't fit. Go for it now, he thought, you can deal with life later.

Maybe he should go look for Karie. He could say he would visit her every month. More promises? Lou sat down heavily. Perhaps it was best to wait till Monday. It was going to be a long weekend.

*   *   *

"I think you should apologize to Coach Gertz." Rafael put his arms around her.

"It was all a trick to stop me from going to L.A. with Andy." But now that things had quieted, Karie had to admit that it didn't sound very convincing.

"Maybe the coach is upset too, for himself," said Rafael. "Maybe he really wanted to go to Arizona. Now he's stuck in Goodland."

Karie looked at him; she really couldn't think about that now. "I'm not going."

"Why not? Maybe they have a good coach?" He drew back from her. "No, you feel that would be a sham, yes? Well, what do you really want to do?"

"It's been almost five years now, Rafael. Five years that I've thought about being coached by Andy. He's supposed to be the best. I want to be the best. I just need to see if I can do it." Karie kept talking on into the late afternoon, hoping to get it out of her system. She was just so tired of indecision. Yesterday, everything was fine. Today she was back to where she was at the Wichita meet.

"I'm going to go run," she said. "Can I leave my bag here?"

"Sure," he said.

Later she returned and wrote her time in her book. She pulled out the Wonder Woman drawing and held it up.

"Too bad I can't turn into her and fly to L.A.," she said.

Rafael smiled. "You wouldn't have to go to L.A. You'd already be faster than everyone. Superhuman strength."

"You could be Clark Kent and we could fly around together righting wrongs whenever we took a break from designing and running."

"So let's do it," he said.

"Do what?" Her voice resounded.

52

"Do what my Dad said. Go for it. Go to L.A.—train with Andy."

"Rafael," she tossed her head in irritation. "L.A. takes money. I probably don't have enough for the ticket, let alone a place to stay, food...can't you understand, I'm trapped. Or is your Dad going to show up and give me the money?" Karie stopped and clapped a hand to her mouth. "Oh my God, I'm sorry, I didn't mean it. I'm just so tired."

Rafael cradled her head and said, "I've got money. So let's go for it."

Later, they made a plan. Karie would check the evening flight on United Express to Denver, and the connection into L.A. Then she would call Andy, and they would get the money from Rafael's bank. He didn't really have it to spare—this was his tuition for the next semester at Tech—but if he had to postpone, so be it. He had to do it for her, even though he dreaded the thought of not seeing her face almost every day.

He sat in darkness with tears on his cheeks. He could not imagine what Mr. and Mrs. Johnson would say to him. Or what his father would think if he were still around.

* * *

Karie went through the day in a daze. The strength she always summoned in an emergency was nowhere to be found. The emotional overload had probably shorted out the synapses of her brain somehow so she wouldn't have to think too much. As a result, she didn't dwell on the hesitancy in Andy's voice when she told him that her parents didn't know about her leaving.

That night, Mom and Dad left for a charity bingo game in the basement of the Lutheran church, and Annie was in Kansas City, spending the weekend with Bonnie. Karie and Rafael borrowed Annie's car on the pretense of going to a movie. Now they headed for the airport, with the battered cloth suitcase that Rafael had first packed up in El Paso and Karie's Goodland High track bag.

Suddenly she stiffened. "We've got to turn back." Rafael glanced at her and braked. "I forgot to leave a note."

"Can't you call from Denver?" He was afraid that someone might come home early.

They stopped at a 7-Eleven and Karie grabbed a get well card with caricatures of smiling faces and Thinking About You on the inside. They drove back to the house. She used a thick pencil to write,

I HAD TO. LOVE K.

She left the note on her bed, closed the door and ran back to the car.

Karie sat by herself in the airport waiting room in front of the darkened window. She was wearing a tank top, jeans and loafers; on her lap she clutched a canvas tote with her track jacket and her Tummy bear. Rafael had wanted to wait with her, but she made him leave. She didn't want to make him any more of an accomplice than he already was. She wondered if the other passengers could tell that she was leaving home.

She had made her move. If Dad walked into the departure lounge, she would get up and follow him. If the plane took off, she would go. It was no longer up to her.

Chapter Five

Karie awoke in the early light, rolled onto her back and began to sift through the images. She could clearly pinpoint the rising fear she had felt at de-planing in LAX because, although she had flown on her own before, she had always been met by her parents or Coach Gertz. She had moved out into the crowd at the gate, looking around wildly, and then came slowly to a stop. What if Andy had gotten the flight number wrong or was late or had forgotten? But then Andy and a woman he introduced as CeeCee had come up behind her, hugging, joking and handing her a Pace Track T-shirt and flowers.

They had driven in Andy's Porsche with the top down. CeeCee let her sit in the front, saying, "Girl, you have longer legs than I do."

Andy agreed by pinching her knee and said, "Yes, she's our new little colt."

They drove to a restaurant in Santa Monica where all kinds of small, thin gourmet pizzas were served. A slim hostess with crisp movements and bright red lipstick kissed Andy on the cheek and showed them outside to a brick courtyard, where the tables were close together and people tended to look around constantly as if savoring a communal experience. Karie sat down and tried to take it all in. A man with an open-necked shirt at the next table seemed to include her in his conversation as much as he did his friends. CeeCee looked the place over, pointing out a man with a motorcycle jacket who was slouched at a table in the corner.

"Look, that's Mickey Rourke."

"Who?" Karie asked.

"You know, the actor," CeeCee insisted.

Karie looked again. He seemed familiar but she couldn't place him. She turned back around and peeked at CeeCee over her menu. CeeCee was older, maybe late twenties, with frizzy dark hair that was combed out, eyes like black diamonds and skin darker than Rafael's. Andy Nagy had introduced her as a sprinter, but CeeCee just laughed and asked, "Did you have a good flight, hon?"

A waiter came up to the table and listed the specials so fast that Karie didn't catch a thing.

Karie said, "I'll have—" and pointed to the *Pizza Napolitana.*

The waiter repeated the item in a nasally voice, and Andy leaned across and said, "Karie, I think you should try the vegetarian pizza. The Napolitana has a lot of fat—you know, cheese and sausage."

She hesitated, looked across at CeeCee who nodded encouragingly, and said, "Okay."

"Very good," the waiter said as he took her menu, closing it with a snap.

"Did you see?" Karie asked. "He had an earring."

"A lot of guys do," CeeCee said with a shrug.

Karie watched a leggy blonde with her hair piled up stride in ahead of her escort and sit at a table across from them. She wore a white shirt tied off at the midriff, blue jeans with holes in the knees, red cowboy boots and large silver hoop earrings, and she seemed unaware of anyone else. Karie noticed Andy glancing in her direction. *Those legs are not for running,* thought Karie. She could probably lap her in the 800 meters. Though she had to admit people did look healthier out here, she still hadn't seen anyone who could handle a really stiff exercise routine. Instinctively she straightened her back and flexed her legs. She could hardly wait to hit the track and show her stuff.

A busboy with long, bleached hair and tan shorts refilled her water glass and winked at her. She was wondering whether to reply when Andy handed her a half-glass of red wine and he and CeeCee toasted "To Karie." Andy rested his arm on her chair and patted her back. "We've been waiting a long time for this. But now," he brandished his glass, "you're here."

People were looking at her. She smiled self-consciously.

"And what does the newest member of the Pace family have to say?" he said.

Karie opened her mouth to speak. Suddenly she was reminded that she wouldn't be home in Goodland tonight, or tomorrow, or for a long time. She felt cold and dry-mouthed. She stood abruptly and looked helplessly at CeeCee who said, "I'll come with you."

Karie bit her tongue until they got to the restroom. "It's been so hard," she said and burst into tears.

CeeCee put her arms round her. "Listen, you're going to be okay. I know it's tough, but believe me, it does get better," she said soothingly. "Besides, it's all set up. I need a roommate, so you can stay with me. Just relax a bit, hon, and concentrate on getting that head straight."

Karie nodded and hurriedly washed her face. She didn't want Andy to see her like this.

By the time they'd gotten back to CeeCee's place in Marina del Rey, it was after 4 a.m., Kansas time. Karie was so beat that, as soon as CeeCee showed her to her new bedroom, she had dropped her clothes on the floor and gone straight to sleep in her Pace T-shirt.

Karie stared at the streaks of light radiating through the slits in the venetian blinds. As she reached back in her mind, she sat up and sucked in her breath. She realized that Mom and Dad would have read her note by now. Karie could see it clearly. First the gentle knock and Mom peering in. Then the bewildered cry that would bring Dad running, to take the note from her numb fingers. Hurt. Sorrow. Then anger? *What had she done?* She scrambled out of bed to put on a pair of shorts and grabbed the phone, hoping Mom would answer.

"Yes." Dad's voice startled her so that she pressed the phone cradle with her free hand. He always answered with a careful, "Eigel Johnson here." He must have been expecting her to call. She couldn't speak to him—not yet, anyway. Dad would have that how-could-you tone in his voice that always knocked the wind out of her.

From her window she could see the tops of a cluster of palm trees. She opened it to get a better look and was struck by the pleasant, salty smell of the ocean, which wasn't at all like the grass-scented air of a Goodland summer. She went downstairs and ran two blocks to the beach. At the water's edge, Karie turned and jogged upwind, chasing the waves, her bare feet sinking into the wet, gray sand. Her focus had been on leaving town, not on how to handle things afterwards. Now it seemed like everything she came in contact with reminded her how far from home she really was.

Come on, Karie, she thought, *there's no turning back now. What did Rafael's father say? Go for it.* She'd been thinking about coming to train with Andy for five years now, but jogging barefoot on some L.A. beach couldn't chase the guilt from her mind. She kept on running, hard. By the third time she came to the turnaround at the pier, her feet were hurting from the sand.

Karie looked for the ramp that had led her down onto the beach and realized she couldn't find it. The streets and houses were a blend of low-rise pastel shapes. Again she felt the hollowness in her stomach that had engulfed her at the airport, but this time anger mingled with her confusion. She didn't even know the name of the street or if CeeCee was in the phone book.

Trying to keep calm, she ran across the sand to the first street. Using it as a landmark, she began to jog back one block and then another street forward. At the second street downwind she saw that one palm tree in a cluster had only one frond, and instantly she recognized it as the one she'd seen from her window. Karie walked slowly back up the street to her apartment, incredulous at her foolishness, and said out loud, "You ain't in Kansas anymore, and tapping your heels together won't get you back—so you better watch out."

CeeCee was not up when she got back. Karie got a glass of water from the tap, took a big gulp, and then spit the water out. Now she understood why she'd seen so many people carrying around plastic bottles of water. Karie went to brush her teeth. Last night, Andy had suggested that they go look at some clothes today, which was a good idea because they sure dressed differently here. He was going to come around at 5 p.m. to take Karie up the highway to a place called Gladstone's. When he wrote the name down on a book of matches, CeeCee clapped her on the back and said, "Girl, you're sure getting the treatment." Maybe she could wear some new clothes, even a dress, to surprise Andy. The rest of the day seemed almost too much to think about. Karie decided to call Rafael.

"I was hoping the plane had mysteriously turned around and brought you back," he said, half joking.

"No such luck. I made it. We went out to dinner last night and I didn't get back till late or I would've called. It's really different here. I've got so much to show you."

"I can't wait," he said.

Karie felt a lump rise in her throat. "I promise to come visit you real soon."

"Me too," he said, "and Karie..."

"Yeah?"

Rafael paused before saying, "Be safe."

Rafael did not tell her that he had walked around to her house about an hour before. Mrs. Johnson must have seen him coming because she had opened the door and stood inside the threshold as he came up the stone path.

He had walked up to the top step and said, "Mrs. Johnson, I came to tell you that I borrowed Annie's car last night and drove Karie to the airport." At first he thought that maybe she hadn't heard him, but then he noticed that her face was trembling. "She went to Los Angeles to train with Coach Andy."

At this point he had realized that Mr. Johnson must have been listening behind the door. Eigel suddenly appeared over his wife's shoulder and shouted, "Get out. And never come back here again."

Rafael forced himself to walk down the steps and was relieved when he heard the door slam. He'd thought Mr. Johnson might come after him. As he made his way slowly back to his trailer home, Rafael could readily understand their grief. When he made it home, Rafael collapsed on the small sofa that doubled as his bed, crying because he knew that he would miss Karie more than anybody would.

Hearing Rafael's voice was like finding shelter on a cold day, and Karie decided to write the letter to Mom and Dad that she had wanted to leave behind. But as she hunched over the page she tore from her training notebook, she realized that there was no easy way to explain what she had done. Her need to run was a separate thing that lived inside her, and it, more than anything, created the need to measure herself with the best. She had long ago outrun Goodland, though she knew that was no justification for sneaking away in the middle of the night. Her head was spinning. Finally, she wrote:

I love you both very much and I miss you.

She stared at the notepaper and the words stared back, hollow and mocking. Karie crumpled the note and picked up the phone.

"Hello?" Dad's cautious voice said.

"Dad. It's me. I just want—"

Now it was Mom. "Karie, where are you?"

"I'm in Los Angeles, Mom. I'm fine, Mom, and I want—"

"What's the phone number, Karie?"

She read the number off the phone. "It's Marina del Rey, Mom. Everything is fine and I'm sharing—" she ignored the click that meant the line had gone dead— "a nice apartment with this great girl called CeeCee and I need to stay here for awhile and train and I love you guys very much and I'm going to write—" the loud, intermittent buzzing sound made her hang up.

Karie pictured Mom writing the number on the pad by the kitchen phone with Dad standing over her and then pressing down on the cradle. There would be no name or initial by the number— only the 213 area code.

He cut us off, she thought. *Mom would have been desperate to talk.* Dad would blame Mom for what had happened, maybe even Coach Gertz. Karie lay curled up with her Tummy bear and when CeeCee knocked and suggested they go shopping for clothes, she didn't answer.

When Andy picked her up for dinner, he came dressed in a white polo-neck and a blue linen blazer. She caught the flicker of distaste in his quick look at her clothes before he embraced her theatrically. She did not want to displease him, but she had done enough explaining for one day.

60

CeeCee decided that they would drive to the Pace track for the Monday morning workout rather than risk the 15-minute walk. The two of them drove through Venice with Anita Baker blasting on the stereo, and they got there on time. The entire team had to sign in, and at 9 a.m., the list was removed and handed to Andy. Late arrivals had to report directly to him. He would stand thin-lipped, record the time, and never say a word. Andy kept detailed attendance records, and he used them to review an athlete's commitment. CeeCee had been with Pace for five years now and said that only three people had been thrown off the team for tardiness because the word got around.

Karie fell in with a dozen other women and went through the stretching and flex routine. Looking trim in a white Pace shirt and tan safari shorts, Andy chose one of them to lead the class while he walked among them murmuring instructions, "Keep the knee flexed...hold it longer...you're bending your back." He had developed the elaborate routines because he was convinced that flexibility correlated to performance, more than even the East Europeans understood. Every month he would introduce a couple of new positions from his training book, which he kept confidential to foil any "industrial espionage." Karie, who had always thought she was flexible, found she didn't have the range everyone else did. She even had difficulty in keeping up with the rapid variations, although she was relieved that Andy did not appear to notice.

Andy separated five women for the hurdles and jumps and then addressed the runners. "Tomorrow we do intervals and sprints. Today is distance: 1600 descending, 800 and 400; stagger start, no running together. Remember tempo and work on your timing."

"Coach." A tall chestnut-haired woman with incredibly strong legs took a step forward. "I'm feeling kind of feverish—can I take it slow?"

"No, Tina," he said. "Don't run, you go on home." He paused. "You see, I want only 100 percent here. Otherwise I can't tell if you're being half-assed." He clapped his hands. "After the run we do box drills and stadium stairs."

He turned towards the two hurdlers and then, as an afterthought, came back to the runners. "Karie," he walked over to her.

At least he knows I'm here, she thought.

"Elena," he motioned another girl over. "Take Karie through the grab routine—yes, the whole bit—and show her the log."

Did Coach Nagy think she didn't know how to grab? As Karie watched him walk away, she noticed that Elena considered her assignment some sort of punishment. She replied in kind by taking Karie through an hour of grab time, first walking and then in 50 meter runs. Karie discovered it really wasn't much different than the pawing motion Coach Gertz always talked about. He would tell everybody "Paw, don't land." Jolene always got it wrong.

"Coach Andy wants you to think you're a tiger in pursuit," said Elena, warming to her role. Then she would call out, "Always hit the track with your leg traveling backwards." And occasionally she would shout, "Yes, that's better," perhaps to impress Andy.

Karie was disappointed with the drill. Coach Gertz said she was an excellent grabber and Andy had seen her run enough times to know that. She really wanted to run with the others and show her stuff. Elena passed her off to a chunky crew-cut kid called Hutch, who seemed to drift around the field and wait to do Andy's bidding. Hutch was just as self-important as Elena had been and marched her off to a small office by the locker room to show her the log. He explained that every member of the team had to keep an individual daily training log in which every morning and afternoon workout was recorded in detail.

"Coach Andy expects you to include everything you do and the time," said Hutch.

"Like if I do weights at the gym?"

"Especially that—and the weight lifted."

"What if I go for a run on the beach?"

"Everything."

"How would he know?" said Karie smiling to see if the kid would relax.

"Coach Andy relies on the honor system," Hutch said. "See here in this box? You must record your weight on Monday and Friday. You can use that scale over there."

"So it's with clothes and sneakers then?"

"Coach Andy can bring you in and weigh you himself if he feels the log is not accurate."

"Thank you, Hutch," she held out her hand. It was either that, or salute.

As Karie walked over to join the group doing stadium stairs she saw a black athlete doing hurdles. She had beautiful style, running over them, not jumping, but she hit the last two hard with her lead leg. Karie heard Andy say, "What kind of shit is this, Andrea? We're going to keep at it—" She couldn't hear the rest but turned to see Andrea jog back to the start.

They broke up at noon and as Karie was gathering her warm-ups she saw Andy walking toward her. *Okay*, she thought, *here's where I get some quality time.* She pretended not to have seen him as she stuffed clothes into her tote bag.

As he neared her Andy said, "Nice going," and kept on walking over to his Porsche as if heading for an important meeting. *Maybe the rest of the week will be better*, she thought.

As she and CeeCee drove back, Karie said, "So if you don't feel well, like Tina did, he lets you go home? That's pretty cool."

"I don't know what the deal was there," said CeeCee. "One time this girl was dumb enough to complain about her period, cramps or something. Wanna know what Andy said?"

"What?"

"He told her real women athletes don't get periods or if they do they are so light they can't be bothered with them. He said this in front of everybody. The girl got embarrassed and left the track and I haven't seen her since."

"That's pretty harsh," Karie said.

"Yeah, well, Andy always has a purpose. And maybe she wasn't that dedicated anyway. Believe me, nobody's complained about it since. Besides he's right. When you go real hard, say good-bye to the monthly."

"Just one of the many benefits of training with Pace," Karie joked.

"You said it. Oh, by the way, I had a set of keys made for you. They're in the kitchen drawer. Remind me to give them to you."

Karie set her gym bag on the bed and kicked off her shoes. Sitting on the edge of the bed, she held up the four keys and examined them, remembering CeeCee's complicated explanation.

"The little round one is for the mail box. The big brass round one is for the gate to the complex. This one is for the top lock, which you have to lock up *every* time you leave the apartment, and this silver one is for the bottom lock which locks automatically when you shut the door."

Karie hoped she could keep them straight. In Goodland they only had one key that went for both the front and back doors and the doors were only locked after 10. Karie went to the battered cloth suitcase and rummaged around underneath the clothes she still hadn't unpacked. Not that she'd ever wear any of those thick wool sweaters in L.A. anyway. Karie found her keychain. On it, besides the key to her house, were a key to Coach Gertz's office, an enameled Goodland High Buccaneers emblem and a miniature running-shoe key chain that Bonnie had given her on her sixteenth birthday.

Karie began to remove the old keys, beginning with Coach Gertz's. Then, changing her mind, she removed the running shoe key chain and put her new keys on it instead. *I wonder if Coach knows I'm gone yet?* she thought. Karie could see the coach coming up to the back porch of her parents' house, calling out hello through the screen door. Her father would invite Coach Gertz to sit outside on the swing while he leaned against the railing. Mom would put on more coffee and set out a plate of homemade doughnuts. Karie couldn't imagine what either one of her parents would tell Coach Gertz. Maybe Rafael had gone to see him. If not, she'd ask him to. Karie put her old keys in the top drawer of the empty dresser. She would unpack after her shower.

*　*　*

Every morning for the first two weeks, Karie woke up thinking about her parents and her Dad's reaction to her phone call. She would lie in bed debating whether it was better to let him just cool off or to call and try again to talk. Finally she decided to call Bonnie for advice. When she rang Bonnie's number, she was happy to hear Annie's voice answer the phone.

"Annie? It's Karie."

"Oh, my God. We were just talking about you. Bonnie, come here, it's Karie. It's so great to hear your voice. How are you? How's L.A.?"

"It's great," Karie said, "completely different than Goodland, though."

"Any cute boys? Wait, Bonnie's grabbing the phone."

Karie laughed. *Same old Annie.*

"Karie, are you okay?" Bonnie was on the phone.

"Yeah, I'm fine. I just called to say hi and to find out how Mom is."

"She's fine, as good as can be expected. She misses you," Bonnie said in her quiet, even voice. "We all do. I think she's just a little blown away. You should call her."

Karie was silent for a second. "Yeah, well I tried. Dad cut us off."

"Since when do you give up so easy? Try again. Mom loves you. She wants to know you're okay."

Karie didn't know if she should laugh at being called stubborn or give in to the urge to cry about missing Mom. They talked about an hour longer. At the end of the conversation, she spoke with Annie again who said, "You know, Karie, I think you did the right thing. I think in the long run this is all going to work out."

For the next two days Karie would periodically pick up the phone receiver, dial her parents' number and then hang up before she heard a ring on the other end. When she finally worked up the courage to hang on a bit longer, the line was busy. Karie didn't try

65

again for two more days, and then on the fifth day she dialed as soon as she woke up. Her mom answered.

"Hello?"

Karie could hear the catch of anxiety in her mother's voice, and for a second she couldn't answer.

"Mom, it's Karie."

"Are you all right?"

"I'm fine," Karie began to cry softly, hoping her mother wouldn't hear, but when she heard her mother sniff, she didn't bother holding back.

They spoke and cried for two hours and before ending their conversation, Karie agreed to call back in a week. Karie hung up the phone feeling more exhausted than any workout had ever made her feel. And it was almost time to train. She doubted Andy would consider conversation with Mom a good enough excuse to not work out.

*   *   *

Los Angeles was a fast-forward journey through pastel sunscapes amid underlying tremors of impermanence. A kaleidoscope of experiences, full of cool people who said love-ya-baby at the slightest provocation, or advised you not to sweat the small stuff. There were rock stars in Mercedes convertibles, soap stars on Harleys and starlets who lunched on salad, insisting the dressing be brought on the side. In one day you could shop on Rodeo Drive or Melrose Avenue, head to the beach for a pickup game of volleyball and then go to the Hollywood Bowl for a concert underneath the stars.

Karie was running out of cash, fast. Out of the $500 she had brought along, she had $120 left. She had given CeeCee $300 for rent with the promise to make up the deposit as soon as possible.

"Don't worry about it. The landlord's cool. And by the way, the first two months of utilities are on me," CeeCee had said.

Most of the girls on the team waitressed the dinner shift so they could keep their days free to train. Karie figured soon she'd be doing the same. She wasn't sure if she would want to deal with some of the customers she'd seen in the restaurants Andy took her to. Recently she saw a woman ask the waitress for all sorts of things not on the menu and then threaten to have the girl fired because the chef could not comply.

"Don't you know who I am?" the woman demanded.

Karie couldn't believe what she was seeing. But Andy had barely glanced away from his menu.

"Did you see that?" she asked him.

Andy looked over at the woman for a split second. "Yeah, that's Caroline Hansen, a producer. She always pulls stunts like that."

Not Andy though. He would be the most charming man in the restaurant. So much so that by the end of their meal, their server would be hovering over their table like a bee around honey, kidding with Andy. Usually a side dish or the coffee was knocked off the bill. *Thank God for all those free meals.* If it hadn't been for that and the fact that her at-home-diet consisted of rice, steamed veggies and chicken breasts, some of the cheapest foods in the market, Karie would've been broke already. Now if she could just figure out how to get money for new running shoes. Hers were already past an acceptable stage of wear, and Andy had mentioned it twice.

The third time he asked her straight out, "Karie, do you have money for shoes?"

"No," she admitted.

"You should've said so. If you can't afford shoes, we can. This isn't small time anymore. You need to get used to that."

Andy took her to a sports store where the entire staff greeted him by name and the manager, a bleached blonde named Donna, came out to wait on him personally. After having Karie try on six different pairs, Andy purchased two pairs of the shoe he liked best and a new pair of spikes. As Andy went to pay, Karie noticed a *Help Wanted* sign by the cash register and decided it was worth a shot.

"What shifts do you have open? For the job I mean." Karie motioned to the sign.

"Oh, all shifts," said Donna, "Hold on, I'll get you an application."

While she was in the back, Andy turned and asked, "So you think this is a place you would like to work?"

"Why not?" Karie asked.

"You see yourself stuffing fat feet into running shoes for four dollars an hour? Karie, this is no place for you."

Donna came back with a pen and the application.

"Thank you, Donna, but Ms. Johnson has decided that the hours will interfere with her training."

"But we've got lots of shifts," Donna smiled encouragingly.

"Either way, it will probably not be best, thank you," he said as he took the pen from Donna's hand and signed the credit slip.

Sitting in his parked car outside in the parking lot, Andy turned and looked at Karie with that penetrating gaze that made her think of the first time she met him. "How much money do you have?"

"A bit more than a hundred," she said.

"And your parents?"

"They never wanted me to come here in the first place." Karie spoke slowly, "I can't expect them to give me anything."

Andy nodded slowly. He remembered the Johnsons from the Wichita meet. A hesitant mother, who seemed like a transparent version of her real self, and the stoic father, cold and clamped down tight. Andy knew the types. He pulled out his checkbook and wrote out a check for $1,000 to Karie Johnson.

"You can cash this tomorrow at your bank," he said.

Karie stared at the check. "I don't have a bank," she said.

Andy took the check from her hands and ripped it up. He pulled out a wad of bills and peeled off 10 one-hundred dollar bills. He handed the cash to her but, before she could take it, he pulled his hand back.

"You live in L.A. now Karie. Please get with the program. We can't have you running around like a wide-eyed doe. You might get hit by a car." He gave her the money. "This should hold you over. In the meantime, I'd like you to pay a visit to a friend who owns a modeling agency. That," he continued as he squeezed her knee, "is where you belong."

"Thanks," Karie said softly.

The agency lay somewhere at the edge of Beverly Hills, and it took Karie an hour and one bus transfer to get there from Marina del Rey. Fortunately she gave herself enough time because Andy had arranged a special appointment for her alone and told her she was lucky to have avoided the open call. CeeCee knew a couple of people who did commercials in L.A., and she told Karie that the competition was rough so she better dress really hot. She pulled a black lycra mini-dress from her closet and told Karie to try it. Karie had been pleased with the way the dress clung to her body.

"You'll have to wear a thong," CeeCee said.

"A what?"

"One of those panties that has the string instead of a back piece. You know, butt floss."

Karie had cracked up. She bought one the next day.

As she rode the elevator to the eleventh floor, Karie felt a bit tawdry in CeeCee's dress. Remembering the stares she got on the walk to the bus didn't help to calm her down, either. Her face was sweaty from the heat and the foundation make-up felt strange on her face. Another CeeCee improvement.

When Karie walked in, a receptionist looked her over from head to toe. "Can I help you?"

"I have an appointment with Tanya."

"Name?"

"Karie Johnson."

"All right, Ms. Johnson, have a seat. We're just finishing up open call. Someone will be with you shortly."

Karie walked into the waiting room and saw five other girls in short black dresses waiting around. Karie smiled as she sat down. No one smiled back.

"Ms. Johnson, Tanya will see you now," a woman in a smooth black shirt and jeans and a very short haircut said.

A girl with a black bob stood up, "Excuse me, I believe I was here first."

"Did you have an appointment or are you here for walk-in?" the short-haired woman asked.

"Walk-in, but..."

"Do you have a book?" the woman asked.

The girl handed the woman a portfolio, which the woman quickly paged through. Over her shoulder, Karie could see several glossy shots of the same girl in several different hairstyles and clothing.

"Stand up," the woman said, "How tall are you?"

"Five-eight and a half," the girl answered.

"I'm sorry, you are a bit on the short side, and we're already representing several girls of your type. Thank you."

Karie felt suddenly very inadequate, but the woman turned and smiled at her. "I'm sorry, we were heading to Tanya, right?"

Karie could feel the other girls staring at her as she walked down the hall. Now she knew what Andy had meant by lucky. The woman smiled, "I'm Erin, by the way." Karie followed meekly up to the dais in a large, tiered room, trying to look taller than her flat heels allowed, where she was motioned to a comfortable armchair. This must be Tanya, up close and personal, with a staggering emerald-encrusted diamond necklace that she had probably been born with.

"Karie, this is Tanya," Erin said.

Tanya took Karie's hand. "How nice to meet you, Karie, we've heard a lot about you." She said Karie's name the same way Andy did, "car-ree."

"Can you stand up for me?" Tanya asked. "Move over there by the window."

Karie walked over to the window.

"Okay, turn around." As she did so, Karie heard Tanya make an approving mmmm.

"Tell me, have you ever modeled before?" Tanya asked.

"I did one advertisement for a gym in Goodland. I brought it with me."

Tanya took the glossy poster out of the envelope, "You seem to be very photogenic, a little outdoorsy maybe, but we always have clients interested in that. And do you have a book?"

"Book?" Karie asked.

"A portfolio." Tanya pronounced all the syllables.

"No."

"That's okay. We have some photographers who can shoot you." Tanya smiled encouragingly. "And what do you do, Miss Johnson?"

"I do track and field." Then, seeing the raised eyebrows, Karie said, "Sports, you know—I compete in athletics."

"And what brought you here—because you are from...?"

"Goodland. From Kansas. Yeah, that's why I'm here."

"Well, that's a refreshing change. Most girls I meet from Kansas want to model but end up running. I think we should get you measured."

Erin was summoned and soon she had a tape measure wrapped around Karie's bust, waist and hips. Karie thought about telling Erin about her "hips, don't grow" phase, but something about Erin seemed too cool to see the humor. Next Erin helped her fill in forms and asked whether she would do cigarette ads (no) or lingerie (yes). Tanya came by and patted her shoulder, "Erin will be your booker. You'll talk to her about setting up appointments and interviews with clients. They're called 'go-sees.' Here's my card, call me if you need anything else." When Karie left, she couldn't avoid the envious looks or believe her extraordinary good luck.

"Good luck, my ass," said CeeCee, "You're just a natural, girl, and that's what they're looking for. Midwest-wholesome, blue eyes, honey blond, fresh, unspoiled, no-smog, Grade A beef." She picked Karie up at the agency and they decided to head out to dinner to celebrate. They ate at Il Forno and Karie enjoyed looking around at the other tables and picking up riffs of conversation. CeeCee suggested that just this once they get a whole glass of wine each, as opposed to Andy's regimented half glass. Karie giggled and nodded. They talked for a long time after that, drawing together under the conversational quilt with some help from the wine. CeeCee was an army brat, born in Alaska, who had traveled continuously until her parents retired in San Diego five years ago. She told Karie about her friendship with a maid in the Phillippines and the shock of leaving. The even bigger shock of going to a street carnival in Rio with her ultra strict father and watching him dance with topless carnival dancers. By the time she was a teenager, the family moved again, that time to Wiesbaden, Germany, where CeeCee said she fell in love for the first time. Karie was surprised to learn that CeeCee spoke German and some Portuguese.

"Why didn't you speak German to that chef the other night? The guy who came out to say hi to Andy?"

"Wolfgang Puck? Andy doesn't know I speak German and I don't want him to know. He would think it was...well, uppity." CeeCee tossed her beautiful head of tight black curls as if she were showering sparks among the diners.

"Oh," Karie said and CeeCee realized, looking at Karie while she ate her Caesar salad, that this heartland sweetheart had yet to discover the subtle treacheries of race relations.

"I'd like to go back to Germany so I can brush up. My parents thought I should study in Heidelberg, but I wanted to go to UCLA. We fought about it a lot."

"Yeah, I sort of had to fight with my parents to get here," said Karie.

CeeCee thought it of little consequence. "You never lose family," she said, "but a gold...girl, that's tricky."

Chapter Six

Karie's test shoot went so fast that at first she thought she had done something wrong and the photographer was quitting early. When she asked was that all, he answered, "Yup, you're a natural," and said it was the best work he'd done all week, thanks to her. His name was James McKinley. He was Australian, and his laidback manner and interesting accent put Karie at ease right away. They shot two rolls of black and white film at his apartment in West Hollywood. He'd told her to come at five because late afternoon sun was best and to bring some nice clothes and makeup. When she arrived, he selected a simple red top and then studied her face. "Looks like we don't need any makeup. You've got a glow all your own." He placed her in a patch of sunlight and instructed her to, "Find the light. Let the sunlight caress your face." Karie turned her face to the sun and he said, "Okay, tilt a little towards me...chin down. Yeah, that's it. Good. Good." He brought the proof sheet to the agency the next day, and when Karie got back from her morning workout at the track, there was a message from Erin, raving about the pictures.

Within a week Karie was contacted for print work on a Milk Board ad—"Milk does a body good." James McKinley was the photographer; he had liked working with her so much that he booked her for the campaign. It was Karie's third week of training with the Pace team, and she was late for an afternoon session because of a photo prep meeting with the agency. She was prepared to apologize and explain, but it turned out to be unnecessary. Andy completely ignored her, spending his time pointedly congratulating the other girls on the results of their workouts. Karie did her stretches and waited for Andy to explain her program, but suddenly he was gone and most of the other athletes began to drift off.

The next morning, she arrived over an hour early, so she could explain what had happened. But Andy was busy with the multi-event women and, apart from a distant wave in her direction, she had to be content with watching him moving briskly from high jump to hurdles to shot and back again. When it was time for the runners, Andy sent Hutch to tell Karie to get ready for an 800 meter time trial. Normally she would have known about the trial at least a day or two before.

Karie was upset at having the welcome mat yanked in such an abrupt fashion. Yet, despite the humiliation, she felt a countervailing wave of anger because she had allowed herself to be caught off guard. She had been around her Dad's construction crews enough to recognize the acceptance/rejection syndrome. She was used to being "Karie, dear," one day and dog shit the next. Why didn't she see it coming? Anyway, it was more than just wanting some attention. He was her coach, and only he could get her to the Olympics. In the past six weeks, not only had he not given her any individual critique, he didn't even seem to be watching her.

Yet as she waited for him at the end of the morning's workout, she had the feeling that he was expecting her to confront him.

"Coach, I want to apologize for yesterday afternoon. I had to go to this meeting and—"

He waved his arm brusquely. "So how are you doing here in our Pace family?"

"Well, I was kinda lost in the beginning." Karie smiled and fell into step with him.

"So—very different from your Coach Gertz, yes?"

"Well, some of the routines are similar but—" Suddenly she realized her mistake.

"Really." Andy stopped to face her. "Then perhaps you should consider running back to him."

She caught up with him as he was about to get into the Porsche. "Coach, please, I didn't mean it that way at all."

"Karie, what am I to think? All I ask for is commitment. Don't I always tell you that?" He opened the door of the car as if loathe to go on. "What do I get? I get this Milk Maid stuff—"

"But you suggested I go to Tanya, to do modeling."

"Then your time trial—five seconds slower than Elena, when

74

you could be level with her. And I watch you all the time. You think I don't, but they'll tell you, 'Andy has eyes in the back of his head.' But you must give me 100 percent. Then I give you 100 percent."

She nodded, having decided not to say anything more.

"Yes, I'm happy to see you doing well with your modeling—but you must not let it interfere. Otherwise, you have to choose." He spread his hands. "Either a star model, or a star of track. We must be together on this—you and me."

Andy leaned forward and patted her shoulder. "This has been a good talk?"

"Very good," said Karie and watched him drive off. Even though Andy was not being very fair, he was her coach and his early apathy frightened her. Was she really not that worthy of special attention? Had she cut herself off from home just to become a member of a team? Karie vowed to work hard and get Andy's attention. First thing, she was going after Elena. *No wonder she was bitchy that first day*, Karie thought; *she sees me as competition in the 800 meters. She's got that right.*

*   *   *

Andy Nagy once heard the head of the Athletics Department at UCLA use the expression, "God tempers the wind to the shorn lamb." Andy concluded that God would have been a good coach; furthermore, He would have understood the need to teach the lamb that it belonged to the flock.

The Pace Track Team was a business. Even the renowned Coach Nagy had to answer to a syndicate and then to the Gazelle Equipment Company which, in the best spirit of benevolent capitalism, would never weigh his past contributions, but would have his nuts if he evidenced any future loss of touch. Athletics and coaching had been his life and, he hoped, were a possible springboard into show biz. It was said that everybody in Hollywood had a script, but only Andy Nagy had Pace Track, the most successful team in history. He had athletes from Bakersfield and San Diego—some who could only make it on weekends, and a few Olympians who came to him from overseas. Last year he'd started a Masters program and this year an evening program for businessmen and professionals that he called Personal Training, and charged accordingly, for the suits who sought proximity to his athletic royalty.

It was Andy who controlled the Karie Johnsons of this world. They came to him just like the sick sought a famous doctor or the greedy knelt before the gnomes of finance. Sometimes he saw himself as a conductor because he could summon from his players that fine pitch that would allow them to soar above all others. Maestro Andy could not imagine any other life. When he stepped onto the field he felt a particular exhilaration as he watched his girls preen and dance like exotic birds: they were the finest examples of human flesh and blood anywhere. The thrill he felt when he watched them move was like the action shock wave that rocked you back when a lineup of sprinters came blasting off the blocks. Who wouldn't yearn to fondle such exclusive merchandise?

Andy was tired of the debate in which parents, friends or even loser-coaches bemoaned the influence that a coach exerted over an athlete—almost always a woman athlete. Because that was the way it would be, and should be. Any coach worth a damn would demand it, and the athlete would accept it. Parents had to learn that they were largely irrelevant. The more they fought to regain control, the more they lost. Andy would not tolerate any form of outside interference, and he especially resented boyfriends. Luckily, many parents were dual-income achievers who were only too happy for Andy to take over, however young their child was.

In Karie, Andy saw a larger purpose. Since Montreal, the Russians and East Europeans had dominated women's athletic events, except the sprints, with their physically developed contestants. Andy longed for the opportunity to win a middle distance event with an American thoroughbred—someone who was a pure exponent of his development. He had his chances, but many of his charges had tended to shy at the final gates. And now he had Karie, a naturally gifted runner, a fugitive from home and easily molded.

He realized that Seoul posed a problem. It was October '86 already—less than two years to go—really not enough time for her. She would be 20, that was okay, but it was the mental prep that came from experience that she needed. Meet mettle, he called it. You can't teach it, can't simulate it—you just earn it. And Karie had this independent streak that he had begun to notice over the last several weeks. She always wanted things explained to her, as if she were capable of making a separate decision on her training. Last week she had come bounding up to him as if she'd just done a PR or something. But it was no Personal Record, she just wanted to yak about the workout.

"Coach," she said, "why do I need all this plio work?"

"Why d'you ask?" *Maybe she doesn't like hopping around like a bunny rabbit*, he thought with annoyance.

"Because that way I'll know better—or maybe I could do weights instead."

There it was, she was questioning his program. He was so surprised that he said he'd think about it. What she needed was a damn good spanking. Although her enthusiasm was a plus for her training, it could cause difficulties in control. That could be a real problem.

If you thought about Seoul—and he certainly did—then sooner or later he was going to have to talk with Karie about "enhancers." And Karie would be just ripe for it. She had matured in a dramatically attractive way. He found his gaze often wandered over her, more so than with some of the other girls. He wondered how she never seemed to be caught in an awkward move or overstressed effort—he who had seen and coached some of the best. She could take a couple of cycles of steroids and no one would notice. She could pack it into those splendid legs. Her butt might be a little more pronounced and it might add some extra definition around the upper arms and shoulders, but nothing her frame couldn't carry off. He'd already seen the heads snap around at restaurants as she walked ahead of him in that light-footed prance. Imagine what would happen once the entire package was a bit more defined. Men all over L.A. would be suing her for whiplash.

All that, plus four seconds off her PR—she would be in medal territory by then. Yet if she were questioning the stupid plio, what would she say about the needle? Another thing he'd noticed lately: Karie wasn't the slash and burn type. She could beat Elena any day now but refused to rub Elena's nose in it. He would have to handle the enhancer thing very carefully, but then what's a good coach for? He would assert more control when the time was right. For now, he was taking Karie to the movies in Westwood every Wednesday afternoon at four and then to the pasta place on the corner for dinner. It was their special time together.

*   *   *

After three months in L.A., Karie's life settled into an easy routine of training in the morning, heading out on go-sees mid-afternoon if she had any, and then going back to the track in the late afternoon to train some more. One day Erin left a message on her machine saying that she was booked for the Paris Bleu jean campaign, which would include four billboards and several bus stop kiosks. Erin congratulated her. That was two major campaigns in less than four months. Tanya was very pleased.

The photographer was Digby Nichols. Karie had heard his name thrown around quite a bit. He'd had spreads in both *Paris Vogue* and *Harper's* last month and was billed as the next Steven Meisel, so Karie was pretty surprised when a scruffy looking guy with a goatee and horn-rimmed glasses, wearing a baseball cap backwards and black fingernail polish, introduced himself as Digby. There was also another model named Vandalyn, a hair and makeup artist named Katja, and Brice the stylist. They drove a motor home on 10 East out to the desert just before dawn. The freeway seemed to stretch out forever, and it looked to Karie like a long vein feeding back to the heart of the middle of nowhere. She had never seen the desert before. The ever-expanding landscape reminded her both of

Goodland and how she abandoned Coach Gertz and her plans at Arizona. She still hadn't talked to Gertz, but she resolved to drop him a line soon.

The shoot dragged on all day. Katja made her up in a few different ways: first very natural, then with some more colors added to the eyes and lips at Digby's request. Karie was beginning to enjoy it, and the constant touch of the makeup brushes against her skin made her sleepy.

Vandalyn sat on the bed while Karie was made up. She was edgy and restless and kept sniffing a lot. Karie didn't want to catch her cold because she couldn't afford to miss any days from Pace. When Vandalyn left for the bathroom, Katja rolled her eyes and shook her head. Vandalyn came out and Katja told her not to go anywhere, she would be ready for her in a second. Katja did the final dusting on Karie and smiled, "All done. You look beautiful."

"My turn," Vandalyn chimed, and she plopped into the makeup chair.

"Do me and everyone else a favor, Vandalyn," Karie heard Katja say, "leave the nose powdering to the makeup artists."

Vandalyn giggled, "Yes, ma'am."

Karie and Vandalyn spent the next four hours intertwined in poses wearing Paris Bleu's jeans and T-shirts. Digby kept telling Vandalyn to stand still, and Karie could tell he was getting really pissed off. Finally Brice said, " I have an idea," and he asked the girls to take off their T-shirts. Vandalyn took hers off right away, but Karie just stood there staring at Brice.

"Don't worry," Brice said, "Your back will be to the camera."

Karie took off her T-shirt. Brice told Vandalyn and Karie to stand next to each other and look over their shoulders, Karie over her left and Vandalyn over her right. Digby shot two rolls and seemed the happiest he'd been all day.

Digby said, "Okay, that's it for now, go get something to eat if you want. The next shot is going to take some setting up. Hey Karie, could you come here for a sec?"

Karie put her T-shirt back on and walked slowly to where Brice and Digby stood.

"Karie, you've been a real pro. We'd like to use you for the next shot because Vandalyn's a bit spacey today," Digby smiled.

"To say the least," Brice huffed.

"Just tell her your idea. I'm gonna go get some food," said Digby.

"With the desert landscape in the background, we want to pose a model in just the jeans holding a bouquet of roses to her bare breasts. Your breasts will be covered by the roses. We'll tape over your nipples, of course. No one will be able to see anything."

Of course, thought Karie. *This guy wouldn't last a minute in Goodland.*

Digby came back with a plate of food. "What'd she say?"

"I'm still waiting for an answer," Brice said.

She looked from Brice to Digby and wished she could call someone for some advice, but whom? Erin? Rafael? Andy? Coach Gertz? Karie felt foolish, then annoyed. She'd come to L.A. on her own. Why couldn't she figure this out?

"Sure," she said.

Digby asked Katya to give Karie's face another look and to meet him back outside. Katja gave Karie strong eyebrows and pouty red matte lips. As promised, Brice taped her nipples and instructed her to hold the bouquet with both arms, "like a homecoming queen." Then he took a spray bottle and spritzed her hair and face and the bouquet lightly with water droplets. Digby took about 45 minutes shooting close-ups and then about an hour doing full length shots. By the time he was done, the sunlight was fading fast.

"Looks like we're through," Digby said.

It was 11 o'clock by the time the motor home lumbered up in front of Karie's Marina del Rey apartment. They'd had dinner, and Karie fell asleep as soon as they hit the road, though she'd come to a few times. Vandalyn was always yakking, as far as Karie could tell, to no one in particular. When she got inside the apartment, the place was quiet and CeeCee was already asleep. She'd left a note by the answering machine saying Rafael called. Karie took it and put a polaroid she'd brought home for CeeCee in its place. After a shower, Karie sat on her bed, wondering what the people back home would say when the pictures showed up in magazines. It had been bad enough when she'd been wearing a leotard. Karie thought about how Coach helped her out then and how she'd wanted to call him during the shoot. Karie got out her notebook and ripped out the two last pages. She wrote *October 23, 1986* at the top and *Los Angeles, California* after the date. She began her letter:

> *Dear Coach Gertz,*
>
> *I'm sorry I waited so long to write you or call, but I've been really busy. I train twice a day and I've been modeling a bit to pay rent. Everything here is pretty different and people aren't as friendly as the people in Goodland. My roommate is cool though. She's a sprinter and she's been showing me how to manage on the team. Coach Nagy's a good coach, but his style is completely different from yours. He doesn't let us run together and he doesn't like to explain the workouts to us very much, unless he's giving us new instructions. I don't mind so much about not running with the other girls. I never did much of that anyway, but I miss talking to my coach. Modeling is cool. So far I've had two jobs and they pay pretty well. I wanted to work in a sporting goods store, but Coach Nagy said I could do better and sent me to this lady who owns the modeling agency. Today I did a photo shoot out in the desert. That reminds me, did you hear from Arizona yet?*

Karie paused and then scratched out the last line. For a second she was about to crumple up the letter, but instead she chided herself for being such a sissy and quickly wrote,

It's getting late and I have to get up early.
Practice, what else? Keep in touch.

Love and kisses, Karie

*   *   *

Karie drove to the agency in the 280Z she bought secondhand from a friend of CeeCee's. Erin had called last night to say her check would be ready the following day and that there were still some papers to sign. Then she went on for two whole minutes about how fabulous the pictures looked, how they were using the bouquet pictures for all four billboards and the company liked her so well they were considering renting two more billboards, including the one on Sunset behind the famous Marlboro man. Did she realize that she got paid *per* billboard?

"She's gushing," Karie said as she listened to the message.

"That's gushing?" CeeCee asked, standing behind Karie, waiting to hear her own messages.

Karie laughed, "It is for Erin. Did you hear about the billboard on Sunset?"

"Yeah, good thing. The Marlboro man needs a girlfriend. This is from the desert shoot, right?"

"It's not too...well, fleshy?" Karie asked.

"Nonsense, you see less of your skin in that photo than you do when you wear your uniform," CeeCee said.

"Yeah, but my uniform's not so sexy," Karie replied.

"Well I'm sure not everyone would agree with you there, including our coach. I've seen the way the guys who work out at the track look at you, and some of the girls. They'd all like a bit of Karie."

CeeCee was trying to get her to laugh, and it worked.

Karie waited for the elevator, still worried that the photos were a bit too wild. As the doors opened, Vandalyn stepped out and

82

Karie could tell she'd been crying. Vandalyn hurried by without saying anything. When Karie saw Erin, she asked her what happened.

Erin closed her office door, lit a cigarette and said, "Don't spread this around. You're a sweetheart so I know you won't, but Vandalyn's been having some trouble lately and she's been doing a few too many drugs, especially cocaine. Digby said if it hadn't been for your professionalism, they would've had to scrap the whole shoot. We had to let her go."

Karie didn't know what to say. "How could Vandalyn do that?"

Erin marveled at Karie's innocence. "You athletes. Your bodies are your temples. Thank God you'll never be in that sort of rut."

*   *   *

When Karie added everything up, she realized that she would have more than enough money to pay Andy back and live comfortably for the next six months. She could send Rafael the money he gave her for her airfare and a ticket to come visit. The front door opened, and when she saw it was CeeCee, Karie tried to hide the blouse she'd purchased as a surprise gift. She'd seen CeeCee fawning over it at Pole, a boutique on Melrose, but it wouldn't have made much difference if Rudolph the Red-Nosed Reindeer had been standing in the living room. CeeCee seemed too upset to notice anything.

"What's wrong?" Karie asked.

CeeCee walked straight to the kitchen and banged through the cupboards till she found a glass. She grabbed some water from the fridge and took a big swig. She rummaged through the cupboards some more before saying anything.

"Our lovely coach...shit, don't we have any clean plates? Fuck it, I'll eat later."

"What did he do?" Karie had never seen CeeCee like this.

"Just something he said. Listen, did anyone call for me?"

"What did he say? Was it about your times? Was it about me?" Karie wanted to know.

"No, it wasn't about you. Not everything is about you. No, it was all about me and how I can forget about training for the Olympics," CeeCee paused. Karie could tell she was trying to hold back the tears. "Coach said I should start thinking about my Masters."

Karie watched the face she'd come to rely upon break into tears. "Are you sure he meant it?" she asked.

"Coach isn't dumb. Where have you been? You know, you don't know when to shut up, do you?" CeeCee went to her room and shut the door.

Karie took the blouse from the Pole bag and hung it on CeeCee's door with a note that said, "Sorry."

CeeCee didn't go to practice on Wednesday, but when Andy took Karie out for pasta and a movie, he asked her if CeeCee was all right.

"She was pretty upset last night, but she didn't really say anything to me," Karie lied.

Andy held up his hands. "I don't want to hear what she said about me. 'Coach is a big meanie,' right?"

"No, she said something about you telling her she should train for her Masters."

"Oh that. That was just a cockamamie thing that got said in the heat of the moment. She didn't want to follow my game plan. I gave her the week off."

"Oh," Karie said.

"Andy knows his girls and he knows when they're slacking. CeeCee is a fine sprinter, but she needs to do things my way. If I'd thought she wasn't good, she would've been off the team."

Andy drove Karie home and watched her unlock the gate and run up the stairs to her door. When she had the door unlocked and the light on, she waved and Andy pulled away. He reviewed the evening and decided it had gone pretty well, all things considered. Maybe he'd call up his friend Carmen, promise to take her dancing next week and convince her to come over for a little nightcap. She could rub his back and talk dirty to him. Last time she'd read his palm and told him he had two moons on his horizon, one waxing, one waning. *Cockamamie bullshit.* But then tonight he'd thought about Karie and CeeCee. One hopeful on the rise and one on her way out. It had a certain poetic symmetry he liked. He never figured that CeeCee and Karie would get along as well as they did. He thought they'd be complete opposites—one from nowhere in particular and one raised in the heartland. But they were both lost, and this bound them to each other like moons around Saturn. At least CeeCee knew the code, and it seemed pretty clear she didn't squeal to Karie. What would the dear little colt say if she knew that he'd tried to talk CeeCee into steroids again?

Karie found a note from CeeCee explaining how sorry she was, thanks for the blouse, she'd be down in San Diego for the next week or so. She left the number and Karie decided to call in a couple of days just to make sure CeeCee was okay. Karie also realized there was a silver lining. In a couple of days Rafael would be here, and she'd have the place to herself.

*   *   *

Karie could barely sleep the night before Rafael came. He was due on Saturday at 2 p.m. Karie was glad he didn't care what she looked like because she was sure she had bags under her eyes. Thank God she didn't have a shoot or anything. She ran for about an hour at the track with the professionals in Andy's personal training program to calm her nerves. Andy noticed how tired she looked and told her to take care of herself, he couldn't have anyone getting sick. *Never lets up,* she thought. She hadn't told him about Rafael. She figured he'd just get mad.

Karie got to the airport with 15 minutes to spare. She hadn't been able to decide what to wear and then realized it didn't matter. As she rummaged through her clothes, she happened upon the cut-offs she wore when they painted the barn. They were still covered with green flecks of paint. She paired them with a white men's shirt and a pair of Doc Martens boots she bought on Melrose, pleased with the results.

Waiting at the airport she thought about how much had happened since they saw each other last. Karie had to admit that she had stepped over a different threshold. This was no longer high school, where athletics and running track were sexy add-ons to the main event of education. She was now surrounded by women, some stronger and even taller, who struggled to eke out a living and stay on the Pace team. The beautiful pink tartan track was an arena for female gladiators. It was instant recognition to make the Pace team; everyone knew that Andy only trained the best. Karie knew she had lucked out big time by not having to claw her way up in either modeling or track. But she also knew that she'd have to fight to keep her place. So she'd won her third junior national title. Big deal. It didn't mean a thing if she couldn't maintain that type of performance. Those who didn't were shipped out to Yakima, or wherever.

Rafael's plane landed and she moved a bit closer to the gate. He must have seen her first, because he was already smiling when she saw him. They embraced, then kissed for a full minute. Karie felt overcome by the heat and scent of his skin, and she realized how much she missed him.

Rafael stroked her hair the entire drive home. When they got to her apartment they dropped his bags in the living room, and Rafael took her hand and started leading her to the back of the apartment.

"Do you know where you're going, young man?"

"I'm hoping the beautiful lady will tell me when I'm getting warmer."

Rafael pushed the bathroom door open. "Good to know where this is." He walked down the hall, and started for CeeCee's door.

"Colder," Karie said.

"Well then it must be this one." Rafael pushed open the only remaining door.

"Warmer," Karie said.

He moved closer to the bed. "Now?" he asked.

"Warmer," she said.

He pulled her down on the bed.

"Very warm," she said.

He pulled her close and Karie could feel his full erection pressing against her.

"Pretty hot," she said.

Rafael began to take off her clothes and, somewhere in between his kisses and caressing, Karie stopped talking. They pushed the clothes and covers off the bed and made love in the afternoon heat. Rafael entered her, slowly thrusting in and out until she came. When Karie came the second time Rafael came with her, calling out softly, "I love you, Karie."

Karie buried her face into his neck and replied, "I love you too, Rafael."

All weekend they were either in bed or at the beach. For the first time since she'd arrived in L.A., Karie didn't want to get up for her 9 a.m. training session.

"Come on, I'll take a shower with you, then we can go to the track together," Rafael said. After practice, Karie introduced him to Andy.

"Nice to meet you," Andy said, "Do you mind if I borrow Karie a second? I need to speak to her about some of our rules."

Rafael gave Karie a puzzled look, and she shrugged her shoulders and handed him her car keys. "Go on, I'll meet you in a second."

"Karie, no boyfriends at the track. Ever. Period."

"Sorry, Coach, I didn't know. He's just in town this week and I thought—"

"Don't think, just do as I say. And I say no boyfriends. Got it?" He walked off.

"Fine. I just thought you'd like to meet the person who lent me the money to train on this team in the first place," she called out after him.

Karie went to her car. She wasn't mad, really. She just hated it when Coach questioned her dedication. Couldn't he see what she was living for? She forgot about it as soon as she saw Rafael leaning up against her car.

"Everything okay?" he asked.

"Yeah, no big deal. I'm just not supposed to bring boyfriends to the track. I'm sorry. I didn't know."

"It's okay. Your coach seems a little uptight."

"No, he just wants to make sure we're 100 percent. Why should he bother otherwise?"

Andy knew he had to play it cool with Karie, so when she came back for the afternoon workout he gave her a pair of tickets to the Hollywood Bowl with a smile and the warning, "Just don't stay out too late." Her smile was enough of a reward for him—at least for now.

During the rest of the visit, when Karie wasn't training, she and Rafael went roller blading at Manhattan Beach, combed through Westwood, went over the hill to Magic Mountain, played together in pickup games of beach volleyball, and drove up to the snow as a reminder of Goodland.

On the last night Rafael and Karie lay together in bed with the radio playing softly in the background.

"Does Dad say anything about me?"

"No," said Rafael. He hadn't told her he was forbidden to visit her parents, and he saw no reason to tell her now.

Rafael had brought all the news from Goodland, and Karie was surprised at how distant she felt. It wasn't a matter of golden beaches or the palm trees that she could see from her window; she had simply closed one door and opened another. She was in L.A. doing what she had to do, and she had come to accept the aching loss of family contact as the price she had to pay. But Dad's silent rebuke she could not handle.

She squeezed Rafael's hand under the sheet, "Why can't Dad accept what's done is done? Why can't we start clean?"

"You ran away," said Rafael.

"I had to."

"That's not how your Dad sees it," he said. "You left." He turned to her and stroked her head.

"It still hurts," she said as she felt the tears on her cheek.

The next evening at the airport they stood clutched together in a corner at the gate until the flight was called. Then Karie drove slowly home and slept the clock around.

Chapter Seven

Karie did her last push-up and brought her face down to brush the fresh-cut grass. She bit off a stalk and rolled onto her back, chewing. It wasn't Kansas prairie vintage, but it was acceptable. She arched her back and murmured, "good color, nice balance, smooth," then spat out the grass, "but not much bouquet, lacks finish." She began to laugh through her stretches, remembering Andy's serious discourse over a glass of red wine.

"You doing grass again, girl?" asked CeeCee. She was on her knees working on leg curls.

Andy came up and asked, "Ready to go?" It was more of a statement than a question; he knew she had only started her warm-up. "When you are, we'll start with the 1200 meters descending routine." He made it sound like punishment for her bantering with CeeCee, but Karie didn't mind because she was now strong enough to handle any of the training schedules. And Rafael was coming Labor Day weekend.

Today would be one of the tougher workouts, so she concentrated on stretching her calves, Achilles, hamstrings, glutes and then on up her back to the shoulders. Then she'd work on quads, abductors and the hip flexor. Finally she went through her technical sprint drills, some six 100s. Karie felt that she understood the temperament of her major muscle groups. They would always come through for her as long as they were treated with respect. Most of the time they liked to curl up along the bone and take it easy, like cats by the fire. If you called on them for some serious contractions or a demo of furious fast twitching, they demanded plenty of notice. Then they would call up their own reserves, see that the glycogen fuel was properly deployed and make sure that everyone was warm, tuned and ready to go. As Karie walked sinuously over to Andy to start the drills, her body was shouting that all cylinders were fired up and ready. *In fact*, she thought as she walked over, *I could kick him in the ass and be into the first corner before he even turned around.* The 1200 descending routine was an emphasis of speed over stamina in the week leading up to a race. Karie started by running 1200 meters in acceleration/deceleration mode. She ran the first 100 at faster than race pace, the next 100 slower than race pace, then continued alternating. Karie knew that this developed her intuitive sense of speed so she could run a good race plan. When the workout was over she, like everyone else, would check her individual lap times. Andy liked to say, "To control time is to win," and Karie translated that into her pain threshold. Coach Gertz used to tell her the body gives a great readout, unless you screw it up with too much adrenalin.

After the 1200, she walked a lap to rest, and then she was ready for the 600 tempo. Karie took her cadence to way over 200 steps per minute, and it blew the hell out of her hamstrings. After she walked the next lap, she did 300 meters of lift-snap-grab exaggerated motion. As some stopped to watch, Karie high-stepped around the track like a circus horse, even though her hip flexors were screaming. Once more round the track at a walk and she let it all out on a clenched-fist 150 kick with the crowd roaring as she blasted through the tape.

Andy remembered the dictum: When God made woman, He knew exactly what He was doing. Karie walked toward him with that light prancing step, arms on hips, head down and chest pumping, sweat streaking her tank top and on down those long, gloriously powerful legs. One female animal. It was almost better with your eyes closed. It practically made his heart stand still. "Good, Karie," he said, falling into step beside her. "Now do some plio, but go easy. You're ready."

For the rest of the morning Karie did her pliometric workout. Holding hand weights, she hopped up the stadium stairs on one leg and then the other and then hopped with no weights. Next she did double leg hops over four low hurdles, with repeats, and she finished with a set of standing long jumps into the pit. Karie liked racing the other girls up the steps, but she couldn't get motivated by the jumps—until Andy had brought out a tape measure and said, "Imagine you're bounding across the finish line." Now she was a full 18 inches beyond where she first started.

Karie showered after her workout. She wanted to catch a quick bite and a nap before heading to Century City at 4 p.m. for a meeting with some people from a beef campaign who were looking for an athletic type. It was a call-back for a major campaign, so Andy let her have the afternoon off. Karie toweled and put on her robe. Since Goodland, the intensity of workouts had slimmed her breasts, but weight training had given her a broad swimmer's back and she still wore a C-cup bra. Her hips had not rounded; she was slim and tucked, with dimples on her glutes that were even more pronounced. Karie felt primed. Tanya noticed the improvements and called her Miss Vitality. She sent her out for commercials and prints ads for casual sportswear where a healthy look was essential.

Karie went into the kitchen and fixed herself a plate of tuna salad and dry toast. Modeling was not the real issue now. Numero uno was the Seoul Olympic Trials in Indianapolis one year away, in August 1988. She had covered a lot of ground at Pace and was now the fastest 800 meter runner on the team, with a PR only five seconds off the American record. At every meet she analyzed her opponents as they stretched and warmed up, just as people examined the style and stamina of horses as they paraded in the ring before a race. She had worked out her Plan A with Andy: go out strong, then cruise and see who catches up; stay with her and be ready to kick for the last 200 meters.

Plan B was initiated when someone went out even stronger. She would keep the pace to push her and see if she could hang in for the long haul. Not many did. Karie could tell by the sound of the breathing who would be in at the finish. The real thrill came when she reeled them in. Every step brought her closer to their frantic shoulders till she was level. When she began her steady pull away, there wasn't a thing they could do about it.

Karie frowned as she began to brush her teeth. She intended to make the U.S. team. If she really trained all-out maybe she could go all the way; then surely things would change at home, especially with Dad. She didn't think she could ever go back to Goodland, but she could do what she had set out to do and maybe then he would take that stupid, hurt look off his face. She would not become lost in the false glitter of Tinsel Town, as he called Los Angeles. Even the Paris Bleu billboards hadn't changed her. Someday she would tell Dad the pressures of L.A. were nothing she couldn't handle, and it would take more than Andys and Tanyas to get her to bend. *No*, she thought as she spit mouthwash into the sink, *Dad's silence is the only pressure I cannot take.*

Karie was stubborn like her father. She could no more give up on her ideal than he could abandon his frozen reproach. The tableau was set, but an Olympic Gold would break the impasse. That was why she was weighing Andy's suggestion that she give up modeling to concentrate even more on her training. "I'd be doing it for you, Dad," she said to the mirror, remembering how Dad would run up and hug her after a good win. But she was getting way ahead of herself. She had to be in Century City by four, and then she would go to Gold's Gym and put in an hour of weights. She lay down in her robe for a nap and was immediately asleep.

*   *   *

Fall was a time to turn around, look back and scope the field. The outdoor race schedule had tapered off, so Andy shifted workouts to emphasize style and technique; for his star girls, this included biomechanicals. The Pace Track Team spent two full days doing tests at the brand new Exercise Physiology Lab at UCLA in Westwood. Karie most loved the series that involved running fast on a treadmill, with cameras taking front and lateral shots that were then fed into computers which analyzed the critical kinetic points and could simulate theoretical improvements. A coach could take the computer outline on the monitor and tweak it. He could punch in a higher arc of armswing for a sprinter, maybe change the body posture to align head-hip-ankle, or shorten the stride and increase cadence for a middle-distance runner and receive a readout of what this would do for time and/or distance.

"Try tightening your sphincter and sticking your tits out, girl," whispered CeeCee as they watched Andy reviewing Karie's sequence.

"You know what the technicians said about yours?" murmured Karie, trying to keep a straight face. "Let's get a shot of those buns and peddle it to the porno shops." Andy turned around in annoyance, and CeeCee grabbed her shoulder. They walked off, ready to break up.

They were also tested on the Magnetic Resonance Indicator that showed vibrant color images, like Technicolor tie-dye prints, of the blood pulsing through the chambers of the heart. Another new device, consisting of an electronic footpad, measured the "Gs" of force at impact and produced a diagram summarizing medial, tarsal and lateral roll. The equipment was operated by a Ph.D. student who confided to Karie that his doctoral thesis was on impact correlations between humans and race horses.

The whole area of exercise physiology was simply another element of Andy's program, and he had the same faith in it that most American coaches did. Americans relied heavily on technology and simulation. The East Europeans were more hands-on. They made the athletes try the new methods, instead of buying some billion dollar machine to do all the work. Andy thought that they were both right and wrong. He would have reduced the number of tests and cut back on the athletes tested, except that the syndicate that owned Pace was impressed by all the high-tech applications. Andy believed that he could tell at a glance what major adjustments had to be made in a runner's style, just like he knew when it made sense to bring on the cameras.

Most of the tests provided the team with a pleasant strut-your-stuff interlude in which they hardly broke a sweat. But during the second day, they had to deal with the dreaded Exhaustion EKG.

"Don't eat much," warned the discus champ, "because you may lose your cookies. I did," she said cheerfully, "but Coach Andy seemed to think puking showed my commitment."

CeeCee said, "No way this should be for sprinters. I'm telling you, girl, this is the last time I do this shit."

At least the test was in a closed room, thought Karie, as a nurse attached four electrodes on her chest with cables that fed into the electrocardiogram equipment. A doctor with a "Cantwell M.D." badge on his white coat helped her onto the treadmill and arranged the cables against a side bar.

"Ms. Johnson, this test measures maximal stress." He sat at his console. "Every three minutes I will increase the speed and incline, so put your hand up when you're at your limit and we'll take the VO2 Max measurement."

The rubber mat started rolling at a pleasant walk. *Why does Andy have to be here?* she thought. *He gets the EKG printout.* But she knew he was there to make sure she didn't wimp out early. He gave her a thumbs-up, but she ignored him. Karie knew that the treadmill went to Stage 7, so that between the eighteenth and twenty-first minutes her heart would be at a max, and Dr. Cantwell would be hovering over her. Her plan was to get through Stage 6 for eighteen minutes, when her heartbeat would be close to 200 per minute, and then flop on the table as the equipment calmly registered her body's frantic recovery mechanisms.

Dr. Cantwell called, "Stage 7," and she immediately felt the surge of the added incline and the dragging fire in her chest. *Come on Karie, another 30 seconds...*she tried to keep her back straight and her knees up...*just a little more...don't stop now...let's do the record.* Suddenly she remembered that she had to keep going for another minute after she signaled. Her hand shot up and she felt the plastic cup over mouth. Above the roaring sound in her head, she forced herself not to quit.

As she felt the treadmill slow, she lurched against the side and almost lost consciousness. Then she lay on the table in a daze. Dr. Cantwell was saying, "Good job, good job." Her chest felt like it was exploding. Five minutes later she wondered what all the fuss was about.

Andy took her arm as she walked out. "That was 100 percent *plus.*"

She was happy to see him so pleased. *I'd better not tell him I screwed up and went longer than I meant to,* she thought.

But Andy knew perfectly well that Karie had overdone it. When she went googly-eyed at the end, he could tell she was running on empty. The VO2 Max measurement told how much oxygen she could suck in. It also showed guts. It meant that if Karie went out too fast on a lap, she'd hang in better than most. He was convinced that she could not only make it to Seoul but, with the right treatment, could even medal. He decided to move her program up another notch.

*   *   *

Karie stood with her feet together, right shoulder to the wall outside Andy's office, and reached up to make a blue mark with her fingertips.

"Now," said Andy putting more chalk on her fingers, "do a full squat and leap for the moon."

"Just like the Toyota man," she said and leaped up to touch.

"Good job." Andy eyed the new mark. "Okay, one more. Come on and slam dunk."

He extended the metal tape measure, nipped it and read out, "Twenty-three inches. That would be good for hurdles or even high jump." He made a note on her log sheet.

Karie smiled. It was mid-morning Sunday and she had Andy to herself, although he'd said another girl was scheduled for noon. This was his Star Program for Seoul, and only Karie and seven others from the team were on it, though Andy knew natural selection would play its part and not all of them would make it past the trials. Karie had already done the standing long jump, eight feet, which he said was above average; and then the 50 meter dash, 6.1 seconds, which was great for an 800 meter runner.

"Next trick," said Andy and walked towards his office. The body fat calculation was the important one. Andy considered the other tests of only marginal interest, but they helped to put the girls in the right spirit. He motioned to the massage table. "Skin folds now. I need you to take your track clothes off—bra and underpants for this one."

Karie hesitated. "But I've got on short tights."

He picked up the skin caliper and turned to her. "You mean—that's it?"

"No," Karie flushed. "I've got a thong. I can roll the tights up on the leg."

"Oh, okay," said Andy. "We should be able to get a decent measurement with that." He shrugged as if this were the first time he'd been confronted with such reticence. Actually it was—all his star girls shied at this gate, but Karie was the first one to refuse outright.

Karie took off her racing singlet. She had on her tight running bra and even though it was less revealing than a bikini top, she crossed her arms over her chest. The only other time she'd had skinfold measurements taken was at Goodland High by a female nurse, and then she'd worn a tank top.

"Okay, lie still now," said Andy. "I say that because sometimes I get complaints that the caliper pinches too much—or it feels cold." He allowed a brief smile and measured the back of the upper right arm, then to the side of her left breast, where he let his hand rest ever so lightly on her nipple. Moving to the lower abdomen, he said, "Hitch it down a little, please," touching the top of her tights. This was Coach Andy's privilege. He could read a lot from their reactions. If they objected, he would be taken aback. If they didn't, it was a step in the right direction. Twice he'd gotten lucky and managed to finger fuck the girl right there on the table. And as far as Karie was concerned, Andy didn't mind how many steps it would take, just so long as he got there.

He finished with her front thigh, then her calf and patted her leg lightly. "All done," he said, "now for the math." She was a real turn-on, even with the tights.

Karie put on her singlet and sat attentively on the side of the table as Andy made his calculations. *What's the big deal? I took my shirt off in the desert, didn't I?* Karie thought back to the time in Goodland when that guy at the gym wanted her to rub oil on her body for the photo session. She remembered the guy's mood as intense and a bit spooky. Andy had seemed that way too, when he turned and looked at her with the caliper in his hand. She was probably being oversensitive. He was her coach, and he must have tested a lot of women this way. He had been so nonchalant about it. She felt a little foolish now. Maybe it was just some more of this California thing which she couldn't quite accept. It wasn't really a question of his integrity.

"Guess what?" He looked up. "You're a perfect 10. Well," he glanced down, "ten-point-two exactly. I always want my stars to be in the eight to 12 percent body fat range." He knew she would take that as a challenge to go lower. Although Karie had a strong, full-breasted body, she had tested even better than he expected.

"I can do better," she promised. *This is great. This is the kind of edge I need,* she thought.

"Here." He handed her a sheet of paper. "You will need to get a urine and a blood test. It's all written down there. I think we'll want to repeat these tests every three months at least." *I wonder if she'll be as skittish about the caliper next time?*

"That's fine." Karie wanted to keep talking but now she saw him glance at his watch and frown.

"One more thing. We'll need to talk about some supplements that our team physician, Dr. John, is working on." Andy began to clear his desk.

"Supplements?"

"They're the kind of additives that help you work out harder and shorten recovery time. That sort of stuff."

"Cool." Karie jumped down from the table and smiled. "Thanks, Coach."

He watched her jog lightly over to her car. These tests were a critical baseline measure before starting a cycle of steroids. That's why he had set up the Star Program. He wondered if she would figure that out.

*   *   *

Andy had been observing the development of steroids and the overall world of doping ever since he came to America. Watching and waiting. Yet, ironically his first breakthrough came as a result of the 1980 Olympics in Moscow. Three Pace girls and one male athlete he'd been training separately all qualified but were unable to attend due to the U.S. boycott. Andy went on his own, with credentials from the Hungarian Olympic Committee, and saw the event from the inside. What he saw changed much of his thinking. His ex-colleagues had been busy in all areas of performance enhancement. Not only did they have access to the latest information from East Germany at the Leipzig Institute but to a lesser extent, due to tighter security, from the Institute of Physical Culture in Moscow.

What interested Andy most was that they seemed to have moved from the pursuit of the latest hot substances, such as stimulants, to a far more comprehensive approach. As his old friend Lazlo told him, the athlete was to shut up and sit in the corner while the coaches and doctors and scientists huddled around the blackboard. In their methodical way, they had studied the effects of speed, diuretics, beta-blockers, even narcotics. They churned through the vast area of steroids and had come up with several new products as well as new areas for future research. They looked beyond steroids to other drugs and at ancillary fields such as electro-stimulation. Although many of these findings had not yet been validated by what they called "field testing," Andy came away with the feeling that he needed to do a lot of catching up.

He quickly concluded that stimulants, indeed any kind of speed, were dead. There was nothing wrong with the products. They effectively reduced fatigue, dampened pain and enhanced aggressiveness. The athletes felt that speed increased acuity, endurance, reactive time and a whole lot of other attributes, despite concrete scientific proof that said otherwise. And if benzedrine didn't do the trick, there was always cocaine. Cocaine definitely was stronger stuff. It could buzz the brain in less than a minute if injected or smoked.

But the trouble with all speed was that it had to be taken just before competing, and even the most primitive testing system would pick it up in a urine sample. So Andy decided to soft pedal the use of stimulants in general and only recommended a little ephedrine if he knew there would be no doping control at a race or if the athlete could be relied on to cheat successfully when providing the urine sample. He liked to point out that speed was only mind-jolting stuff, and he wanted his athletes to have enough control not to rely on it.

He wanted the emphasis elsewhere. Making it to the big event meant muscle power, so Andy Nagy began his affair with the new and improved world of steroids. In Hungary, he had known the shadowy people who worked on testosterone and its derivatives. The initial experiments resulted in some of the Iron Curtain countries showing up at Munich and Montreal with grotesquely masculine women. He remembered meeting a promising young female athlete when he was still at the Institute who had been inducted into the state program. She had been stuffed with so many hard steroids from the age of 13 on that by the time she became gold medal material in discus, her medical tests cast doubt on her femininity. Andy had wondered how it felt, after spending her entire teens training and dutifully consuming the dangerous cocktails, for her to learn that she was no longer considered female. The cruel system led an East German women's swim coach to say, when questioned about the deep voices of his team, "Ve have come here to svim, not to sing."

Shortly after returning from Moscow, with his eye on the 1984 Olympics in Los Angeles, Andy decided it was time for him to go to school on steroids. He was convinced that they would eventually become a primary tool of his trade. Because some substances were already banned, it created the temptation to cheat. Some, he knew, could cheat better than others.

*   *   *

When her phone rang Sunday morning at 8 a.m., Karie thought that it was probably Rafael because he usually called while his mother was at church. She was surprised to hear Bonnie's voice bridge the distance and even more surprised when Bonnie announced that she and her boyfriend Jack were engaged to be married. Bonnie also mentioned that Annie had told her Rafael's mother was ill and had been in the hospital for tests. Karie told Bonnie her news. The Beef Council had been so pleased with her first Protein Kid campaign that they were planning a second, and the residual checks from the first were still arriving weekly.

As soon as she hung up with Bonnie, Karie called the airlines and booked a roundtrip ticket to Kansas. She'd been back last Christmas, but that trip had been a rushed three days of dividing her time between her family and Rafael to no one's satisfaction.

When Karie visited Bonnie's apartment, the floor was covered with swatches of fabric and sample invitations.

"Jack's father owns a printing shop, so naturally he's going to engrave our invites," Bonnie said.

"Naturally," Annie chimed. The wedding was scheduled for December of '88, and Karie was secretly glad that it came after the Olympics.

"Karie, what do you think for the bridesmaids' dresses? The teal or the aqua silk?"

"I like them both. Besides it's your wedding."

"But I want you and Annie to be happy with the dresses."

"I say teal," said Annie, "It's more evocative." Bonnie and Karie giggled at Annie's description.

"What did Mom say when you told her?" Karie asked.

"She was thrilled and got all teary-eyed. So did Dad. Especially when I told him the ceremony was going to be traditional and that I wanted him to give me away."

Karie grew silent. She had expected Dad to be distant, but the reality hit hard and she'd been reduced to one angry cry in her bedroom. She did not know that her father later drove off to a construction site and sat gripping the wheel of the truck, talking to himself. She showed Dad a series of her competition shots from the summer season, but she kept all the things she wanted to share with him about the team and her training bottled up inside her. Rafael suggested that she let time pass.

Her sisters were also testing the champagne Karie had picked up at LAX. As Bonnie talked about her plans, Karie noticed a definite change in her. Her hair had been cut to a crisp and swingy bob. Though she still spoke in her quiet, methodical way, Bonnie's hesitant mannerisms had been replaced by an almost worn-in casualness, as if a sudden lightness had infused her. It made Karie relax and, at the same time, ache for home. Karie didn't want to be back in Goodland—she knew that was impossible—but she longed to define the shapeless future beyond her Olympic goal.

Mom was overjoyed to see her. Karie caught her frequent sidelong glances and it made her nuts how many times Mom said, "My, you've grown." But she wouldn't have traded their time together for the world. Karie showed Mom the proofs of her three-page magazine ad for Irish Kiss liquid soap. In each shot, Karie looked as if she'd just stepped out of a shower and shrugged into some casual clothes. Each page had a message. Clean. Pure. Healthy.

"Look at this," said Mom, picking a photo that showed Karie, relaxed and happy, in jeans and a beige chamois vest. "Are you wearing a bra?"

She laughed. "Can't you tell? No."

"You look so natural, Karie."

"Mom, it took about three hours from makeup to finish."

"But it doesn't look like you're wearing any."

"You get a touch-up before each shot because of the studio lights."

"Look at your hair, all straggly and wet." Mom wanted to be taken through the whole process, step by step. She promised to visit Karie at the first opportunity and asked, among all the things she'd done, whether she had room service and breakfast in bed.

Karie visited Coach Gertz's office unannounced. She sneaked up to the door and nearly blew her cover when the familiar sight of his feet propped up on his desk almost made her giggle.

Karie popped her head in, "Hey, Coach," she said.

Lou practically fell out of his chair. He stood up and gave her a big hug.

"It's the Protein Kid," he said. "My word, you feel strong."

"I'm still at it, Coach."

They walked around the track as Karie told him about the summer meets and her training regime. She explained her countdown to the trials next year and how she was focusing on making the U.S. team.

"Coach, you should come to a meet."

"Maybe. That athletics job in Arizona—looks like it might happen next summer."

"Great. Then I'll come and train with you."

Lou shook his head. "You're big-time now—and Andy's a great coach."

Karie nodded. Coach seemed happy for her. Everything seemed to be working out for him too.

Then he put his arm round her as they walked. "Do me a favor, Karie. You make the decisions. Coaches can get carried away. But you're doing the running—not them. It's your body and your life."

"There's more to life than track, right? I won't forget."

Karie went for long walks with Rafael along the trails she had run as a kid. They made love behind a turret of tall leaves, close to the patch of mondo grass where she used to pick crocuses. During their walks, Rafael talked about Cooper Union, the art school in New York he planned to attend as soon as his mother got better. For him, the great thing about Cooper Union was that all tuition costs were covered by the school once a student matriculated. The teachers there were so excited about Rafael's work that they agreed to hold his place until his mother was well again. Karie noticed how frail she looked although she kept the same work schedule.

"I'll still be only a plane ride away," he said. It was their last afternoon together and they had borrowed Bonnie's apartment.

"Let me know, and I'll drive you to the airport." Karie smiled; it seemed so long ago. "And buy your ticket."

"Then you can come and visit me, Karie. You could model my latest creations."

"We'll go into business together. I can see it now—the House of Rafael." She smiled and put her arms around him. "It's less than a year to go now for the trials—then we'll have plenty of time."

Rafael began to unbutton her blouse. He always insisted on taking all her clothes off, slowly and between caresses. Once, when they had come home late to the apartment in Marina del Rey, she had kicked of her heels, shrugged off her clothes and jumped into bed. When she glanced up to see his look of disappointment, she had dressed again and let him take off every stitch.

Rafael kissed her ears, her neck and the hollow of her throat. They stood close together as he unhooked her bra, gently licked her nipples, and embraced her. Then he dropped to one knee, removed her panties and burrowed his face between her thighs until she fell tremulously back onto the bed.

Later, as he helped her dress, he said, "In these last months of training, I want you to be careful."

"What do you mean?"

"Sometimes you get stubborn. Forgive me," he kissed her shoulder, "but you might train too hard. Don't overdo it."

"Promise," she said. That was the second piece of advice she'd had.

*　　*　　*

The day after returning from Goodland, Karie went to Andy's apartment in Playa del Rey. She had been there once before at a team celebration. This time, it was just the two of them.

105

They sat together on a couch, watching video race sequences that Andy had put together, 800 and 1500 meter tapes, men and women.

"Watch Lane 5 here in the 800 meters," Andy instructed. "She's from Texas State."

Karie watched number five start in the lead pack, fall off a little, begin to threaten the leader on the final back straight, and fade badly to sixth place. She couldn't tell what the race was, but the poor woman looked devastated.

"Poor strategy, bad finish." Andy rewound the tape. "Look at the arms and the body position in the first 200." He hit the pause button. "Not smooth and no control."

Karie thought she looked hyper—like she was trying to run through the early-race jitters.

"The mind must control the body." He went through the strategy as they watched the sequence again. "Okay, so now she's got problems, she hears the bell and she's thinking, 'I've still got a lap to go, I'm hurting and I'm way off...' So look—she speeds up. Wrong!" He banged the coffee table for emphasis. "Watch her fade on the last 200."

Karie felt sorry for number five. A bad race was tough, but the postmortem was worse.

"See." Andy froze a frame on the final straight. "The shoulders have dropped, the arms are loose—she's dead." He pushed a notepad over to her. "You should make notes. You must study the tapes. I want you to *learn* racing." He grabbed the pad, wrote on it, and pushed it back.

Karie read out, "3 equals 1:59." She looked up, puzzled.

"If *Andy* had *trained* her, she would have been three seconds faster, at least. She would have run a 1:59," he said.

Karie shrugged, "I guess." *Andy is beating this one to death*, she thought. *So the poor woman had a bad day; it happens.*

Andy jumped up, "I know what you're thinking—too bad, big deal, do better next time, right? No!" he stabbed at the image on the TV screen, "There is no next time for her because this race was the finals of the trials for the 1984 Olympics. If she ran a 1:59, she comes in third," he paused, "and makes the U.S. team."

Karie looked again at the screen—the last desperate effort, the frantic look. She heard Andy say, "That was Tina Venturi. She had to remember that race for the next four years, maybe forever."

He dropped down beside her and took her shoulders in his hands. "Now you see why Andy wants you to watch his cockamamie tapes. Because there is no next time." His face was so close to hers that Karie could see the different shades of gray and white hairs in his eyebrows and the spittle in the corners of his mouth. He sank back on the cushion as if the video sequence had wearied him.

"So when you line up for the big race, and the other women look strong and tough...and you get that shitty, hollow feeling... and you wonder if you've peaked just right...but you want so much to win...stop." He sat up. "And think. The body doesn't matter any more. It's the mind. Take control. Focus. Run smart."

Karie's eyes strayed back to the TV. *He's right*, she thought, *I need to practice mental blocking. I don't want to end up like her.*

Andy watched Karie concentrate on the tape. The light played on her lashes and his eyes traced her profile to the cut of her jaw, down her long neck to her taut and sinewy body. "That's why we have to be together, Karie, so that I can protect you from failure," he said. "It's you and me. I will teach you the mental games." Something in the urgency in Andy's tone caught Karie off guard, and she turned to him. Andy muted the sound of the TV. Speaking softly he continued, "It will be a wonderful partnership. We must become one. You must trust me completely. Share everything with me. If not, how can Andy protect you?"

Karie smiled and nodded, thinking how long she had worked for this, for someone to really be there, in her corner. Finally all her hard work had paid off.

Andy bent to kiss the top of her forehead and stood up. "It is good," he said.

The next day after the workout she went to see Tanya and, on impulse, took a computer printout of her running on the treadmill.

"Look," said Karie smiling, "I thought you might like it for your gallery."

Tanya glanced at it and, with a wintry smile, put it aside. "You have not been using sunblock on your face, my dear. If we wanted a weathered look, we would hire fishermen," she said severely, her own pallor attesting to the importance of serving only one calling.

Karie was about to head out and check with Erin on her bookings when Tanya said, "Sit, dear. We need to talk."

"So you weren't able to make it to the L'Oreal Shampoo casting?" Tanya quizzed.

"It was smack in the middle of my afternoon practice. You know I can't miss that."

"And you know that they asked for you specifically." Tanya shook her head. "What you don't know is that they yelled at Erin for an hour because she told them you were working, that she'd misread your sheet. The cost of delivering your book to their hands before 4 p.m. will come out of your paycheck."

"No problem," Karie said, beginning to bristle.

"You've only had two commercials so far this year. This is no time to miss go-sees."

"What's the problem with that? I've got plenty of money."

"You could be making six times what you're making now, and that's not even counting what you'd be able to do if you went to Paris or Milan. You healthy American types are all the rage since the Olympics."

"But I don't want to look like someone who *should* be in the Olympics. I want to *be* in the Olympics." Karie felt exasperated. With the advent of Seoul, Andy was making them work harder and would not allow for time off.

"Well, maybe you should reconsider your commitment with us then," Tanya said icily.

"I'm fired?"

"Karie, we work for you, not the other way around. It's just when you don't make it easy for us, how can we help you? You go do your Olympics thing and call me when that's over."

Later, Erin left a message saying the shampoo people did want to use her. The shoot was early November. Could she make it? Karie called back and accepted. She didn't want to burn bridges. When she spoke to Erin, she thanked her for taking up the slack. Cool as ever, Erin said, "No problem, that's my job. I'll be looking for you in Seoul."

Karie couldn't wait to break the news to Andy. "Surprise, surprise," she said. "The Protein Kid will take time out from modeling at the end of the month." She didn't say that it had really been Tanya's idea.

"Good, Karie. Good. So now you give me 100 percent. I have a surprise for you too." Andy smiled slyly, "No, I can't tell you now. We'll save it for Saturday."

Karie was glad Andy was pleased. She had returned from Goodland savoring her love for Rafael, but feeling slightly disoriented in terms of her life in L.A. Her disorientation made her realize how much she'd come to rely on Andy's opinion and guidance.

When she considered the advice of Rafael and Coach Gertz in regard to her training, their words, though sweet, seemed misinformed. It was unrealistic, she knew, to expect Coach Gertz and Rafael to know how dedicated she needed to be when they were in Goodland. They just didn't understand the rigors necessary to achieve her goal. But Andy did. If Andy's Old World possessiveness sometimes became overbearing...well then, it was only because he shared her dream and believed in her Olympic goal. If he didn't tolerate interference, it was because he needed to know that she gave 100 percent. She could accept that. So on his last two visits, she had kept Rafael away from the track and had not told Andy he was in town.

Andy doted on her constantly, pushing wayward strands of hair from her face, insisting she sit next to him when they were in groups.

Karie wasn't the only one who noticed his attention. She had become aware of CeeCee's look of vague displeasure whenever Karie said Andy was coming to pick her up. It didn't make sense that CeeCee felt left out. Every time she was invited, CeeCee opted to stay home. Whatever the reason, Karie couldn't figure it out and decided to ignore CeeCee's mood swings.

On Saturday, Andy promised to reveal his surprise at a special dinner. They went to Michael's, where he knew the manager and most of the staff, and sat in a courtyard filled with oriental shrubbery and the sound of tinkling water. Karie was glad that she had chosen her sleeveless blue silk dress; it was shapely, and yet felt loose enough for her to stretch and flex. She felt deliciously aware and in control.

Karie was tasting the kiwi sorbet, curling her tongue around the chilled spoon, when Andy said, "I don't think I told you but," he paused and looked around, even though the tables were set far apart and the waiters seemed to disappear into the garden, "we ran some numbers on the exercise physiology tests." Andy went on to explain that the lab at the UCLA center in Westwood had a software program for comparing athletes. Karie's running physiology had been compared against all others in the L.A. area for the 800 meters and, although the athletes' identities were not revealed, Andy had access to the results.

"Congratulations. You won." Andy smiled and raised his glass. "Top of the class."

Karie said, "No way," and then to mask her feeling of elation she added, "Do we get a prize for Pace?" She sipped her wine lightly. Never more than one glass, and only because they were celebrating.

Andy laughed and shook his head. But it sure had helped him with the suits that owned Pace—and would he make the most of it.

"The margin was good too," said Andy. "Should stack up well against any other competition here or back East. And now we've got to focus entirely on the trials—"

Andy was ticking off a list of events and deadlines, up to the trials in Indianapolis, set for August 1988, and all of a sudden Karie felt lonely. She should make it to Seoul, but then what? Andy would find someone else to train. She could go live with Rafael when he moved to New York, she supposed, but she'd miss her life in L.A. Karie thought about Dad. Would he be proud of her? *Running, that's what it is*, she thought. *This is what it's all about. I've got this thing inside me that keeps shouting run-baby-run. No way can I reign in, hold off or turn away. I've got to hang in and let it go. And I've got the best coach for the ride.* She turned to her coach and realized she hadn't been listening.

"We must think together on these things," Andy was saying. "We must be closer. No interruptions, no boyfriends, nothing to come between us. It's like a marriage," he smiled to smooth the analogy. "Then we will go all the way for the gold."

Just more of Andy's commitment talk, she thought.

"There's one more thing you need to do," he said. "We need to arrange for you to go and see our doctor." Andy paused and tilted his head.

Karie shrugged and smiled. "What for?"

Andy shifted, cradled his chin and became serious. "Karie, you need to talk to the doctor and listen to what he says. Dr. John believes that an athlete, most athletes, can only go so far by all the conventional means of training, however hard. He believes that if you really want to win—" he paused awkwardly as a busboy refilled their water glasses—"that if you really want to go all the way, you have to use enhancers."

"What d'you mean, enhancers?"

"It's stuff that builds you up and lets you train harder," he said.

"You mean drugs? Steroids?" Karie suddenly felt as cold as the sorbet.

Andy stiffened and held up his hand as if she had thrown something at him. Patiently now and looking around as he spoke, he said, "Dr. John believes that a very mild cycle may—"

"What do you believe, Andy?" She leaned forward incredulously, gripping the table. "You're my coach."

Andy sighed and wiped his lips with a napkin. "Karie, Karie, all I said was that you may want to talk to the doctor. If you don't want to, that's okay, it's your choice. All I thought was you might want to know what's going on all around you." He signaled for the bill.

"But it's cheating?"

"Technically." He nodded.

"Are some of the team doing it?"

"I don't know, Karie, and I don't need to know."

She shook her head sadly. "Okay. Then I don't want to know." She sure wasn't going to see any Dr. John.

"Well it's not okay, really." Andy tried to keep his tone reasonable. "It's not okay to be in the line-up for a big race and know that some people have a few seconds on you." He signed the bill.

She stared miserably at him. "What are you saying?"

He faced her, hands on the armrest of his chair. "I just thought you might want to know what sort of a playing field it is out there. I thought that it might even be helpful to know what you are up against." He rose and came round to help her up, and they stood together looking out at the soft night. "Whatever you do is your business. It's your choice—your medal."

Then he was guiding her out, his hand on her arm, as if she were in need of assistance. Karie kept a wretched silence on the way home, as thoughts crashed like waves within her. Is this what it took to become a star? Was that what Andy had promised at the Wichita meet? Hadn't Coach Gertz tried to warn her about drugs? Andy was speaking briskly about her schedule, but she wasn't really listening.

Twenty minutes later, Karie unlocked the door. CeeCee was in the living room watching TV. Karie walked in and sat down on the couch without setting down her things.

"Hey, you, how'd your evening go?" CeeCee asked, barely looking up.

"Andy brought up the subject of doping. Do you think he was kidding?"

"Andy never kids about doping," said CeeCee.

Chapter Eight

Andy did not take Karie's refusal easily. The more he thought about it, the more it annoyed him. He had used a really soft sell, and still she was appalled. That stricken look of hers, which he could still see, that said, "Watch out—here's where the wolf shows his ears." And at Michael's? He never went there with one of his girls without a positive outcome. Well, Little Miss Karie from Kansas would just have to learn that nobody was allowed to pick and choose. Coach Andy Nagy was all or nothing.

He was willing to invest some time in convincing his star athletes, even stroking egos when necessary. He didn't mind hustling a bit because every athlete eventually capitulated. Karie would have to get it through her head that there would be no shying at the gate. He was not about to let her cockamamie Midwestern values get in the way.

He could still recall the shrill lectures of Herr Doktor Ziegler at the Institute, a self-important little prick who enjoyed titillating his students by drawing very anatomically correct male and female versions of the human body on the chalkboard during lectures. Andy could still hear his voice.

"When a young boy reaches puberty, the hypothalamus organ in the brain sends a signal to the pituitary gland to secrete a hormone into the blood that causes the testicles to go into sustained production of testosterone..."

Steroids duplicate the male sex hormones, synthetically. Andy could remember the exact moment he realized that a teaspoonful of cells in the nether region of the brain could determine whether you were competitive material or a wimp. One moment, Andrei Nagy was looking out the dirty windows on a gray November day, thinking about the tits on the girl in the tea shop. The next moment, he was considering the possibility that steroids could trick the body into working overtime, serving the same purpose a doctor's smack on the rear serves a newborn. Andy began to breathe in the new wide vistas of the steroid world and hung on every word of old Ziegler's lecture.

"For the next few years the testosterone goes to work in developing a man's muscular physique as well as the other sex characteristics, such as body and facial hair," Doktor Ziegler shrilled, "the deepening of the voice, development of the genitals, and arousal of the sex drive." Chalk squeaked. "Once the appropriate development is achieved, the hypothalamus perceives this as a result of a feedback system and eases off on the throttle. That's all there is to it," said the Doktor. His truncated and simplistic explanation was deliberate. The scientists at the Institute were jealous of sharing their research. It drove Andy nuts the way they purposely withheld information, and he had to resist a strong temptation to try the wonder drugs himself.

In the wake of the 1980 Moscow Olympics, Andy decided his knowledge of steroids was primitive, and he decided further study was in order. Dr. Brantley John of Ventura, California, became his tutor. When Andy met the doctor through a decathlete he was training, he recalled him as a shadowy figure who hung out on the fringes at most L.A. meets. Even though his office had wall-to-wall certificates from Europe, South Africa and a portfolio of countries in Latin America, Dr. John, President of Medical Research Inc., did not overtly claim an M.D. degree. He had originally trained as a veterinarian at the Manchester Polytechnic in England and acquired an honorary doctorate in applied psychology in Paraguay. With heavy, tinted spectacles and a red, slightly chapped complexion, flanked by Hippocratic emblems, he dispensed advice in all fields of medicine but gently demurred from providing prescriptions, as if this were something that you had other people do.

Despite Dr. John's lack of bona fide medical training, he had impressive knowledge in the field of performance enhancers, especially steroids, because, as he put it, "Mr. Nagy, that's where the money is."

He had developed his knowledge in the field of animal husbandry, guided by the demand in America for lean meat. He then moved on to studying what made horses swifter and stronger and jump higher and had naturally progressed to the human animal.

The first time Andy met with Dr. John had been the last time he'd seen his office. The address was on Wilshire, just east of Beverly Hills, in a medical building. The door to the suite was locked, which Andy found odd. He knocked and a lilting voice called out, "Who's there?"

"It's Andy Nagy for Dr. John."

The doctor himself opened the door.

"Ah, Mr. Nagy, how very nice to meet you. Do come in and have a seat."

As the doctor lowered the window shades part way and flicked on a light, Andy glanced around. The office was meticulous, not a paper clip out of place. It reminded Andy of the petty bureaucrats in Hungary whose offices were immaculate only because they had nothing to do all day.

"Care for something?" Dr. John seemed disappointed when Andy shook his head, but got down to business fast. "The trick, Nagy," Dr. John lectured, "is to get the testosterone to bind with the muscle cell." Dr. John took up a child's toy lying on a corner of his desk. "You cannot get this square peg into the round hole—or indeed the triangle, rectangle or semi-circle. But once you have the right fit"—he kept jerking two blocks together for emphasis in a gesture of copulation—"you have connection. The steroid enters the muscle cell and causes the DNA to wake up and crank out more protein. This makes the muscle," he paused expectantly, "bigger." He took off his spectacles and polished them with a cloth. "Yes, it grows in size and strength.

"Now," Dr. John continued," when the free steroid molecule in the bloodstream mates successfully—"

"What if it doesn't?" Andy asked.

"Let me come to that," said the doctor irritably. "When it binds successfully, a number of other reactions take place. First, the volume of blood can increase by up to 20 percent."

Andy understood that. More raw power and more fuel. What a combo. He could see the pro body builders at the gym with biceps like grapefruit rippling under the skin. The doctor droned on about

115

nitrogen retention, increased glycogen storage, and how steroids somehow inhibited the cortisol entering the muscle tissue—which was an added plus, because cortisol reduced muscle size. *Is this a great product or what?* thought Andy, but he carefully hid his enthusiasm from the doctor.

"Matchsticks, they're called," said Dr. John, "or to the cognoscenti, creatine phosphate. They fire up the muscles." The doctor interlaced his fingers over his soft belly and glanced obliquely at Andy. "Have you ever really looked at the start of the men's 100 meters—the race for the fastest man alive?"

Andy hated it when people pontificated, but he kept his patience because he needed the goods.

"See how the winner blasts out of the blocks like a rocket? He's got more matchsticks, that's why. Either because of superior genes or," he paused, "through a good dose of steroids."

Net, net, Andy concluded, the numbers were awesome. A successful cycle of say 12 weeks—steroids plus intense training—yielded bulked, "ripped" muscles and faster recovery time. *A kid adds 25 pounds of lean muscle and increases his lifts from 175 to 225 pounds. Not bad for about 250 bucks. What's an American gold medal worth? One million? Five million? Hell, you could take baths in steroids and still have plenty for a penthouse and a stable of Porsches.*

"To your question, now, my friend," said Dr. John. "The free steroid floats along the bloodstream, looking for a friendly receptor with which to bind, but there's no way of directing it solely to a muscle cell. This is the fly in the ointment." The doctor folded his arms and shrugged. "I wouldn't be honest if I didn't say there can be considerable side effects."

Andy nodded slowly. He had heard as much.

He is enamored with the entire process, thought the doctor. *The side effects would have to be devastating to keep this one from having a change of heart.* He leaned forward enthusiastically, "Look, Nagy, we all have a delicate balance of testosterone and estrogen in our systems. So the ingestion of varying forms of testosterone can derange the body chemistry."

These goddamn doctors can be very glib about the downsides, thought Andy. *They don't have to deal hands-on with the consequences, like a coach does.*

"First thing that happens," said Dr. John, "is that the hypothalamus finds out about the foreign invasion and promptly orders the testicles to shut down production of testosterone. This leads to testicular atrophy and decreased sperm production. The balls shrivel up—adios, gonads," he laughed. "In fact, when you have a serious case of the shrinks, the only cure is to jumpstart production with a hormone called HCG, which is purified from the urine of pregnant women."

"I thought you went around feeling very macho," Andy said.

"You mean wanting to screw anything that walks?" he chuckled. "Yes, heightened libido occurs, but through a little trick in our DNA, this is then followed by impotence, even sterility. The athlete can't get it up, or hold it up, which is probably worse." He laughed unpleasantly.

"I thought that was only for large doses, or some special cases?"

"You want to try it, Coach?"

Andy shook his head. No way was he going to take that risk.

Dr. John stared moodily at Andy.

"There's more," Dr. John continued. "Remember those free steroids floating around in the blood? At least two things can happen, and neither is very good. One possibility is that the steroids can bind with receptors in the brain." Dr. John paused. "Have you ever heard of 'roid rage'? Some of the heavy users are human time bombs, quite ready to beat the stuffing out of anybody at the slightest provocation."

That would apply to the body builders, thought Andy. Bunch of baboonaroids who seemed to be locked in combat with weights. "Can't they fix it—reformulate or something?" Andy asked. But the doctor ignored him.

"Then again, by another strange process, the steroids can end up being converted to estrogen."

"The female hormone?" Andy could not imagine the results.

"Quite so," said Dr. John. "The estrogen scurries off and starts doing women's work, like developing the fatty tissues around the nipples. Now picture this, Nagy," the doctor stood up. "Here we have our budding Mr. Universe who has so much muscle he can hardly move when, presto, he starts to develop tits—and a high voice." The doctor continued in a ridiculous falsetto, "So the poor slug has an operation to remove the bitch tits, as they are called. Either that or wear a bra."

"Score one for the women," said Andy.

"Touché, my dear fellow. But that," he looked at his watch, "is for another class."

Dr. John watched through the wooden louvers as Andy got into his Porsche and drove off. He'd told Andy enough today. He could tell Andy was hooked by the possibilities, and Dr. John didn't want to spook a lucrative connection. So why bother the coach with the minor derangements, such as acne, facial hair or premature baldness—they were cosmetic anyway. But there was one potential side effect he'd deliberately avoided discussing. The bigger a muscle grew, the more likely it was that the athlete could overburden and tear the tendons which attach the muscle to the bone. Coaches got real nervous just thinking about that.

*   *   *

Andy stood in the infield and watched Karie go through her 1200 meter descending routine. Right now, he would like to march her into his office, bend her over his desk, pull down her tights and squirt some steroids into those buns of hers. By summer he could guarantee she'd be feeling pumped and wouldn't have any problem with the lactic, or the pain, or whatever. *Christ, by now she could have packed away a couple of cycles of the stuff and would have been really outstanding.* Goddamn, it pissed him off. It was already too late for Seoul.

It was March of '88, four months since they'd gone to Michael's, and she still didn't realize what she'd be up against in the trials. He

118

had to admit that she was working real hard. She should be top three material for the U.S. team in August, but that wouldn't guarantee a thing. She might be the Great American Hope—America's chance to wrest back the 800 meters gold medal. Or the 1500 meters. Or both. *Christ only knows how, but that girl is going to get on the juice, so help me,* Andy thought bitterly. He just wished to God it could've been in time for Seoul.

Karie walked toward him, hands on hips, breathing heavily, and glistening with sweat. What was it his friend Milos said? Little beads that tasted like absinthe—that was it. They fell into step just inside the track.

"You eased off a little on the last 200," said Andy.

He's got eyes in the back of his head. "My left calf felt a little stiff by then. I didn't want to push it."

"You haven't been playing volleyball again?"

"No. I —"

"Or anything else, Karie? You know the rules."

"No way, Coach."

He believed her. The last time, he'd almost reduced her to tears. None of his Star Program girls was to risk a sprain or a twisted ankle— he didn't even want them jumping off a curb.

"I think my calf tightened up because I was working real hard today."

Even Karie needs some stroking, he thought. "How'd it feel?"

"I thought I was fast today."

"You were." He put his arm around her shoulders. "Faster than ever," he said and felt her relax. *Of course if she really wanted to please me, she could get on the juice, then she wouldn't feel stiff. But the season was about to start, so it was too late anyway. Shit.*

"Karie, we've got 10 days until the first meet. It's San Diego. Fast track. I want you thinking PR." He stopped. "Look at that kid Marcia—what's she doing?"

Karie watched their newest recruit, a 400 meter runner. "Leaning forward?"

"Well, that too—but it's her arms. Looks as if they're just along for the ride."

"Yeah, yeah," said Karie, smiling now. "Every part of the body runs, right? Nothing gets a free ride. Even the ears—you can hear your speed."

"Right." He gave her a high five. "So think PR," he said briskly. "It helps to blow 'em away at the start of the season."

"I'm ready."

"Go ice the calf. And you need to taper off for San Diego—but no volleyball."

She turned abruptly.

"Just kidding," said Andy. "And Karie—I've got another tape for you."

"You have? I want it. Where is it?" Excited, she stutter-stepped in front of him.

"On my desk. It's the '86 World Championships 800s. I want you to study the women *before* the race. See if you can pick the winner. We'll watch it tomorrow. Now, what did I tell you?"

"I know, I know. Everything communicates." She ran off toward the office.

"No cheating," he shouted. *Karie was doing well with the mind games.* Telemetry, he called it. She would study the video of women stretching and warming up for an international event, and he would quiz her on what kind of a race they ran. Then they would watch the actual race on tape. She needed to learn the language of the body, to be able to smell fear in a competitor. Karie lacked feral aggressiveness toward other runners. Andy discovered long ago that the desire to tear the competition apart and pound them into the ground was instinctual and not easily coached. But what Karie lacked in aggressiveness she made up for in intelligence. She was becoming very good at reading body signs. Sometimes she picked up things even he had missed.

Once again he felt a flash of irritation at her resistance to enhancers. Here he was opening up the tent on his best techniques, and she didn't want to discuss them. Maybe this was something that cockamamie Lou Gertz had put in her head. Andy had considered spiking Karie's isotonic drinks, but rejected the notion as impractical. He could try and strong-arm her, but he knew that wouldn't work. Besides, he would lose her admiration, so evident every time she pranced up after a workout just to say, "Hey, Coach."

Andy took one last look around the field. He didn't like the idea of a Pace Track Team without Karie, and the realization annoyed him. Even the suits in the syndicate had congratulated him on her recruitment. Well, the way she's going, she should make Seoul. And if she didn't, he'd use that as future leverage.

*   *   *

Andy liked having periodic updates on the latest doping products, and Dr. John was happy to oblige. They no longer met at the doctor's office. He had leased a Mercedes and a car phone and was maintaining a mobile relationship with most of his clients. He met Andy at Ships, a diner at La Cienega and Olympic. As they walked in, Dr. John turned and asked, "It's Thursday, isn't it?"

"Yes," Andy replied.

"Goody. Today's special is turkey with gravy."

They sat down at a booth and a busboy brought ice water. Dr. John began to play with his fork and continued the conversation they started in the parking lot.

"First, you have the water-soluble derivatives," said Dr. John. "Just pop them in your mouth—things like Anavar, Winstrol or Dianabol."

Part of this was familiar ground, but Andy knew the doctor was scrupulous about covering the whole field. Hell, you could get D-bol at the local gym. Even the pugs knew it would clear your system in less than a month.

"Then you have the oil-based esters which are stored in the fatty tissues. Remember that I recommended Deca-Durabolin to you," said Dr. John. "It's smoother and less risky because the steroid is released over time, when your athlete burns fat through exercise."

Andy consulted his notes. "But it can take up to six months to leave the body. Why can't the backroom boys come up with a good masking agent?"

The doctor sucked air through his teeth and sighed. "Look, Nagy, if avoiding detection is the main objective, then shoot them with straight testosterone. Of course, it has the most negative macho effects."

A waitress came to the table. Dr. John ordered two coffees and the special.

"I would like some tea," Andy said. "Milk, no lemon."

"So one coffee and one tea?" the waitress asked.

"No, two coffees and one tea," Dr. John replied. "They never refill it fast enough," he confided to Andy.

"Where were we? Oh yes, to testosterone, or not to testosterone, that is the question." Then he badgered Andy by chanting a Gilbert and Sullivan ditty about the enchanting paradox. He paused on the high note and said, "But I have the solution—stacking. A mixture, my dear Nagy, a bit of this and a dash of that, makes the goulash more palatable."

They paused while the waitress brought their beverages.

"Stacking?" Andy said.

"Yes, stacking," Dr. John replied. "By stacking one drug on top of another, you blend the most desirable muscle-building characteristics while tempering the negatives and reduce the chances of getting caught."

Andy could put up with Dr. John's patronizing attitude and even the show tunes because the little shit of a horse doctor knew his stuff. Andy wondered if anyone at the Institute had thought of this.

"What we could try, Coach," he said, looking sideways at Andy to judge his reaction, "is to begin the cycle with some Deca injections." He put up his hand, "Bear with me...and move to Winstrol pills and some aqueous testosterone—then, for the final month, taper the Winstrol and turn up the Testex. An excellent cocktail, if I may say so." He took out a pad of Medical Research Inc. paper. "I'll have to calculate the right dosages. Oh, and after the full 12-

week cycle add some HCG, just to get the balls back in business."

The waitress brought out Dr. John's order. "Can I get you anything else?" she asked.

"We're fine," Andy said, "What's the latest stuff for the women?"

"For the Amazons, as I told you before, we need to be more careful. Atrophy of the old gonads is not a problem," Dr. John chuckled, "but we need to watch out because the virilizing effects tend to be permanent. We don't want her shaving for the rest of her life, or singing baritone in the choir."

"We could interrupt the cycle of enhancers?" Andy offered.

"Primobolan," said Dr. John, "good stuff. We could start with these tablets, together with some shots of Deca."

Andy started shaking his head, and the doctor looked annoyed.

"Look, if they shy away from the syringe that's not my problem—I'm telling you what's best."

Andy knew injections were a problem, especially with the women. It took half a second to wash down a pill along with your pride. The prick of the injection needle, on the other hand, might as well be the sting of conscience.

Dr. John continued. "I would hold off after the first four weeks and see what's going on. If everything's okay, I would resume on week eight and continue with Deca, bag the Primo, and switch to a half-dose of Anavar."

The doctor felt he'd told Andy enough for the day. He put the pad away in his briefcase. "I'm not ready to try straight testosterone—not yet anyway. Unless you've got a bull dyke in the traces, Nagy."

As the doctor drove off and Andy paid the bill, Andy was already considering another alternative. These new products enabled a smart coach to tailor the combinations to meet an athlete's individual needs. Anyone who understood enhancers could charge big money for such a specific program. Come get your complete enhancer system at Andy's Full Service Station. What an opportunity.

*   *   *

As Andy considered the start of the '88 season for Pace Track, he had to admit that things looked good. He felt Pace would win another national title by late summer and could have a record crop of his athletes qualifying for the Seoul Olympics. He had six men training on the side, including one from Boise, and figured two or three should make the U.S. team. The number was more than likely double that for his Pace girls. The word was out. If you want to win, go with Andy.

So far—touch wood—the doping issue was being handled well, and Andy felt he'd worked out most of the kinks from 1984. Even though he pretended to an arm's length relationship, he knew from the doctor who was doing what. They had started with the men because, as Dr. John put it, "The side effects won't be as noticeable, and besides, the dear ladies don't have much testosterone raging around in the blood. Even a low dosage could give them a serious jolt." Andy had given a lot of thought to his initial approach. He had settled on a couple of attention grabbing one-liners, reliable standbys from peer pressure days, which could function in tandem like one-two slaps to the head. He led with you-want-to-win-don't-you? followed by everybody's-doing-it.

It turned out to be easier than he expected.

He had misjudged the athlete's visceral need to try anything that held out even a vague promise of improved performance. *To hell with the consequences* seemed to be the credo of the contemporary athletes. They just wanted their places in the sun.

After an initial period of success with the men, Andy's next step was to try and hook some of the women. CeeCee Thomas was one of the early ones. He spotted her great potential when she was a freshman at UCLA and her coach had her trapped in the relays. Andy moved her to the 200 meters and she became one of his star girls. She was slow out of the blocks, but when she swept around a curve it was an act of grace.

Black wasn't his favorite color of the rainbow, but he liked

CeeCee's high spirits. Her army brat upbringing, in a household where even the shag carpet stood at attention, meant not only did she respond well to orders but also that she lacked a place to call home and would know how to pick up and go quietly when it was time to move on. Maybe it was the time spent in Europe, but CeeCee had few problems taking off her clothes when Andy offered a sports massage. A little while later, she was spending entire weekends, day and night, at his apartment. CeeCee was a hot lay, but Andy found himself wondering what she'd be like if given the right doses of Dr. John's cocktail. Perhaps when he'd perfected the use of steroids in athletics, he'd move to the civilian market and sell certain combinations as aphrodisiacs. One Friday evening after a tough workout session on the track and another one in the bedroom, Andy found a way to bring the topic up.

"Coach, I'm going to take a shower before dinner," CeeCee said.

"Fine," Andy said. "Hand me that journal before you leave."

CeeCee picked up the slim magazine and glanced at the cover. "You read medical journals? I'm impressed, Coach," CeeCee said as she brought it over.

Andy normally would have been irritated by the hint of sarcasm, but he managed to smile. "Yes, there happen to be some really good studies out lately on steroids and athletics."

"Great," CeeCee yelled from the bathroom. More sarcasm.

"Surely you want to know about enhancers," said Andy. "To know what you'll be up against."

CeeCee came out, a towel wrapped around her body, and shrugged. "Why? Maybe I'm better off not knowing."

"I don't make the rules, CeeCee. I have to live with them."

"So do I—and I can get caught. Maybe they'll change the rules. Or enforce them better."

Andy sighed. "Don't hold your breath. Athletes have always used enhancers. Concoctions of strychnine and alcohol, heroin, cocaine—whatever." Andy believed most athletes were pitifully insecure and that being part of a long tradition of doping was comforting. He held back on some of the more grisly references—like the use of testosterone by some of Hitler's troops or the Japanese kamikaze pilots—he saved those for the men.

CeeCee said, "If I'm caught, I'm banned, finished."

"Like I said, it isn't a level playing field. Next thing, they'll ban hypnosis or electro-stim. You tell me what's fair." It always helped to commiserate.

"I could have side effects and complications. Why risk it?"

Andy shrugged. "Suit yourself. But I think I've been very generous with my time and knowledge. It's you and me, CeeCee, all the way, but I can't do it without you. I happen to know the guy who wrote this article. His name is Dr. Brantley John. At least go talk to him." He knew CeeCee would not look at the magazine. The thought of Dr. John being published in a reputable medical journal, or any medical journal for that matter, amused Andy.

In the end, CeeCee agreed to a trial period, provided she was tested every two weeks. Initially, things went well, and she made the U.S. team for the Los Angeles Olympics. But then there was an accidental screw-up in the dosage, and she was told the steroids wouldn't clear her system in time. She had to tank her preliminary Olympic heat, even though she was considered to have strong medal potential.

CeeCee was devastated. "Maybe I could have made it without them," she sobbed to Andy. CeeCee always treated steroids as if they were a separate host that temporarily inhabited her body. "Now I'll never know." She never took anything else again and refused to discuss her experience.

Since then, the products had improved and Dr. John had become much better at gauging the correct dosages. Andy was elated by how positive and confident some of his girls became. When he increased their training load, they took it in stride and displayed an assertiveness that bordered on truculence. But the best effect the enhancers had on the girls was the way it made them strut.

Over at the Olympus Club in Santa Monica, his girls preceded him like a praetorian guard heralding his arrival. Uninhibited, they would range through the cavernous, dimly-lit premises full of insecure people jockeying for position. They would return to his side, having scoured the hall, leaving many bruised egos in their wake. Andy kept a zealous watch over his charges. He was immensely titillated by the envy he observed as he sat drinking Perrier and lime with his adoring retinue. Beautiful women at his command. This was America.

Chapter Nine

It was six months until Seoul, a little over four months until the U.S. Olympic Trials in Indianapolis. Karie felt good. She was right where she wanted to be in her spring training. Her times for the 800 meters were only a couple of seconds off Houston's Marie Stevens, and Stevens was the current front runner. Karie planned to peak in time for the trials. She couldn't believe how warm it was already; the weatherman said over 70 degrees. There was still snow on the ground in Goodland. Barefoot, in jean shorts and a Pace T-shirt, she tacked a calendar to the back of her bedroom door and marked the key meets and check points in her training schedule. Her life now revolved around training and competing, and she was happy. She could see the light, and it wasn't a very long tunnel.

Andy never again raised the issue of doping and was increasingly supportive as they reviewed her schedule leading up to the trials. It was clear to her that Andy meant what he said; he only wanted her to know what she might be up against. It was true that this had come in the context of his recommending a mild cycle, but, much as she abhorred the idea, she couldn't really blame him. After all, he merely offered her the option; there had been no pressure attached, neither then nor subsequently. In fact, Karie had to admit that she had been very naive about drugs, and it was just as well that Andy had raised the issue. Maybe she'd overreacted. She trained harder than ever because she didn't want Andy to question her commitment.

Actually, Karie was glad to know what was going on. The real eye-opener came when a competitor who'd never been in Karie's league before came close to beating her for first in the 800 at a regional meet in Oregon. Karie had been really upset and asked Andy what she did wrong.

Andy shrugged, "You ran a clean race, Karie, and like I said, not everybody does."

That night, as Karie and CeeCee sat up late talking, Karie worked through her frustration.

"Whatever you do, girl—and I don't need to know—don't ever take chances and never get caught."

"Cee," said Karie, "it's me you're talking to. Remember how upset I was? No, I won't tell you because I won't ever have to."

"I would know anyway. Because I can tell. You'd be walking around like this—" CeeCee strutted aggressively around the room in her bra and panties.

"Hey, looks good," Karie smiled, "can you do that bit again where—"

"That too, girl. I'd have to watch my ass because you'd be so turned on you'd have to go around with your clit taped down." Karie started laughing and CeeCee dropped the act and sat back down on the bed.

"But seriously, girl," said CeeCee, "just before your sweet little corn-fed buns came sashaying into town we had this 400 meter woman who was doing some serious stuff. She was trying to make it into the Goodwill Games. You know what her trick was? She stuck a condom full of urine—not hers of course—up her vagina. She ran the entire race with that piece of sausage in her, and then when she gets hauled off for testing, she scratches the rubber with her fingernail and presto—pure, unadulterated piss. Probably her coach's."

Karie's hand strayed protectively to her lap, trying to imagine what it would feel like to run with a bag sloshing around between her legs—it was bad enough with a period. "No way," she said.

"Bet your ass," said CeeCee, "but there's a problem. She gives them a nice warm sample—she'd done it before—and here she is ready to book her ticket to the Games. But some smart prick in the lab notices that her urine is identical to another woman's, in the long jump I think, and they're both from the same team. So, adios Goodwill Games."

"What happened?"

CeeCee stood, rubbing her stomach. "Oh, they both got DQed, suspended, never heard of them again. But can you imagine the dumb-assed coach? Probably had the clap and it blew the testing equipment." She sat down on the bed. "There was a guy called Norton, huge mother, threw the discus, and he'd show up and train with Andy. He told me that he carried a little sachet of liquid soap taped between his cheeks, so every time he gave a sample he would rub some soap around the cup. It completely screws the test. In the end they told him, 'We don't know what you're doing, but you better quit.'"

Karie stood up. "But how could she do it? You know, how could you stuff a condom...it's so—"

"So what?"

"Awful."

CeeCee said, "Let's split a beer."

"But what about training?"

"Here we are talking 'roids and you balk at a beer. You're right, let's make it one each then." CeeCee raised her right hand. "I promise it will clear our systems before the trials."

They went into the kitchen. CeeCee popped open a couple of bottles of Heineken and sat down opposite Karie at the counter.

"Are you nervous about the trials?" Karie asked.

"Hell, no, I figured I already managed one—it's the Games I worry about."

"What are you talking about?" Karie asked, "You made it to the Games."

"But not to the finish," CeeCee took a swig of beer and Karie wished she hadn't said anything. CeeCee was quiet for a moment. "Listen, girl, you've had it easy, okay. No, I know leaving home ain't easy—but if things don't work out here you can always go home. Or you can wiggle that cute little fanny of yours or—anyway you've got opportunities up the kazoo. What d'you think some of these other girls have?" She took another swig of beer.

Karie shook her head.

"This is it. There's no going back. They'll take any deal. Offer them a medal, they'll do any stuff, even if it kills them."

Karie nodded and looked away.

CeeCee leaned across and took both her hands. "Look at me,

girl," she said softly. "I know you think you've got it figured out, but between here and an Olympics there's a long road. Even for you. So you best watch out." She tightened her grip. "You're too good to mess up."

*   *   *

Andy was eating breakfast on his balcony and, as he reached for his coffee, a morning headline caught his eye: "Atlanta to Represent U.S. in Bid for 1996 Olympics." No way. *What a cockamamie idea*, he thought. *That's Magnolia Land. Must have mixed it up with Atlantic City.* "Atlanta joins the competition with Athens, Belgrade, Manchester, Melbourne and Toronto for the right to host the Centennial celebration of the modern Olympic Games."

The USOC was putting a small bet on a slow horse. It was the 100th anniversary and Athens was in the race. No way the Greeks could screw that up. Even if they did, it would be only 12 years since L.A. The Games wouldn't come back to the U.S. that soon.

But what if the others self-destructed and Atlanta won? The benefits of Los Angeles '84, both to Pace Track and to Andy, had been considerable. With that experience under his belt, he could capitalize on this one big time.

He skimmed through the chronology of Atlanta's bid. Originally 14 cities had their hats in the ring, but the group quickly narrowed to four in December '87. Nashville inexplicably dropped out and San Francisco capitulated to a threatened gay boycott, which left Minneapolis/St. Paul and Atlanta.

There was a sidebar on the last-minute lobbying of the two rival cities at the meeting of the USOC Executive Board in Washington, D.C. Both rivals hosted events to entertain the board members in the week preceding the final formal presentations. The Minneapolis/St. Paul contingent bet on a poolside reception with a water ballet show, but a vicious cold snap drove the guests indoors, so they got only occasional glimpses of the frozen performers. Atlanta hosted an elegant dinner at a private home, with a marble staircase that evoked comparisons with Tara. The White House Strolling Strings, a violin ensemble, had been prepped to play each board member's favorite song. The reporter, exercising 20/20 hindsight, speculated on the importance of such soirees in the final outcome.

Andy decided to write Billy Payne, the leader of the Atlanta delegation, to offer his services. Maybe they could meet in Seoul. It would be over two years before the International Olympic Committee chose the host city for 1996; meanwhile, Andy could be a consultant. His mind began to fill with possibilities as he answered the ringing phone. Dr. John had also read the news. Andy held the phone away from his head as the doctor tried to sing the song from *West Side Story* about liking to be in America.

Perhaps the Atlanta bid could be the impetus Andy needed for his full service station for doping. If so, then the insufferable doctor would be just the guy to work up a menu. Choose your own cocktail. Andy spoke into the phone, "We need to talk."

*　*　*

As Andy drove from Playa del Rey to Ships on the 10 freeway, he indulged his full service station vision. What an opportunity to build a better mousetrap. He was particularly pissed off by the smooth operations of his ex-colleagues in Eastern Europe and Russia—they seemed to handle doping with tacit official blessing. Andy felt sure that the same would be true of any countries seeking to make an athletic impact, like Cuba and China. Only America had to be so goddamn honest-to-goodness all the time.

Andy cut off a white BMW, ignoring the honking horn and the finger flipped in his direction. The thought he couldn't stand was that someone could very easily be working on the same plan as he. If that were the case, all his research would be for naught.

His approach was simple and efficient—do what you have to do and don't get caught. This meant that you could fine tune your athlete by using the whole array of steroids, as if you were preparing a Formula I car for a Grand Prix event, monitoring the results with both urine and blood tests to ensure that the athlete would not test positive at a target meet.

The whole system of drug detection offered ample opportunity—the trick was in customized screening. To detect straight testosterone doping, the testers had been obliged to develop a special system because the hormone existed naturally in the body. The urine test consisted of determining the ratio of testosterone to another hormone that was its chemical mirror image. Normally this ratio was around one-to-one, but in order to allow for abnormalities, the International Olympic Committee decided that an athlete with a ratio in excess of six-to-one was considered to have taken synthetic testosterone and was judged positive. An athlete could probably shoot up as much as 100 to 300 milligrams per week for a six-week cycle and still not move the needle beyond a five-to-one ratio.

In East Germany, the doping program was in the hands of Stasi, the secret police. They would stoke some athletes up to a 20-to-1 level, or more, and then monitor the clearance curves as the ratios declined. It was simply a matter of getting the steroids in and out of the athlete's system before the big events. All you needed were good endocrinologists and a bunch of lab technicians.

The smart athletes could get away with doping; those without access to proper screening got caught. All you had to do was offer the kids a full-line, comprehensive service, at a price, and everybody would win. This was American enterprise at its best. The need was clear. Fulfill the need and reap the gold. Atlanta being in the running to host the games heightened the interest of American athletes and bolstered their need to win. It was time to put the case to Dr. John. They met for lunch at Ships.

"The kids here are going to go for the stuff whether we like it or not, right, doctor?" said Andy.

The doctor lowered his eyelids and nodded.

"Most of them haven't any idea what they should be doing, where to get it, or how much is enough. Chances are they end up talking to Pepe at Bazooka's gym, and they're lucky if they come away with anything that vaguely resembles what's on the label. They might even endanger their health."

"My, my," said Dr. John.

"I believe that if an athlete is willing to enhance competitiveness, then we should lend our support. Then all the athlete has to worry about is training and competing."

Dr. John held up his hand, "Nagy, old fellow, hold on." He sat up and looked at Andy with a pained expression. "In South America they have an expression, 'Gypsies don't read their own palms.' So spare me. Now what is it?"

"What these athletes really need," Andy closed his eyes as if he were summoning a vision, "is a full service program. A network where they can get good advice, the right products, proper checkups...that sort of thing."

"Are you going to advertise in the *L.A. Times*?"

"We know how to do it."

The doctor tugged at an ear and looked thoughtful. "Look, Nagy, I'm sure your thinking is right and that it would be a jolly good thing for your athletes and," he shrugged, " there's probably good money to be made." He cocked a look at Andy and said, "Count me out."

"I've talked to people who can supply us —"

"Mr. Nagy," he said in a tone that made Andy wonder what else Dr. John might have done in South America, "full service means supply. That means Mexico, at least. There's a border to be crossed. My sources tell me that the DEA, the FBI, the Justice Department and perhaps a few others are waiting for just such an opportunity. Washington has decided that steroids are a gateway substance that can lead to harsher stuff, hence their interest. Also, it's far less risky to go after a bunch of ex-jocks than the real dealers. As I said, I'm out."

With that, Dr. John checked his watch and, begging Andy's pardon, left for another appointment. Andy paid the bill, wondering how he might revisit the issue. No way could he pull it off without the doctor.

A few months later, the Feds nabbed a ring of conspirators bringing counterfeit drugs in from Tijuana. The leader, an Olympic medalist known as Dr. Roid, went to jail.

*   *   *

Karie sat in the locker room at the Indianapolis track on the Sunday of the U.S. Olympic Trials for Seoul and gently kneaded the sartorius muscle in her right thigh. She tried to visualize the long muscle fibers releasing the soreness trapped there as she massaged with her thumbs along her quad, pressing where the sartorius attached at the knee. *A little warmth and TLC, that's all it needs.* She murmured soothingly, "Keep me in line this last time, and I'll give you all the rest you need."

She was warmed up, although she would do a few speed bursts once she got outside. This is what she'd come all the way from Goodland for. Her family would be watching. Annie and Bonnie had sent flowers and a letter with news from home. Bonnie and Jack were moving to a bigger house so they could start a family, and Annie had decided to go back to school to eventually study law. Karie missed them and planned to visit as soon as she was back from Seoul. Rafael promised he would run in front of the TV and keep pace with her. He had sent a hand-drawn card and a love letter.

She glanced at the wall clock. At 2:18 p.m, just over 30 minutes from now, she would be in the 800 meter finals, and the first three places would qualify. The locker room was surprisingly hushed as each athlete focused on her own preparations. CeeCee told her that everyone would be concentrating so hard that no one talks or looks at anyone else. Karie was glad nobody she knew was around to break her focus. She marveled at how charged the room was, yet how quiet. Shoes were tied with the greatest attention. Athletes brushed and pulled their hair back into ponytails or braids. Women stretched or mumbled quiet prayers. This was it. The best women in America, vying to make the U.S. Olympic Team. Racing for the chance to wear the uniform and parade behind the Stars and Stripes in the Opening Ceremony. The right to say, "I was there."

Karie was not really nervous—not that gut-churning, hollow-legged feeling—just a little apprehensive about running a good race. Mostly she felt hyped and ready to go. She sipped a diluted isotonic preparation and reminded herself to go to the restroom just before the race. Karie smiled as she looked at the toilet stalls in the far corner. Could anyone be stuffing a condom-full of urine between her legs, or trying to dilute whatever forbidden substance was still lodged in her body? She shook her head and thought, *she's welcome*. Yesterday, after the prelim, a young black girl named Janet had attached herself to Karie while Karie was still tapering off in the infield. Janet had shown her badge, said she was an escort, and asked Karie to sign a paper agreeing to show up for testing within the hour.

Janet walked with her to the testing building and explained that until she was handed over to the testing staff, she could only drink water or soft drinks out of sealed containers. Karie signed another statement and was directed to pick a sample jar from a large bin. Her name was called and she was accompanied into the stall by a big, frazzled-looking woman in a pale blue uniform with a name tag that read "Meg." Karie had closed her eyes and was trying to quiet down, ignore the hulking presence, and think of passing water when Meg yelled over her shoulder, "Roz, tell her she can't leave until she does."

After a few minutes Karie felt she was getting further from the objective. She looked up from the seat, still holding her jar, and said, "Can I drink some water?"

"I don't recommend it," said Meg who continued to direct business, staring fixedly at Karie's nude lower body.

There's no way I could use a pin or a fingernail here because old Meg would be on me like a flash. "Well, Janet, the girl that brought me here, said I could drink as long as the container was sealed."

Meg tossed her head impatiently. "She's just a courier. Look, hon, if you drink too much water, you'll end up with a weak sample.

Then if the doctor says it's too diluted you have to keep on here until you give us a proper concentration—even if it takes all night."

"Okay," said Karie reaching for her uniform. "I think I'll drink a little and take my chances." Imagine spending the night with Meg—she had goose bumps on her thighs as she stepped into her damp Pace tracksuit.

Meg shrugged. "You can sit on that chair in the lounge. Make sure you keep the sample jar where we can see it. If you move away, we'll have to DQ you."

Christ, this old bag could blow me away. Contritely, Karie drank a little water and sat back in the chair, thinking of tinkling streams in fern-filled glades. Ten minutes later, not even Meg's probing look could stop her from filling her jar and continuing noisily to pass water. She then signed her container and cheerfully let science take over.

Karie walked around the locker room, testing her legs. She was fine. The muscle wouldn't bother her. Everyone came to the finals with aches and pains. She was in better condition that any of them. She was the youngest of the top contenders and had better style, better technique and a better coach. Her first prelim time was 1:58.25, which was fine because no one had gone all out. She placed second, about three paces behind Marie Stevens. Then in the next prelim it was Sandra Miller, who won in 1:58.39. Sandra, a big, bony woman who looked like she cut her own hair and never smiled, had blossomed late in the season to come within three-tenths of a second of equaling the American record of 1:56.90. Sandra was originally a 400 meter specialist and had only moved to the 800 meters this season.

There were two other girls who could be a problem: Tina Delgado from Florida and Elena Begg from Seattle. Even though Karie had beaten them both at Mount San Antonio College early in the season, she knew better than to get overconfident. She discussed all seven women in the finals with Andy last night. They broke down the women's times. On the basis of PRs, Marie should win; then it was a toss-up which of the next two places Karie and

Sandra took. Tina and Elena would probably come in next, and after that nobody would threaten from the pack. They explored the possibility that some of the women might team up against her, but there didn't seem to be any combos. They looked to the obvious problem of getting boxed in and considered who might trip or fall or spike. Karie felt that she could take Sandra. Sandra was strong, but she didn't kick well. It might be possible to beat Marie. Andy reminded Karie that Marie was 24 and had a lot of experience.

When they were finished, Andy squeezed her shoulder and said, "Karie, I think we've got it. But this is the finals. Everyone wants to make it. They will knock you down and run over you to get there."

Karie looked at the clock. Twenty minutes. Every few minutes she sipped the isotonic drink by her side. It was important to stay hydrated and maintain good blood sugar. Karie watched Marie stretch her legs. *Hell, I'm ready to blow them all off the track.* Nobody was going to get in her way. As Karie laced up her spikes, a tall, slim black woman in a Northwestern tracksuit came in, streaked with sweat. She looked like a 400 meter runner and had a wild, chilled look. Karie was going to say something to her when the woman collapsed on the bench. Suddenly the woman crumpled forward and hugged her knees as huge sobs racked her body. She was beyond consolation. *At least I made it to the finals,* thought Karie, but she felt a sudden twinge of apprehension as she hurried out to the track.

Andy stood waiting. "How is it, champ? Ready to go to work?"

Karie shook her legs so that the muscles quivered and bent her back forward and around. "Piece of cake."

Andy put his arm around her as they walked. "I think Marie and Sandra feel that they can rely on their kick, and they might hold back a bit, so take the lead if you think it's a little slow. I'll be in the same place I was yesterday." Andy made sure he caught her eyes in a locked stare before he said, "Karie, don't let anything stand in your way."

*   *   *

Lou Gertz took a seat in the stands that was almost level with the finish line and checked his watch. Karie's race would be in about 20 minutes, so she would come out soon. He had watched her preliminary race yesterday on television at the Arizona University campus. Later, he took the red-eye flight from Phoenix to Chicago and caught a connection to Indianapolis. He wouldn't have missed the finals for the world, even though this evening he would retrace his flight pattern to make a meeting he had with the athletic director on Monday morning. He had started as the track and field coach only this month. It was the job he'd promised Karie he would take during their last days together at Goodland High, only he was two years late.

Andy's done a good job, Lou thought. He'd taped the preliminary run in his University office and replayed it several times before leaving. On the flight he was able to sit back, close his eyes, and recall the images. Karie's wonderful fluid style was still there, no need to tinker with that. Certainly she looked stronger, more experienced too, in the deliberate way she came to the starting line. Her arm movement was definitely more disciplined The overall performance was more focused, more molded, but Karie's exuberance was still there.

What if Karie had trained with him over the last two years? Would she look as prepared? Would she even be here, on the verge of making the U.S. Olympic Team? Reluctantly, he admitted that he was not at all sure. The Pace experience was a unique thing. He tried to tell himself, as he had many times since she left, that Karie had made the right choice. Yet he took little comfort from the thought.

He watched the finalists move onto the track as the announcer called the race. God, he felt nervous. *She doesn't even know that I'm here*, he thought. She looked so poised, as if this were the moment she was born for. That was Karie, all right. He knew she could blow them all away, but the anticipation was killing him. He wished

140

somehow that the next few minutes would be over already, so he could head back to Phoenix, knowing that Karie had made it.

* * *

As they moved toward the start, she could feel a few flutters in her stomach. Karie had drawn Lane 8, the outside. She preferred the low numbers so that she could keep an eye on everybody else, but they would be into the cross-over after the first turn, and then it didn't matter. The track was hot to the touch, and there was only a slight breeze. Karie felt that any records—trial, American or world—would be tough in this weather.

"On your mark." She stepped up and leaned forward, arms hanging loose, left leg behind the line, her head nodding slightly.

"Set."

She sprang forward at the puff of smoke as the sound bounced around the stadium. Karie wanted to make sure she could cross to the inside lane after the turn, and she made it easily. *Don't go easy now*, she thought. *Make sure it's a good pace that strings everybody out. That way we won't have a mass sprint in the final stretch.*

At the 200 curve she looked back. The field seemed to be lagging a bit, except for one woman who was a couple of paces back. *That's what Andy had said to watch for, an attempt to keep the pace slow so that they can rely on a strong kick at the end. No way. Just keep the power on and make them hurt.*

As she came round the bend into the 400 meter straight she was going good. "Keep your line, keep your style," Andy always said. She heard the bell and the time of :55 as she took the curve. Less than 400 meters to go. She almost stumbled at the thought of :55. *It can't be…*she'd never done :55, :58 or :59 was what you wanted… *Christ, I'm too fast.*

Andy saw the problem early and knew the lap time before it appeared. *It's the curse of the outside lane. I told her to watch for the slow start and she's over-corrected.* He watched her swing into the back stretch. *Karie knows she's in trouble. Son of a bitch, this is not*

141

her kind of race now. He clenched his teeth and watched the gap narrow.

Karie glanced back. Marie and Sandra were about 15 meters back. *Shit, what do I do, I can't ease off, I'll lose the pace.* She could feel the hurt now. *Must have been all the adrenalin at the beginning...gotta hang in now...take it 50 meters at a time...think finish.* The blood was really pounding in her ears now. *Only 200 to go.* The woman who was just behind had dropped way off. *Just a little more...keep pushing.*

At the last curve she saw Marie 10 meters back and gaining. Karie tried to kick but couldn't. She could feel the burn in her whole body. *Don't trip, just keep pumping through the straight.*

Lou realized he was on his feet, shouting her name in desperation. Maybe the sound would reach out and carry her forward just a little because it was going to be a matter of inches. He was scared. *She must feel like she's tearing apart,* he thought.

In the press room at the far west end offices over the track, journalists and reporters listened and watched the race from one of several TVs placed around the press room. Their colleague Randy Boyd announced the race: "They're in the final stretch now and Karie Johnson is still in the lead, but can she hang on after that blistering first lap? Here come Marie Stevens and Sandra Miller, with Elena Begg hanging with them. They're at the 50 in record time. Stevens is level now...doesn't seem like Johnson will be able to hold on, with Miller and Begg just behind for now, it's coming down to the wire...that's it, Marie Stevens wins, Sandra Miller second and...hold on, let's see if we can replay that...it looks like a tie for third between Karie Johnson and Elena Begg. Marie Stevens from Houston, Texas, wins the 800 meters in 1:56.32, a new American record. If it holds up, that's six-tenths off the old mark, ladies and gentlemen. Seems as if Miller is also a record breaker today, with Johnson and Begg tied at the previous mark of 1:56.90. What a race! They'll be sending this one up to the judges to see who makes it...Elena Begg or Karie Johnson."

It's Elena, thought Karie, *I just know*. She had staggered at the finish and thought she would black out. But the tearing pain in her chest had eased now. She had walked straight over to the testing office with her courier. She just wanted to get it over with and get out. As a tie for third she had to be tested until the judges blew up the photo-finish images and decided whether Elena's or her torso broke the plane first.

Even in that respect she had shown inexperience by dropping her head at the line. If you drop your head, you pull your chest in. Push your boobs, pull your head, how many times had she heard that said? Of course, she almost lost her head in those final steps anyway. Everything was ready to go. She lost her head, her step, her cookies. *What a race—yes, what a way to blow it.*

She had inadvertently served as a rabbit for everyone else. Was it first time nerves? No, she was just too hyped to realize how fast she'd actually been running. Bolting off like a rabbit for a first lap :55. Now that's probably even a record for the men's 800 meters. Marie and Sandra killed the old women's record, and she and Elena did a pretty good number. But she had believed she might win. Second, for sure. Qualify, piece of cake. Zilch, she was nothing. She couldn't even bear to think what she would do now. *So you blew it. Just don't break down. No tears. Cool.*

She signed the statement and took her sample jar. Right now she was so pissed she could go right back on the field and give a splendid sample in front of 50 thousand people. Bare, corn-fed buns from Goodland on national TV. *That's it*, she thought looking up at Meg. *Call Rafael and call home. Then get out of town.* She never even considered that any of the other three women might test positive.

*   *   *

From his position, Lou thought that she'd made it. She was going to Seoul. What an incredible race. Sure she had gone out way too strong. But he knew that the :55 first lap was not the story.

143

It was the :61 plus final lap. When you go out too fast like that, you blow up, the machinery slows to a crawl, and most people end up jogging at the end. It takes big-time guts to hang in and beat your own PR.

Lou was suddenly reminded of his Marine coach leaning over him and rasping, "The real ones, the real ones who make it, they've got it in their blood; they've got the pepper. They don't quit, they hang in, even when they're burning up. Pepper." Karie would make it. She must have wanted it real bad to handle that sort of pain.

Lou couldn't bear to sit and spent the next hour walking around, halfway hoping he'd run into Karie. He ended up at a press lounge, complete with a full bar and TVs set up to monitor the race. Lou hung out just inside the entrance and watched the monitors. Not interested in any other event but the outcome of Karie's, he wanted her to be confirmed and then head the hell out. Lou paced back and forth in the entranceway of the lounge and was about to go find Karie when the announcer stated, "The results from the record-breaking women's 800 are in. The judges have declared that third place belongs to Elena Begg. Begg will join Stevens and Miller in traveling to Seoul next month to represent the United States."

"Shit!" Lou yelled.

A few people looked over in his direction. Lou couldn't remember ever feeling so disappointed. He headed out of the room and walked around, looking for Karie. Knowing her, he guessed she was already gone. He walked out the front and grabbed a cab from the line.

From a distance, Andy watched him go.

Chapter Ten

Peter Bernier crushed out his Pall Mall into a butt-filled ashtray and took a swig of scotch from a jelly glass. The windows of his dinky, wood-paneled office were open. The electric fan didn't stop the sweltering Miami heat. The throb of the cursor on his computer screen seemed to match the throb in his head as he searched for an angle. The results of the U.S. Olympic Trials for track and field trigger the gold count for the coming event, and every sports publication has easy copy and guaranteed readership for at least eight weeks. Two women had broken the American record and two others equaled it. Further, the new mark was now at least within a respectable distance of the world record, in a race where the U.S. traditionally struggled to even be represented in the Olympic finals.

Bernier got the assignment for *Runner's Weekly Journal* by calling in a favor from a friend. "Come on," he had said. "Give me a reason to shave." Peter Bernier—"Bernie" to his friends—had been a political analyst in a time when a Presidential assignation referred to antebellum history, war was an act of glory, and the threat of Commies was discussed over the tinkle of cocktail glasses. He'd casually shifted to sports writing as a way to promote his son and his son's new hobby, race car driving. One day the boy made a tiny miscalculation in a turn and took it too fast and too sharp. The car spun out of control for what seemed like years. Hit a wall. Exploded. Bernie's usual scotch turned into a double, then a triple, then a bottle, then two. The wife left after the party invitations stopped coming, went back to school, burned her bra, and never spoke to him again. Bernie realized, decades later, that the million tiny fragments his son became were nothing compared to the billion fragmented pieces that described his life. As far as the Indianapolis thing went, two new American records were good material for any journalist, soused or otherwise. But what fascinated Bernie, in a perverse and macabre way, was that the records had come about due to a tiny miscalculation in speed.

Bernie mopped his brow, considered the women's 800 and its final moments, lit another cigarette, and typed furiously. Indianapolis did not yield much in the way of breakthroughs, as far as the journalists were concerned, other than the usual speculation about continuing U.S. dominance in the sprints, decathlon and heptathlon. The Johnson/Begg tie was glossed over until Bernie's article, titled "Rabbit Revisited," came out in *Runner's Weekly Journal* three short days after the race.

The thrust of "Rabbit Revisited" opened up new fields for the modern media's Great American Gold Rush, suggesting a new racing strategy that the U.S. had pioneered. *Runner's Weekly Journal* retraced the entire race based on video clips, with a breakdown of the 200 meter splits and a detailed commentary on the precise strategy as Bernie saw it. The article called what happened a new twist on the old strategy of having a "rabbit" set a fast pace and then drop off for the benefit of the favorite. The trick was to go out fast, almost as if the race were only one lap, and then hang on for one more. Peter Bernier laced the exposition of his theory with comments such as, "Is it 800 meters or two 400s?" and pointed out that the strategy would physiologically take the kick out of contention and psychologically cow the competition and destroy elaborate race plans.

The four phases of 200 meter splits showed Karie Johnson leading in the first three and in a photo-finish for third place. The captivating grace of Karie's style caught the exact spirit of America's quest, and photos of her were destined to be pinned to the walls of coaches' offices and gymnasiums all over the country. Peter Bernier was careful to point out that Karie had gone out perhaps a little too fast and that her early speed cost her the race, but the concept that must have been devised by her coach was clearly the wave of the future. There was a sidebar that reported on Pace Track's impressive national victories and Super Coach Andy Nagy.

"Bullshit," said Andy getting up from his breakfast table, "cockamamie bullshit." He scanned the article again, still standing. "What a pile of crap." He sat down delighted, considering the possibilities. Andy knew that the real purpose of the rabbit, whenever you could find anyone dumb enough to do it, was to help the favored athlete gauge the right pace and run a smart race. Any time you ran too close to maximum pace—he called it "red-lining"—you ran the risk of the body shutting down. Hell, they'd tried it in East Europe 10, 20 years ago and had given up on it. There was something about muscle mechanics that, once you strayed into that red zone, didn't allow you to pull back or ease off. Whether it was lactic acid buildup or creatine phosphate depletion or whatever, the whole system seemed to get progressively gummed up and your nerves literally fried the brain with electric impulses to stop.

The real trick, Bernier, Andy thought, *is to know how to keep just below maximum pace and then have an explosive kick at the end.* Any time you stepped over the red line your body became an inefficient processor of energy and the progression was geometric. Anyone who had passed through the Institute knew this; presumably Peter Bernier was unaware of what "hitting the wall" meant. Moreover, Bernier couldn't be a runner himself; otherwise, he would have experienced it. The more Andy ridiculed the theory, the more he relished the sensationalism an article like this could create. It was great copy, and he was sure that some dumb-assed U.S. coaches would pick up on it. Maybe some Europeans might wonder whether Andy had somehow broken the code. Now that would really screw them up.

Andy would have to tell Karie not to take any interviews. It wouldn't help to have her spoil the fun with her relentless honesty. Once again he found himself wondering how Karie had managed to hang on after that :55 first lap. She must have an incredible pain threshold. Either that, or her max could be stretched further than they both realized. If only he had got her on a mild steroid cycle, she would have blown them all away—and Andy would have his Great American Hope.

                    *   *   *

As Andy had hoped, *Inside Track* requested an interview, then broke with a story on "Power Running." It borrowed heavily from Peter Bernier's concepts, and Andy was only too happy to push the misconceptions along. Andy, whom the magazine called, "arguably the best athletics coach in America today," spoke of the customized training that he had devised for the Pace Track women to permit them to run fast for longer periods of time. He coyly declined to elaborate on the precise nature of the workouts. There were photos of Andy and his girls at the Pace workouts and quotes from other coaches supportive of the power running concept. As he prepared to go to Seoul with four of his girls, Andy couldn't have been in better spirits.

Karie had no problem with declining all interviews when she returned from the Indianapolis trials. She also refused Andy's suggestion that she keep up her training, in case she were summoned to join the team. She dropped out of the Pace workouts altogether and ran the hills at Will Rogers Park instead. There she could get a good view of downtown L.A. and, when the weather was clear, of the San Gabriel Mountains and Catalina Island.

She believed when one set a goal for the Olympics, as she had for Seoul, that it was a commitment. It was something to count on, something that allowed you to make future plans. The fact that she now had to wait another four years or abandon her goal left her feeling disoriented. But the worst part was knowing how easily it all could've been avoided. The race had been so close. If she had only thrust her chest forward at the finish or even run an average race, she would've qualified.

Karie tore her calendar down from the door. After Seoul, she had planned to spend whatever time it took to restore her relationship with Dad. She had rehearsed the words in the weeks leading up to the trials. "Dad, I left home because I wanted to go to the Olympics. I've done that, now I'm back." She would show him the photos and have him live her experiences. Then she could get on with the rest of her life.

Rafael came to stay for the first week of the Seoul Olympics—he would have stayed for the full schedule of the Games, but his mother was now seriously ill. After the third day of his stay, Rafael was finally able to get Karie out of the house to a small pasta place in Playa del Rey.

"I had planned for us to go hiking through Mexico," she said.

"Whereabouts?" asked Rafael.

"All over, not just the tourist spots. I want to see that place where they dive from a tree with the liana tied around their ankles—"

"Papantla, near Veracruz."

"And I would learn Spanish. We could go to that place where your father is from."

"Oaxaca," he said.

"Maybe he's gone back there?"

He took her hand and kissed it. "We can do that sometime soon."

"I know," said Karie. "It just would've been different, if I had the Olympics behind me."

Rafael called for the bill. "Promise me you'll go for Barcelona. No, don't shake your head. You've got to get it out of your system."

She groaned. "Another four years of training?"

"Do something else for a while. Call Tanya. Be the hostess here."

"I don't know. It's too much to think about now."

"Then think about me holding you for the rest of he week," he said.

"I think," Karie smiled briefly, "I can manage that."

Next day, after a late afternoon run, Karie came back to the apartment. She and Rafael had planned to eat in and catch some of the Olympics broadcast—swimming was featured. The phone rang and she answered.

"Karie Johnson?" the voice paused, "This is Peter Bernier. I'm calling from Seoul and I'd just like to ask you some questions."

"Sorry. I told you no—"

"No, this is not an interview," said Peter. "I just wondered if you'd heard the news? About Sandra Miller?"

"What news?" The picture of Sandra at the trials came to Karie's mind.

"She tested positive after her preliminary," said Peter, sounding officious. "Sandra has been disqualified and kicked off the team."

Karie said nothing.

"I wanted to ask you how you felt about it…seeing as how you could have made the team…"

Bastard, thought Karie. "She beat me clean," she said, and hung up.

Six days later, Ben Johnson, gold medalist in the 100 meters, was DQed for testing positive for Winstrol. Peter Bernier wrote a comprehensive report on doping. The article's headline was Karie's comment, "She Beat Me Clean."

* * *

Karie called up Erin at Tanya's a month later, like Rafael suggested. She wasn't hurting for money yet, but she would be in a couple of months if she didn't do something soon.

Erin was glad to hear from her, "You know what, you lucked out. My lunch date just canceled, so if you're not doing anything how about Chianti's at 1:30?"

"Sure," Karie said. "See you then."

At lunch Karie told Erin about the trials. Erin talked about agency gossip and said Karie's timing couldn't have been better because three blonds just left Tanya for L.A. Models and Talent.

"Was Tanya hurt?"

"No, she's too tough." Erin leaned back in her chair and pushed her hair out of her face.

"Do you think Tanya will let me come back?"

"Are you kidding? She'd love to have you. You made money for us. Healthy is always an 'in' look in L.A." Erin lit a cigarette. "And personally I'm missing the commission you brought me."

"Then why did Tanya cut me loose when I wanted to train?"

"Andy and Tanya are old friends, but they're so competitive that when he brings her a girl from his track team, she tries to woo the girl away from him completely. You held out for track. You're the only one who ever did, too."

"Well, I'm going for Barcelona. It's going to be the same story in a couple of years."

"As you should. Whatever doesn't kill you makes you stronger, and that goes for Tanya's attitude as well. Plenty of girls work part time; there's no reason you can't. Listen, this industry is filled with muck up to here," she held her hand above her head. "You are different, genuinely sweet. If we get you back, even with the year off, it's a blessing. But now I've got to get back to work. This has been fun."

"I can't tell you how much you've raised my spirits. Can I call you before my next big race?"

Erin laughed, "Sure. Listen, don't worry about Tanya. Leave her to me."

*   *   *

Karie tried to get some sleep on the plane. It had been a rough week. She'd spent the first four nights consoling Rafael on the telephone as his mother lay dying in the Goodland hospital. Rafael spent his days nobly fighting the hospital bureaucracy to let him take her home to the trailer as she wished and his evenings sobbing to Karie. Two days after he brought Teresa home, Rafael called Karie to say Teresa had passed on. Karie packed and left within the hour. When the ticket clerk said, "Getting away for spring break, huh?" Karie just nodded.

She had managed to make it back to Goodland almost every Christmas, but it was the first time in a long time she'd seen Goodland in the late spring. The lush greens overwhelmed her almost as much as the humidity. She realized she'd grown accustomed to the light tones of L.A. as well as its even-keel cool, and although Goodland would always be Goodland, L.A. had become home. She remembered sitting at the table in the trailer, the familiar smell of caramel blending with the formaldehyde of protracted illness, as Rafael made plans to sell everything and move to New York. Karie had cried, not out of sudden grief, but because she felt that a door had closed and she wondered whether she had left something on the other side of it. Was there anything more to be gleaned from memories of running up to the trailer with Bo barking in the snow, or from the long summer days when she and Rafael were covered in dust and paint thinner? Was there still a talisman to be extricated from her jumbled memories of Goodland?

Mom had come with her to the wake and seemed glad to see Rafael again. Karie watched her mother mix easily with Teresa's friends from the beauty salon and her catering jobs. Karie noticed how kind and assured Mom was with everyone. Karie's dad was poignantly absent. Dad held Rafael partly responsible for Karie's leaving, and he curmudgeonly refused to put aside the past. Karie and her Mom were the last to leave the wake. When Karie told Rafael she'd come by tomorrow, he told her not to. He wanted to be alone. Karie understood and they said goodnight.

As they drove home, Karie watched the dusk settle into night. She cracked the window of the car to smell the grassy air, still warm but cooling fast. The cicadas were singing, and Karie wondered what she was going to do tomorrow. Maybe she could help Dad like she used to.

"It smells so different here. When I first got to L.A., I couldn't believe how great the ocean smelled, salty and warm, but now I don't notice it."

"I hardly notice what Goodland smells like anymore, though your Dad likes to say he prefers a deep breath of Goodland air to early morning coffee. Maybe it's the smell he likes."

"Mom, why does Dad still hate me for going off to L.A.?"

Her mother stiffened and pulled over to the side of the road before she answered. "Karie, what a terrible thing to say—you know your father loves you."

"But he's so distant."

Nancy nodded and said, "He was terribly hurt, we all were, it was just—it was just that we couldn't understand how you could do that to us, to run off in the middle of the night." Nancy burst into tears. Karie took hold of her mother's hand, alternately trying to speak and pat her on the back.

They sat together for a long time, sniffing and wiping their eyes, until Nancy spoke again. "I know your father wouldn't hear of me telling you this, but for years now he has had the L.A. paper sent to him every day just so he can keep up with you. He has all the newspaper clippings and those articles from the running magazines in an album in his desk. And you know all those prints that you send us from your modeling? Well, he keeps those inside the doors of a cupboard in his office. I came into the office the other day without knocking, and he was standing there looking at all those photos—I think he was talking to you. He was very cross with me."

As Mom pulled out on the road, she told Karie about her father's wanting to go to Indianapolis to be with her at the trials and how upset he had been with the result.

"But why didn't you just say so? I could've sent you tickets," she said.

"You know your father couldn't ask you for anything like that."

Early the next morning, when Dad came downstairs to go to work, Karie was dressed and waiting with a thermos of coffee.

"I thought I'd help you at the site," she said.

"Suit yourself. Not like I could stop you from doing what you want anyway," he answered.

They rode to the site in silence, and Karie started thinking this may not have been her best idea. Dad gave her the job of sweeping the concrete floors of every home in the site. It took her all day, and she skipped working out to stay on the site with Dad. When they drove home together in the late afternoon, Karie tried again.

"Dad, I'm training for Barcelona. I was wondering if you could come to the school track and time me."

"When?"

"I was going to head out tonight, after supper."

"I have some contracts to look over," he looked over at her, "but they can wait."

"Thanks, Dad."

Karie spent the next day with Rafael at the trailer. He had cleaned and packed the whole place up. The emptiness startled Karie. It was as if all the color had been drained away, and when she looked at Rafael she began to cry. As they embraced, he started sobbing too. They sat on the steps and held each other till the late afternoon.

"I'm going to New York next week," Rafael said later. "Why don't you come with me?"

"I can't," Karie said. "I've got practice and a job next week. Maybe I can come later." *If only I'd made Seoul*, she thought. *Then I'd have this dream out of my system, and I could go with Rafael.* Karie wrapped her arms around him and stroked his back.

* * *

"What ailest thou, knight at arms?" said Dr. John, walking into Andy's condo in Playa del Rey. "Alone, and palely loitering." He came up to Andy, who stood on the balcony, and patted him lightly on the back.

"A sprinter tested positive at a meet in San Diego on Saturday—no, not one of ours, one from Northridge. So close to home."

"Now, Coach, only the dumb ones get caught. Natural winnowing of the herd. Got any decent wine?" The doctor headed for the kitchen, and Andy wondered if he had been popping his own stuff.

So far, the doctor was right. If an athlete followed the program, there should be no problem—barring surprise checks, and Dr. John had a pretty good nose for those. On the other hand, the individual athletes who weren't with a team, or could not afford good supervision, were asking for trouble.

"Remember that tall, lanky girl you sent me?" said the doctor.

"Becky. She's our 10K runner."

"She may be a lot of things to you—but she's not very informed. She bounces in and wants to know all about blood doping, as if she's going to add it to her shopping list at the drugstore." He sighed. "So without batting an eye I told her it's easy; draw a liter of blood 12 weeks prior to race day, quick freeze and store. Two days prior to the competition thaw the blood, separate the red blood cells from the plasma, prepare blood in saline solution, and inject. She almost passed out." He smiled and sipped his wine. "What did she expect, the silly little twit? Some pills—take two after your evening meal?" He sat at the balcony table.

Andy retrieved the bottle of Silver Oak 1985 Cabernet Savignon that the doctor had so generously poured and set it down between them. "I hope you told her it's more complicated than that," Andy said. "Becky's not the brightest..."

"The principle behind blood doping is simple," said Dr. John. "It's the execution that's difficult." He continued, "When the muscle goes to work, it burns sugar—or glycogen as we high priests call it—with oxygen to produce energy. Oxygen comes to the muscle courtesy of the red blood cells and their supply is limited, representing about a 40 to 45 percent concentration in the blood. Imagine," he said, "going up a steep hill in a Volkswagen Beetle. You make it up to the top, but the engine has to work like hell to do it. A Mercedes cruises up without breaking a sweat. With more red cells, the body has more capacity for energy and endurance, so it experiences less stress."

Andy wished the doctor had explained it this way to Becky, rather than spooking her.

"One of the best ways to improve the human engine," he continued, "is precisely what psyched Becky out of her shorts. You draw off about a quarter of your total blood supply, and after some 12 weeks, when your body has replenished that blood, you infuse the red cells from the blood you drew off originally. You have 25 percent more red cells, and your engine is that much more powerful. Sounds simple, doesn't it, Nagy?"

155

Andy looked up from his notes and nodded.

"But, of course, it isn't. Quite apart from the medical team required, there's always the opportunity for infection and adverse reactions."

"What about a donor?" said Andy. "Somebody from the same family, same blood type. That way the athlete can keep training without loss of blood."

"Can be done." The doctor stroked his jaw. "But donor blood increases the risk of allergic reactions, and there's always the danger of passing on something else with the red cells, if you catch my drift. But here is where science comes galloping to the rescue of our anaerobic brethren." As Dr. John poured more wine, the setting sun glinted ruby through the bottle.

Andy remembered a story after the '84 Olympics in L.A. about a team of American cyclists who set up a blood doping operation using donors. He made a note to check it out, although the practice was now banned.

"The trick, as always, dear fellow, is to see if you can't nudge the body to do it on its own, and then you don't have to bother with all the paraphernalia. No people, no risks, no getting caught—no problem. There is a natural hormone produced by the kidneys that stimulates the bone marrow to increase red cell production. Isn't that wonderful?" Dr. John took his glass and stood gazing out to sea.

Andy realized he was referring to the sweeping sunset, now infusing the horizon with its own red blood.

"Just lovely. Do you realize that our lovely red sunsets are a by-product of pollution? Each day we take in more carbon monoxide and lead into our lungs and bloodstreams, but we have such lovely sunsets." The doctor paused. "Where were we?"

"Blood doping," Andy said.

"EPO," said the doctor, "short for Erythropoietin, works like a charm. Inject some synthesized EPO into your marathoner and you know what it does?" He paused. "It gets on the phone right away. 'Hullo, bone marrow, EPO here...we need you to get cracking on some red blood cells…yes, we've got a spot of extra work to do, about 30 percent more should do it.'" He sipped his wine.

"And it works?" said Andy.

"Takes at least a minute off a 10K."

"And it can't be detected?"

"No. Not yet anyway. That would involve blood testing, not urine. It's what I keep telling you. Only the dumb slugs get caught." He glanced at Andy, "If you want your precious Becky to rev up a bit, I'll tell her what to do. But watch out, you might not be able to catch her after that." He chuckled to himself.

"Any problems?" said Andy.

"Always a possibility, old boy, when you tinker with the old system. But then," he grinned and pointed a finger at Andy, "you want to win, don't you?"

Andy waited patiently for the doctor to continue. You couldn't push the old fart because he loved his pulpit. *This was dynamite stuff. A minute off a 10K was three percent.* Andy knew people who would kill for less.

"The red cells are solid, you see, so they thicken the blood and increase the possibility of clotting. The blood becomes more viscous, and it increases the load on the old pump here," Dr. John patted his chest. "And remember, when you're at maximal exercise levels, the blood is sloshing through the body five times or more per minute." He became pensive. "Our marathoner, who is also dehydrating, can get red cell concentrations of well over 55 percent, maybe 60. It can get," he paused, "sludgy, at the end. And we know the engine doesn't work so well then…" He turned to Andy, "Got any crackers and cheese? Need to stoke my own engine, you know."

When Andy returned with a tray, he asked, "What's new on growth hormone? I hear conflicting reports."

"Ah, my friend, I knew that was bothering you ever since you saw those prominent foreheads in Seoul."

"Well, does it work? I heard it builds muscle like steroids?"

"It works on animals—the four-legged kind. I worked on a

project in Paraguay with the bovine growth hormone, for President Stroessner."

Andy remembered when their paths had crossed in São Paulo, Brazil. Dr. Brantley John was visiting from Asunción, and Andy was on a Pan American Games visit. The doctor explained they were working on special breeds of Nelore and Santa Gertrudis cattle that could not only exist in the sub-tropical scrub, but produced meat that was exceptionally lean and of good flavor. This was not for local consumption—although the little runts were in need of some good protein—it was an opportunity to take a bite out of the world market. They were way ahead of the lean beef kick.

"The beauty of it was that we were doing our own sort of recycling, Nagy," Dr. John said reflectively. "What the growth hormone does in you or in me or my animals is it commands the body, muscles, bones, tissue to grow. It's secreted by the pituitary gland, most heavily in the teen years, and controls growth. Too little, and you're a dwarf. Too much, and you're a giant. Just as well Hitler didn't get hold of it. In the Paraguayan jungle, I didn't exactly have access to recombinant DNA technology—hadn't even been invented then—but I did have access to the pituitary glands of cattle. The President offered me *human* growth hormone if I wanted, said why not try it out with humans before bothering the herd? A real sweet guy, that Stroessner. I should have known."

What Dr. John discovered was that an extract of the pituitary gland produced a marked increase in muscle and a decrease of fat in cattle. No one knew why or how, not even the doctor. It wasn't till much later that scientists deciphered the complex reactions and synthesized the hormone in a lab.

"It was like taking a swing in the dark and landing one on the chin. I became a hero, at least down there anyway. And I had set it up like a chain operation. As the animals were slaughtered for their lean beef, we could extract more of the gland, and it became a cycle. That was the trick." Dr. John now sat staring at the faint feathers of pink cloud that hung like exclamation marks over the dusk.

"Did it work?"

"Of course it bloody worked." He fell into a moody silence. "It's a long story. I was railroaded out, that's what—the greedy sods. Even took my medal away. So now I'm back to humans, just like the president suggested."

Andy recognized the signals. Whenever the doctor got testy, it was best to move on. "As far as athletes then?"

"Look, Nagy, it's not clear how well it works or doesn't work. In fact, you might want to try some yourself. Won't shrink your balls or give you the hots, I promise. Tell you what though, it's got a lot of promise as a cure for obesity and for osteoporosis. I might set up my own fat farm one of these days. Meanwhile, the athletes seem to like it. Perhaps because they don't get caught. But overdo it, and you can end up looking like a Neanderthal. And it's very expensive. But," he put down his glass and got up, "growth hormone is said to potentiate the action of steroids." Dr. John looked at Andy over his glasses, "Just a fancy word that means there's a synergism, makes them more effective. I know what you're thinking, Coach," he walked with his hands clasped behind his back, "here's an opportunity for Andy's Combo Cocktail."

"Anyway, what, or who rather, do you have in mind from your little flock?" The doctor stood close. Andy smelled the wine on his breath, realizing Dr. John had finished the bottle. "Not that blonde bombshell that I saw at the track the other day—Karie, isn't that her name?"

Andy turned away.

"Why you randy old bastard."

* * *

On September 18, 1990, the International Olympic Committee gathered in Tokyo to select the host city for the 1996 Summer Olympic Games. With the solemnity of princes of the church, the 86 members were called to order by President Juan Antonio Samaranch. The ceremony was held in the brand new Pamir Convention Center of the Takanawa Prince Hotel. Robert Helmick rose to the podium to lead the bid for Atlanta, with support from President Bush (on tape), Billy Payne, and Ambassador Andy Young, ex-mayor of the city.

In presentations worthy of this United Nations of sport, Atlanta was followed at one hour intervals by Athens, Toronto, Belgrade, Melbourne and Manchester. Still later, the members listened to reports by various technical commissions that assessed the acceptability of the venues. Finally, at 6 p.m., the voting began—by secret ballot and with the abstention of the president. To win, a city had to receive an absolute majority of the votes cast, with the lowest city eliminated from each successive round. It took the maximum five rounds for a winner to emerge.

At 8 p.m. the Hokushin Ceremony Hall was filled with well over a thousand people—delegates from the six cities, functionaries of all levels and press from all over the globe. As the assembled delegates reassured themselves of the success of their city's presentation, the IOC members filed onto the stage under the hot scrutiny of world TV. President Samaranch began speaking in his heavily flavored English, "The International Olympic Committee has awarded the 1996 Olympic Games to the city of..." As the world waited, he struggled with the envelope and then, pausing as if with incredulity, said, "Ah—." The delegations of Athens and Atlanta heard the same clarion call and prepared to leap from their seats and dance in the aisles. "Aht-lanta."

Andy heard the news on the radio while he was shaving, and he ran into the living room to see news clips of the celebrations around Underground Atlanta. As Atlanta's finest hailed the centennial Olympics as the panacea that would vault the city to prominence in the twenty-first century, Andy made his own pragmatic assessment. It was an absolute win-win. For the next six years, the athletic world would be knocking on his door. He would even use the history of Atlanta's bid as an inspirational theme—of perseverance? of strategy? Whatever.

It was a pity about his full service station idea. Smart doping would really be in demand, but it was too dangerous. One thing for sure, Andy's retinue would be the best athletes that he and science could turn out.

*   *   *

Andy had given a lot of thought to how he might approach Karie on the subject of performance enhancers. It had to be done well ahead of the trials for the Barcelona Olympics in the summer of 1992. For most of the girls that Andy targeted, it was like shooting ducks at a fair. If his arguments were shot down, the duck merely went around and reappeared, wearing a different coat of blandishments, until eventually he succeeded. But Karie didn't give him another chance. She got that brittle look in her eyes which made him feel uncomfortable, sort of tarnished.

He felt that he'd recovered well from the dinner at Michael's, and his current plan was to do a reverse fake off of it. As soon as they started going over Karie's outdoor schedule for 1991, he began to talk about time lines.

"Now, Karie, I want you to start thinking in terms of where we want to be now and in the future for our 800 meter times. We can start now for the spring and set 1:59 and draw the line on that. Then I'll work something up for the summer. Then there'll be some tapering before the winter indoor meets, and so on until the trials in New Orleans. Does that make sense?"

Karie nodded. "Yeah, that would be helpful."

"Okay, I'll work on it. So cheer up. You had a good season last year, and this one should be great. I just think we need to establish where we want to be. Don't worry, we're not talking steroids here." He grinned and flung up a protective arm, as if she might attack him at the very mention of doping.

At the same time, Andy played up the competition. He would tell her repeatedly how strong and fast they were, while withholding any praise in her direction. He would never accurately assess her performance but would make half-assed comments like, "You *should* be able to make it," or "*Seems* like you're getting faster." He wanted to shake Karie's belief in her own ability.

At the end of the 1991 summer season, Andy told Karie they needed to talk seriously about Barcelona, which was less than a year away. Karie wanted to go over her future time lines anyway and was glad to have Andy so involved. Andy suggested that they get together at her place because he felt she would be more at ease there.

They had just sat down at the dining table when CeeCee came rushing in, "Hi, guys, I guess I'm getting forgetful in my old age." Andy looked annoyed as she fiddled with the answering machine in the corner and wrote some things down on the pad next to the phone. "Hey Karie, I'm stopping off at the store after work, anything we need?"

"Dish soap."

"Okay, I gotta run, I'm late. Ciao."

Karie said, "Like I told you, she works two afternoons at her boyfriend's office. Real estate."

That's why she seems so nervous, Andy thought, *she doesn't want me to know she has a boyfriend*. Then he shrugged. "Okay, where were we?"

"Well, so far I'm okay with the time lines," she paused and looked at Andy, "as long as you think that's going to cut it."

They were sitting on the same side of the table with the schedule laid out in front of them. He reached over and patted her hand. The warmth of his touch caught her off guard. For a split second, she wanted to spill her guts and let all of her balled-up anxiety unfurl into the moment. But Karie held back, knowing it was not the time to let her guard down. Andy and Pace would be relying on her to strut her stuff and pull through the season. She would have to wait for another time to share her bad memories of the trials.

Andy was still patting her hand and saying, "...you've done well this summer season..."

Karie stood up and began pacing the room. "It still doesn't feel like it's enough for Barcelona."

"Look, you've got the best style, you know the techniques, the rest is for us to emphasize speed and endurance."

"Haven't you forgotten something?" said Karie severely. Then she broke into a smile, "I've got the best coach. What did they say?" she adopted an officious voice, "'arguably the best coach in America today.'"

"Well, we've come a long way—"

"You remember, in Wichita, with your cowboy hat—"

"And look at you now—"

"That's it," she dropped back into the seat beside him. "I took second at the Santa Clara meet last month, remember. I should've been first...these time lines..." She clasped both hands together, "I need to know. Is it enough?"

Andy sighed. "Maybe."

"Maybe—just maybe?"

He snapped his pencil down on the table. "So now all of a sudden you want to know? If you want it straight, I'll tell you, but don't pull my chain. Last time you got mad, and we didn't get very far." He paused as if surprised by his own words, "I really shouldn't be talking about this."

"Go on, I promise I won't be such a jerk this time."

"Karie, you should have gone to Seoul. No," he held up his hands, "don't say it, I'm not talking steroids. But that girl Sandra was on the juice and she took your place. And I'm not sure about the others."

Andy stood and walked over to the window. "I don't want you on steroids—however mild—I don't even want to talk about them. But I don't want you to have your head buried in the sand either. The trials are going to be tough, and some girls are going on the juice for an edge—a five to 10 meter edge."

He turned from the window. "What we need to do for New Orleans is to train real hard to make sure you peak just right. This will probably be your last shot, you know."

Karie sat with her head bowed, going over the training that would lead up to the trials. Barcelona was it for her. No way Atlanta—she'd be 28 by then. Anyway, all she'd ever wanted was to get to the Olympics. After that, she could get on with her life. She already had too many things on hold. "Barcelona, here I come—without steroids." She shrugged, "I don't need it that bad."

"Actually, some of them won't be on steroids," he said. "There's a new product."

She looked up.

"Well, I don't know too much about it, except that it's definitely not a steroid with all the problems. It's called growth hormone. It occurs naturally in the body—maybe that's why they can't test for it, because it's supposed to be there."

Karie said, "So there's something that helps your training that occurs naturally in the body. But it's banned?"

"In a way, yes. It's banned, but they can't detect it if someone takes it." He shrugged.

Karie looked at him. "Tell me about it."

*   *   *

"Here's what I think we should do," Andy said to Dr. John. "Start her on a mild dosage of growth hormone for, say, four weeks, and then four weeks off." He paused. "She is likely to be monitoring herself carefully for the slightest adverse reaction, and I want this to be smooth."

Dr. John smiled. "No doubt you will tell her that her training has improved significantly."

"Then, for the next four weeks, a blend of GH and testosterone, or Primo if you think—"

"Aha," said the doctor, "this is where the wolf shows his ears. Bait and switch. Andy's cocktail, no less. What dosage?"

"Mild. No, wait." He'd had enough trouble dragging her this far. "Make it a full dose."

Dr. John looked at him and shrugged. "You're the coach."

"And then another four weeks off." He thought for a moment. "I'd like this to be customized, so can you arrange blood tests as well, at the beginning and end of each cycle?"

"Of course."

"You'll handle this through your usual source?"

"Got a new lad," said Dr. John. "Bradford Barnes. College grad—very smooth." He took out a pad of his paper, wrote KARIE JOHNSON at the top and began making notes.

Chapter Eleven

Karie sat in the visitor parking area of the Windrift condos in Westwood. The property bordered the huge playing field of the UCLA campus and a faint October breeze stirred the jacaranda trees. *Here I go*, she thought, *less than a year to Barcelona. Hard to believe that just over five years ago I was waiting in the airport departure lounge.* Now Karie was waiting again. She was 10 minutes early for an appointment with Bradford Barnes, and she used the time to let her nerves settle.

Two days ago she'd met with Dr. John at a place called Ships that reminded Karie of the diners back in Goodland. She arrived after the doctor, breathless and anxious, and found him in the parking lot by his red Mercedes where they had agreed to meet. When they got a booth, the doctor suggested some chamomile tea to soothe her nerves. He chatted idly about a film he'd just seen and then grew silent as he watched Karie cup her tea in both hands and blow on it to cool it down.

"No doubt you have questions," said Dr. John.

"Yeah," Karie nodded sheepishly and wished that they could've met someplace else.

The doctor leaned forward. "Look upon it as insurance, my dear lady," he said. "It's like a sort of anti-freeze. The growth hormone makes sure the body is in tip-top form."

I've never been called a dear lady before, Karie thought. *I'll have to tell Andy.* "And it's natural to the body?"

"It is the *essential* hormone for growth. Even as we speak, medical authorities are testing it on senior citizens—as a sort of fountain of youth." *They want to recapture a little of you*, he thought. She really was a splendid creature.

"Then why is it banned?"

"To be perfectly candid, my dear, I don't know. Misguided zeal, perhaps? I understand they were considering a ban on vitamin supplements recently, if you can believe it." In the spirit of candor, he could have assured her that her dosage of growth hormone would have little effect on her, but what came later would. He imagined she would become positively leonine.

"And it can't be detected?"

"Not at all." He stroked his chin. "I dare say there is little interest by the medical people either. I mean, what for?"

"This, cycle—is that what you call it?"

Dr. John nodded.

"It's mild? So I can see how it goes?"

"I will go through the test results with you myself." He stood, left some money on the table, and took her elbow as they walked to the door. "Karie, dear, if it's any added comfort, it is my considered opinion that all of the major athletes have considered this option."

"Considered?"

"Karie, please," he gestured in apparent frustration, "medical etiquette forbids me—you know?"

Dr. John referred her to Bradford Barnes—actually, he insisted on saying he merely suggested she call Barnes—who would be able to supply her with the growth hormone. She had been very relieved to find out the suggested Mr. Barnes occasionally worked as a part-time trainer at Global Gym and had, at times, spotted her on weights.

So here she was in her 280Z a little early for her 2 p.m. appointment, ready to go for it—and the only people in the know were Andy, Dr. John and now Mr. Barnes.

Earlier in the week, when she had just about decided to take the growth hormone treatment for a trial period, Andy phoned. He wanted to discuss her training, he said, so she listened until he came around to his real purpose.

"How are you coming along with your thinking?"

"There's one thought I've had all along," she said.

"Yes?"

"It's cheating."

Andy was silent. "So you're not going to do it?"

"I didn't say that."

"Karie, it's a shading of the truth. Just like people shade their tax returns. Give your cockamamie Midwestern values a rest."

Karie had been stunned and a bit hurt. She knew what Andy meant by Midwestern values, and she didn't think of herself as that uptight. She could tell he was losing patience.

"Call it what you will, Karie. I think you should take it so you can be sure of competing on a world stage. I think you've earned it, and you deserve it. You might even consider doing it for your country, as I know others have. But it's your decision." He hung up.

Karie thought about her old coach, Lou Gertz, at that moment. She hadn't spoken to him in a while, even though she knew he was now at AU. She wondered what would he say about what she was going to do. She'd heard plenty from Dr. John and Andy on the subject. Gertz was a better moral compass than both of them, and she trusted his perspective on the world of running and the level playing field Andy always talked about. Her head felt heavy. Would it matter to Lou Gertz anymore what she did? It didn't seem important to Coach Gertz when she needed him to go to AU with her. It was up to her then, and it was up to her now. Karie got out of the car. She made the right decision five years ago. She hoped her luck would hold.

Karie found the apartment with little trouble. She knocked on the door and rang the bell. Within seconds a man answered the door.

"Bradford Barnes?"

"Karie, right? Call me Brad. Only my parents call me Bradford."

The hall opened onto a combination kitchen and living room that was light, airy and surprisingly neat. A TV with the sound turned down showed the Los Angeles Rams at work in the stadium, and there was an open book, face down, on a side table. *Of course they could be props*, Karie thought. She had heard at the gym that Barnes was into acting. *This could be a set for a Dewars Profile, complete with Latest Book Read. Another actor/stud.*

"Can I offer you something?"

She smiled and shook her head. "I just finished a late lunch."

She had seen Brad at the gym. Looking at him now, in faded jeans and a white undershirt, she could see why CeeCee said, "Girl, he's the definitive source from which all hunks flow."

He cocked his head to one side, "Excuse me, but do I detect a slight Midwestern tonality?"

"Kansas."

"I'm from back East. I came here three years ago. For a visit, of course." He gestured to a room with a desk and chairs, "Shall we?"

"I'm ready." Karie thought she sounded too eager. *Cool down,* she thought.

Brad grinned and adopted a businesslike tone. "GH has to be kept refrigerated at all times, both before and after you mix it. You're going to start with two shots a week for a four-week cycle. These," he held up two small bottles, "mix up into two doses, so you only have to mix a batch up once a week. Once you see how it's done, you can inject yourself, or I can do it. Sundays and Wednesdays, unless I'm out of town or on a job. Payments should be made weekly, in advance, in cash.

"First, we draw off two cubic centimeters of distilled water." He held the bottle and the syringe up so that she could see. "Get into the habit of eliminating any air by flicking the needle with your little finger. Then you can expel it with the plunger."

"Let me try that," said Karie. She did.

"Okay?" He took the syringe back and picked up another bottle which contained white powder.

"Why are they separate?" she asked.

"It degenerates over time," said Brad. "Now we mix the water and the GH." He held the bottle of the powder on its side and inserted the needle. "Watch this, Moneypenny," he said in a passable imitation of James Bond, "the elixir must be stirred, not shaken." He rolled the bottle carefully and the solution became milky white.

Karie took the bottle and held it to the light. This was it. This is what constituted cheating. It looked innocuous enough. "Okay," she said.

"It's always best if you stand, say, on your left foot, and bend the right knee, so there's no weight on this butt muscle." He took a new syringe and drew off half of the GH solution. "Pull down your jeans."

Karie unbuttoned and pushed her jeans down to expose a demure area of her right cheek. "Is that okay?" *Andy would have suggested I drop my pants to my knees,* she thought.

"Fine. Now I swab quickly."

She felt a cold tingling sensation, then the jab of the needle.

"Good, you're not a jumper. Now inject slowly." She watched the plunger move down. "Okay, quick dab." He pulled the needle out and pressed her skin with the cotton. "Here's a trick that helps. Take two fingers and rub around the prick point, to dissipate the GH."

She could feel a dull presence around the point, but no pain. "One last thing," he spread his thumb and finger from her hip bone, "You want to be about four inches from your hip bone. If you move too much over towards the spine, you might hit the sciatic nerve—and you'll never forget it."

Karie pulled up her jeans. "It's not easy to measure—"

"Tell you what I did at first, for myself. I used a tape measure and marker. No kidding."

Karie twisted round to feel the target area in her rump.

"That's right," he said. "And give it a good jab so the needle goes into the muscle, about an inch."

Brad walked out to the kitchen. "Here," he handed her the two used syringes. "Just stub them against metal and break the tips. We don't want any druggies scavenging in the garbage."

Karie held out her hand. "You've been a great help." She smiled. "I was a little apprehensive..."

"So was I." He affected a solemn, Dr. Kildare voice, "I just try to look professional." As she turned to go, he said, "It's *Promised Land*, by Robert B. Parker."

"Sorry?"

"The book I'm reading. I thought you were looking at it."

"You caught me," said Karie putting up her hands. Relaxing with a book was on the list of things she wanted to do after the Olympics.

"I like Spenser mysteries," he said. "And in these chartless times, 'there is no frigate like a book.' I don't know who said that, but somebody did."

Karie walked to her car feeling embarrassed that she had chalked up Brad as an actor/stud type. *I have now broken the rules and could be banned from running, now that I have this GH swimming around inside me.* "Technically," Andy would say. "For insurance, dear lady," Dr. John would put it.

Brad waved from the balcony as Karie drove off. So this was the special case that Dr. John had cautioned him about. Not bad. Start with a mild one cc of GH, then after an interval, go to a mix with a good slug of testosterone. And she's not to know about the switch. No discussion, nothing. *Strange—but the show goes on.* He gripped the rail and declaimed: "Theirs not to reason why, theirs but to do and die."

And the money was good. Brad went back to Spenser and the Rams.

* * *

Karie had always wondered what a singer felt when she hit a high note and held it. She imagined feeling exalted and borne aloft on a ray of pure sublime sound, then brought safely to earth as the note faded and applause crashed all around.

When she had completed Andy's program, Karie would add her own crescendo. She would start a 400 meter lap with an easy bouncing stride and gradually increase her speed, like a singer winding up for the big note, until she hit the final curve and reached the ultimate high of sustained motion. Then she would lapse into her easy stride and slowly build until she was ready for another. As she flashed down the straight, she would keep perfect pitch until the applause broke around her. Thinking like this helped manage the

172

pain. The trick was to concentrate on being Barbra at Lincoln Center and not let anything else intrude.

Andy watched Karie going through her extra laps. Her kicks were explosive, each with the same fierce intensity. Andy noticed other team members paused on their way home to check her routine, and he knew that Dr. John sometimes came and watched from his car. Andy couldn't recall when a steroid cycle had worked so well. Karie's muscles were not overly bulked or ripped, although Brad Barnes reported that she was now lifting an extra 20 pounds with ease. Her power seemed smooth and effortless. There was no shading on her upper lip, and her voice showed no change, although—he smiled at the thought—she was a little irritable sometimes.

As he watched her build up to another high, he wondered again about her sex urge. He felt sure that they were destined to become intimate. Their mutual dependency would bring them together, quite apart from the insistence of the hormones. He decided to bide his time and not make any crass moves. He could never be quite sure with Karie. She still insisted on wearing tights when he took her skinfold measurement with the caliper. Even so, the last time he was embarrassed to feel an erection coming on.

Andy came up to her as she completed her sixth lap. "Looking great, but I think you've done enough for today." They continued walking on the track; the rest of the team had left.

"You said the medicine," he had told her not to say growth hormone, "would help me recover faster, so that I could train harder. Well it has, and I am." She pranced around him and then started high-stepping backwards. "I can do more."

"No," he said.

"Hey, here I am all fired up and ready to go—"

"I don't want you overtraining or risking an injury. I mean it— all it takes is a twist or a sprain."

"Okay, Coach." She hung her head and pretended to sulk.

"And that meet in Portland, at the end of the month, I think we can skip it."

"What? I thought we were going to kick some serious ass there. I feel like competing—"

"Look Karie, we can go to the meet, but I don't want you to run, that's all."

The doctor had said Portland was still too close to the last cycle and not to risk it, but of course Andy couldn't tell her. It was a pity he couldn't talk to her about the cocktail. Make her understand that her fast recovery times should not lead to heroic training bouts. She was such a quick read and so damn principled. Anyway, it wasn't long now. They were already at the point where they could plateau on the steroids. "We're only 10 weeks from New Orleans, and we don't need too much exposure. I want you to think of yourself as the stealth candidate."

She nodded. "But I need competition."

"Don't worry, we'll do the regionals." Andy caught up to her and massaged her shoulders. "Drop by later if you can. If not, *hasta mañana*."

Bummer, thought Karie as she drove home, *what does he think I am, a porcelain vase? Maybe I'll run to the gym and back this afternoon.* Later Brad was taking her to a Billy Crystal gala benefit at the Dorothy Chandler pavilion. She hadn't told Andy because she knew he would get very uptight. He could really get tiresome at times. Brad was good company, except when they were with his actor friends and they all started doing imitations. Tonight should be fun. She had splurged on a Norma Kamali outfit, so they would both look sharp.

She toweled off after her shower and stepped up to the mirror. Her legs were looking really strong. It wasn't just definition, there was a cut to the quads and calves when she flexed. The growth hormone had really done the job. She scampered into the room for her bra and pants. Karie put on her bra and accidentally brushed her hand against her nipple. She felt a shiver go up her spine and was suddenly covered with goose bumps. Instinctively she rubbed her thighs together. Too bad she was running late, otherwise she'd lie back for a little relaxation. Lately she'd discovered some very interesting uses for the personal sports massager she'd bought to relieve leg cramps. Karie blushed; she hadn't been that discreet about it either and was pretty sure CeeCee had overheard her moans on at least two occasions. Maybe that's why CeeCee kept giving her funny looks and staying out of her way. Fine. CeeCee spent the night at Robert's practically every night anyway. Rafael could only make it out once every two months. Good thing he was coming tomorrow. Brad's subtle hints were getting harder and harder to ignore.

*   *   *

Karie watched Rafael sitting beside her at the table, the candle-light playing softly on his features as he talked about New York with CeeCee's boyfriend, Robert. Rafael wore a black and white striped shirt with no collar that he had designed, black jeans with a silver buckle and short black boots. She pressed her knee against him as she smiled and cocked her head in a possessive gesture. They were dining in the patio of the Trattoria Il Forno, and it seemed to Karie that their table was bathed in a warm glow that cocooned them from the surrounding diners.

Rafael had become established in New York and was making good on his promise that he was only a plane ride away. When Karie went back to Goodland at Christmas and for the birth of Bonnie's son, Timothy, she had run past the trailer. It was now occupied by a young couple and their four-year-old daughter. *Things have changed and are definitely falling into place*, she thought, as she reached impulsively to rub Rafael's neck.

Rafael was saying, "I was the skinny little kid in school, you know—the easy target—and then I saw Martin Sheen in *Apocalypse Now* doing tai chi. So I started doing the moves at home."

"So you got respect?" asked Robert.

"Self-respect." He nodded. "I'm into it pretty much now. I find it blends into so many things, like in design work, perhaps because of the stylized movements that it teaches."

175

Karie put her hand on his thigh. He seemed harder and stronger than she remembered, and she wondered for a moment if he was onto some juice. She leaned back and smiled at CeeCee, who raised her eyebrows in a questioning look, but Karie shook her head slightly. She just felt good. She had never been as confident and competitive as she was now. She closed her eyes, flexed the muscles in her legs and shoulders, and knew that right now she could kick off her heels and burst into a sustained high-pitched sprint down the street. Even Andy seemed a little in awe of her training schedule and fussed about it, and he didn't know about her evening runs. She was going to be ready for New Orleans and for Barcelona, and now with a level playing field she could see the Stars and Stripes billowing at the end of the last straight.

Robert was saying "...last weekend I went with a friend of mine on this yoga retreat in Korea Town. You start off having to sit in a circle for a couple of hours, without moving."

"Did it work?" said Rafael.

"I don't know—I got kicked out. There's this old guy who said I was screwing up the group, said I wasn't supposed to breathe while I was connecting with the 'ying'—"

CeeCee excused herself to go to the bathroom. She wanted to get out of there, because she was upset by what she was seeing. Karie was all over Rafael, and Rafael was obviously uncomfortable. Earlier, as the hostess took them from the bar to the table, Robert had breathed in CeeCee's ear, "What's up with Karie? She's so hyped." CeeCee couldn't very well look into Robert's big brown eyes and say, "Oh, don't mind her, she's just on steroids. I can tell 'cause I took them." CeeCee ran the faucet and held a paper towel underneath to wet it. She dabbed her face and tried to calm down. Robert was some kind of man, hot and sensitive in all the right places. He was also thoughtfully showing her the ins and outs of real estate. Now that the Olympics were behind her, she wanted something to fall back on. She'd still train, but it would be on her dime, not Andy's. If she got her broker's license, her life would be that much more rounded. Especially if Robert made good on the marriage proposal he'd hinted at. CeeCee gave herself a once-over in the mirror. The meal was almost finished. She could make an excuse, go back to Robert's, take a nice long bath with her man, and forget all about Karie.

Back at the apartment, Karie locked the door, put a finger to Rafael's lips and began to unbutton his shirt in the darkness. She dropped his clothes around them at the entrance and, taking his hand, led him into the dark of the bedroom. Then in a quick kneeling movement she put one hand behind his knees, the other around his back and swept him off his feet. She took a few quick steps and laid him on his back and with quick fluttering hands began to massage his legs and torso, like they did at the Soft Tissue Center. Karie slipped out of her clothes and knelt over him so that she could trace her nipples from his stomach up over his chest. She began to tremble with desire and pushed her tongue between his lips. As Rafael moved his hands up her body to stroke her back, she grabbed his wrists and held them above his head. She lowered herself onto him and in rhythmic movements, snaked her tongue into his mouth and pushed down onto him, with increasing reach—until her whole body was flailing against him.

After, as they lay together, Rafael asked, "Did CeeCee seem in a hurry to leave to you?"

"She just kind of stresses," Karie said. "It's the first Olympics in eight years she's not going out for."

Rafael said, "Remember when you told me that Andy had suggested you take some stuff to help with your training—it was about three years ago?"

"What stuff?"

"Steroids."

"He didn't suggest I take them. He wanted me to know what was going on."

"Has he talked about it again?" Rafael asked.

"About what?" Karie sat up on one elbow.

"Taking steroids."

"No." She climbed on top of him and straddled his body. "Anyway, what is this with you?" But before he could answer, she was nibbling his lip.

Next day they took a picnic and drove up the coast north of Zuma to where a cluster of tall, black rocks formed a natural shelter.

Karie did a series of 200 meter interval sprints on the beach as Rafael sketched. The sand was too uneven for her to get up any real speed, but it was a good workout and soon she was sweating freely. She decided to go to the track in the evening, maybe do some 400 meter builds, even though it was supposed to be a rest day.

After lunch Karie lay on the sand, thinking she would send Mom and Dad airline tickets for the trials in New Orleans. Money was not a problem. She had done a lot of modeling in the last two years, although she had now stopped almost entirely except for sports prints, which never took much prep work. Erin had been right. Tanya had welcomed Karie back with open arms, but Karie had a feeling that Tanya would probably not take her back again. Her words, when Karie said, "See you after Barcelona," had been, "Well, we all have to make choices." No problem though, there were other agencies. Karie knew she'd be in demand if she medaled.

She opened her eyes to see Rafael sitting up and looking at her. "Hi," she said softly, and reached for his hand.

"Hi," he said and squeezed her fingers.

"You look as if you've lost something?" She smiled.

He stroked her leg. "You're looking very strong. I don't think I've ever seen you this...developed."

"I'm training harder than I ever have." Although her tone was reasonable, she felt a spark of irritation. It stayed there, smoldering, as she began to think where the conversation could lead.

Rafael lay down close to her and put his arm across her waist. He spoke quietly, "You know how we always tell each other things. Well, I can't help but tell you that you seem different."

"I said I'm training harder." Her voice sounded loud.

"What I was trying to say last night was…if you're taking something…please tell me."

Her anger was rising. *Lay off*, she thought. *I make my own decisions, not just about what I choose to do, but most of all about to whom or what I choose to say. It's my business, my training and my future.*

Karie's eyes were flashing, and Rafael could tell she was angry. He took her shoulders gently and said, "You can tell me. Hey, it's okay. We can work it out. It's just that we need to talk—"

Karie sat up suddenly, saying, "Why do you keep at it, when I said no?" She paused for a moment. Rafael looked stricken but she couldn't contain herself. "And since when are 'we' going to the Olympics anyway? Just drop it. I mean it." She sat up, clasping her knees, and looked angrily out to sea.

Rafael lay back on his elbows looking at the muscles on her arched back and was silent for a while. "So you have been doing something."

Karie tightened her grip. The flat judgment caught her by surprise. "What if I have—let's just suppose—what in hell has that got to do with you?" She turned to face him. "If I do, or if I don't, it's none of your damn business."

Rafael stood up, shrugged, said, "Okay," and walked to the water's edge.

His apparent belief that he had caught her kept her seething. She got up and began to gather her things. *It's my decision and my body.* She wanted to say, "And it's not steroids," except that it sounded too much like an admission.

As she drove back, Rafael kept a miserable silence. *As well he might*, she thought, *he brought it up*. When they drove up to the apartment, Karie patted him on the knee and said, "Leave it alone." Then she drove to the track for her workout.

She trained hard and then kept walking around the track to cool down. She felt sorry that she had to deal so sharply with Rafael. She couldn't remember ever arguing with him about anything. But if he insisted on questioning her, she had no course but to slap him down. It was her decision. She never intended to talk about it with anyone else, and she had never expected to be confronted. What business was it of his? As she got into her car, she admitted that she should not have allowed herself to get angry—but even now, she felt annoyed.

But Rafael wouldn't give up, and he was waiting for her when she returned from the track. She could tell immediately by his earnest look, which was now beginning to bug her.

"Karie, please don't get mad, just listen."

I have to admit that he's got balls to bring it up again, she thought, as she made an elaborate show of putting away her Pace bag and pulling up a chair to sit opposite him. In the past...well, of course, in the past this had never occurred.

"If nothing's going on, you know," he said awkwardly, "then I'm sorry, I apologize. But if you have been taking some stuff—"

She exhaled loudly and continued to stare at him.

"—then please be careful."

It was the same thing that CeeCee said, only she had said it better.

Now Rafael continued with his most concerned voice, "Sometimes these things have side effects that can—"

Now wait a goddamn minute. "If," said Karie, "if I were taking 'these things,'" she mimicked his tone, "I can tell you I'd know all about them and a hell of a lot more than you." *Christ, don't get angry,* she thought looking up at the ceiling of the kitchen. Rafael just sat there with a mournful look, as if his mission in life were to keep coming back for more abuse.

He said, "It's what you don't know that can hurt you."

Great, now we have some tai chi talk. Karie stood up and said, "Just leave me alone. Get it?" She walked to the bedroom and shut the door. Later she heard Rafael and CeeCee talking, and she wondered if they were talking about her—no, Rafael would never do that.

She drove him to the airport the following afternoon, and for the first time, she was anxious for him to go. She had not slept well and her workout was sluggish. She knew she had to put everything out of her mind until New Orleans. Then they could have it all out. They could have a wonderful, big argument, maybe even a little wrestling, and not come up for air until everything was straight between them. And stay in bed for a whole weekend.

How strange it is, she thought, *that we can hug and kiss at the airport and say, "Take care," and, "Love you too," when this big chasm has opened up between us.*

*   *   *

The Mount San Antonio College Relays, held in April, are a harbinger of talent for the full season. Although they are too early for any record times, the two-day event draws strong competition and establishes a good base for runners who will try and peak that summer. Because 1992 was an Olympic year, the competition also attracted a number of journalists and sportswriters, including one sober Peter Bernier.

It seemed to Bernie that Karie Johnson ran a perfect race in the 800 meter finals. Not only did she look confident—in fact, almost impatient—in the silver and blue Pace colors, but she led from start to finish. It was as if this were some preliminary event that needed to be completed before moving on to more important matters. With her strong kick she finished in 1:57.34, which clearly established her as the early favorite for New Orleans. He watched her walking like a thoroughbred after the race with her coach to the press conference where a throng of journalists stood in a group, throwing out questions to this new track princess.

"Karie, tell us why you run."

"It's what I do best."

"Can we talk about that?"

"I think you have to follow your own path. Establish what you want to do first, and then do it."

"How did you do that?"

"Everybody has to ask herself, 'Can I do it? Can I break two minutes in the 800 meters? Can I press 170 pounds? Can I write a sports column?' If you can't—move on."

The last question from Bernie. "Can you do it in New Orleans?"

Karie laughed. "If I can't, I'll follow my own advice and move on."

Bernie's piece on the press conference with the headline "Can You Do It?" caught the attention of Gary Neal, the marketing director of Acceleration sports drinks and power bars. Gary was fed up with the introspection of the Me Generation and the cynicism of Generation X. What he wanted was a challenging statement that not only bespoke the true attitude of his target users but also extolled the values of his product. His department had already spent a weekend at La Costa, huddling with their advertising agency, with very little success.

The more he repeated "Can You Do It?" the more Gary believed it caught the mood of the '90s. People today were in a cut-the-crap, no-BS mood. Put up or shut up. Can you bike 100 miles, or break 40 minutes in a 10K? If not, move on. The implicit promise was that whether you could or you couldn't, Acceleration drinks and bars were there to help you try. The theme had legs. He could even see a photo of a student hitting the books with a 32 oz. bottle of Acceleration to keep the blood sugar up under the caption *Can You Do It?* where the copy referred to breaking 1200 on the SAT.

The campaign offered an invitation. It dangled a carrot, threw out a challenge and provoked discussion. The kids would eat it up. Damn, he felt good. Karie was signed to do promos and the campaign broke in a wide variety of sports and nutrition publications with a photo montage of her at the relays.

*   *   *

It was now three weeks since Rafael left, and still Karie could not summon the remorse to call and make amends. It was best to leave things on hold for now and not risk another blow-up over his pesky intrusiveness.

She had a job to do, and Rafael, of all people, should understand that. She was in the tunnel now, and nothing and nobody should get in her way. At the end was New Orleans and after that, everything would be okay. If Rafael didn't understand, too bad.

For now, she had never felt so clear and purposeful, so physically primed for the goal ahead. Even when she was bare-legged in shorts, her leg muscles strained and pulsed against their outer casings, as if she were wearing tight jeans. She quit wearing her old blouses because they made her restless, wanting to stretch against the seams or pop the buttons.

Sometimes Andy could be a little heavy, control freak that he was. Yesterday was a case in point. She'd been at his place watching tapes when he started rubbing her back and came up with this cockamamie idea.

"Karie, I've been thinking maybe you should move in here."

"Why?"

"We've got only a month until the trials, and I need to make sure you're doing everything right."

"I am."

"Otherwise, I'm going to be calling you all the time wanting to know if you've stretched properly, or if you've iced down, or if you're eating just right." He paused and gave her that hard stare of his. "If you need a rubdown, I've got a table right here."

"I don't need that, Andy, but thanks." *Boy, is he pushing it*, she thought.

"I don't want to have to check that you're getting your rest and that you're in bed at nine. We need to be together now all the time, to become one, so I can do the thinking and leave you to train and not worry."

"Time out, Coach," Karie jumped up. "Let's get something straight between us." Suddenly she caught her own double entendre, and she gritted her teeth and shook her head to keep from smiling. "I know what you're saying and I appreciate it, but I don't need any mothering. I'm giving it all I've got, and you even want me to hold back sometimes. I need your help, especially now, but I also need my space."

183

Andy stared at her, then shrugged. "I thought it would make things easier for you, that's all."

"Coach, believe me, everything's fine. Listen, I gotta go. Don't sweat it, Coach, I'll be okay. I promise."

The guy's overboard on control, she thought. *Of course, I could tell him that old one about I'm always in bed by nine and then I get up to go home, except that he'd have a fit.* That surely was one aspect of the GH that she hadn't counted on. In fact, if she didn't know Andy better, she might have accused him of mixing a little aphrodisiac into the shots. Lately she'd been feeling so damn horny. Normally, when training became intense, she burned off her sex urge, and all she wanted to do was crawl into bed and fall dead asleep. GH was hot stuff.

It was just as well Brad was around. They had been hanging around a lot, and not just on the days she needed her shots. Karie managed to put aside his lack of ambition or any fixed goal in life. As Brad said, in his best Sly Stallone imitation, "Yo, you got a problem with that?" He drifted like tumbleweed, and his great looks and hard body kept him living in fine style. Karie loved to hear him talk about crossing the country on his Harley, with excursions into Mexico, even though the experiences were probably embellished. Meanwhile, he continued to get good print work, most recently for Calvin Klein jeans and Drakkar Noir cologne.

Every time Brad made a pass, she cut him off real quick. But a couple of weeks ago, her blood raging, she decided that she needed to do something so she wouldn't short out her vibrator. Acceleration held a big promo bash at Loew's Hotel in Santa Monica where Karie made a brief speech and signed autographs. Halfway through the evening, she led Brad upstairs and took him to bed. Then she rejoined the proceedings.

Karie sipped champagne and felt happy at how well things were going. She was finished with the growth hormone. It was all over, finished, dead, buried, no more, not ever again. It certainly seemed to be a hell of a lot more than the insurance Dr. John made it out to be. In fact, she had to wonder, if the growth hormones were this good, what else could those notorious steroids bring to the party? Someone else asked for her autograph, and Karie signed with a smile. So, she thought as she posed for a photograph for the umpteenth time, if Mr. Rafael Jimenez thinks it's time to see other people, well, he probably knows best. She had his letter in her evening bag. It had arrived that afternoon. *It's not forever, it's just until the Olympics. It's for the best. Rafael just didn't get how much was at stake.* Brad walked over smiling. *Good boy*, she thought, as he handed her another glass of champagne.

*   *   *

Andy felt good about Pace, about Barcelona and even about Atlanta. They were two weeks from the trials and, apart from his usual crop of sprinters, he had two new young kids that surprised him. One was a girl he'd found in Abilene, Texas, who perfectly filled the 10K gap in his line-up. There was another kid, a boy from Chula Vista, who blitzed the 110 meter hurdles. And there was Karie in the 800 meters. The Great American Hope.

Karie easily had the fastest times and was not only the favorite to make the U.S. team, but, with any luck, could go all the way. The toppling of the Berlin Wall in 1989 had played havoc with the athletic programs of the Iron Curtain countries, and the really good coaches had migrated to other nations that now sought international recognition. But Barcelona was too soon for the new programs to take root, and Andy felt that the women's 800 meter field offered the rare breakthrough opportunity for an American Olympic champion, though he had deliberately played down any such speculation by the sporting press.

Andy focused heavily on the trials, allowing them to consume all his waking thoughts. Above everything else, Karie needed to peak just right.

"No more heavy track workouts from now—just technique."

Karie made a face.

"You don't need any buildup."

"I know, Coach." She jogged lightly by his side. "Just maintenance, right?" *But I don't want to lose any power either*, she thought. She could always do some evening intervals by the beach, on her own. That way she would sleep better. "What about weights?"

"Just for toning." He smiled, "I've already told Brad what the program should be."

"Okay." But Brad would do what she wanted. She just didn't want to leave anything to chance.

"Tomorrow I want you to do some easy 400s. I want you to get the feel of the lap times."

"No more :55 first laps, right?" *It's funny how the Indianapolis disaster had faded*, thought Karie. Now she could kid about it, because she was really going to show them.

"You got it; :58, or even :59, will be just fine." Andy turned to go.

"Wait," she said in dismay, "what about the visualization session?" He'd started her on a program where they went through the whole race, from the sound of the crowd to the feel of the track as she thrust herself through the finish line, with arms raised. Andy called it "mind grooving," and she really dug it.

"I didn't realize you liked that," he joked. "This afternoon at four."

Karie gave him a huge bear hug that almost knocked him off his feet. "That's my coach." *He could be a real pain at times, but he was the best.* She ran off laughing to herself, then turned and waved to him.

We've become a team, he thought. After New Orleans he'd be able to tell her about his doping cocktail. She would understand and be appreciative because it had gone so well. Then they could plan for Barcelona and really be together, sporting like young tigers under the sheets. But more importantly he wanted to plan a good celebration. Maybe he'd buy her something. They had come a long way together.

*   *   *

To make the U.S. trials in track for the 1992 Olympics was to be in very tall company, whatever the event. This was the cream of the strongest team in the world, and you didn't get there by being lucky. To be there for the second time, as the favorite in the 800 meters with the fastest time for the year, was to be unique. *As Brad once quoted, "What's past is prologue,"* thought Karie. Beyond this June Saturday and Sunday in New Orleans lay the Olympics in Barcelona, and beyond that there would be other mountains to climb. As badly as she wanted to make up with Dad, she couldn't see herself moving back to Goodland. Maybe New York. She'd have to wait and see.

But for now, Andy made her focus on the task at hand. None of the front runners from Indianapolis was here, and there wasn't anyone that Karie had not met during the season. During the last month she had done most of her training in the San Fernando Valley so she could get used to the heat, and they had come to New Orleans a couple of days early so that she could get to know the feel of the new tartan.

Together they had gone over her race plans, thought through any eventualities, worn in an alternate pair of running shoes, and psyched each other up. So if Andy called out, "The hotter it is...?" Karie would shout, "The faster I go...there's less wind resistance, dummy," and when he said, "If they go inside...?" she would respond, "I'll zap them on the curve." Karie had even been on a local TV station news flash, where the commentator introduced her as the Can Do Kid and asked if she had any thoughts about her upcoming race. "Just tell them I'm ready," said the Kid with a smile that made the Saturday newspapers.

Her preliminary race was set for 4 p.m., and thunderheads were building over Lake Ponchartrain. Looking at the dark clouds in the distance, Andy said, "It's a sign of good luck, Kid. It means there are plenty of ions in the air, and that's when records are broken."

Karie knew that he was just keeping her psyched and she gave him a hug. "Like the Kid said, 'I'm ready.'"

*   *   *

Some races feel better than others, and by the first 200 meters Karie felt that this one was going to be okay. By the 200 mark, your body was telling you how much it was going to hurt—and you also had a good read on who was going to challenge you. As they came to the curve before the final straight of the first lap, Karie was running just behind the lead pair, two women from the east coast. Patti was a known fast starter with no kick. Kelly was already pushing it. The occasional catch in her breathing was a red flag. Andy had reminded Karie to play it cool. The top three qualified for the final tomorrow, but if she were feeling good…"Well, Kid, it's up to you if you want to show them a good time."

Just after the bell, Karie prepared to pass after the turn and pull ahead on the back straight. *Andy was right, a good time would psych out everyone else who qualified and make it easier for the finals. I'm ready, so let's see if we can hit the high note on the final stretch. Let's go for the good time.*

As Karie came round the final curve, now almost 10 meters in the lead, the crowd was hushed. Something was about to happen. Maybe it was the ions in the air that everyone was breathing, but here was the Kid with her head flung back and going so smooth it was like she was on wheels. Now the crowd was on their feet, not that the race was even close but because they knew that they were being treated to something special.

As she was flying to the finish with her chest high, Karie felt a slight knock in her right hamstring, as if someone had tapped her with a relay baton, and then she cut through the electronic beam and the announcer was yelling "…at 1:56.13, if confirmed, this is a new American record…Karie Johnson, ladies and gentlemen." She walked up the track, with everyone rushing over to her, thinking, *Wow, that's my fastest ever and it just sort of happened.* She put her

188

hand on her hamstring, just above the knee where she had felt the tap. There wasn't any pain.

Lou Gertz was at the race and couldn't stop jumping around like a kid, shouting, "Way to go, Karie!" She'd be going to Barcelona for sure, and she might just go all the way. He had three kids from AU in the trials, which was pretty good for a start, but above all he wanted to see Karie nail down a position on the U.S. team. He wanted to find her now, but he knew he should not come between her and Andy until it was all over. *Tomorrow*, he promised himself, *I'm going to hug the Can Do Kid off her feet.*

*　　*　　*

Grover had been the therapist with Pace Track for at least two coaches before Andy Nagy—and he had disliked them all. They all pushed the kids too hard, filled them up with all this bullshit about it's-all-in-the-mind and you-can-be-a-star-if-you-want-to, and then, sooner or later, their bodies snapped and they ended up with Grover. The team had an M.D. on retainer, but he never came on field trips. He was only useful for authorizing the ultrasound or the electro-stim; for anything else, they had to go to an orthopedist.

Every now and then you came upon a real pisser, when you wished you had another profession, like postal worker. "Karie says she feels fine," he shrugged and looked at Andy. "We iced down and put on a pressure wrap. Told her to keep doing that every hour, gave her Motrin, told her not to go dancing. We'll see to-morrow."

"Grover, cut the shit, I need to know."

Grover liked to drag it out a bit. After all, it wasn't like your car was making a funny noise, but he could see that Andy was a little stressed. And Karie was one of the great ones. It really was a pisser.

"It's the biceps femoris," he said. "You know how the ham-string muscles divide and attach on either side of the knee?" Grover turned sideways and touched his leg above and behind his right knee, "The biceps is on the outside."

"Is it the short or the long head?"

I keep forgetting, he thought, *the coach knows his shit.* "It's the big part of the muscle, the long head. Karie said it was like a tap. That could be a slight rupture of the tendon, not a strain..." He let the words hang. "I didn't want to go pressing around there too much."

If it had only been tomorrow, thought Andy. Break the record at the finals and then we can handle any injury before Barcelona. But here she is, having broken the American record, a potential Olympic medalist, and she still has to qualify tomorrow.

Grover said, "Coach, the only way to find out the damage is to do an MRI at a hospital, but I'm not sure what good that would do now." They both knew that the only purpose would be to determine if there were a tear, and how dangerous it might be, but it wouldn't stop Karie. Andy shook his head.

Later, Andy phoned Dr. John in California.

"Nagy, old chap, did you put gunpowder in her drink? That was a fantastic performance."

"We've got a problem. Grover says she's sprained her hamstring, maybe even ruptured it. It happened right before the finish, for Chrissake."

The doctor was quiet for a moment and then said, "It's always the risk, isn't it?"

"All I can think is she must've been over-training big time. Suddenly she doesn't have any recovery pain, so she starts doing extra workouts and the muscle bulks up but the tendon doesn't—"

"Didn't you tell her—?"

"That, or too many squats in the gym and the quads get stronger than the hamstrings—"

"You didn't tell her?"

"Didn't I tell her what?" His voice was flat and angry. "That we had a little Testex in with the growth hormone? And that she should go to church on Sunday and not to the track? Give me a fucking break, Doc."

"Hold on, old fellow, this is not getting us anywhere," said Dr.

John. "Though I thought you would've at least mentioned it to her." But there was not much to be done now, except wait and hope for the best. That, and cover your ass.

"Sure," Andy said, and hung up annoyed. *As if Dr. John were ever honest about anything*, he thought.

* * *

Karie was sitting on the examining table, grabbing her right knee with both hands. "Sure it hurts when I press right here, but I've hurt before and still run well, haven't I? I figure that once I get going I won't feel anything until after the race."

Grover looked at his watch and said, "No more ice. Keep the wrap on until you start to warm up. Everything else okay?"

"The Kid's ready," said Karie. "After all, it's for less than two minutes."

"Just keep it at 90 percent, and you'll be fine," said Andy.

"Hey," she said, "just don't expect me to coast into third. I'm not running any risks here, and I'm not going to have some college kid spook me on the blind side."

"Karie, Karie." He put his hand on her shoulder and shook it gently. "All we're saying," he looked at Grover, "is to do enough to qualify, then we'll get you all fixed up. If you do too much, then it may take longer. So don't try and blow them all away. Save it for Barcelona."

Karie shrugged, "No problem." They were making too much of this.

"And if you feel any real pain—Grover, back me up on this— then quit."

Grover looked at him. He had never heard Andy say that to anyone.

"Yeah, yeah, Andy, like we've come all this way to crap out." *He's worse than Dad.* She had spent the evening with her parents in their hotel room so she could keep icing her leg, and Dad kept hovering around her as if she were about to go into labor.

She stood up, feeling the pencil of tightness just above the outside of her knee. Right now she wanted time to think about the race. Then, in about half an hour, she would go change and begin a very gradual warm-up. She knew what to do. She'd been here before. She didn't need any more attention or talk. It was all up to her now. She was on her way to Barcelona, and she'd run right over anyone who got in the way.

*   *   *

Andy had insisted Grover sit next to him. He looked over to where Karie was lining up at the start.

"What d'you think?" said Andy.

Grover shook his head. "Should be okay. Just keep your fingers crossed."

They watched the starter raise his gun.

Karie felt so calm she figured she had at least a half step on everyone when the gun sounded. But there was no call-back, and by the time they were on the back straight she was into her rhythm and breathing well. She could tell they were on a :59 pace, which was where she wanted to be. As long as her hamstring didn't feel any tighter than it was now, she would be fine. Karie Johnson had received a special burst of applause when she was introduced in Lane 3, and she had turned to wave in the direction of her parents. She figured Rafael caught it all on TV.

As the bell sounded she looked back. There were three women a good five meters back and only Kelly Baskin in front of her. Karie felt a flood of adrenalin as she realized she was only 300 meters away from the Olympics. If she pulled ahead, she would grab a flag and do a victory lap and go up into the stands with Mom and Dad. But stay loose, don't kick. She tightened up on Kelly, just off her right shoulder, and realized that Kelly was really hurting.

"She's going great, Coach," said Grover, trying to sound calm. "The Kid's a real pro."

"Keep your fingers crossed." Andy's hands were clenched tight.

He watched the rhythmic cadence of her arms and legs. *Now she's visualizing the finish just like we worked it out.* He whispered, "Come on Karie, another 20 seconds."

Just before the final 100 meters, she eased past Kelly and used the curve to look back. Two others had begun to kick and they were coming up on Kelly...Karie kept her stride and slightly increased her cadence...she had the inside track and about five meters, and she was not going to let anyone sneak up on her right...and now there was only about 50 meters to go...all the way to Barcelona. Karie felt a loud smack in her right hamstring and half turned to see who might have hit her from behind. The momentum carried her right leg forward again and she felt a knifing pain behind her knee as her leg gave way. She crumpled forward, hitting the track on her right shoulder, with runners passing on her right.

The medics were later congratulated for their efficiency. Before the winner crossed the line, two paramedics were sprinting to where Karie lay writhing on the track, her cries clearly audible in the shocked silence of the stadium. She was strapped on a stretcher and heading for the emergency room before the announcer could make a statement.

Rafael could see her face, contorted with pain, and he yelled, "Karie," at the TV screen, then stumbled to the phone without knowing whom to call. Nancy and Eigel Johnson stood up with the rest of the crowd, then turned to each other and fell together, their faces ashen and expressionless. Lou Gertz ran from the stands and hurdled a gate in front of a startled guard. He went through the tunnel into the yard but was fended off by the medics as the ambulance pulled out. He turned and ran to the cab stand.

The accident made national TV news with spectacular footage in freeze-frame format prefaced by the caution, "You may wish to avert your eyes as we show the closing seconds of this historic race." It was a front page photo in most newspapers, with sports page photos showing progressive shots of her fall, down to a close-up of her face contorted with pain, which one former athlete claimed to be "worse than giving birth." The sound of the tendon snapping—

causing the muscle to bunch back like a window sash cord—was later described as being like "the crack of a rifle." *Sporting Life* even made the analogy of the shot heard coming from the book depository in Dallas. As one TV reporter put it, "You cannot listen to a commentary on this accident without wanting to feel your muscles just behind the right knee," as her hand dropped to touch the back of her leg.

Sports columnists agreed that Karie's injury was a key loss to the U.S. Track and Field team. Karie Johnson had been an odds-on favorite for U.S. Olympic gold in a category that hadn't produced America winners. And as Peter Bernier told his editor, "It's a personal tragedy as well. She'll never run competitively again."

Chapter Twelve

Karie eased the needle of the 280Z back to 70 and shifted her position at the wheel, wishing she had cruise control so she could rest her right leg. Up ahead on the left was a windmill farm that looked like a flock of long-legged birds with large silver beaks staring in her direction. They reminded her of the sandpipers on the beach that Rafael had been so fascinated with.

It was six years to the month since she had set out for L.A. with the intention of giving full rein to her running career and her vision of the Stars and Stripes at the finish line. Now she was driving I-10 East, bereft of any dream, with no destination in mind other than leaving L.A. behind. Someone had told her that as one door closes, another opens, but hearing that brought Karie no comfort. Running had been her life and her abrupt and dishonorable transition had given way to the sensation of falling into a black hole. The only thing to be found in the void was the phrase that punctuated her every move: She would never run competitively again.

Dr. Christian Laforet had brought a book with him when he came to visit her on the Monday morning after the trials. He drew up a chair so that they could face each other. "I'm the one who stitched you up yesterday." He smiled, "So I thought we might talk about it."

Karie nodded. He spoke softly, as if they were sharing confidences.

"It hurts?"

"Yes," she sighed and arched her back for relief.

"And the shoulder?"

"Not too bad. Just uncomfortable."

"You have a lot of bruising there," he leaned across her, "yes, quite a sight." She could smell his cologne, a metallic, lemon scent so clinical that she wondered if it were standard issue for doctors. "I was looking at the photos and you hit hard…track burn on your shoulder and the palm of your right hand that saved your face…I was going to put the arm in a sling." He sat back. "Lucky, really."

Karie looked at him and waited.

"Now, about the leg." He made it sound like something they might face together. "I brought this medical book so I could explain the procedure, if that's okay?"

He took out a marker and opened the book to show a color drawing of the tissues in the rear upper leg. "The hamstring is really three separate muscle bundles. Two of them attach down here at the knee on the inside. The other, the biceps femoris, which is our culprit, goes on the outside and attaches in two separate places, two heads, to the bone..."

Karie stared. She wondered if muscles were really that pink and stringy looking. When you feel a muscle it is compact and smooth, like a power-pack, something that can explode into action and hurl a heavy body down a track. What she saw here seemed an amorphous work still in progress, unable to support a box of toothpicks, let alone her entire skeletal frame. And were the tendons really white, like the base of a celery stalk?

She realized Dr. Laforet had stopped talking and was watching her. "Karie, when I was in medical school, a doctor once told me not to worry about how things look, but to think about what they do. If you look at an electric motor, it looks powerful—yet take off the cover, and all you've got is something like a ball of twine. So think of the muscles as a motor."

There you go, she thought, and smiled.

"Where your biceps femoris tore is right here at the tendon and, when that happens, the muscle snaps back like a rubber band."

Karie shuddered inwardly, and the movement caused a stab of pain in her right leg. She remembered grabbing the back of her leg and the terrible feeling, like having a snake bunched up under the skin. Then hands had taken her arms and legs, pulled her up and lifted her away in a slow-motion sequence. The realization that the race would be won without her was like when film gets stuck in the projector and a tiny pin-prick-sized spot of light bubbles and melts, flaring into a gaping hole with burned edges, until nothing is left but a blank screen and the flapping sound of the projector.

"So we stretch the muscle out, sew it up good and tight and, in time, the fibers knit together."

Karie looked at him. "Why did it snap, Doctor?"

"Too much strain," he looked at her. "It might have begun to fray. You didn't feel anything before?"

Karie said, "Well I felt this sort of tap at the end on Saturday." She reached down under the sheet to feel the spot and then pulled her hand away when she felt the cast. "I mentioned it to my coach and the trainer who travels with the team."

"And you went ahead, with that kind of warning?"

"Well I was feeling pretty good...and I was going to stop if I felt any real pain, just drop out."

"What I mean is," he looked up and raised his hands imploringly, "they should have stopped you. Never let you run."

Karie stared. *This guy doesn't have a clue*, she thought. "Nobody could've stopped me. I would have crawled over the finish if they hadn't grabbed me. This was the finals, understand? This is for the Olympics, see?" She felt the rush of anger as the words seemed to erupt from her. "I came pretty darn close, too. If I'd held together another five seconds, I would've made it." She bit her lip. "I almost made the team." She closed her eyes as tears overwhelmed her.

She calmed down and opened her eyes, surprised to find Dr. Laforet still sitting there, holding out some tissues. *Screw him anyway, what difference does it make whether he stays or leaves?* These people had no idea what it was like to train and compete, to start at the bottom of a very tall ladder. How at each step, things only got harder, how the slightest imbalance, even a bad night's rest, could make you forfeit, and yet you had to keep moving up, because by then it was such a long way down. And what was at the top? Probably another ladder, but at least you made the team. At least you got to strut on that platform which set you above everyone else. She felt sorry for Dr. Laforet. He would never feel those juices in his veins. "They are spectators," Andy would say. "They watch, they chronicle and discuss—but they're never in the game."

197

She turned to the doctor, as if he were the patient, and said, "There is something you should know. I have been taking some growth hormone injections." She told him when she began and when she stopped, the precise dosages and the intervals between cycles, and then the step-ups in her training schedule as a result of her quick recovery time.

The doctor did not seem surprised by her admission, nodding with an understanding expression on his face until she had finished. "Yes," he said smiling, "I could see the needle marks. But I would like to run some more tests. I need your permission."

How quaint. "Test away," she said, lying back on the pillow and closing her eyes. "I'm not going anywhere."

*   *   *

In a couple of days Dr. Laforet had the test results. This time he rolled Karie in a wheelchair to an examination room. He helped her on an examination table and patted her cast. "If you can, keep flexing the muscles in your leg; it helps to keep the fibers knitting in a straight line." He demonstrated by interlacing the fingers of his hands. "But don't do it if it becomes painful."

"I can handle pain."

The doctor ignored the remark. "When you feel up to it, we have some equipment in the hospital that lets you exercise your good leg. You'll find the benefit transfers over to the muscles in your right leg and limits any atrophy."

Neat, she thought, *maybe I can make Barcelona after all.* She knew she was being harsh, but he was a spectator.

"You never took steroids, Karie?"

"No. Of course not."

"Did anyone ever offer any?"

She shrugged. "I refused to do steroids."

The doctor looked at the young woman in front of him and considered what she was telling him. She looked worn and beaten, her skin dull and her eyes puffy, the mouth pulled into a tight pout like someone trying hard not to cry. What did she have to lose by lying? Besides, something about her suggested the real thing, not one of those in-your-face, make-me-a-star type of athletes but a pure competitor interested in winning fair and square. He wondered how the hell the coach was able to talk her into growth hormone. Must be quite a guy.

"When you were taking the growth hormone, did you go for any tests?"

"Every two weeks."

"Why?" he asked. "Growth hormone can't be detected in the testing at athletics events."

"I guess it was just part of the monitoring my coach set up."

"Did your coach ever tell you not to compete in any events?"

Karie said, "No," then hesitated. "Well, he did suggest I not participate in two events, but that was to limit my exposure, to keep a low profile before the trials."

"A low profile," the doctor repeated, "even as the American champion?" He turned away, as if not expecting an answer and reached for a file. "Tell me, Karie, did you ever feel any of the characteristics associated with steroids?"

His voice had turned soft and confiding again, and it took Karie by surprise. "Like what?"

"Increased sexual urge, irritability, a take-charge attitude?"

Karie sat up. "What are you saying?" She really needed to get another doctor.

"Karie," he said, "you have been dosed with steroids, testosterone, mainly, and quite a lot of it. Here's the lab report." He handed her the file. "It's not in your name, of course."

Karie pulled into a rest area where the land stretched away on either side of the interstate—flat, ribbed and desert brown, shimmering in the noon heat. In her backpack she carried water, a convenience-store tuna sandwich, an apple and some Motrin pills. She was now walking for one hour at dawn and sometimes up to two hours in the afternoon when not even the lizards or rabbits were stirring. Then by dusk she would crash at a motel.

199

When Dr. Laforet had passed her the file—he had dropped it in her lap and walked out—she remembered not looking at it, not even bothering to touch it. She remained immobile, propped up on her elbows, both legs outstretched on the examining table. She had always clung to the belief that taking growth hormone was different, and everybody accepted that. It was like food and all the other things athletes did to fortify their bodies. So it had been banned, but that was only recently, and that was a sham because what was the point of banning something that you couldn't test for? As she lay staring at the folder, she realized that even this thin veil had now been snatched away.

She, who had constructed an elaborate mental wall between growth hormone and the tainted world of steroids, now found herself on both sides. She shuddered at the thought of the brutish testosterone molecules that cruised her blood...not just lodging in muscle tissue, but manipulating her genitals, invading her brain and tampering with the sensitive mechanisms inside her. What had she done? She felt an urge to run as far and as fast she could, to leave this poison behind. Awkwardly she tried to swing both legs off the table, letting the contents of the file scatter on the floor, until the sharp tug of pain from the cast arrested her motion.

When Dr. Laforet returned, he picked up the file and drew up a metal stool to sit beside her. "When you take steroids, the muscle bulks up and puts an added strain on the more unyielding connective tissue, like your tendon." His voice was quiet and earnest, as if he very much wanted to share his knowledge. "Normally, this is not a serious problem—unless you overtrain. Some athletes can get carried away by the quick recovery from muscle teardown and pile on extra hours of training, which definitely increases the risk of injury." He looked at her. "You knew nothing of this?"

Karie shook her head wearily. She had been a little puppet on a string. True, Andy had not been aware of some of her training and had at times even suggested that she ease off, but even if he had known he could not have told her of the danger without telling her the reason. It was a fair paradox, a parable on cheating.

"What I find so inexcusable is that your coach did not properly advise you on the risks before the final. No," he held up his hand, "it's not whether you would have competed anyway or not—it's that you should have been told about the steroids."

Karie wondered what would she have done if she had known before the race. If she'd been honestly warned about the seriousness of the risk of injury, she was pretty sure that wouldn't have stopped her. You have to go for it. Even the tap sensation the day before did not deter her. But what if Andy and Dr. John, or even Brad, the whole conniving bunch, had told her they'd been pumping her with testosterone— more than GH—what then? Would she have had the courage to walk away? Or would she have been too much into the 'roids to shrug it off? It was easy for her to say now that she would have quit and pulled out, claiming legitimate injury. But what about then?

"Your coach probably didn't tell you because he feared you would withdraw," said Dr. Laforet appraisingly. "And, of course, all that monitoring was to measure the presence of testosterone in your urine and make sure you would be sufficiently clean for the testing."

How did they go about it? she wondered. Did Andy and Dr. John get together every few weeks to review the lab tests and map out her results? Had they made projections on a race calendar, complete with check points, safety margins, peaking and tapering? She imagined a file somewhere with dosages and cycles and colored graphs that charted the progress of Karie Johnson, the guinea pig. Meanwhile, the real flesh-and-blood Karie kept doing her workouts and running around the track like a hamster in a cage.

"There is another aspect that you must consider," said Dr. Laforet. "Your coach has engaged in criminal activity. This report," he patted the file, "was submitted by an independent lab. There can be no doubt about their conclusions. Mr. Nagy doesn't know we have this information. In fact, I only decided to request the analysis because of the nature of your injury." He smiled briefly. "I am an advisor to the Athletics Director at Tulane, and I've seen a similar case with an athlete who transferred from Rice."

"But I agreed to the growth hormone—"

"First, to induce an athlete in your program to take a banned substance is serious enough. Second, to deceive and administer steroids to the point where it causes critical injury is"—he paused, his face flushed—"is criminal. The man cannot be allowed to get away with this. He must be stopped." He got up abruptly and walked to the foot of the table.

Perhaps he is not such a spectator, she thought. "What do you suggest I do?"

"I'd put him in jail," he said. "But that's for a court to decide."

She had a vision of Andy being lead from a crowded courtroom by federal marshals—and yet she felt no satisfaction.

"Karie, I want you to understand that you have a choice. I ordered the tests, with your authorization, for medical reasons. Now that I know the circumstances, I think this is an outrage. These people and their drugs, they don't care about the athletes, they destroy careers—" He stopped abruptly, as if he had said too much.

"So you want me to sue?" said Karie.

"I will certainly support you if you do."

"Andy, my coach, will deny everything."

"There's no way," said Dr. Laforet. "He will be finished—"

"No," she said.

"Whatever he says, he would be tarnished."

"No," she said, "I'm not talking about the outcome. It's just that I'm not going to do it." Karie sat up and dangled her left leg off the table for balance. "I'm responsible for what happened. If I hadn't started on the GH, I wouldn't be here. Everything else," she shrugged, "is just tough luck."

Boy, her coach really trained her well in the loyalty department, he thought, as he checked his temper. *What this guy Nagy did is sickening*. If Dr. Laforet didn't think that it would have impeded her recovery, he would've given Karie a good talking to. Laforet patted her cast and said, "I'll do everything I can—but I'm not sure how it will work out, okay?"

"It was good while it lasted." Her voice cracked.

"I'm going to prescribe some things—one of them will be some GH—and then we'll talk about rehab."

"You're the doctor."

As she was wheeled back to her room, she thought of Brad. Was he at risk of going to jail? Certainly he was the most hands-on perpetrator in the whole scheme. She imagined him preparing the weekly dose then turning to that chaste little area of cheek that she so willingly exposed. He must've drawn off a small measure of GH and topped it up with testosterone so that the volume remained the same. Did he really have no feelings of remorse, as he pushed the plunger down and sent those ghastly steroids coursing through her veins? Or later, when they became lovers, as he shuddered beneath her and called out in the sexual storm, was there no shame at the dirty little switch?

Presumably not. Why should she expect any decency from Bradford Barnes? Obviously, he was strictly business and did what he was told. Maybe his Mexican connection would catch up with him some day. He made enough trips to Tijuana on his Harley. *So look at the bright side, Karie*, she admonished herself. Brad had been there for her when she needed to slake her 'roid lust, to impale herself and bang away at his nice, hard body. At least she hadn't fallen in heat with anyone else, and Brad had been a good foil against Andy's advances. Brad was a rolling stone. Sooner or later, he'd go over a cliff.

* * *

Karie found a flat rock where she could sit and stretch her leg while she drank some water. She took a couple of bites of her sandwich and threw it away, wondering what little creatures would feast on it once she had gone.

She had gotten to like Dr. Laforet even though he didn't understand her reasoning. Not that she blamed him. He had staunched the wound and sewn her up. Now he was obsessed with finding and punishing the culprits. She was satisfied that she had found both. She was the primary culprit, and she surely was being punished. Falling to earth and hitting hard just before the finish had, at least, knocked some sense into her. She went to the hospital because she was a cheat. Adding steroid use to the list, albeit against her will, was further insult to the injury.

How could she ever have fallen so low as to agree to take GH? Her failure to qualify at Indi was a factor, as were Andy's skill at arguing for "a level playing field," the advent of the new growth hormone and, of course, the biological clock and the "last chance" suggestion. Not that they added up to anything. How could her mind have been so turned around that she, of her own free will, agreed to cheat? She was not desperately seeking to keep a place on the Pace team. She also had her modeling. Karie Johnson could not lay claim to any crutches.

So what if she had been deceived and tricked? They had spiked her cocktail and treated her like a lab animal because she was too dumb to catch on to what was going on. Too dumb to realize she couldn't train her ass off all day long, pushing past her old PRs, and then wake up the next day and be ready to go out and do it all over again with gusto, and not say, "What's with this GH stuff anyway? What's going on here?" That's like believing someone who says, "the check's in the mail," or "I'll only put the head in."

She remembered feeling so horny that she climbed all over Rafael when he was in town until he waved a white flag and asked her what was going on. And she just kept on thinking GH was really great stuff. Because how could she believe that dear Andy and Dr. John might be up to something? They wouldn't mix an aphrodisiac into the juice, would they? Certainly not any steroids, not after she told Andy she wouldn't take them. Why would she suspect Andy would do such a thing? How could he? He could.

During their six years together, he had shown her a total commitment to winning and a total disregard for how it was achieved. Whenever one of his girls stumbled, she could imagine him saying, "Next," and moving on. He had vowed to make her a star, but he didn't say how. But she never imagined him deceiving his beautiful

"Car-ree." He never got her between the sheets, but he screwed her anyway.

Karie thought about a guy from back home who used to get girls drunk to take advantage of them. Steroids were a different drug, but the game was the same. Or maybe not. Those girls had said "no." Karie had said "yes"—at least to the GH. Karie's head was spinning.

The Magi had been lavish with her—a body that left people breathless and a running style like a gazelle over the veldt. Yet she had sunk lower than all the girls in Goodland, those girls she looked down on for their big hips and low ambition. She alone was responsible for ending up with a gammy leg, out in the Arizona scrub, with no idea where she was going. The bitterness and humiliation still hurt as much as when she first took stock, and she realized they would be her companions until she understood why she had thrown it all away.

Karie got up and threw the apple core as high and as far as she could. She shouldered her backpack and walked back toward the shimmering horizon.

Chapter Thirteen

Karie turned off the road at Luna in the foothills of the Gila Mountains in southeastern Arizona. At first it had been comforting to be a part of the flow of vehicles all purposefully heading east on I-10, through towns like Indio and Blythe, traveling to a promised land somewhere up ahead. A black Nissan truck with a camper top drew level with her and then went ahead. She recognized the driver and his white Alsatian—the dog growled at her at a service station outside Palm Springs. *I'm just like any of them*, she thought, *we're all going in the same direction*. Soon after crossing the Colorado River into Arizona, she began her detours off the main road.

She knew what she wanted: a small town where she could rent a room for a week or so and go for long hikes, preferably toward a line of mountains on the far horizon. Now it was best to drive in the morning, stop off around noon when the water temperature gauge on the Z was redlining, and then continue on in the late afternoon. Karie liked to walk and explore in the heat of the day, when no one else would dare be out because then she completely owned the landscape. She thought it would be nice to keep walking in one direction, so that she could venture even farther, and then be picked up, rather than having to turn back. Past Quartzsite, Karie had taken a "primitive road" that was supposed to parallel I-10 and then rejoin it. She had ended up spending the night where the road ended in a pile of stone, dozing fitfully through distant flashes of lightning and strange nocturnal noises.

At Phoenix, she stayed east on Route 60, heading toward the mountains. Then it was Globe, where she opted for the right fork on 70 to the San Carlos Reservoir. She hiked for a couple of days and slept in the car, curled up in a blanket. She decided she wanted to be somewhere more remote and decided to try New Mexico, but by the time she reached Luna, the Z was making ominous noises. Along the way, the trouble had been traced to the differential and diagnosed as old age, so when the groaning from beneath the back seat sounded really painful, she turned into Oscar's Repair Service.

The man she assumed was Oscar wore a faded Grateful Dead T-shirt and worked on a spreadsheet with help from an Olivetti adding machine whose roll of paper was down to its core. The desk was covered with grease-stained receipts and stacks of auto parts catalogues. The man's hairy arms rested on top of the clutter as he bent his bald head over his work in a posture of full concentration. The centerfold art above his desk was only slightly less raunchy than that in the mechanic's bay, where Karie had first gone looking for him. For a second Karie considered tapping him on the head, but instead, she cleared her throat.

"Yep," he said looking up and then glancing immediately down at her legs.

Karie walked right up to the desk so that he had to lean back. "The 280Z out there," she gestured through the grimy window. "I think it's the differential."

He nodded. "Yep."

"Can you check it?"

He scratched the back of his neck. "Maybe if I drive it round the block. Wouldn't want to say yes unless I know for sure."

He made it sound like major surgery. She hesitated and then handed him the keys, knowing he couldn't get very far. Karie sat in his chair until he returned.

He was back in five minutes and approached her at the desk a few seconds later.

"It's the differential, all right."

Looks like I ruined his day, she thought.

"I'll have to put it on the rack and take a look."

"A look for what?"

He shifted awkwardly. "Could be the universal. Could be the ring and pinion...you've got 140 thou on that, you know."

"Couldn't just be a bearing?" *Here's to all that time spent with Dad and the construction crews*, she thought. "A bearing from one of the small gears...so they miss-mesh?" She knew that was a real shot in the dark, but she didn't want him pulling her entire car apart for nothing.

Oscar straightened up and nodded. "Could be."

"Tell you what, Oscar." Karie leaned back as if to think it over. "We'll put her on the rack and take a look—then I'll decide. But if I want to keep on going, we just put her back together."

"Might take a while."

"Tell me about it." She put out her hand and, with a surprised smile, Oscar shook it.

It took most of the afternoon to disassemble the differential housing and then take off the rear axles. Both the other mechanics joined in. The parts were laid out like entrails. At the final count the universal joint and the ring and pinion passed inspection, but the ball bearing on one of the spider gears had gone and the teeth were badly worn. As Karie wiped differential fluid from her arms with a kerosene-soaked rag, Oscar asked, "Sure you don't want a job?"

That night, Oscar let her sleep in a dingy office space above the garage, and Karie woke up at dawn not knowing where she was. She took a sponge bath in the sink and then walked through the main street section of Luna feeling nostalgic for Goodland. She went to a diner and ordered cereal and coffee. A burly Native American who'd been sitting next to her at the counter got up and left his newspaper. Karie picked it up and scanned the help wanted section, but all the jobs listed were located in other towns. As the waitress refilled her coffee, Karie asked if there were openings at the diner.

"No, honey. You may want to try the bakery down the road."

Karie said thanks, paid and left. She walked down the road expecting to find a small storefront but was surprised to discover a fairly large operation that supplied bread to all the grocery stores and restaurants in the area, as well as the Rancho Las Colinas Spa five miles up the highway. Karie got a job, starting the next week, working from 4 a.m. till noon, with Tuesdays off. She also managed to find a small apartment over a real estate office. Luna was as good as any place to stop off for a while.

As Karie picked up two postcards from a convenience store, she thought about the get well card she'd left her parents the night she left for L.A. Karie addressed one card to CeeCee and wrote,

*I'm okay. Sorry to leave it all hanging. Hope
everything goes well for you. Bye. Love, Karie.*

She had left CeeCee a check for two months' rent and the deposit, but still felt weird taking off so suddenly. CeeCee hadn't really been around much anyway, so Karie had the place to herself as she moved out. She was thankful she'd been so busy these past few years. Since she never got around to buying much of anything, she could leave L.A. as light as she came.

The second card went to Mom and Dad. She told them she was okay and wrote the address of her place with strict instructions to give it to no one. Karie underlined the last words twice.

When she got back to the garage it was a little after two, and Oscar said the Z was fixed. Karie asked him to sell it after she moved her clothes into her new place. A couple of days later she negotiated with the owner of a bike shop for an almost new Trek with a carbon alloy frame and front shocks. In the lowest of its 18 gears, she could ride it up the steps of the town clerk's office. From then on, she would only travel as far as the bike would take her.

*   *   *

Karie reached for the bedside light. Some nights were not as good as others, so she might as well get up. She canceled the alarm on her clock—it was almost 3 a.m., anyway. Swinging her legs out of the warm bed, she began massaging around the knot of tissue at the back of her right knee. It felt like a lump of modeling clay that had to be kneaded and squished into action. Perhaps it would be better today.

Dr. Laforet had warned her there would be scar tissue where he'd sewn the muscle and tendon back together. "Your leg will tend to stiffen easily," he said. "And you will not have the same arc of flexibility as your left leg. Initially, of course."

"Doctor, could it—might it—you know?" The thought of that terrifying pain stopped her.

"Could it rupture again?"

She nodded.

"Definitely not." He sounded offended. "That spot is stronger now than before."

Which doesn't mean it can't happen somewhere else, she thought. "Doctor, will I run again?" She watched his face change expressions. "Come on, Doc, all I want is your honest opinion."

"I see no reason why you can't start a light program of jogging—"

"Run, doctor. Run?"

"I can't promise anything. It's too early to tell."

She was being perverse anyway. What did she care? That part of her life was over. But now she found herself wondering, just what was it he couldn't promise? Was he unwilling to promise a full recovery? She could understand that. Or was it an intimation that she would always have to favor the leg as a weaker member of the family, as she now did? *I should call Dr. Laforet sometime*, she thought, *rather than lying awake at nights*. But for now she was probably better off not knowing.

Karie took off her T-shirt and brushed her teeth. She noticed the ribbon of flesh at her waist and arched her back till it disappeared. Clamping the brush with her teeth, she cupped her hands under her breasts and pushed them together so that they swelled out, abundant and heavy. She spat foam into the basin. "Flab. Goddamn flab."

She pinched her thighs and ribs. *Three months ago my legs felt like steel coils and my guts were ribbed*. What was it she'd got down to on the body fat—eight percent? She thought of Andy and his lewd little caliper games. It seemed so tawdry now, like a headline from a supermarket rag. "Super Coach Gets His Jollies—Has His Own Little Peep Show." Shit, he'd really had the hots for her, a little paw here and a friendly little pat there, all in a day's work.

With her current bloat she would probably measure 20 percent fat, easy. Karie sighed. She really was damaged goods now. She still had the note Andy delivered to Dad at the hospital. Dad had refused entry to all visitors, suggesting that they write notes.

"That son of a bitch Nagy went off in a huff," Dad said to her in one of her moments awake, "but he came back the next day with his tail between his legs."

Perhaps he'd talked to his lawyer, Karie thought when she read the bland message.

> *Dear Kid, All of us at Pace are hoping that you will get better real quick and will be back with the team, ready to go....*

The upbeat, on-with-the-show theme also suggested that she might consider assisting Andy with some of his coaching duties. Nothing like a little money to heal your wounds.

Dad told her he'd allowed Coach Gertz in to see her, but she was still under the effects of the anesthesia. Later, Rafael had come. He left a handmade card, with a rose on the front drawn in six bold ink strokes. Inside was written,

> *I know you will find your strength again.*
> *Love, Rafael.*

They had seen her, but she hadn't really seen them. She felt very vulnerable, almost naked, when she realized that they had also seen the coverage of her fall, and she wondered what it must've felt like to watch her go through it. She knew she'd disappointed everyone.

She also remembered that, in those first days, Dad would relieve Mom in the evening and sit by her bed. When he thought she was sleeping, he would hold her hand or stroke her hair. Sometimes she thought she heard him crying. When that happened, she bit her tongue and tried not to move. Letting Dad feel his sadness was more important to Karie than her own healing. Funny how she'd had it all wrong. It wasn't winning, it was failing that had started things moving back in the right direction. When they knew she was on the mend, Eigel and Nancy had gone back to Goodland.

Karie finished her cereal and grabbed a banana—she really had to lay off those pastries, even if they were free at the bakery—and wheeled out her bike. This afternoon she would ride out into the scrub, along the dry riverbed and then up toward the distant summits. By dusk she would have covered enough ground to endorphin herself into a good night's sleep. She didn't expect much from the routine simplicity of her life. She wasn't consciously seeking expiation, and she hadn't set any goals. Intuitively she felt that this was a time of waiting, that the routine was the message. Just keep plugging along. So many sunrises, so many sunsets.

*   *   *

As Karie pedaled through the sleepy streets to the bakery, she hoped that the blood that now sluiced through her veins was fragmenting whatever molecules of steroid still lurked in her system, much as the cleansing movement of the sea eventually atomizes the blight of an oil spill. What she really wanted was to recover her former strength, like Rafael's card suggested. That accomplished, she would have a platform from which to survey the residual damage.

It was hard to think about work when the early morning desert looked so beautiful. By spring, wildflowers had appeared almost overnight, and Karie was promoted to driving a delivery van for the bakery. Her route included a number of restaurants and the Rancho Las Colinas Spa.

Afternoons and days off were spent exploring the desert and the hills on her bicycle. She still hadn't mapped out all the trails that networked over the hills. One afternoon Karie was riding out along a back road when she accidently ran over a chollas cactus burr and flattened her front tire. Because she'd been riding pretty fast, she also bent the wheel when the sudden flat caused her to lose control of the bike. Since the bike wouldn't roll, Karie tried lifting it over her shoulder, but only succeeded in straining a back muscle. She wanted to scream. As Karie was trying to figure out what to do, a car slowed down.

Karie looked up to see a woman with curly red hair and wraparound sunglasses leaning over to the passenger window. Karie thought she looked familiar. *Probably someone from the bakery*, she thought.

"Do you need a lift?"

"That would be great," Karie said.

The woman opened her trunk and tried to help Karie lift the bicycle inside.

"I can do it," Karie said. The woman grew silent and stepped back. Karie felt a twinge in the muscle in her back as she lifted the bike into the trunk.

As they got into the car, the woman said "Let's start again. Hi, I'm Julie."

"Karie."

"I've seen you at the spa. You work at the bakery, right?"

"Yeah," said Karie.

As Julie drove, she told Karie about her job as a massage therapist, about how she moved to Arizona from New York, and a little bit about the Indian history of the area. When they got to Karie's place, Julie said, "You don't talk much."

"Guess not," Karie said. "Thanks for the ride."

Karie hadn't meant to be unfriendly, especially after Julie's kindness, but the bike accident reminded her of her injury. She wondered if she'd ever feel invincible again.

She felt she owed Julie an apology, so the next day when she made her delivery at the spa, she put a fat-free muffin in a bag for Julie with the note:

> *I'm sorry I was so unfriendly. Bent out of shape by a bent wheel. I swear I've had a bran muffin since then. Karie.*

Karie checked her reflection in the mirror behind the bar. Normally she wore her hair loose, but tonight it was combed straight back and braided for a more serious look, although it was hard to be serious when your uniform was a sleeveless white blouse, a red bowtie and a black mini-skirt that hardly covered your butt. The outline of the uniform flashed on the neon sign of the Change o' Luck Casino on the Indian reservation at the outskirts of Luna.

Tony, the manager, had stressed in his indoctrination speech that his cocktail waitresses had to be a class act—"like models on a runway at a fashion show" was how he put it. Karie doubted Tony had ever seen a fashion show. Still Karie had to admit that the waitresses, stepping carefully with their trays borne aloft, cut a distinctive swathe through the general scuzz. It was all just plain folks, pumping the slots in green-lit rooms, ogling the chicks, listening to some old timer who thought he was Tom Jones, grabbing a little ass in the press at the bar or having a few belts and haggling with the hookers Tony allowed in. Everyday people just kicking back and having a little fun.

Karie had started at Lucky's—that's what the locals called it—at the insistence of Julie, the massage therapist at Las Colinas Spa. Although it was three months now and she felt like a veteran, she had almost quit the first night. As she was trying to edge through the crowd with her tray in both hands above her, someone had deliberately jostled her, and the three bottles of Bud Light and two Old Grandads on the rocks had tipped to the floor. She noticed that the crowd parted like the Red Sea as the tray clattered. A woman customer squealed, "I've got beer in my hair," as Karie grabbed at the bottles still glugging on the floor. Tony had hurried over. "Maybe I'll have the boy with the mop follow you around, Princess." Then, as she was refilling the order and enduring her sudden notoriety with the clientele, Tony comforted her with the reminder that the replacement order was on her ticket. As she continued through the evening, Tony watched. When she paused at one table to answer a where-ya-from-hon question, he took her arm and breathed in her ear, "Princess, just because you've got a cute ass doesn't mean you don't have to move it."

Later, when the bar closed and the die-hards were still floating around the parking lot with their paper cups, Karie sat in a corner trying to settle up her cash and tickets. Julie had already settled and, after assuring her that Tony was always a pain in the ass with the new girls, went to the locker room to change. Karie wasn't sure how to complete her sheet, but she wasn't going to ask Tony, who was talking with the bartender and shafting glances in her direction. Then she heard Tony say, "Princess," and saw him start towards her.

Karie jumped up, grabbed her tray and, using it as a breastplate, pushed Tony to the wall. She leaned into his face and said, "Just one more word," she shoved him with the tray for emphasis, "and I'll break this over your fucking head. And that'll be just the beginning. No more crap, Tony. Ever." She turned and walked back to her table. Goddamn, but she must still have some of that testosterone in her, because she hadn't felt this good since she was running with Pace Track. Wasn't it funny how, when the chips are down, you can flush all that humble shit out of your system. Even though Tony was a spineless little fuck, she had been on complete alert and was ready to reach for that bottle of Bacardi to smack him. She grabbed Julie, and they went down the street for a few brews before she was ready to call it a night.

Now she looked forward to cocktailing on Fridays and Saturdays and came to understand the divided loyalties of her Lucky's family. "Either you screw the customer, or you screw the house," Julie had said. "I do both, but I feel bad about Charlie at the bar." But after a while Karie realized everybody got to drink at the trough, from the Indians on the reservation to the sheriff in the parking lot.

A customer running a big tab with a credit card was an easy mark. A waitress could put a cash order on his bill and pocket the payment. When things got real busy, a girl could call in an order to Charlie and then forget to write it up. Charlie was sure to short a few drinks if necessary to even the talley. Karie did not pull any tricks, but she was queen of the tips. She knew how to spread the customer's change on the tray and then smile sweetly. She had a knack for appearing at a cardholder's elbow when his pen was poised, as if she were officially there to witness the signature and inspect the gratuity. On a weekend night she cleared $100, easy.

Last week, Tony had beckoned her over as soon as she came in, and they went to his office.

"How's it going, Karie?"

"Fine," she said.

"You're doing good." It sounded like he had access to her personal finances and a customer satisfaction survey. "Well, I shouldn't be telling you this," his gesture bespoke the confidence of the confessional, "but I think you could pull in a real big number."

Karie thought she knew where this was heading, but she nodded attentively.

Tony leaned forward and jerked his head, "Up the road, at the Top Hat. Five hundred a night, minimum." He let that sink in. "A real classy place, good security, nice uniform—but, you know," he gestured awkwardly.

"Topless?" she asked.

"Yeah, topless, but with a bowtie," he said seriously.

Karie wasn't quite sure how to handle this. She wasn't angry, but she didn't want to smile. Tony was looking strictly business, as if it were his duty to advise her that she could make more money by shedding a garment or two. It was also clear that it would only be through his influence that such a future opportunity might occur. She assumed that he would take his cut somewhere, just as he did with the pros that came into Lucky's.

For want of any other reply she said, "Would Julie be able to apply also?" Then noting his displeasure she added, "She introduced me here."

"She could apply but," he shrugged, "like I said, it's a class place."

Karie stifled a smile and said, "I'll have to think about it."

She couldn't wait to drag Julie into the restroom and then break the news that, in Tony's opinion, she wouldn't cut it at the Top Hat. "You don't say." Julie fluttered her eyelids. "Reckon we'll sashay on down there sometime—see if the li'l cocksucker knows shit."

Karie wondered about the Top Hat more than she thought she would. It bugged her that she would even consider working there. Was she simply titillated by the dare? She had heard that people went around topless on some beaches in the Mediterranean, and in that situation, she was sure that she would join in. Did her reticence spring from the taint that was associated with partial nudity, the implication of easy virtue? And that what was considered okay in some places was not-okay in a bar in a small town in Arizona, and certainly wasn't worth a crusade. Mostly Karie felt that she would be revealing herself in a way that she would wish to save for more intimate moments.

But the real revelation was that two years ago she would have been offended by the Top Hat suggestion, yet here she was pondering the question as if it were really an option. Was nothing really sacred? What good had her so-called morals done her anyway? She was no longer the Golden Girl. She might as well get used to that.

As she lifted her tray and cut through the crowd at Lucky's—all you had to do was walk straight at the customers and they got out of the way—she wondered what Andy would think. He always preferred the glitzy places with plenty of stardust, where beauty was trussed and pushed into shape and he could parade his girls as the Real Thing. Andy was the original no make-up, no tucks, no cellulite man. He would have hated the occasional brawls at Lucky's. It was the suddenness of the fights that always got to Karie. One moment she was calmly serving a table, her body on idle while her mind concentrated on change and drink orders. Then there was that silence that seemed to precede the punch or the shattering glass, and suddenly adrenalin was flashing through her body and she felt she could leap up and grab the chandelier. After that, she was so hyped that she walked around on a champagne high.

Tonight, at quitting time, Karie saw Julie hanging around a table by the band, talking with Oscar and the two young guys who worked in his shop. As Karie paused at the table, Oscar stood up and Julie said, "I'd like you to know that these fine gentlemen have volunteered to escort us to the titty club."

The Top Hat was surrounded by its parking lot, as if it might have been a fast food franchise in an earlier life. There were a couple of heavies at the door who welcomed the ladies and took five bucks each off the men. Inside, it was dark. There was a distinctive odor to the place, innocuous yet pervasive, like mouse shit sprinkled with pine air freshener. They were led to a table by a 30-something woman with a deep cleavage and a full-length dress. "She's probably the Selection Committee," Karie whispered to Julie as they sat down. When the cocktail waitress came up, Oscar didn't seem to know where to look, and the two young mechanics were google-eyed.

The main room looked larger than Karie had expected. Maybe it was the black velvet walls and banquettes. There was a five-piece band in a back-lit flamingo pink shell with a willowy brunette singing R&B, a tiny parquet dance floor, and a general air of hushed expectancy.

"So what d'you think, guys?" said Julie. "How about the uniforms? How about the talent?"

"I prefer Lucky's," said Oscar loyally, although it might have been because he had just paid for the first round. The Top Hat was more expensive. *It's the kind of thing Dad would say*, thought Karie, *if he ever went to a place like this.*

"Oh you're just saying that," said Julie teasing him coquettishly. "But aren't you just the cutest little thing."

But Oscar is right, thought Karie. She preferred Lucky's too. There was something restraining about bare breasts cruising around the room, and there were at least a dozen pairs. They seemed to float around, stop, circle back and stop again, all on their own, like fish in a tank. It was like sitting in a big aquarium.

219

Karie remembered talking with a model at Tanya's who had done a pictorial for *Playboy*. The girl said she was a mess of nerves at the shoot, but then she felt liberated and now was sorry for people who didn't feel natural about nudity. Karie imagined herself topless, gliding out in front of everyone here, turning and bowing, serene and liberated. She couldn't do it. She wouldn't do it. Not for the money, not for anything. Because if she did, she'd stop being Karie. That's what had happened when she'd started injecting growth hormone. She didn't want to stop being Karie ever again.

"What do you think, Karie?" asked Julie.

"I think the girls are cute," said Karie. She really did. They had to be. The uniforms—black hot pants with large pink buttons up the front and the pink bowtie—were a little saucy, but the girls looked good.

"Not bad for Luna," said Julie. "But you could put all these broads to shame, Karie dear, couldn't you?"

Karie glanced at her. Earlier in the evening, at Lucky's, Julie had brought a Jim Beam to a customer instead of a J&B, and she'd had to replace it. But she put the reject in a paper cup and drank it in the restroom because she'd paid for it. Now Karie wondered whether there had been any other misorders.

One of the mechanics—this one was Rick, the other was John—asked, "Would you, Julie?" He was piqued by the idea.

"Me, topless?" said Julie with one hand over her heart. "No."

"You wouldn't do it," said Rick, nodding understandingly.

"No—it's because I can't," she said in a loud stage whisper, "I have a problem. I don't really talk about it, but I'll tell you. One of my breasts, my left one, actually," she touched it to ensure the correct identification, "points out a little. It's not straight. Sort of like having a crossed eye. A sidewinder is what they call it."

Rick grinned and nudged his pal, "Looks pretty good." Oscar nodded in assent.

"You don't understand," said Julie, "I have to use an anatomical support. It's called a rodeo bra."

"Huh?"

"Rodeo. You know, round 'em up and head 'em out." She laughed and said, "Can't leave home without it."

"I'll drink to that," said Rick, signaling for another round. "To the sidewinder."

Chapter Fourteen

In mid June 1994, Peter Bernier checked his computer calendar and saw a note he'd filed four months earlier, at the conclusion of the Winter Games in Lillehammer. Lillehammer was history—that was the point.

He'd posted the reference as an antidote to the reigning euphoria over Koss the Boss and the parade of exultant gold medalists. Now he opened the file, "Where Are They Now?" and went over his notes. How quickly the candlepower of athletic fame faded. It was all just one unbelievable high, shared with the world, followed by a long descent into anonymity. Yes, Bonnie Blair, Dan Jensen, Nancy Kerrigan, et al., were already on the long glide down.

And rightly so. If there was anything that pissed him off more than futzing officialdom and archaic rules, it was the athletes. Just because they were the shining examples of superior breeding didn't mean that they could treat you like a sack of shit. Such prima donnas led him to formulate Bernier's First Law of the Athlete—to wit, If I Didn't Win, Something Was Wrong. "Has anyone ever noticed," Bernie would ask sarcastically, "how the real stars never lost when they were completely fit? Or when the conditions were right? Or the organization efficient, the officiating fair?"

Let them have their day. Let them prance and preen and dangle their medals. He would accept their condescension because he knew their dreams were ephemeral. What did you do with your medal once the applause had died? You couldn't eat it or use it to keep the home fires burning. It was a reminder that the world had already moved on, and now you were only capable of looking back. And he, Peter Bernier, would always have the last word. He could resurrect, and he could bury. He had just done a piece on Mark Spitz, the swimmer with seven golds at Munich in 1972. Spitz had tried to come back for Barcelona, but he didn't make it. Bernie chronicled his attempt in a story titled, "Mark Who?"

As a prelude to the Atlanta Games, Bernie was researching former Olympic greats for a continuing series. He had already done outlines on Bruce Jenner and his infomercials, Greg Louganis's acting career, Mary Lou Retton of Wheaties and Revco fame, and Edwin Moses, who was moving into the financial world. He had file references on all American medalists as well as the current record holders. As a gesture to fairness and balance, he planned to include one or two profiles on those who had made graceful transitions from athletic life, but Bernie's real goal was ferreting out those who were ill-prepared for a life beyond the starter's gun.

As the current record holder for the women's 800 meters, Karie Johnson came under his scrutiny. He remembered the sensational coverage she got at the New Orleans trials in '92, and he also scrolled back to Indianapolis '88. This little filly had been his ticket to a new life with that story called "Rabbit Revisited." He didn't see the harm in playing the card again. Popular young girl from the Kansas wheatfields, a star from Andy's Pace Track racing stable, a real natural, attractive, articulate, good copy source—it was a lot of promising print for someone who had failed to make the team twice. Then she disappeared. No record of teaching or coaching or married-with-kids. Nothing. He remembered hearing something about Andy Nagy a few months ago. Something about doping, but nothing concrete. Trouble was, thought Bernie, she should have at least made it to the Olympic starting line for there to be a real angle. I mean, if you want to report a fall, it has to be from a decent height. He checked back. There had been quite a lot of expectation for Karie as America's answer to the middle-distance dominance by the Europeans—at one time, Nagy referred to her as The Great American Hope—but that's all it ever was, hope.

A pity, because there was a lot of good material in the file. Great visuals, good quotes, modeling career. Yet it all ended up as a mouthful of feathers. What he had in mind was a sidebar, a counterpoint to the medalists, something like the rocket at the fireworks show that soars upwards and then just fizzles. He would have to massage the idea to come up with the right angle. Reluctantly, he put her file aside.

* * *

"Refreshments up ahead," Karie called out and stepped off the path to let the women file by. "Just over the next rise—champagne and caviar."

"She's just saying that," said an older woman with blue hair who was on her first five-mile hike.

"And Clint Eastwood's doing the honors, right?" said a 50-something who came every year.

"Trust me," said Karie, "and it's all downhill from there."

Karie took a shortcut through the scrub to catch up with the lead and make sure they found the flat rocks where she had stashed the Evian and fresh fruit. She felt like a sheepdog, making sure the hikers kept a good pace and stayed on the trail, keeping track of stragglers. She also was the St. Bernard, with a backpack of emergency medical supplies and a two-way radio. There were 18 women in her care, all democratically turned out in teal shorts or warmups and the white T-shirt with the Rancho Las Colinas crest. It was ladies' week at the spa, which came once a month. Today was Wednesday, so most of the kinks were out, and the women were serious about getting some exercise, forgetting the family, dropping out of the routine—whatever other reason had caused them to come to Las Colinas in the first place.

Karie had been in the pool at 5 a.m. for 45 minutes of lap time and then assembled her troops at dawn for the hike. She always tried to think of these sessions as an expedition in which it was her responsibility not only to bring them all back safely but also to reward them for the achievement. Wednesday was her "awareness day," the day when she offered brief comments on the surrounding Gila Mountains, the wildlife and indigenous Indian culture. Now she moved among her flock, collecting the water bottles and cups.

"That's Bryce Mountain and over there is Webber Peak—"

"A little over 7,000 feet, I think—"

"The New Mexico border? About 50 miles—"

225

"It's sabroso grass, supposed to be a remedy for aches and pains, but I wouldn't try it right now—"

"No, the cliff dwellings are on the northern side—"

"Looks a little swollen, would you like me to bind it? Okay—"

"Saguaro cactus, sure you can eat it—"

"I said downhill? So I lied." She led them up the slope on the long loop back. "We're over halfway now, believe me. And Paul Newman's waiting to give you a rub-down." There was more laughter.

"Arnold," said the first-timer.

"Whoever—as long as it's not my husband," the regular replied.

Karie wished she could get Mom to come. She had it all planned. She would set up her whole program and arrange for a special hike up to Hope Lake with a picnic, and on Mom's last day, she would put on an apron and bring her breakfast in bed. But Mom wouldn't come without Dad, and Dad said he couldn't get away. So she consoled herself by saving up to send Mom a ticket and pay for the week at Las Colinas—it was a lot of money.

Karie fell back to encourage a stocky woman from Chicago who always looked worried and didn't leave her room without a made-up face.

"Karie," the woman said in a low voice, "I have a pain right here."

"Those are the abductor muscles," said Karie, "that means you're getting a great workout. But see me when we finish—we're almost there." She jogged back up front.

As they came down the slope to the bridge where they had started, Karie said, "Hey, everybody, don't go away. I've got a surprise for you."

She ran to the bridge, took off her backpack and gave each woman a card from the Luna Curio Shop, good for a free cactus charm made from green onyx. Karie suggested the idea to Oscar. He was part owner of the shop, and so far they were getting over 90 percent redemptions. She showed them the charm she wore around her neck and said, "It's supposed to bring good luck."

Now they would go off to breakfast and a full day of activities: aerobics, weights, swimming, tennis, volleyball, racquetball, yoga, self-defense. Karie was on from 6 a.m. till 2 p.m, and when she was through, she would get on her bike and ride the five miles back to Luna. She had been at Las Colinas for six months now, after bugging Gayle Sherman, the director, for a job more or less every week since she'd started making deliveries for the bakery. It wasn't the money she needed. Living expenses in Luna were low. Karie needed to fill the time that training used to take up.

She and Julie became fast friends, despite Karie's rudeness at their first meeting, and they hung out together in the sauna during employee hours. Julie told Karie she'd escaped from New York in the early 1980s, after a broken engagement. She'd spent her young life living in different places, always on the cusp of moving on, till harmonic convergence brought her out to the desert to stay.

Julie dug Karie's positive energy. She had done Karie's astrological chart one night. Western sign Pisces, Eastern sign Monkey—which meant Karie was creative, mischievous and driven. When she did Karie's Tarot reading, the Chariot had shown up as both her life and soul cards. "You've got a long road to travel," Julie told her, and Karie laughed, saying, "Don't I know it." The reading had been in fun— a way to break the ice.

"I can't figure these people," Julie once said. "They come here because they want to get away—but then they have to go back. If you really want to get away, then go, and keep on going."

Karie felt that perhaps one week of pampering could get you through the other 51—something to look forward to and something to cherish—but Julie seemed to be struggling with something that the regulars had intuitively figured out. People sought a common thread. When you knew the wife of an entertainment mogul or an eastern power broker shared some of the same warts and blemishes in life, then everyone could go home happy and endure.

"This place is so unreal," said Julie. "All clean linens and fresh-cut flowers and Golden Girl Karie to take you on a hike. After your yogurt, it's time for an herbal wrap and nice, sweet Julie will squeeze out the lactic. Then it's time for some Deepak Chopra, a light lunch and a siesta."

"Screw reality," said Karie. "I'm for a little illusion." Ever since leaving Goodland, Karie felt she'd had plenty of reality. "They'll get reality when they go back to New York, or wherever."

"Hold it," said Julie. "I'm not ready for that. But it's strange, you know, how you change. I came out here to get away from it all, and then—after a while—I end up doing time at Lucky's for my dose of sleaze."

"We all need to recharge our cultural batteries." But it suddenly occurred to Karie that if Mom came, she would not do cocktailing that week. It would be easier than explaining.

* * *

Peter Bernier sat across the desk from Jerry Matier, editor of *Inside Track* magazine, and tried hard to look detached. Jerry, his elbows on the table, hands cupped over his ears, was hunched over the draft of an article Bernie wrote for the August 1994 issue on Karie Johnson. Jerry insisted on reading the article in the presence of the writer, and Bernie considered it a disconcerting and unnecessary practice. Someone once told Jerry that Bernie had been a mean son-of-a-bitch when he was a lush, but sober, he was pissier than ever. Occasionally Jerry would jerk his head up and look at Bernie, as if he were the subject of the piece rather than its author.

Now Jerry shook his head, snorted, and said, "Has Dr. No seen this?" Dr. No was Jerry's name for the magazine's legal counsel.

"Yes. He initialed the checklist, there on the front."

"Don't shit me," said Jerry rearing back in his chair.

"Well, he asked me to change some things—small stuff. He thought it was really good—"

"Bernie, let's keep this simple. I don't care what a goddamn lawyer thinks about your story. I want to know what he made you change—or this goes into the trash." Jerry once told Bernie that the only way you knew whether you had really gone far enough on a story was if you were threatened or sued.

The phone rang. Jerry picked up, listened and agreed to take the call. It always annoyed Bernie when this happened. He felt that the work of a journalist should be read and discussed without interruption, but he had not yet shared this view with his editor. Jerry Matier had come to *Inside Track* a year ago, transferred from the entertainment side of the publishing division with clear authority to shake things up. There had been rumors at the time that the sports section would fold if it continued to lag far behind *Runner's World*. Jerry had cut staff and indicated to the survivors that a market share of "second with power" was a minimum requirement.

Inside Track left the traditional reporting of track and field athletics to the more responsible publications. It concentrated on poking a stick at rules and officialdom, gave generous coverage to unusual training methods and unproven medicinal claims, and maintained a flexible editorial stance. Six months earlier, the magazine had argued strongly against random drug testing, claiming that it was an unwarranted invasion of privacy. Then, when the Chinese women swimmers started cleaning up at international meets, claiming special training techniques, *Inside Track* did an abrupt 180 and championed testing—even blood testing, if necessary. Even Bernie had to admit that the change in editorial focus had been successful—at least in terms of paid circulation, which was now loudly bannered as being 250,000 copies per month.

"What changes, Bernie?"

"He made me frame the whole story as a question."

"I hate question marks," said Jerry. "It's faggot writing. Sit-on-the-fence crap."

Bernie wondered whether he had an ally, or whether Jerry was being oblique. "Dr. No said it was all circumstantial—you know, just opinions—and that he wouldn't sign off if I didn't hedge."

"Typical. Did you talk to the parents? See them?"

"They're in Goodland, Kansas, for Chrissake," said Bernie. "I talked to her mother but she didn't say much. Didn't know where Karie was living. Didn't know shit."

"Where is she?"

"I don't know—"

"Don't you start now," said Jerry, his face flushed.

"Look, she took off from L.A., driving, around the time of the Barcelona Olympics. She's somewhere in the Southwest, I guess."

"Can you find her?"

"I guess. Take a little time—but sure. I thought it best not to look too hard," said Bernie.

"Tell me about the coach."

"Andy Nagy is a classic case of CYA." Bernie paused. "He'd sell his mother—but he can't sing about the drugs because it puts him in the crapper."

Jerry stood up and circled his desk. When he got the circulation up some more, he'd demand better offices. "You have a source, I suppose?"

"Sort of," said Bernie.

Jerry raised his eyebrows, questioningly, but Bernie ignored him. Bernie had met with Grover on two occasions after Grover was fired from his physical therapy job at Pace, but he hadn't been very helpful. Grover hated Andy. He said Karie was a natural and shook his head sadly. He had the annoying habit of repeating, "I ain't saying no more," which had prompted Bernie to offer him good money. Bernie thought that maybe Grover would spill his guts to the people at The Athletic Congress—which, journalistically, was throwing it all away.

Jerry shrugged and sat down. "Well, maybe it will sell a few copies, but I need to go over it some more."

Bernie knew that this was as close to a compliment as he would get. Recognizing that it was now time to discuss just how his story would be featured, he said, "Jerry, it's going to be big, especially with these great visuals." Bernie wanted it to be a cover story, but Jerry had the hots for a piece on Michael Johnson.

"You know that phenomenal sprinter who is going for double

golds at the 200 and 400 meters?" Jerry asked. "Well, the power structure of the IOC is reluctant to change the Atlanta schedule sufficiently to accommodate such an historic attempt. Pretty idiotic, huh?"

Bernie nodded. He was running into a brick wall, he could tell. He took a deep breath. One day at a time.

Jerry continued, "How about a five-page spread and a cover highlight?"

*　*　*

Karie had just brought her flock back to the bridge after another five-mile hike. There had been 26 men and women this morning, a record for her. As with most mixed groups, it was far less cohesive, and she had to do a lot of herding. The men seemed quieter, more relaxed, although one asked peevishly, "Don't you get tired of doing this?"

Today was Thursday, and as soon as she finished at Las Colinas, she would bike back to town, stuff her backpack with provisions, and take the trail up Bryce Mountain. She would bike as far as she could and then hike—her goal was to go way higher than last time and be home by nightfall. As she was walking to the cafeteria, another employee handed her a note. It was a summons from Gayle, who wanted to see her right away. Karie sighed. Gayle always seemed uncertain. Like the time they needed to redo the women's sauna. Teal or white tile? The entire staff had been polled. Karie wondered what it was now.

When Karie entered the office with its wonderful view of the Gila Mountains, Gayle appeared to be absorbed with some papers. She was a handsome woman in her forties who perpetually overdressed. Today she wore a gray pinstripe suit with a ruffled pink blouse.

Gayle looked up and, patting a magazine on the side of her desk, asked, "Have you seen this?" Then, without waiting for a reply, "You certainly never told me about your past."

"No, I haven't—"

"Well then you'd better read this." It sounded like the reading would be indictment enough. "No, not here—use the office next door."

Karie glanced at the yellow highlight on the cover with the black letters, "A Great American Failure," and felt the empty jitters she got before a race. *Be calm*, she thought, *you've always known this might happen*. She found the page, glanced at the photo of her falling to the track at New Orleans, and began to read.

A Great American Failure
by Peter Bernier

This is an American Fairy Tale for the '90s. A young Olympic track and field hopeful from the heartland of America travels to Los Angeles to train. She becomes a star model and a star of the track. She breaks the American record for the women's 800 meters, only to succumb to a terrifying injury in the 1992 Olympic Trials in New Orleans. Then she disappears. Her name is Karie Johnson, and she's still missing.

Johnson was born in February 1968 and raised in the wheatfields of Goodland, Kansas. Family, friends and coaches confirm her early promise as the kid who loved to compete and win against girls much older than she. She won all the regional meets, became state champion and then won three national junior titles in a row. "A great athlete is an accident," says Steve Delaney, Oregon State coach. "I used to see this kid run against my girls and it was awesome. The whole field would stop and watch her run."

Delaney was not the only one watching— Karie's prowess came to the attention of Super

Coach Andy Nagy of Pace Track, who set out to woo her to his famous team. After graduating from high school in 1986, Karie spurned the offer of a full scholarship at Arizona University and went to live in L.A. and train with Andy Nagy. Under his skilled tutelage, Karie became a star at Pace and helped the team continue to win its string of national titles.

At the Indianapolis Trials in August 1988, we saw the first crack in the mirror: Karie ran a sensational 55-second first lap in the 800 meters, only to fade and not qualify for Seoul. What happened? Here was a Great American Talent, our first real hope in the middle distances, coached by the man who has sent more women athletes to the Olympics than any other coach in history, and she doesn't make the team. Was it bad preparation? Poor strategy? Or were we seeing the first murmuring of a lack of heart? Did Karie Johnson have the heart for world-class competition, or were the attractions and distractions of Hollywood beginning to sap her juices?

Son of a bitch. She looked back to the beginning of the article— Peter Bernier. The same Peter Bernier who had written about the Indianapolis trials and later phoned from Seoul. That was the article Rafael had framed for her, with the four photo splits of the finals. "Rabbit Revisited," Bernier had called it. He'd raved about the technique and said it was the wave of the future. He'd written about her "indomitable spirit." She remembered his words because she'd looked up the precise meaning in a dictionary. Now this. *The two-faced son of a bitch.*

"She had it all," said Bob Jones, a senior TAC official. "Her style was," he pauses, then with the smile of a man who has discovered an elusive truth, says, "flawless." But even Jones may be accused of selling her short in not mentioning that she was a top model with looks that might have inspired the popular song, "My Baby's American Made." In Tinsel Town, where the line-up at any modeling agency goes around the block, Karie hurdled the queue to become a top moneymaker with model agent Tanya, the doyenne of L.A. fashion luminaries. What did a successful modeling career have to do with success on the track? Everything. Putting her body on billboards gave Karie the time and money to dedicate herself completely to the teachings of Andy Nagy and the excellence of the Pace women. She had everything going for her.

Fast forward now to the Olympic Trials in New Orleans, June 1992. Enter Karie Johnson at center stage, the reigning favorite in the 800 meters. She has dominated the season with the fastest times; she has become the darling of the circuit and earned the media sobriquet the "Can Do Kid." She enjoyed the indulgence of sitting out of a couple of prestigious meets to heighten the drama. For starters she blitzes the field in the Saturday prelims: people who witnessed the event still talk about it. Out in front and pulling further ahead, she was in a class of her own—world class. Her time? 1:56.13, the current American record.

Karie looked up and narrowed her eyes in remembrance of that day in New Orleans. If only she could feel that way again. And that evening, as Mom and Dad fussed over her ice packs, she had said, "I don't want you two to worry about things in the future—because I'll take care of you." Steroid bravado.

If there ever were a case for mailing it in, this was it. But to make the Olympic Team, an athlete must finish in the top three at the finals, and prior times are irrelevant. So no problem, have her breeze round the track a couple more times. Instead, Karie stumbles and falls—spectacularly. Most people in the U.S. track and field world know where they were that Sunday at the fateful moment, for such was her magnetism...and nearly everybody in America saw the photo that marked the spot where Karie Johnson fell to Earth. A shocked and silent stadium witnessed America's hope flame out with a ruptured hamstring within meters of the finish. And this is where this story should end, with Karie Johnson living—athletically speaking—unhappily ever after.

But why? Should she be allowed to be remembered as the victim of a most capricious Fate? Or is there another story? Was Karie responsible for her own downfall? Were we witnesses to a Faustian pact?

Dr. James Feldman, a noted orthopedic surgeon at University of Chicago Medical School, maintains it is extremely unusual for the hamstring muscle to rupture in such a way. In his experience, Dr. Feldman says, the muscle needs to have bulked up considerably —perhaps by the ingestion of anabolic-androgenic steroids—to sustain such an injury.

What does Coach Nagy say? "I have no reason to believe that Ms. Johnson was taking any banned substances. We have strict rules at Pace Track regarding substance abuse, but we cannot control our athletes absolutely." Sound like a lawyer to you? With good reason: the coach is currently under investigation by the Doping Control Committee of TAC because of complaints filed by two former Pace female athletes. They claim Coach Nagy not only condoned the taking of steroids, he encouraged it.

That's my coach, Karie thought bitterly. *The one I left home for.* How pathetic that Andy doesn't have the balls to stand up to them—give them that spiel about a level playing field. Who blew the whistle? Maybe she would track down CeeCee and see what she knew.

Before reading on, Karie studied the photos interspersed with the copy. There she was, standing skinny-legged on a platform to receive her trophy at the junior nationals, smiling with Andy at a Pace meet, winning at Mount SAC, leading the field at Indi, and a poster shot from the milk commercial series on the last page.

The fact that Karie did not participate in a couple of key meets for the Pace team is also unusual, and significant. An athlete on steroids may have to sit out a meet at which drug testing takes place for fear of being caught. When asked, Coach Nagy could not recall specifically but said it was not unusual for him to sideline an athlete either for recovery or because it was part of the program to peak for the trials. It is also important to picture the milieu that Karie moved in: the world of a star athlete in L.A. or a top model—and she was both—can be a Garden of Temptation for recreational drugs and casual sex. There are many who say Andy and his girls enjoyed a code of behavior on the order of "Run hard and play hard, who says you can't burn the candle at both ends?" You can, of course. But when you stretch vital tissue to the limit, it snaps.

> It's sad that a beautiful young talent, who rose
> up like the dawn over the wheatfields of Kansas,
> should come to a shuddering, heartbreaking end.
> But even worse is the real possibility her talent
> was debased by substance abuse and weakened
> by a licentious lifestyle.

Karie shook her head in disbelief. It made her yearn for one more good cycle on the juice, so she could kick the shit out of Peter Bernier.

> This writer's effort to establish the truth reads
> like a B-movie title: *The Coach, the Doctor & the
> Athlete*. Only nobody wants to appear in the cred-
> its. The coach isn't talking. Dr. Christian Laforet
> at Parkview Hospital in New Orleans, where Karie
> was treated after her fall, refuses to disclose his
> patient's medical records. After leaving Parkview
> Hospital, the athlete disappeared from sight. So
> we issue an invitation, "Will Karie Johnson please
> speak up?"
>
> Is yours a case of monumental bad luck, de-
> serving of our sincerest sympathy? Or are you
> truly a fallen idol, a talent so squandered that
> Baron de Coubertin would thrash in his grave?

Karie slammed the magazine on the desk. She could imagine the pain the story would bring her parents. *Dad*, she thought, *we just turned the corner, we are on the mend.* Would he pin this article in his cupboard with the others? *Come on, Karie, don't lose your cool—this is their best shot.* She got up, walked into Gayle's office without knocking, and sat down.

"I've read it." She kept the copy on her lap.

"Well, what do you say?" said Gayle.

"I will want to talk to my lawyer." *Too bad Annie was only in her first semester of law school.*

"You never said anything about this—"

"About what?"

"About the drugs, about taking steroids," Gayle's voice rose plaintively.

Karie shook her head.

"You deny it? You say you didn't—"

"I don't think I have to answer."

Karie saw the sudden indecision on Gayle's face, and she almost felt sorry for her.

"This spa has a select clientele and very high standards." This was what she told to all the new recruits. "We simply can't risk our good reputation by employing someone with your background."

Karie looked past her at the mountains, rising up over the haze.

"I had Cindy pick up all the copies of the magazine. Imagine if our clients found out one of our assistants had been involved in drugs."

That's it, thought Karie. "Are you asking me to resign?"

"Well, surely, you can't expect to stay—"

"Because I don't quit."

"Administrative leave, at least—"

Karie stood up. "I'll be back to work tomorrow, for the afternoon shift."

"And I'll be talking to Mr. Lorelli." Gayle made it sound as if bringing it to the general manager were the kiss of death.

Karie shrugged and walked out. She saw Cindy in the hall. "Wow," she said. "I didn't know you were such a star."

She went to find Julie. "Didn't you tell me your ex was a lawyer?"

Julie nodded.

"Any good?"

"Oh sure. It was in other areas that we had problems."

"Read this—and then we can talk."

"You're going?" Julie knew she'd get the scoop later.

"Bryce Mountain." Karie replied. *All the way to the top,* she thought.

*　*　*

Karie was on the mountain when night fell. She knew when it had been time for her to turn back, but she kept climbing steadily through the scrub, until even the distant lights of Luna were hidden by the brow of the last steep rise. When she could no longer make out the trail, she decided to stop and wait for moonlight. Although she was still warm from the climb, she put on her sweats and sat down with a Powerbar and a bottle of water. No way could she stay home tonight. As she looked down into the surrounding well of night, she hoped she might put things in perspective.

Had she really thrown it all away? Her mind was still frazzled by Bernie's images. Did she have it? Or was she just a good runner who could never quite make it to the top, not even with steroids? She put her arms around her knees as she crouched in the brush. She had always believed she was destined to be a champion, and yet here she was, a nobody on top of a mountain. What if she never made it? The thought scared her. *Don't let go, Karie, you're not a failure. You've done a 1:56.13 time. You're the American record holder, for Christ's sake. Hold on.* Twice she had come close, and twice she had failed. Was this it for her?

The article was a real backstabber, and setting the record straight would be like blowing in the wind. She hugged her knees and stared up at the stars. She remembered being at a construction site with Dad when he was recounting a fight he'd had with the lumberyard. He stopped in the middle of the scaffolding to deliver his dictum, "Don't get mad, get even."

But as she wished Dad a silent thanks, she was again overwhelmed by the grief that she had caused those who loved and cared for her. She could see their faces, numb and vacant-eyed, heads bowed down by her dishonor. And what about Coach Gertz, who always insisted there was more to life than track? And dear Rafael, leading with his chin and coming back for more. They warned her, and she spurned them.

She had been born with a gift—an exhilarating, soaring, blood-pounding gift—and she turned that gift into an instrument of shame. Circumstance and duplicity had ganged up on her. Although she was not wholly responsible, Karie knew she had to find a way to wipe the slate clean. She felt an immense weariness at not being able to retrace her steps to where she had taken the wretched wrong turn. She was cut down, unable to start back again.

The moon was now high enough for her to see her way. Close to the last approach she angled over to the east to avoid a vast scree of loose rock. It had been two years since she had turned off the road at Luna, but she was still adrift, her albatross still around her neck. Perhaps she was waiting for something that would not come. What had she really been doing in the desert anyway, if not hiding out? Maybe she was still a failure.

Karie decided to hold off her final climb until first light, which she guessed to be less than three hours away. She was well above the line of vegetation so she hunkered down in a natural hollow, using her backpack as a headrest. It was cold now, and she slept fitfully. Once she jerked awake, thinking she heard a voice, and went back to sleep. She dreamed of running through corridors, searching for something just a turn ahead. There was the voice again—an insistent voice, urgent and righteous. "Show them," it said. "Go show them." She was running again like she used to run. Exhilarated. Fast. Easy.

Karie jumped to her feet. The top of the mountain was bathed by the first golden shaft of dawn. The eastern face watched over the ancient cliff dwellings across the valley. She could see the flat head and one of the eyes on the crest that the Indians called Lizard Head. As she hurried forward, it was as if someone had just thrown a switch to illuminate a stage set. She wanted to get there before it went dark again.

She stood on Lizard Head as it floated brilliantly over the timid hues of dawn. Turning slowly, she filled her lungs and shouted, "Go Show Them!" to the landscape. It was time to go to work.

Chapter Fifteen

Lou Gertz sat at his desk at Arizona University, feet propped up on his desk. *There had been better days,* he thought wryly. Again, he glanced at the memo stamped, "CONFIDENTIAL: Attorney Client Privilege," and addressed to Mr. Louis Gertz. "I think it is appropriate to review your options," it began. Litigation wasn't a legitimate option, as far Lou was concerned. He had never sued anyone; that was for others. But again, no parents had ever accused him of exerting too much control over their kid. Now that his head was on the block, he'd counted on the court as an ally. How naive. He was still hanging on, weighing the cost of fighting back and the penury of losing—but the lawyer's meter was running. Soon he'd have to decide.

Wearily, he pushed the memo aside. He needed some exercise and a good night's sleep. He picked up the latest issue of *Inside Track* to take home with him, glanced at the cover, and then sat down abruptly. He flipped to the photo of Karie falling at New Orleans, checked the length of the story, read the last paragraph, then went back to the beginning. When he had gotten through the piece a second time, he put the magazine down and sat still. What a terrible crock.

He had expected something like this ever since Peter Bernier called, only what he had read was much worse. Such a professional hatchet job would be widely noticed. Lou chuckled despite himself. He knew you couldn't sue or hope to force any retractions. How easy it was to offer legal advice when you weren't sitting at the poker table of litigation. When it wasn't your reputation at stake.

Lou tried to recall what Bernier had said on the phone.

"Thank you for returning my call, Coach. I'm doing some research for a story we're doing on a star ex-pupil of yours, Karie Johnson."

Lou hadn't heard from Karie in quite a while, but he was immediately suspicious. "What sort of a story?"

"I believe that she had a great talent but never quite realized her potential."

"She still has the record for the 800," Lou paused, "despite her accident."

"I would like to talk to you about the early years, which was perhaps when her talent was molded. It would be good exposure for you, Coach."

"Would I be able to review the story before publication?"

"No, Coach, that is not our policy."

They sparred for a while, but Lou didn't really say much. Bernier promised to get back to him after talking to his editor, but didn't.

Lou sat forward moodily, his head in his hands. He could still see Karie standing at his desk, bitterly reminding him of his promise. It was eight years ago, and time had only sharpened the image. He knew now how badly he had failed her and how, by waiting to tell her, he had lost her trust.

He had last seen Karie when he peeked into her hospital room while she slept. She looked so forlorn and immobile he couldn't bear it. He said good-bye to her parents, and on his way out, he ran into Rafael in the lobby. The kid had looked good, thought Gertz. He barely recognized him. Rafael wore an expensive leather jacket. His hair, grown out to a neat, chin-length bob, was tucked behind his ears, revealing a small silver hoop in each one. Rafael was holding hands with an Asian woman whom he introduced as Amina.

"How is Karie?" Rafael asked.

"She's asleep," Lou said. "Her dad isn't letting everyone in."

"You should go try. I'll wait down here," Amina said.

"I was going to get some coffee," Gertz said, "you're welcome to join me."

"Thanks," she smiled and turned to Rafael. "Go on, I'll be fine."

Lou bought Amina coffee and talked with her until Rafael came back down. She was bright, and talking to her cheered him up. Actually, Amina did most of the talking. She told him that she and Rafael were living together. They had met in design school. When

Rafael saw Karie's accident on TV, it was Amina who convinced him to come to New Orleans.

When Rafael came back from Karie's room looking depressed, Amina turned her energy to him. Rafael was quiet. Lou said good-bye, wished them luck, and spent the plane ride trying hard not to think about the accident.

Karie must have washed up somewhere to rest and lick her wounds. Lou picked up the magazine and stared out of the window at the AU campus.

Maybe it was his turn to do the right thing. Bad news travels fast.

* * *

Karie started with calls to Erin at Tanya's ("I'm afraid she can't come to the phone now") and Eddie at World Sports Agency ("Yes, Karie, of course. Look, I'll call you back"). Days later she finally got through to Tom Norton, the manager of Global Gym in Venice.

"Hey, Karie, what's going on?" She could hear the clacking of metal over Sheryl Crow singing "Run, Baby, Run." Sometimes when she worked out late, Tom would spot her on the free weights.

"I'm hanging out in Arizona, and I thought I'd give you guys a call—catch up, you know, it's been a while."

"We're keeping busy."

"I'm starting to train again."

"Excellent. Come on in, and we'll work out a deal so you can train with us."

"No, Tom, I'm going to be here, but I'm going to need a sponsor and I was wondering if you knew—"

"You looking for a sponsor?"

"Yes, I called Eddie at World Sports, and he's going to get back to me."

"Kid, did you see that thing they did on you in *Inside Track?*"

"Sure, but I'm starting training—for Atlanta."

"Kid, read it again. You're dead meat. Nobody's going to touch you. Even if you went clean and started winning again—" Karie held the phone at a distance, shaking her head in annoyance, then listened again "—dude came in with this poster, 'Drugs Are a Deadly Game' or some such shit from the Boy Scouts, and I had to throw his ass out. It's bad."

"Well, thanks anyway," Karie said.

*   *   *

Karie had been waiting for half an hour at the First National Bank of Luna when a kindly, gray-haired secretary said, "Mr. Burlington will see you now, Miss Johnson."

Karie felt uncomfortable as she walked past the row of desks. It wasn't being in heels, hose and a dark suit—it was the thought of having to plead in open court. She had expected the personal loan officer to rate a private office, not to be presiding over a room of people where you could hear somebody cough. Perhaps that was the point. Any histrionics would be like raising your voice in church.

"Edward Burlington," he said. "How may I be of assistance?"

You know perfectly well, she thought, I *want to borrow money*. Karie opened the briefcase she had borrowed from Julie and took out a slim file with her bank statements. It was like opening a garage door to wheel out your bicycle. "I have had a checking account with your bank for two years now—"

"Yes, Ms. Johnson, I'm aware of your record."

Which means a few minimum balance charges in the early days. "I'd like to apply for a loan, as you can see," she pointed to the application form in front of him.

"Yes, and the stated purpose is that you wish to train for the next two years to compete in the Olympics in Atlanta?" She wondered if everyone else in the room had heard.

"Right. You see, I'll have expenses for coaching and training and treatment—and I'll need time off for my workouts. I don't mean right now, but in a few months I'll have to be training twice a day."

"So your income will decrease?"

"Yes, but then I'll start competing and I'll get sponsorships—"

"And if you don't?" he paused. "Don't do well enough to get sponsorships, I mean?"

I'm the American record holder, goddamn it. These bones have been around the track a few times and brought a stadium full of people to their feet. "It's not an option," she said.

"Of course. Now your current employment is at the Rancho Las Colinas Spa and you also mention hostessing?"

"I'm a cocktail waitress at the Change o' Luck Casino. Come round, I'm there Fridays and Saturdays." It was the first time he'd looked unsure of himself.

"You haven't had any of these jobs very long. The bakery for instance...you were only there seven months."

Karie wasn't sure if she needed to explain that a 3 a.m. wake-up call for minimum wage couldn't compete financially with cocktail waitressing. But Edward Burlington continued.

"Miss Johnson, I think you should wait until your financial situation is more secure."

He was serious. "What about training for Atlanta?" she asked.

"Perhaps you could wait another four years."

What the hell am I doing here? She thought of the time she spent pressing her suit, choosing the right blouse and rehearsing her lines.

Mr. Burlington was leaning forward earnestly, "We try to help folks make the right financial decisions, so that they will not be faced with any unfortunate situations down the road." Now he sat back and smiled, "That is the kind of service we try to provide our valued customers."

Karie smiled back. Of course, if she were secure financially, she wouldn't need to borrow money. She snapped open Julie's briefcase and replaced her file. "You've been most helpful." She took a few steps, turned and called out, "Ed, don't forget. Lucky's Casino—Friday or Saturday."

More out of perversity than hope, Karie sat on the phone one afternoon until she got through to Erin at Tanya's.

"Hi," said Karie, "I just wanted you guys to know that I'm back."

"Back from?" said Erin.

"I had an injury, but now I'm okay, same weight, same stats." So I'll starve for the audition, she thought.

"Hold on," she said and Karie imagined her bringing up the file on the monitor. "Karie you must be—26 now?"

"Right."

"Karie, let me be straight with you. You're too old for us now. Listen, I'm sorry. I'd love to have you around. We just don't make money on the older girls."

Damn, so they have an age cut-off as well as height. "What I wanted to know is if Tanya had any clients that might be interested in athletic tie-ins—like for the Olympics?"

"We don't do referrals," said Erin. "I have to go."

"Wait—" but Erin had hung up.

Karie put the phone down and murmured, "The Great American Failure is moving right along."

Suddenly it hit her that she was completely on her own. Without proper coaching and training, she might not even qualify for the trials. Maybe her fast-twitch fibers would not respond, and she would never again be borne aloft on a moment of pure sound. She sank into her pillow, sobbing, and gripped the side of the bed until she was quiet again.

Slowly, she put on her sneakers, then massaged the back of her right leg. If she ran long enough, she would be too tired to care.

* * *

Eigel Johnson found the path that snaked through the woods up to old Mrs. Kratohvil's place. Mrs. K had died a few months ago in early spring, alone in her cottage. She lay there until she was discovered a couple of days later. If Karie had been here, it might never have happened that way. But then things don't always happen the way they should; that was the lesson he learned at his doctor's earlier in the year. Dr. Samuelson had always been straight with him. This past visit was no different.

"Eigel, you better get in shape or you won't last another winter."

Dr. Samuelson called it a "silent heart attack," said it had happened while Eigel was sleeping. He'd lost a quarter of his heart's strength.

The thought of dying provoked him to lay out over $60 for a pair of Nike walking shoes. He set out to find Karie's old trail, the one he remembered she called the Big Loop. As the days lengthened into summer, he found most of her landmarks. He was still searching for the patch of mondo grass by the stream where she had picked the flowers, one of which he kept pressed between the pages of a book on taxes. His health willing, he would walk in the season of the quiet snows and hear her footsteps from afar.

He turned onto Chester Lane and picked up the afternoon mail. Among the pieces was a large white envelope from AU, which he took into his study. He locked the door before opening the envelope. A note was clipped to the *Inside Track* article. It read,

Let's talk. Lou Gertz.

Eigel sat down heavily with a sick feeling and began to read.

He knew he really needed to get out of his damp clothes, but he re-read the article slowly, trying to suppress his anger. "That's it. Enough." He opened his cupboard doors so that he could talk to Karie directly. "This Bernier man is a liar, a fraud. The story is BS, pure BS."

Heart, he thought as he paced the room, *Bernier says she doesn't have heart. Everyone knows Karie has more heart than anyone.* He was never the champion wrestler at college but, win or lose, they had to pry him off his opponent—they called him "The Grip." Bernier had been at Indianapolis, what did he think it took to hang in for the final lap after the first :55 split? Bernier had been at Mount SAC—Eigel took out his album and flipped through the pages—that's it, he'd done the profile on Karie as an Olympic hopeful and started that stuff about the Can Do Kid. Now he's trying to say she can't.

That story was a pack of lies, and Eigel decided to talk to Coach Gertz about Bernier. Maybe he should call Annie, who was now in her first semester at Boalt Law School in Berkeley. Bernier should be drummed out of the profession. Eigel turned to stare at the many images of his youngest daughter. The poor kid had put up with enough and sadly, her own father had not helped. The more he followed her footsteps along the old trails, sometimes breaking into a jog to feel his pulse quicken, the more he realized what a fool he'd been.

Now, he looked at his watch and picked up the phone.

"Coach Gertz." Eigel stood tall. "I want you to visit my daughter." He cleared his throat. "I want to know she's all right."

* * *

One Saturday afternoon in late August, Karie biked over to the Luna High School track. She had been running for a month now, mainly easy distance runs, and she now wanted to get a sense of her times for 200 and 400 meter splits. Except for the first week, when she had to ease off, her leg was doing okay. She was taking plenty of Advil and icing three times a day. The crunch would come in the later months, when she began her heavy workouts.

She leaned against the fence and watched. One girl, probably a junior, was circling on the outside track with an easy stride but leaning forward too much. Some other kids were doing 200 meter intervals, and there was a football squad in the infield doing stretches, twists and jacks under the supervision of a bulldog figure with a whistle. The track was a crusty black asphalt that would fry an egg and the white lines zagged a little, but as Karie began walking around it, she felt like it was an energy field. That boom-boom feeling and the desire to pump those arms and churn the wheels until the wind started tugging on her hair began welling up inside of her. Her new mantra, Go Show Them, came to mind.

As the squad was breaking up, she walked over to the coach who stood there looking fierce, his arms akimbo like handles on a pot.

"Hi," Karie said.

"Can I help you?" the coach asked.

"I'm from out of town, and I hear you've got a great track and field program here."

"Who says?"

Oops, better be careful, she thought, *forgot about all that coaching rivalry.* "Heard about it at AU and Mount SAC—I used to be in L.A."

Satisfied, he said, "Yep."

"Do well, huh?"

"Damn right. Our kids do well in the city meets. Do well in the states. Probably send a couple to the nationals next year. We got a real fine bunch of kids."

Yeah, I bet. "Look, Coach, I used to do track, and I was wondering if I could do some training here."

He didn't even consider it. "Nope. Can't do it. Insurance won't allow it." He turned and began to walk stiffly towards the single stand of bleachers.

Go Show Them. "Look, Coach, you got a good kid for the 800?"

He stopped and turned his whole body round to face her. "Got Murray. He's faster than a prairie dog."

"Coach, let me run against Murray. If I win, then you let me train here. Come on, Coach, I need a break."

"If you lose?"

"Hey, I'll fix your hurdles, paint the bleachers, chop wood—whatever."

The coach looked her up and down. "Tomorrow, this time. Be here."

As she biked out to the field on Sunday afternoon with her track shoes, Karie wondered how fast a prairie dog really was. Maybe this Murray kid was a natural. *Screw it*, she thought, *just go do your thing. If you can't clear this hurdle, you ain't going anywhere.* She was glad to get her stretches and warm-ups done before the coach drove up with the kid.

Murray was a tall, cocky and blond. He obviously had never been beaten by a woman before, so he was sure to try and smoke her on the first lap and then cruise. The coach had brought his gun and a stopwatch. He made them line up properly and told them anyone who stepped off the track got DQed and his word was final. Then he said, "Remember, we got a bet, young lady."

The kid started off at a good clip, and Karie hung on his right shoulder. He had a surprisingly fluid style, but his stride was too long and bouncy, and he wasn't using his upper body. By the 200 she knew he wasn't going to be a problem, and she started watching him more. As they came into the first straight she said, "Murray, try swinging your arms like this." She pulled ahead slightly, "It makes your legs come through quicker." She fell back, "That's right, you're doing great."

The coach called out, "One ten, bell lap."

On the back stretch she said, "Keep it up, Murray, but don't swing too high. You can only run as fast as your arms. Do that and you'll win big."

The kid was really hurting on the final 200. "Come on, Murray, this is it, keep going strong. Head up man, show your stuff." She pulled ahead a little at the finish—a bet's a bet—and kept running lightly into the infield.

She saw the coach put his arm around Murray, who looked as if he were about to puke. "Great job, Murray, you did 2:17. That's PR time for you, man. I'm proud of you." Only when Murray was nodding and smiling at his PR did the coach look for her.

He walked up and smiled. "You're okay."

As she walked to her bike, the kid came up and said, "Thanks."

They shook hands. "I'll see you around, Murray."

Karie rode home slowly. It had felt good to race, better than she expected. She almost wished she hadn't started the ball rolling because she could feel the urge to compete overwhelming her, and she considered that maybe she had let it lie dormant too long. Right now Karie needed to relax. She decided to call Julie and go out for a couple of beers.

*　*　*

Karie was in Tony's office at Lucky's, talking with Tony before her shift started. There was a sharp rap on the door and Julie stuck her head in. "We got another one," she paused, "asking for Karie Johnson. Big. Dark-haired."

"I'll take care of the scumbag," said Tony.

Since the *Inside Track* story had broken, three reporters had shown up at Lucky's, and Karie now screened all her phone calls. She wasn't going to say anything, so it was easier if she avoided them. Karie had hoped to keep the story a secret, but a young freelancer for the *Phoenix Sun-Times* had come asking questions, and Julie couldn't contain herself any longer. "These legs have run circles round every other woman in America," she told the staff, "and now they need a little privacy." Championed by Tony, the Lucky's family had closed ranks around Karie and were only too ready to tar and feather anyone who came snooping. The story had gotten more complicated. Karie was amused to learn that now people in Luna were saying she was a legitimate star who had been screwed out of her reward by the drug Mafia and was lying low until things cooled down.

"Wait," said Karie, "let me take a look at the guy." She had a strange feeling. Karie looked out through the two-way mirror behind the bar. The man's back was to her but she recognized him immediately.

"Know the guy?" asked Tony.

"Yes," she smiled, "he's—he's my high school coach. I can't believe he's come to see me."

Lou and Karie sat in Karie's kitchen drinking Red Dog ale. Her apartment was sparsely furnished, just a few chairs and a second-hand table, worn but clean. He raised his glass in a toast. "Eight years," he said. "For you at least. I saw you run at Indi in '88."

"You were there?" Karie seemed flattered.

"Professional jealousy. I wanted to see what Andy had taught my star pupil."

"His training didn't come through in that race, that's for sure," said Karie. "Unless I had been taught to start off like a designated rabbit, and then realize I had another lap if I wanted to qualify." She took a sip of beer, shaking her head.

"I imagined what you were thinking, like, 'Oh shit, you mean this is two laps?'" Lou looked quickly over at Karie, "I'm sorry, that didn't sound right."

"That's okay," she said. "Andy had this theory. He calls it 'the natural physiognomy of the race.' Part of it is BS, but the message is right. He said most of the key runners in any race have this linkage between them, so if you move out front," she gestured with her hands, "you need to watch out for the accordion effect when you bunch back up again. The moral is, if you go out too fast, then just try to keep the tempo, and gut it out."

"Best race I've ever seen."

"You know, Lou, that's the one I can't forget. It was like I was caught in this awful vice, between this terrible burning in my chest and the feeling that the others were pounding up behind me." She shuddered involuntarily, "I still get clammy hands. Then Sandra Miller tested positive in Seoul and was kicked off the team."

"So she was on the juice?"

Karie sipped some beer and nodded. "From my deep experience in the matter, sure." She paused. "So you found out about me?"

"Dr. Laforet sort of let me read between the lines. I think he hoped that I would change your mind about going after Andy."

She shook her head. "I can't see going after him when I said yes to growth hormone."

"What's it like—the doping?"

"It's wonderful," Karie said. "You feel immortal. You know how paranoid runners are? Suddenly—no doubts. You strut around feeling real cocky. Train all day and wake up ready to go. Any sucker wants to challenge you, you're just going to beat her ass into the ground. You're the Terminator and you can do anything. Chug-a-lug, rag-a-tag-tag, great balls of fire."

"Should feed it to the coaches," said Lou. "We're the neurotics."

"I must have been on high octane stuff for some of the later cycles. I slept well, ate well, trained well. Any excess fat on my thighs, stomach and boobs just dropped away. I felt so in touch with my muscles that I thought I could talk to them."

"You didn't feel any side effects?"

"One thing right away," she started laughing, "your buns get like a pincushion. And you get a lot of scarring. One of the heavies at the gym was trying to find some daylight and he hit his sciatic nerve. He couldn't sit down for a day."

Lou straightened and rubbed his rump. "I've heard of that."

"I think maybe I was a jump ahead of any serious side effects. I was probably getting to the shadow on the upper lip and the voice change, you know." She sat with her head propped in her hands. "I had a pretty short fuse. I guess I got pretty bitchy."

Karie stretched her arms. "Well, there you have it. Oh, I left out the best part—you get pretty horny from the steroids."

"Just like regular guys," said Lou.

"But it's strange because you want to be in control. It has to be on your terms."

"Won't take it lying down."

Karie laughed. "But I understand that for a man it can work the other way—he withdraws."

"I think I need another brew," Lou said.

"So what brings you my way? Shouldn't you be at AU for the new season?"

Lou shook his head.

Karie stared at him. Something was up. "What is it, Lou?"

"I got kicked out." Technically, he had resigned, all charges dropped, but "kicked out" was what it was.

"I can't believe it."

It was nice to see someone so genuinely concerned for a change. That's what had been missing all these years. Now he wanted to open up to this serious young woman who had last chastised him for not keeping a promise. "The parents of a sophomore athlete issued a formal complaint against me for causing their daughter's alienation or, as they put it, for 'orchestrating the estrangement.'"

Karie watched him, wide-eyed.

"Sue Kowick," he shook his head sadly, "was a promising athlete. National Junior Olympic Champ in the 1500 meters. NCCA title holder in the 5,000 meters cross-country, just the right combination of speed and stamina for all the middle distances. Initially her parents—both are lawyers by the way—were supportive. But then the kid stopped talking to them and left home. All she wanted to do was train and compete." Lou looked up. "I guess they blamed me for whatever went wrong."

"But what about AU—didn't they back you up?"

"The father, who is on the board of trustees, threatened legal action against the university and against me personally. He alleged undue influence on my part, and even intimated sexual involvement. Then Sue dropped all her classes and asked me to train her independently; the university, while finding no evidence of misconduct on my part, privately put the bite on me to leave."

Karie watched him as he pulled on his lower lip, a gesture she remembered from Goodland.

"So I hired a lawyer and hunkered down for a fight. I was tired of moving and thought I'd make a stand—until I found out how long it might take and how much it would cost. I feel sorry for Sue. She must hate the whole world now," he said.

That's my coach, she thought, *more worried about his pupil than himself.* She hoped Lou would stick around for a while.

He leaned across the table and touched her hand. "Now, what about this piece of shit Peter Bernier did on you?"

254

"As I said, parts of it are true."

"It's not the parts, it's the whole, and it's bullshit."

"Lou, don't whitewash and say I'm not responsible—"

"Don't be so damn noble and understanding. This is a hatchet job. First the Can Do Kid, now the Great American Failure. Come on, Karie. And then there's dear Andy. He nearly maimed you for life, and he takes a dive when the heat is on. The super coach gives lessons on covering his ass."

"So what d'you want me to do? Shoot them?"

"Yes," he said, smacking his hands on the table so that the empty bottles jumped, "I want you to mow them down and grind them into the ground." He exhaled. "Spoken by a man who just threw in the towel on his own disgrace."

"Lou, I don't know how I'm going to handle Bernier or Andy—it's too much to think about. But I've decided I'm going to run again, and I'm hoping you'll be my coach."

"What about your leg?"

"Dr. Laforet said he couldn't promise anything," said Karie. "It's this knot of tissue right here," she pressed the back of her right leg, just above the knee. It may let me know as soon as the training gets heavy."

"Then what?" said Lou.

"I don't know. Maybe I can work through it."

Lou shook his head. "It'll restrict the flex—like a bicycle with one brake rubbing. But then again the body can do amazing things—and there's a lot you can do to help it heal. Some guys at AU go to a Chinese doc for acupuncture. Some use homeopathy. I'll check it out."

"Hey, I'll try anything, and all at the same time if necessary. But you know what is supposed to help?" She touched his arm. "The GH. It strengthens tendons, muscles, bones—everything. We'd be watching a big meet on TV and Andy would say, 'Look at that forehead, no way he isn't on GH—probably needs braces.'"

"Braces?" Lou asked.

"Yeah, braces for your teeth. If someone has been doing a lot of GH, their teeth can spread out and then they need braces."

Lou shook his head. "Is that how Andy sold you on it—by saying everyone was doing it?"

"I guess the line on cheating got a little blurred when he kept saying they'd banned something they couldn't control." She wrinkled her nose, "But I was just reaching." Now she felt ready, if her leg would hold out. "Lou I don't know how this is going to work out. I haven't got any money.

"Don't worry. It will work out. Anyway, some of the college kids want me to keep training them on the side."

"Sue?"

"Definitely not Sue."

She watched him from the corner of her eye. Lou must be in his early forties now, and he hadn't changed a bit. He would probably look the same in another 20 years, with a distinctive touch of gray. He had a decathlete's build and a shock of tousled black hair. Mom said his mother was French.

"Were you close to Sue?" she asked.

Lou sat up. "Close—you mean intimate?"

Actually Karie did wonder, but she didn't want to say so. "I mean emotionally close."

"Karie," he smiled reprovingly, "she was my pupil."

She wanted to yank him out of his seat and give him a huge hug. Karie put the empties back in the carton and left them by the trash. "You can sleep on the couch—no, don't be an asshole and say no. It's late." She finished wiping the sink, "As I said, I can't pay you now. But I'll owe it to you?"

"Not a problem. I'll set up a syndicate. That way I can get me a cowboy hat, boots, drive around in a Porsche, push dope on my athletes—"

She punched him in the ribs. "I'm serious. Why are you doing this?"

"Karie, I'm just a technician," Lou said, turning to face her. "You—you're a natural."

Chapter Sixteen

Karie short-stepped through a patch of loose gravel on her path up toward a copse of pine trees overlooking the bluff—it was about 4,000 feet, the highest point on her five-mile loop above Luna. She had not slept well, jerking awake from sudden muscle twitches and then, at dawn, when she swung her legs out of bed, a cramp had seized her left quad like a metal fist, leaving her whimpering with pain as she desperately rubbed her thigh with both hands. She resolved to take four quinine pills per day, until her muscles bowed to the training regime.

This year the period of heavy afternoon showers that were known as the monsoons had continued into late August, and Karie felt like a candidate in a wet T-shirt contest as she struggled on. As if on cue, two flat-iron clouds jumped into view over the brow of the mesa, dark and menacing like helicopter gunships. She caught the pine scent on the wind and straightened her back for a quick sprint up the last rise, but her legs just didn't feel in the game.

Now she could throttle back, cruise a little and get her heart rate down. One thing about running in these foothills was that, however zapped out she felt, her mind was always on the alert for chollas cactus or twisting her ankle in a prairie dog hole. Karie had not seen wild pigs or the mountain lions that favored the higher elevations, but she always had the feeling that hidden eyes were watching her. When she had mapped out this course as part of her base training, she decided to borrow Murray's dog for her runs. Chino was her forward ground controller, ranging far and wide through the scrub, and occasionally bursting out beside her on the path before racing off again with his tongue lolling out.

She was approaching her roller coaster, the part where the path became sandy and heavy, and she tried to sprint the downhill so the momentum would carry her up most of the next rise. From there she would rejoin the old railroad trail for the final half-mile to where the one-armed saguaro cactus would salute her finish. Behind her, the sun must have been caught by the approaching clouds; the sharp ochres and siennas on the flats were dulled to a spectrum of browns. Karie saw Murray, waiting up ahead with Chino by the cactus where she always left her bike. She straightened up and tried to pick up the pace, however painful, to the finish.

"Looking good, Coach K," Murray said, tossing her a bottle of Powerade.

Sweet little liar, she thought. Her face was on fire and her legs were caked in dust. "Just keep telling me that until I believe it, Murray."

He had become her training partner for intervals at the track and joined her on hill runs. She had taken him through the stretching and warm-up routines and had suggested one of the training schedules from Pace. "You have the talent," she told Murray, "but you need to learn how to run." If he took her suggestions, he could drop 15 seconds in the 800 meters in a semester and make the junior nationals.

Karie sat on a flat rock and Chino wandered over to push a cold nose between her legs. She looked up quickly and caught Murray watching her. "I used to have a dog," she said. "My dad had him put down about five years back."

"That's tough. Was he yours?"

"Bo was our family dog, but I took care of him." *Till I left home*, she thought.

"You going to do some weights?" Murray asked.

"No way. Not today. You always want to leave a day in between so the muscles can regenerate. About three times a week is good." *That is*, she thought, *unless you're doing steroids*. "What I'm really saying is that yesterday was a bad experience." She finished the bottle of Powerade and smiled. "Murray, when I was in really good shape I could bench press 155 pounds, easy. Four sets of eight reps, no problem. So yesterday I figured I'd start with 135 pounds; that's the bar plus two big plates. I thought, shoot, that's okay." She leaned back on the rock and raised her arms, "I lift the bar off the cradle, push up, and suddenly I realize I'm in trouble."

"Didn't you have a spotter?" said Murray.

Karie pointed her finger at him, "Dumb, huh? But you know what you do when you can't lift the bar back onto the cradle and it's beginning to press down on your chest?"

"Yell like crazy?"

She laughed. "That, too. You tip it to one side so that the plate falls off—remember, never ever lock the plates, even with a spotter—and then the bar whips up and the second plate falls off on the other side. It makes a humongous noise, like when a waitress drops a tray of drinks."

"Not too hot, huh?" he said, laughing.

"But cool Karie here thought she had a better idea. Slowly, I rolled the bar with both plates on down my chest and onto my stomach. Then I sat up and lifted it off."

"Way to go, K," said Murray.

"No wonder I feel like shit today. I ended up by struggling to do two sets at a miserable 95 pounds." Karie stood up and instinctively turned to look at the wet mark she had left on the stone. At Pace, after a good workout, they would sit on a wooden bench and then compare bunprints. The tighter the glutes, the closer you were to the perfect butterfly watermark.

She flexed her knees and said, "So then for punishment I tried some squats, but I only managed a lousy 135 pounds." She shook her head. "It's hard to believe I could do sets at 205—piece of cake."

Karie did some stretches and said, "Now that you're growing about five inches a week you ought to be doing weights. We could go together."

Murray nodded and smiled. "Sounds like you need a spotter, right?"

"Smart ass," she said. Chino came up and nuzzled her. She patted his ribs. "Chino sure doesn't have a weight problem."

"He's a survivor," said Murray. "Most greyhounds last about two to three years here. When they slow a little on the track—maybe a second per lap—they get rid of them."

She looked at him. Maybe he was trying to put things in perspective for her.

"Chino got lucky," he said. "When the track closed, the handler left town. Just took off and left five dogs behind. When they found them, he was the only one still alive."

She knelt and rubbed his head behind the ears. "You and me, Chino."

There was a roll of thunder and a dust devil swirled along the path. They picked up their bikes and pedaled hard for town.

* * *

Karie walked quickly down the hall and slipped into room 12. She stood quietly as she adjusted to the atmosphere, as calm as an afternoon siesta. She heard the faint sound of waves washing restlessly over a remote beach as she undressed and lay between the sheets on the massage table.

There was a soft knock. "Are you ready?" asked Julie.

"Show me your stuff," replied Karie.

"Good," said Julie. "Now," she said lifting the sheet, "turn over and lie on your stomach." Julie gently kneaded Karie's back and then did a little percussion riff down her legs.

"Wow," Karie yelped, "what was that?"

"Just getting your attention, dear, and keep your voice down or we'll have Gayle joining us." Julie rubbed some eucalyptus scented lotion on her hands and began applying a rhythmic pumping action to Karie's shoulder blades. "What I'm going to do, mostly, is sports massage. It's deep tissue work, so I want you to relax and breathe slowly. Don't try and resist me." Karie felt Julie's strong fingers cornering a kumquat-sized knot in her back. Gradually the knot seemed to dissolve with the combination of warmth and pressure. "I am using cross-fiber friction, because I want to separate the muscle strands where they may have become tangled from exercise. Is the pressure okay?"

Karie nodded. Already the top half of her back felt ploughed over and loose. No way could she keep up training without three or four massages a week. Julie worked on Karie in between her other sessions and wouldn't take any money. When Karie protested, Julie had replied, "What I want is to see you compete again. To get strong and kick some ass. Besides," she paused, "I've spent years in this game, but I've never worked with a professional athlete."

Karie was now on her back with a cloth over her eyes, feeling the exquisite sensitivity of finger-tip pressure on the soles of her feet, when Julie said, "For sure you're going to need some PNF."

"Sounds kinky, what's it mean?"

"It's a trade secret," said Julie. She started to raise Karie's right leg, then thought better of it and said, "Let me show you with the left. Lock your knee and tell me when it hurts to bend it back further. Okay, now I'm going to hold it and I want you to try and push my hand back down—but do it from the hip, don't use the back muscles."

As Julie took her through the exercise, Karie found that each time she could extend the arc of her outstretched leg a little further back, as if the muscle were reminding her that, with the right kind of coaxing, it would agree to unwind a little more. When they repeated the movement on her right leg, Karie felt a similar level of gradual uncoiling, but without the same arc of flexibility.

"Karie, you're going to have to contact your doctor in New Orleans. You know that, don't you?"

Karie pulled a face. "What, and invite him over to the spa and for a few drinks at Lucky's?"

"When you get into intensive training, it's going to feel like one leg is shorter than the other."

"I'm going for it, however it feels," said Karie sitting up on her elbows.

"Come on Karie, don't be Joan of Arc. We can't have you flopping on the track like a dead mackerel again. We need some professional medical advice."

"I'm sorry, Julie," she said. "I just can't bear the thought of not being able to compete again. I feel like they owe me. Damn it, there I go again," she wiped her eyes, "they owe me the right to prove myself. To do it right. Just one more time, to show them some stuff. Surely," she looked imploringly at Julie, "that's not too much to ask?"

"Nobody is going to stop you, I promise." Julie cradled her head and handed her some tissues. "But I want everybody on the same team," she murmured. "We'll talk to the surgeon, and we'll try every alternative therapy. Maybe we'll even try some amulets and get the Medicine Man to offer incantations."

Karie smiled. "What does PNF mean?"

Julie closed her eyes and recited slowly, "Proprioceptive Neuro-muscular Facilitation."

"I love it when you talk dirty."

Julie hadn't told Karie that she had already contacted Dr. Laforet at Parkview Hospital. The doctor had been alarmed to hear that Karie was back training but agreed to share Karie's medical records if she consented. He also wanted to warn Karie of the possible consequences. Dr. Laforet agreed that yoga might be helpful and was not opposed to alternative therapies. He sounded very interested in Julie's work and had plenty of questions about the benefits of massage.

Julie hung up the phone. *What a sexy voice*, she thought, hoping he had a body to match.

*   *   *

"My RDA is at least three," said Lou Gertz snapping a can of Bud from the six-pack he had brought. He had been gone almost three weeks, while Karie started her basic training, and he had now decided to commute to Phoenix. Karie had invited Murray, Julie and Lou over for a pasta dinner so they could discuss her training regimen.

"So what's the word, Coach?" Karie stacked the dishes as they sat around the table in her kitchen. Julie was drinking a glass of her cactus wine, and Murray had left to go hit the books.

Lou folded his arms on the table and looked directly at her. He had let his beard grow, and he looked a bit like the renegade hippies that still populated the region despite the yuppie migration.

"It's more like a bag of tricks, really. I've been doing some thinking," Lou continued with a smile. "I believe that in America we're very good at the technology of a sport, the hardware, but we're not really up there on technique. If we're going to be successful in getting Karie to Atlanta, we want to do things differently. We need to try new approaches, to adopt the latest techniques, to sort of think off the wall. That's why we need a whole bag of stuff, because your competitors don't think that way." He paused and looked at them both. Karie remembered how he used to drop by to talk with Mom back in Goodland. Now she found herself wondering how she felt about him. Surely she considered him more than a father figure.

"What's in the bag?" asked Julie.

Lou laughed. "Okay, number one, you should go for the 1500 meters. That's your event."

Karie said, "How much RDA have you had?" But she could see he was serious.

"When I went back to Phoenix this time, I spent about a week going over the tapes of your major races—I'm convinced that you're a natural for the 1500 meters." As Karie listened she had to admit that he'd done his homework, but that didn't mean he was right. "We don't have a biomechanical lab here to run correlations through a computer," he said, "but we don't need one. You have the speed of an 800 meter runner as your special advantage, so the only question is the endurance, and that should not be a problem." He emphasized the benefit of her experience and how important it was in a longer race where strategy was essential. "On the other hand, in the 800 you would be competing with a fresh crop of sprinters who would break like a pack of greyhounds and try to hang on for two laps."

"I don't know, Lou." She shook her head wearily. By just closing her eyes she could run the videotape of her combined races through her mind, replay the strategy of every curve and straight on the whole 800 meter stretch. That race, that distance was as familiar as an old friend. It was part of her. She knew by her body's dashboard where she was, how far she had to go and what her current readings were. And now he was telling her to throw this out and assume she would become as proficient in almost double the distance, to compete against others who had already grooved the feel of four times around the track into their bodies.

Lou said, "Think of it as cruising the first two laps and then running your 800 meter race."

Julie shot Karie a worried look. "What else is in the bag?"

"No," said Karie, "not tonight. Until I get my head around this, everything else is secondary." She sipped a Diet Coke. "It's a new trick, all right." Then she had another thought. "Is this all or nothing, Lou?"

He put down his beer. "I'll stay with you, no matter what you decide." He shrugged. "But you may not want me."

* * *

Over the next days, after she finished work at the spa, Karie went everywhere with Lou. They biked into the Coronado National Forest, jogged the foothills loop, ran the high school track with Murray, pumped some iron and shot a little pool at Charlie's. Later they would return to the room over Oscar's garage that was their Mission Control. He installed the new video system that was a farewell gift from his AU athletes, and he brought in a large dry erase board, a table and some chairs. She noticed that his sleeping cot and bedclothes were neatly folded behind the old cupboard, and his toiletries were arranged along the windowsill of the bathroom downstairs. He still drove the same '72 Beemer, pristine as ever, that he'd brought over from Europe during his Marine days.

Lou grinned through his beard. "Well?" he asked.

"You still growing that thing?" Karie asked.

"You don't like it?"

"It's just not the coach I remember. You have such a nice face."

Lou shrugged. He knew she was stalling for time. An uncomfortable silence crept around them.

Karie felt uneasy. Today she was supposed to decide on the 1500 meters. Lou was standing at the dry erase board, where they had listed the pros and cons over the last few days.

"I understand your plan—it's good," she began slowly, "but I'm scared to let go. The 800 meters is my watermark—I'm still the American record holder—and that is what my comeback should be measured against." She stood looking out over the rooftops of Luna and up towards Bryce Mountain. "If somewhere, somehow, I can do 1:56 again, then I'll call a press conference to tell *Inside Track* and Peter Bernier what I think of them."

Lou said, "I think you have to have another goal."

"You think I can't do another 1:56, don't you?" Without waiting for a reply, she said, "Is it because of the drugs? Or the injury? Tell me, I can take it." She turned to face him, arms on her hips.

"What I'm telling you is you shouldn't even try to do 1:56. It's time to move on."

"It's the drugs, isn't it?"

"It's time to turn the page," he said matter-of-factly.

"How can you be so sure?" she asked.

"I'm you coach."

"But you're not God," she said, getting annoyed.

"Listen, I'm not Andy either." His look bore into her, "Let me go over this again. The 1500 is your natural event —"

"You don't know what it means to switch, do you?" she said bitterly. "It's easy for you to say—"

"Of course it's easy for me to say. I don't have to run. I just fart around and drink beer all day."

She was startled by his tone.

He continued, "After all, you're thinking, he never did much as an athlete, so he thought he'd try coaching. And now he's crapped out on that too."

"Don't say that." Karie had never seen him angry like this.

"I've got it," he raised his arms in revelation. "Let's find another Andy, someone you can believe in."

"Lou, stop it!"

"Get a second opinion. Go to Petersen in Oregon. I'll pay for it. Can't ask for a better deal—"

"Shut the hell up, Lou." Her head was pounding. "I'm not going anywhere. I'm going to stay here and give it all I've got...but right now, twice around the track is all I can stand."

He sat down, but refused to look at her.

"D'you want me to say yes, just to satisfy you?"

He shook his head. "You have to believe."

She lowered her voice. "I'm not there yet. You want me to decide now. Change horses and off we go. It doesn't work for me like that." She paused wearily. "But I'm trying."

Lou paced a bit in front of the board, then spoke quietly. "I wish you could see what I see. The 800 meters is the past. You will be running against yourself, and you will always have the 1:56 time hovering over you. Let everyone else bust their buns going after your record. You do something new."

She dared not interrupt. She wanted so much to believe him.

"The 1500 meters is your clean sheet, your fresh start. The true test of a champion is to move on and make the team. You're blazing a new trail. No American woman has ever done that. You'd be in a class of your own. You don't try to get even with the Peter Berniers, you leap over them." He stood looking out of the window and spoke as if reasoning with himself, "I don't think you can do 1:56 again—and not because of drugs—but even if you could, that's a been-there, done-that thing."

If he could get her to the 1500 finals at the trials, she'd run till her other leg collapsed. Karie came up behind Lou and put her arms around him, resting her chin on his shoulder. "I'll try." She hugged him. "But work with me, Lou. I'm scared."

On Sunday morning they were all together at Mission Control. Lou was standing by the dry erase board in a scruffy American Eagle rugby shirt and chinos. He had trimmed his beard to a goatee. "Nice," Julie had said when she caught sight of him. Karie still liked Lou's face better without a beard.

"Here's the plan," he said. "I want Karie to be the golden girl in the line-up for the race." He turned to the board and wrote in sloping, neat letters: *Strength + Endurance + Flex.*

"Gives us what?" he asked.

"Kick-ass speed," said Murray.

"Good job." Lou gave him a high five. "Tell you what, Murray," he continued, "after we're through here, Karie can show you some slo-mos of her sprinting. If you watch carefully, you'll see a synchronization with the arm swing, and how it helps pull the knee up and lets the leg snap through."

"Cool." Murray smiled.

"We want mucho macho strength stuff for Karie," Lou said. "I'm counting on Murray for this. Free weight routines on the upper body. Go for the max, with fewer repetitions."

Karie wondered whether Lou had been like this with her in Goodland. Maybe she hadn't listened then. Certainly he had been her protector. She recalled when Bob at the Atlas Gym wanted to rub oil on her and give her a hooker hairdo, and how Lou had set him straight. Funny how she could see that now. But the first time she really felt close to Lou—like a sharing—was when they shook hands on going together to AU. She was 18 then, and he had begun avoiding physical contact. He no longer ran up to give her hugs or rubbed her back. Perhaps he sensed a crack in his reserve. Maybe that's why she was so mad at him when he told her he wasn't going to AU. Had she run away to spite him? Karie shook her head clear of that last thought and turned her attention back to Lou's lecture.

"You're going to have to do it the hard way," Lou was saying, "by getting your buns into the rarified air and stimulating your bone marrow to churn out more red blood cells." He underlined *Endurance* on the board. "Some of your competitors will be blood doping or taking shots of EPO."

Karie nodded.

Murray looked from one to the other. "What's this, " he looked down at his notes, "blood doping?"

"Blood doping is when you extract your own blood, separate the red cells, then re-inject them about 12 weeks later. That way you have a higher concentration of red cells, you get more oxygen to the muscles, and you can run faster," Lou answered.

"How much faster?"

"They say three to five percent or more," said Lou squatting down to be at Murray's eye level.

"Wow," said Murray. He turned to Karie, "And they're going to be running against you?"

"Some athletes will do it," said Karie. "But as the coach says, if I train in the mountains, I can probably get my red cells higher too."

Murray looked at her, then turned back to his notes. "EPO?"

Lou said, "It's an artificial substance that makes your body do the same thing."

"Like steroids, you mean?" The kid looked at them. "Shoot, there are guys at the gym doing all kinds of stuff." Lou sighed and stood up.

Julie said, "Coach, how much would Karie expect to increase from altitude training?" Karie looked at Julie. She knew that Julie had doubts about Lou, but mostly she kept them to herself.

Lou started writing on the board. "A normal hematocrit is about 40 to 45, so say 50 to 55, anything in that range would be great." He turned to Murray, "Hematocrit is just a fancy word for percent of red cells in the blood."

"Wouldn't it be good to get a proper initial reading then? I mean, she's already started her base training now." Julie was thinking of Dr. Laforet.

"What if she got up to 60 or so, Coach?" asked Murray.

"Too much is bad. The blood gets sludgy, and the heart could just stop pumping." Lou turned back to the board.

He's left handed like I am, Karie thought. *How strange that I never noticed. Perhaps if I hadn't been so obsessed about training with Andy, I might have given Lou another chance—and what then?* Certainly he was the right man for her now. A fresh start, a new event and a new coach. Lou was right—to try and repeat in the 800 meters would be like going back to Andy's Star Program and not coming close. She would no longer leap for the moon on her vertical jumps, and she shuddered at the thought of her body fat calculations. Did Lou use calipers? Had he taken Sue's measurements?

"Now what have we left out?" Lou was pacing in front of the board, holding the back of his head with both hands. He looked like a coach should look, she thought—very much the man you wanted on your side in a fight.

"Yoga for flexibility?" said Julie.

"Thank you, Julie," he said. He wrote it on the board. "About six months ago I met this guy, Dr. Morris Mann, who is an expert in flexibility. I mean, he can do contortions like those performers in the Cirque du Soleil. Turns out he coached Pablo Morales when Morales was training for his great swimming comeback. So Pablo learns all these great moves and when they're all on the platform just before the Olympic final, he does this incredible back bend— hell, I can't do it—and it psychs the competition right out of their Speedos.

"So I'm free-associating here," Lou smiled, "but I can see Karie just before her race. She's doing this amazing stretch, and all her competitors are thinking, 'Jesus, she looks strong and she's got that kind of flex, I'd better cut her some slack.'"

"Yeah," said Murray. "Just like that boy in *The Karate Kid*."

Julie said, "Yoga will stretch the muscle fibers. She needs that to counter all the contracting from training."

Right, Karie thought, *because the Can Do Kid is going to need all the help she can get.* It was great to have a bag of tricks and a support team, but she knew it was going to get lonely. Switching over from Pace Track's stable of training partners and exercise physio lab to running the trails in the desert with a dog, you give up a few things. Karie watched the eager faces. They looked as if they were at a revival meeting, but Karie knew she was in for some serious hurting. *What if I can't make it? What if I no longer have it? What if the matchsticks in my muscles no longer give me the same burn?*

Karie suppressed a shudder. *Did Lou realize the odds?* One thing she could promise him was that she was ready to show her stuff, to roast the skeptics and to rise above Andy and his cocktails. Shining up ahead, just around the corner, was a glittering image of what she could be. She would just have to apply her internal spurs to get herself over the rough spots. She was good at handling pain.

Murray was scanning his notes. "Coach, what about race strategy for the 1500 meters? Do you start kind of easy and then blow it out on the last lap, or do you go out pretty fast and string them out?"

"Both," said Lou. "No, let me level with you." He rested both hands on the table, "I've given a lot of bad advice, as Karie can probably tell you, and I've now done a 180 on this. Show me a coach who tells you to go with a fixed plan for a race, and I'll show you a guy who hasn't taken a good shit for a couple of weeks."

Murray stopped writing.

"Look, it's okay to have a general plan in case nobody else has one. But in Karie's league, everybody does, so you have to be intuitive and ready for anything. I mean, if she's in a race that starts off real slow, she'll kill them with her kick, but you have to figure they won't be that dumb." He looked at her with raised eyebrows.

Karie nodded, "He's right, Murray." *That's my coach.* She stood up and motioned Murray over to the VCR.

Julie walked over to Lou and asked in a low voice, "What are her chances?"

"Of making the U.S. team?"

She nodded.

"Nobody's ever come back from an injury like hers." They had walked to the other end of the room, "But Karie's Karie."

Julie looked at him. "What if she gets injured again?"

"Her leg's not her only injury," Lou said.

Chapter Seventeen

Sometimes Karie would wake before the alarm, knowing that she had only a few more minutes of rest. Slowly, by feeling with her hands, by flexing, twisting or stretching, she would inventory her body and assess her pain. Then she would run through the demands of the day's events, starting with the long grind up the hill to the spa. And finally, she would ask herself why it had become so hard.

The business of training to an elite level was a simple proposition. To build muscle up, you had to first tear it down. That was the rule. Perhaps that was why it invited such rebellion. Successively, you would exercise your muscles to a point beyond, and then, when rest came, the body would call out its repair technicians and go to work to rebuild the wasted tissue to a level higher than it had before. Once set in motion, this cycle could not be put on hold, short-circuited, abrogated or circumvented. There was a rhythm to the process that never let you get too far in front or allowed for respite. The cycles, in different forms and nomenclatures, were known to athletes all over the world. Karie called them the shit times.

In the shit times, you constantly pressed the ceiling. When you attained one elevation, you tore it down in the hope of building back up to a higher one. You kept pushing up, knowing that the better you were, the closer you were to danger. Stretching and reaching for that last extra little incremental bit, teetering out along the furthest line, something could give and send you free-falling down. You had to learn to approach your pinnacle and caress it, but never embrace it. You had to know merely exhausted from totally wasted.

It always seemed such a pity—a waste even—that you could not build incrementally. Having flogged a particular braid of muscle into fast-twitch mode, it wasn't possible to raise the tempo another beat or so without going back to spur the fibers past their prior high, enduring the lactic acid buildup until the whole regenerative process kicked in again. When you sought a higher note on a string instrument you could just tighten it up a notch, without completely re-tuning. The body was a different instrument.

Karie had come to know the process and understand what was going on inside her. She looked upon the color of her urine as a run-off from the last layer of buildup, and could sense in the fibrillations of a muscle that she might be heading for a cramp. But she had never known training to be this hard. The most difficult kind of pain to handle was the self-inflicted—her own procrustean bed—when all you had to do to make it to go away was stop. She knew that out there now, some of her competitors could be popping a few pills or preparing a needle. That meant that they would be anesthetized to the shit times and would not fall prey to self-doubt.

Lou tried hard to be protective. "No time trials," he said, "no forced marches. Quality not quantity. Listen to your body and let it happen." One week, when he returned early from a coaching assignment in Phoenix—the kind that paid—he cycled up to meet her by the saguaro cactus.

Karie wiped the sweat from her eyebrows and checked her Timex. "It's not happening, Coach."

"Let's keep walking," said Lou.

Even Chino seemed out of sorts, padding softly behind them. "There was a time, after Seoul, when I tapered off for a while, until Andy got really pissed. So I jumped back into some hard training, and within a week I was back burning up the track."

He smiled. "You always were a precocious animal."

"It was like shedding a heavy cloak. After a few days I felt vibrant and ready to fly."

"It'll happen. Remember it's been over two years."

"I just don't feel that tightness where I could call up any muscle and talk to it. My body and I are just not communicating these days."

"Maybe you need a break. Take off for a few days."

She stopped, "Lou—"

"Karie, I'm serious. Sometimes you need to just break the cycle."

272

As they turned back, she smiled. "Maybe." Lou was just being kind. No way was she going to ease off, let alone take time to go somewhere. She'd never felt this barrier before, and now she needed to smash through it. What was it that Andy used to say? "Athletes learn to live with pain, the elites ignore it."

The next day Lou brought her a log book. He wanted her to record the overall time and type of her workouts while he was away. Karie did what he asked, but she also instituted her own code of "make goods." If she felt that a particular training session was below her expectations, she would enter it in the log, but felt free to omit the repeat session when she exercised to cover the deficiency. This was not deliberate deception. She believed she needed to supplement Lou's regimen. As Dad always said, "If you're going to do it—do it right."

As she lay waiting for the alarm, she wondered how much longer it would be before she would break through to her summit. When would she hear the wind in her ears again?

*   *   *

When it happened, it was as if something had sneaked into her bed when she was sleeping. Afterwards she imagined it as a revolt, a sort of town hall meeting of the hamstring fibers, where they set to twitching and jerking in frustration, until the fine network of capillaries could take it no longer. From then on it was a vicious circle. The first few tiny skeins ruptured and hemorrhaged. Then the intra-cellular fluid poured in to the point where the skin puffed up and the pressure shut off, stranding the relief column of white cells which were rushing to the rescue. By the time it was over, the old injury behind her right knee was inlaid with a coagulation of dead red blood cells, plasma and cell debris. When she tried to move, it felt like she was tearing the scab off a wound.

"Looks like you've burst a pipe," said Julie looking at the tight, swollen skin, mottled by dead blood.

Karie lay face down. Today she would not climb any steep trail.

Today she would surrender some of the physical base that had been built so painfully. No warming tired muscles marbled with the dreaded lactic. No clawing feeling in her lungs. No waiting for the body to begrudge the morphine that brought some respite. And no wrestling with the voices that questioned a life drawn by endless goals. Why couldn't she let go?

"Ice," said Julie. "A little ice massage, with compression and elevation. Complete rest. If you move, I'll kill you. And we're going to Phoenix—"

"Phoenix? I can rest here. I've had sprains before, you know."

Julie knelt down beside her with one arm on her shoulder. "Karie, we know you're upset, okay? We all are. But don't be stupid. If this recurs—you're finished." She had already placed another call to Dr. Laforet. He had promised to help. They needed all they could get—and a little luck besides. "We're going to Phoenix, and I'm calling Dr. Laforet to have him meet us there."

*   *   *

"My belief is that she sprained the muscle while exercising that evening," said Dr. Laforet. "Then later that night any slight movement while she was asleep could have caused the biceps femoris— the hamstring—to spasm, leading to hemorrhaging and edema. You must realize that this whole area," he moved to the light box on the wall with the four x-rays, "is likely very sensitive, and constant repetitive stress leads to microscopic lesions...." His voice trailed off as if the corollaries were obvious, even to the layperson.

He's still a spectator, thought Karie, and then realized what an uncharitable thought that was. But here she was back on an examining table in Phoenix with her leg tightly bandaged and propped up, and everyone around her was talking as if she were chopped liver. In the two days since it had happened, she'd been tested, prodded and probed. Now it was time to diagnose.

Dr. Laforet spoke to Lou. "Individuals with a high tolerance of pain," he glanced at Karie, "are often unaware of the body's early warning signals."

274

Now he's being kinder than I deserve, she thought. She had definitely felt a specific hurt over the usual chorus of aches and pains the evening before it happened.

"Yes, so what next?" Dr. Laforet smiled at Julie's unspoken question, as if she were the only sensible one in the group. "First let me explain what's going on. All this in here is the result of trauma and overexertion," he said. "The first stage is the inflammatory phase, which is where she is now. You get a mess of dead cells, fluid, lactic acid and chemical substances that accumulate and cause swelling and pain. The body starts healing right away. Its first reaction is to clear out all the dead cells and other debris. Then it starts to rebuild the ruptured capillary system so that all the proper fix-it materials, like oxygen, amino acids, sugars and vitamins can be brought in."

Looks like Lou has got me to take a break after all, Karie thought. It suddenly crossed her mind that maybe he had meant that they should take off together. They could drive to Phoenix and fly off to clear waters and murmuring fronds. Dash off someplace where they could wear linen, dance on warm sand and sleep with the sound of the surf. Maybe they could talk about all the things that were on hold while she worked so hard for restitution. She looked across at his dark brows, now arched in concentration, and inwardly shook her head. Maybe not.

In the meantime, my muscles will atrophy. She had read somewhere, or maybe she heard it from Andy, that a muscle can lose one-third of its strength in one month. That meant that about 10 percent was already down the toilet, and the doctor had said it would take three more weeks for her to heal. *That's it,* she thought, *just because I have to lie still doesn't mean I have to take this lying down.* "While all this tissue mending is going on, I'm going to atrophy like I'm in a body cast."

"That's not true, Karie," said the doctor, "As long as you aren't in severe pain, you can do pool exercises—pull-buoys, kick-boards, aqua-training, all that—and you can do the Aerodyne by working your arms and left leg. Plus you can do upper body weights." He walked over to her, "Julie can arrange for you to get magnetic stimulation at the spa, so that the muscle fibers are repolarized and will knit properly with a minimum of scarring. I could even come and check up on you out there."

Karie smiled. "Way to go, Doctor." *What a bitch I am,* she thought. *They're all doing the best they can and all I do is whine. But I think I'm falling behind—what Andy termed "the negative side of the power curve"— and I'm scared that I won't be able to catch up. Yet everybody still seems to believe in me.*

Dr. Laforet said, "We can put a man on the Moon, but we still don't understand how the body heals itself."

He walked back to the x-rays. "The good news is that Karie's original injury—the rupture of the biceps femoris right here—is healed. It's as strong as it ever was. What's not so good is that there is scarring, and there is a different density to the tissue that causes it to behave differently when subjected to stress. In that sense it's in competition with the left leg, and she has to be sympathetic to it." He snapped off the light and began taking down the x-rays.

Julie helped Karie off the table and held the single crutch. Dr. Laforet put a hand on Lou's arm, "In answer to the obvious question," he said quietly, waiting for Julie and Karie to leave, "it's a result of chronic overuse stress."

"She can't handle the training?" said Lou.

"No," he shook his head, "it's not that. Look, we know Karie's an overachiever and very tough. She's going to exercise balls-out every day. The left leg can take it, but the right one doesn't have the same tolerance, at least for now anyway, and she will experience occasional flare-ups."

"You're saying she can't make it?"

"Not the way you're doing it," said the doctor.

"You want me to tell her to quit?"

"No," he shook his head, "I didn't say that. I think maybe there is a way, just as long as it doesn't involve the type of training you're doing now."

Lou looked at him. "So what should I do?"

"You're the coach," said Dr. Laforet.

* * *

It was a beautiful afternoon for a time trial. The late spring warmth was tempered by a light breeze, and even the asphalt Luna High track felt resilient. Karie finished up her stretches in the fresh-cut grass of the infield. Her leg had healed, but before she resumed heavy training, she argued with Lou that she needed a benchmark. She insisted on one, because they were now less than a year away from the 1996 Mount San Antonio College Relays where she hoped to qualify for the Olympic Trials in June. It was time to establish a calendar countdown of time check points, just like she did with Andy for New Orleans. She ran through some sprints on the last lap of her warm-up and then signaled to Lou that she was ready. Murray would pace her for three laps, and unless she felt really good, she planned to run at about 90 percent. She was wearing her favorite Pace Track uniform as she put her left foot to the line—Murray was on the inside—and started rocking her head in anticipation.

"Andy Nagy changed her stride a little," Lou said to Julie, "and he taught her that blocking motion with her arms." They watched them complete the first lap. "But he's too good a coach to mess with anything else."

"She's doing good?" said Julie.

"Look at the style. She's so much more efficient; see the leg turnover. The kid's improved too, but he has to muscle it and he's leaning forward too much."

"Will it be a good time?"

"No way," said Lou without looking at his stopwatch, "but she always looks good." Murray had dropped out at the bell and Karie started up the backstretch. "See, she's shortened her stride now—the spark plugs just aren't firing right and she knows it." Karie came into the final straight with her head high. "She's hurting now. Maybe it'll help."

277

"You're a mean bastard."

"Sometimes you have to tear down before you can build up." He timed the finish and turned to Julie. "Sometimes you can't change unless you're really worried."

*　*　*

They were all there at Mission Control over Oscar's shop, and Lou was writing on the board. When Lou told Karie yesterday that her time was a fat 4:42 she almost freaked out. For the first time in her life, Karie felt a pang of doubt. She spent the afternoon worrying that maybe she could no longer cut it. It was unlikely that she could improve enough to qualify for the trials. Just the idea of not making it back scared the shit out of her.

Maybe Peter Bernier had it right. Maybe this was the true aftermath of steroids. They took you up to the top of the mountain, but after that, they buried you alive. Yesterday she had angrily suggested to Lou that they should go back to the 800 meters—at least it would be over quicker, she said. Ever since she had started training again, she was having trouble making it into high gear. She no longer came close to that clean feeling of confidence, of being able to line up with anybody and take them, the way she did at Pace. She could no longer break through the barrier and hear that clear Streisand pitch of sound. Now she was worried about being humiliated by some pig-tailed bopper from the prairies. So why not quit?

Lou had come around for his RDA of beer last night at Lucky's. She still worked there sometimes, even though she didn't stay through the late shift. "I think I ought to quit," she said.

When Lou didn't answer, she wondered whether he'd heard her. Or worse, maybe he was going to agree. She remembered the quick feeling of dread.

"I'll make a deal with you." There was something in his voice that made her put the tray on the table and sit down. "First, you don't quit unless I say so. Second, you don't train unless I'm with you."

"But Lou, you can't—"

"That's my business," he said abruptly. "This is it, Karie. Not one step without me. I know you used to run on the side in high school, and you admitted to doing as much on steroids," his voice softened and he put his hand on her back, "For once I want you to stick to the game plan. This is big time, okay? No extra weights, no swimming, nothing. D'you understand?"

He had insisted on shaking hands. She remembered when Andy had warned her to get with the program. He'd been such a shit and Lou was so...so caring. He had decided to quit his part-time coaching in Phoenix to work with her full time. "Everybody can spare a year," he said.

Lou finished detailing the training schedule on the board. "Half of all coaching is bullshit," he said. "The problem is to figure out which half. Today I want to make a stab at it." Then he dropped it on them. "We're going to cut the traditional run schedule down to half. Look," he said in the ensuing silence, "we know how to do the tear-down part of the training cycle. We've got to have equal time for the buildup."

"From now on," he pointed to the board, "only three days a week of running." He paused, "But we need high altitude—at least 7,000 feet—because we found out in Phoenix that Karie's only got a 45 hematocrit."

"We'll have to go to Coronado for that, Coach," said Murray. "It's about an hour's drive."

"That's where we'll go," said Lou. "Only three to four hours per day—we want intensity, not duration."

"Are you serious, Lou?" said Karie. "You mean only 10 hours a week, between now and Mount SAC?"

"Right. Only 10 hours with your sneakers on. By the way, remind me about that, because I'd really like you to train in something heavier, like hiking boots."

"Time out," said Karie. "I know I stunk yesterday, but your answer is to work me half time?"

"You had an injury because of your current schedule."

"I'm not an invalid."

"I'm saying the optimal program is three days a week—for you or anyone else."

"So more is less?" she said. "It's a big risk."

"It's a bigger risk to keep hammering on."

"You agree that Andy was a good coach, right?"

He nodded.

"At Pace, anyone who didn't put in 25 hours got kicked out."

"That's all anybody talks about—hours. I don't want hours, I want quality. Like it's your last session before the race. I want passion. I want you to leap out of bed and say," Lou flung back his head and shouted for emphasis, "I'm going to *run* today."

"Way to go," said Murray, but he looked around uncertainly.

Lou was walking round the room now. "This decathlete guy, Bill Toomey—gold medal, Mexico, '68—told me about going to Europe to train. The Germans kept telling him his stride was all wrong until he said, 'I'm sorry I can't learn from your runners because they're always behind.' I'm saying they just don't know any better."

"How's that?" said Julie.

"Everybody's stuck in the same rut. Train till you drop—that and doping. There's nothing else in the bag."

He's really serious about this, Karie realized. Images of the strict discipline of Pace collided in her mind with Lou's fairyland ideas until her head spun. But now Lou was back at the board underlining where he had written: *Weights + Aqua + Yoga*.

"Don't worry, Karie," he said, "you won't be bored. You build strength from all these activities and you can do aqua-running. And you have one day to rest—you can walk if you want, preferably at high altitude. But," he came round and stood over her, "ten hours running a week, max, even if I have to tie you down."

"Now wait a goddamn minute," she said. "If I'm going to fail, I wanna do it sweating my guts out, not sitting on my ass. At least then I'll know it wasn't for lack of trying."

"Your body's changed, Karie. Face it."

"You're just taking a stab in the dark."

"Karie—"

"No way, Lou. You have no idea that this will work."

"I know what won't work."

"Try it on somebody else—give it to your precious Sue in Phoenix."

Julie stood up and said, "We'll leave you to work this out."

"Sit down, Julie," Lou said roughly. "Nobody bails out on me. We're going to settle this right here and now."

"Not with me," said Karie. "I'm not buying a ticket halfway to Europe."

"Well where d'you think you're going? You won't even have a ticket into the trials."

"This is my last shot, Coach, if you remember, and I'm not going to miss it for one of your cockamamie hunches. I'd rather go down in flames."

"And you will go down." His face was flushed and his voice harsh. "Because you're too fucking stubborn to listen. Because you've always had your way. And because you can't believe that someone might just have a better idea. You just want to crash in style—and crash you will."

"Lou, please," Julie looked nervously at Karie's shocked face. "Don't talk to her like that."

"That's the problem—nobody has ever talked to her like that. It's about time."

Karie jumped up so quickly that Murray flinched. "Just who the hell do you think you are? D'you think this is how you coach someone? You're not a coach, you're a failure." The words seemed to echo round the room, and she sank back to her seat.

"I can agree with that," said Lou quietly. "For 20 years now I have lived with my failure to make the '76 Olympics in Montreal."

Murray, his head between his hands, looked up. "No shit, Coach."

"Let me tell you what kind of a failure I am." Lou pulled up a chair and sat facing them. "I started out thinking not only would I make it to the finals of the decathlon, but on a good day I could take Bruce Jenner for the gold." He nodded his head in recollection. "Then about two years before Montreal, when I was competing in Europe, I tore one of my adductors —the muscles that run deep from here in the glutes to the knee. In those days you could be sidelined for months, and so I began a long struggle of climbing up the ladder and then falling back down again. All I could think of was just give me one good week, or even a couple of days, so I can get my workouts done. I felt my expectation drop from just making the U.S. team to hoping that somehow I might qualify for the trials."

Julie shook her head. "What did your coach say?"

"I didn't have one—and I didn't know any better," said Lou.

"What happened?" said Murray.

"I entered a qualifying meet in Rochester," he said, "and focused on scoring the 7,600 points I needed over the two days of decathlon competition. I was careful to only try for one good long jump, or one big heft with the shot put, and then pass on the other attempts, so I wouldn't aggravate the injury. By the end of the first day, with five events done and five to go, I was about on track to qualify—but that's as far as I got." He paused. "The next day I couldn't get out of bed. I'd been shooting up pretty good with cortisone, and I guess my whole system crashed. I remember lying in bed, not being able to move, just looking at my watch—and I swear that at 10:30 that morning I heard the gun go off for my heat of the 110 meters high hurdles. I knew then that it was over."

In the ensuing silence Lou stood and looked around. "I spent a month in the hospital." He spread his arms and spoke softly, "Don't expect me to take Karie, who has so much more talent and ability, down that same path."

Karie covered her face and sank forward on her knees. Lou knelt and put his arms around her.

Murray and Julie tiptoed to the door. Lou glanced up and waved them out.

Chapter Eighteen

He got the phone on the second ring. "Eigel Johnson here."

"Coach Gertz, Mr. Johnson. I just wanted to tell you that everything is okay. We had Dr. Laforet, the doctor from New Orleans, check her out and he said her leg had healed up real well."

"That's good." Eigel felt a rising concern. He knew the coach would not have called just to tell him that. "How's her training?"

"Well, that's it. You know how I said I'd found her, and she was really back," Lou paused. "Well, I think I've lost her again."

"What d'ya mean?"

"I mean, she's not running any more."

Eigel hardly listened to the rest of the coach's comments. When they hung up, he sat down heavily.

Nancy looked at him across the supper table.

"She's quit training," he said. "I bet that Bernier article has gotten to her again."

"Did you ever talk to her about it?"

He shook his head irritably. "Wouldn't do any good."

"Did you try?" Nancy's words snapped out of her.

"You know Karie. I mean, what's she doing in the desert working at a fat farm when she could be here with us?"

Nancy stood up abruptly and took her plate to the sink. She felt a flush of anger and didn't trust herself to answer.

"Miss Independent," said Eigel as if Karie's temperament were a genetic anomaly. "That's why she ran away to that son-of-a-bitch Nagy in the first place."

Nancy scraped the last plate, dropped the cutlery in the water and set her apron on the table as she walked away.

"Where're you going?" Eigel twisted in his chair.

Nancy turned, her hands clasped in front of her. "I'm going to pack."

"What for?"

"I'm going to visit Karie." She looked over his head. "I'm going to tell her I'm proud of her." She turned away before the tears came.

* * *

Murray had to stand on his pedals to cycle up the hill to the Las Colinas Spa. He felt the burn in his quads all the way to the top and then relief as he shifted into top gear on the circular drive at the entrance. Julie watched him climb and stepped out into the early afternoon sunshine when he finally reached the top to hug him hello. Anyone would've thought it had been months, not a week. He smiled self-consciously at her as he tried to breathe normally and said, "I'm here."

Julie led him to the garden. "She called in sick on Friday—today she didn't even bother to call."

Murray stopped and turned to her. "Did she leave?"

"No," she said taking his arm, "the lady who lives in the apartment below says she's there. But she didn't show up at Lucky's over the weekend. Apparently she likes to go for long walks in the evening." Julie did not say that while looking for her on Sunday evening, she had seen Karie at the track, walking aimlessly until long after dark.

"I talked to Oscar like you suggested," said Murray. "He said the coach left town Thursday evening—you know, after our meeting."

"Where was he going?"

"He didn't say—Phoenix, I guess."

"Did he take his stuff?"

"Oscar would have said, right?" He looked inquiringly at her. "I didn't want to sound too curious."

Julie nodded.

"What d'you think Karie should do?" he asked.

"About the training, you mean? Murray, I don't think that's what is bothering her. I think she's been carrying a lot of stuff, you know, and she finally snapped."

"You mean she and the coach are not going to work it out?"

Julie didn't know how to answer, but Murray kept talking.

"We've got to do something. Karie is already losing a week, and

284

it's May, so we've only got 10 months before her first race."

"Maybe we should let things be for a while."

"No," he said. "I'll call the coach—Oscar knows where to leave messages. You tell Karie."

"What shall I say, Murray?" She looked at him sadly.

"Tell Karie I need to see her. I know, we can get together at my house on Thursday—Dad doesn't get back till late." He started walking purposefully back to the main building. Julie followed.

"What if she isn't ready yet?" said Julie.

"She already said she'd go with me to my prom. Tell her we need to make plans."

Julie put her arm on his shoulder. "Why not?" She sighed.

*   *   *

Murray's parents' home crouched on the rise behind town. In the living room, Lou stood looking out across the valley to the Coronado National Forest—that was where Murray said you could train at elevations over 7,000. Julie looked at her watch and said for the fourth time, "She'll be here."

"Yeah," said Murray, "she knows where it is."

Shortly after, they heard a bike being wheeled. Karie came in wearing cut-offs, sandals and an old tank top tucked in on one side. She looked around, nodded, and sat down by Julie on the couch. Julie looked at Murray and said, "Go ahead."

He stood up, looked nervously at Karie and said, "I do want to talk after about the prom. But I've missed you guys and I thought we might talk a little, because Karie's the greatest runner I've seen, and the coach has helped me so much...and I was hoping that we could keep training because I want to make it to the nationals next year. I know you guys need to get some things sorted out, but maybe you could keep me in the running. Coach, I can't pay you now—but I'll sure owe you. And Karie," he walked over to her, "Chino sure misses his workouts."

There was an awkward silence and Julie looked around. "Coach, why don't you tell us some more about this Halfway Program."

Lou smiled and reached back to link his hands behind his head. "I was raised in the Hans Selye method. Selye was a balls-out Austrian coach who developed a maximal stress system of coaching. It was a survival course in training overload—and those who survived were the future superstars."

"Not my type," Julie quipped.

"I'm not saying Selye's method didn't inch you up the performance scale, but it took such a toll that we called it the Undertaker System."

Julie shook her head.

"As I told you, I've had plenty of time to think. I want to get away from the repetitive stress regimes that pound the shit out of you, and use more pool and bike workouts that give cross-over benefits. I could be wrong, but I think if you train better as opposed to harder, you can come back to the running schedule with such intensity that you can blow it out way over the top. Of course, I could be wrong," Lou shrugged.

"No," Karie said deliberately, "I think you're right." They looked at her in surprise. "I just don't think I can make it. It suddenly occurred to me that I've been running for way too long—it's time for me to ease off." She smiled at them.

Murray jumped up. "I forgot." He went into the kitchen and came back with a large paper bag. "I biked to Stafford—I'm keeping up the training, Coach—for these." He pulled out a white T-shirt with "Team LunaSi" on the front. "Get it?" Then he turned it around to show a dog waiting by a one-armed cactus. "Because Chino always wins." He passed them out. "You guys are my team for the nationals."

"Way to go, Murray," said Julie. She turned to them with her arms around him, "How about my prairie dog?" They gave him high fives.

Lou said, "Karie, we can start the program real easy and see how it goes. Then we can keep the kid in the running."

She shrugged. "Sure."

"Good," Lou said. "Julie, you're in charge of preventive medicine—care and feeding of the athlete, homeopathy, ayurveda, chi-
ropractic, aromatherapy, ju-ju, whatever."

Murray said, "Coach, I've been thinking. The guys on the football squad, any time they get hurt, they go see this Chinese guy
who sticks pins in them—"

"Acupuncture."

"That's it," said Murray.

"I don't know about that," said Karie shaking her head, laughing finally, "I've done enough needles already."

"They're very small," said Murray seriously. "I've seen them."

"Who is it?" said Julie. "I'll check him out."

"Well, I don't know," said Murray, looking uneasy.

"You don't know his name?"

"I'll find out," he said. "The guys call him Dr. Prick—and I
figure that's probably not his real name."

"Dr. Prick," said Julie shaking her head. "LunaSi...it fits."

*　*　*

"Come on, Murray," Karie said as they approached the mark for
the last of the 200 meter intervals, "try and make this one sing."
The kid's getting fast, she thought as she hung on his shoulder round
the curve and into the straight.

She jogged back towards Lou. Maybe they ought to try Murray
out for the 400 meters. It was a bitch of a race, but the kid was
strong. She stopped dead in her tracks. "Dad?"

Eigel said, "I came to watch you."

Karie ran to him.

Over her shoulder he said, "I walk your old course back home.
You know out west and then round by Mrs. K's place—" he stopped
because he didn't know whether Karie had heard about Mrs. K's
passing away.

"No wonder you look good, Dad."

"So I thought I'd check out your new loop in the hills. Coach told me about it." He turned to find Lou had moved away.

"How's Mom?"

"Very comfortable." Eigel smiled. "She's already checked into the spa—your friend Julie helped us."

"Mom's here, too? I can't believe it," she said, gripping his arms for assurance. "How did you get here?"

Eigel pointed.

"The truck." It sat there like an old dog waiting for them.

He was about to tell Karie that they had brought the truck to leave it with her, but then he remembered something else he had decided to say. "I came," he looked quickly around, "well, your mother and I have been talking," he paused, "and I wanted to tell you how sorry—"

She flung her arms round his neck so fiercely that he had to steady himself.

As they clung together, Eigel thought that after all that rehearsing, he should try to finish his speech, but he was too choked up. It was the same, really. As they drove through New Mexico, Nancy kept insisting that he talk to Karie while he still had the chance. Now he'd done it. Later maybe, he could talk to her about the winter, and about following her footsteps through fields covered in soft snow.

"Let's go find your mother."

*   *   *

They rose up through cactus, aspen and now pine until Hallelujah Road gave up. Lou checked Murray's map again and turned the truck on the two ruts in the grass. They lurched up a final rise and stopped on a patch of hard-scrabble ground. He stamped on the parking brake and left it in gear. "End of track," he read out. "Path starts here. Boy, I'm glad your dad left the truck. Imagine getting here with my car."

Karie grinned at the thought of Lou driving his precious BMW anywhere near an unpaved road. "The kid did good," she said. She opened the door to let Chino out and rubbed the white skin scrape on her arm where he had pawed her.

"That must be Mt. Graham, and over there is Redemption Canyon. Some years you get snow up here." Lou glanced at her.

"Just like Goodland," she said.

Lou was rummaging in his backpack. "And for my next trick," he pulled out the chest strap and wristwatch of a heart monitor. "Behold the athlete's time clock—keeps track of your heartbeat."

"I know all about them," Karie said. She used one at Pace Track. Andy would try and rub up her bra every time he adjusted the strap.

"It really keeps you in the zone," he said. "I wish I'd had one back when."

Karie watched a hawk riding thermals over the soft hues of the valley. "What was it like in Europe?"

He leaned back and closed his eyes. "I wore a blue blazer with the U.S. emblem. It was like stepping into another world—especially in Scandinavia. Imagine a place where you could meet someone on the street who would be happy to take you home, feed you and deliver you to the meet on time the next day."

Andy had discouraged foreign tours. Now Karie wondered if he thought they would undermine his control.

"But there was another reason I was so desperate to make it to Montreal in '76," he said. "Astrid Munson. I met her on my last European trip. Her father was a Swedish cross-country skier turned industrialist with a castle, a family crest and a young wife. It was a separate social universe. I felt as if I had waked up inside a movie. I remember polishing up my Spanish, because it seemed to be the only language she wasn't fluent in. We spent the summer together on the tour. The collage of people and places was different from anything I'd ever known. Life was so exhilarating. Not even sleep was the same."

Karie looked at him.

"We would fall into bed at any hour. Next morning, we were raring to go." Lou sat up and gripped the wheel. "Then I was injured in Frankfurt."

"When was that?"

"It was '75—a year before Montreal. It happened on my last javelin throw, and I had to drop out of the 1500. We kept in touch and in the fall, Astrid came to New York for a week. But it just wasn't the same. Somewhere we had lost the spark. I guess I didn't show up well, on my home turf and without my natty little emblem. Sometimes Astrid retreated into herself. 'Being with her trolls,' she called it. Those little creatures would spirit her off to some dark forest in her mind. She was an only child whose mother had died, and she always seemed to be in competition with her stepmother. Her moodiness made her even more desirable to me. I always thought that I'd be the one to unlock her dark little soul."

I have grown up with this man forever, but I don't really know him, Karie thought.

"Astrid was going to come back for the trials, and we planned to go to Montreal together. I began to train my heart out. I had these wonderful images of her that I used to drag myself out of bed or spur me on for the extra miles. But my injury had never healed properly. I kept struggling up the ladder only to be yanked back down again." Lou shook his head. "I would have made any deal to get well for a few weeks—doping, whatever."

"Lou, you don't mean that —"

"Karie, I was obsessed. I could picture her waiting down at the finish, and I felt like I was crawling there on all fours."

She put a hand on his arm and was surprised at how tightly he was gripping the wheel.

"Eventually, I healed up okay." He began to relax his grip. "I realize now Astrid would have been a big mistake. But back then...half the time I wanted to pick up the phone to call and the other half I was waiting for it to ring."

He stretched and smiled at her. "But I did salvage one little nugget out of the whole mess." He leaned close so that she picked up the scent of his hair. "You must do it for yourself, or not at all." He drew back to watch her. "You can't do it for love, or your parents, or Andy, or country, or Pace or LunaSi—it's for you or don't bother."

"That's sort of what Dad told me when he left," said Karie. "He gave me the keys of the truck and said, 'If you want it—go for it. Don't bother about anybody else.'"

"Smart man." He had never told her that Mr. Johnson had offered to pay him for her training, or that he turned him down.

"What happened to Astrid?"

"I never made it to the trials. Neither did she."

"Didn't you ever wonder?"

"Of course. I hope she did too."

Lou opened the door and got out. "I brought along some canvas boots so you could have good ankle support if you want to check out the trail. I'm going to scope out another site Murray marked on the map."

Karie followed the path along the crest of the ridge as Chino ranged ahead. Across the valley she could see the south face of Bryce Mountain where she once waited for the dawn. It all seemed so long ago now. She had forgotten the heart monitor, but she was only going to walk anyway.

It was funny how all her old reasons for wanting to make the U.S. team seemed to have fallen away. Not even that smirking son of a bitch Bernier could tempt her. The whole shebang was on her dime. Lou was right. God knows she would really like to do it for him, and for Dad, and for LunaSi, but it was her deal—hers alone.

At times like this she missed CeeCee. She remembered the first time she had confided in her about the rift with her parents. She could see CeeCee now, tossing that beautiful head of tight black curls, saying, "You never lose family, but a gold...girl, that's tricky."

Karie broke into a light jog as the track angled up a rise. CeeCee was right, it was tricky. Karie understood exactly what that meant now. But had CeeCee implied more? A challenge, or maybe a warning? Suddenly Karie realized CeeCee must have suffered a cruel misfortune she could never shake, just like Lou lived with his own burden. The two of them readily dispensed advice, as if to nullify their regret. But Karie knew she could never shake the feeling of coming that close. Karie's heart caught in her throat. Would it be the same with her? Karie thought about Murray. Wouldn't it be better to tell him what it was like, not what it was almost like? She didn't want to be an example of how not to win.

She was running now, across the very top of the ridge, bounding through the clean mountain air. She would have to choose names for this route if she were to run here three times a week. There would be no Big Smoky Lake like in Goodland, but there would be a Summit, and a Superstition Ridge, and up ahead a Chino Point. Karie remembered writing RUNNING IS WHAT I DO in her log book 10 years ago. *It's still what I do*, she thought as she charged up the last rise before the path curled back down to the truck.

Lou stood in front of the truck holding out a large beach towel. Karie ran right into it and slumped against him as he folded it round her. She leaned against him while she regained her breath. She felt him give her a light squeeze. They called Chino and climbed into the cab of the truck.

"Now I can tell you this." He started the engine and turned back onto the track. "In June 1975, I came in second in the decathlon at the Olympic Stadium in Stockholm. It was my best performance on the entire European circuit—both in position and in points. As they led us out to the track for the final event of the two days, the 1500 meters, I remembered that this was where Jim Thorpe had won in 1912. They called out our names, and the entire stadium was standing and cheering...and to this day I can see each of the faces of the seven other decathletes."

"After all these years?"

"It's that shared threshold, when we were all winners, that is ageless. They can never grow old to me." He clasped her hand for emphasis. "Perhaps you will find that the real value in life is the moment when you all stand together, uplifted by your collective efforts."

They lurched around a curve and she felt Chino's ribs pressing against her arm. "So now you tell me," she said, half joking.

"I didn't want to influence your decision."

She looked at him in surprise. "What if I'd quit?"

"I've known you a long time."

"You've got to give me all you've got, Lou. I may not be as fast, but I will be a better runner."

He nodded. "So what does it for you?"

"I want to step up to the line one more time." *Yes, CeeCee, it's tricky*, she thought, *but I'm going to give it one more shot.*

* * *

Karie had now cut her work at the spa to a half-day in the morning. When Gayle had balked, Karie suggested she fire her, knowing full well that by the time Gayle decided what to do, the Olympics would be over. Karie did her altitude runs in the early afternoon three times a week, then delivered herself to Julie's hands for a full massage.

"I can't wait to get my hands on you," said Julie one evening, about a month into the new regimen.

"You must have been a sorceress in a prior life," said Karie, lying face down on the massage table.

"Today we will start with some routine cross-fiber stuff—until you are lulled into a feeling of false security—then I apply NMT."

"What's that?"

"Naked Man Treatment," said Julie, thinking she'd have to try that with Dr. Laforet. "I discovered it in Bangkok. You soap each other in the hot tub and then massage one another without using your hands." Julie paused, but her fingers were still at work.

"Wow, I can feel that," said Karie, stiffening.

"That's a trigger point," said Julie holding a deep pressure point with her thumb, "and that's what NMT—sorry, neuromuscular therapy to the uninitiated—is all about." As she slowly relaxed the pressure, Karie could sense the increased circulation. "I swear I'm going to soften up this scar tissue till your right leg runs faster than your left."

"It'll help on the curves," said Karie. "Just as well that we run counter-clockwise."

Well before the trip to Phoenix, Julie took Karie to visit a massage therapist who had retired from the spa. Her name was Ingrid, and she was trained in homeopathy. Karie loved the idea of taking tiny portions of plant or mineral extracts to stimulate her defense mechanisms and healing. As Ingrid talked about unique energy fields and magnetic blueprints, Karie thought that someday she might treat her own family with this vital therapy.

Julie had given Karie the remedy *Arnica Montana* the morning of the hemorrhaging. Karie liked to imagine how those little pills under her tongue, a pure distillation of the humble yellow mountain daisy, had gone to work on the damaged blood vessels and cleaned out the lactic acid buildup.

On another visit, Ingrid said, "Now, dear, you need something for the connective tissue. *Ruta Graveolens*. It comes from the rue plant." Karie had no idea what a rue plant was, but knew homeopathy was a long way from testosterone and GH. Over time, Julie became armed with remedies for sprains, heat cramps and even, she said, the yaws.

She also taught Karie yoga positions. Julie had studied with Irina Pavlovska, who drove to the spa from Tucson to teach a basic yoga course which she called Garden of Eden. Although Irina preached poise and harmony in class, Julie felt she undermined the message by bitching about her fee and the commute. Nonetheless, Julie became convinced that yoga was a critical addition to their bag of tricks. It was the best method for developing flexibility, and it formed a synergistic triad with Karie's strength and endurance training. Julie started Karie off with a mix of positions that she had chosen for flexibility, but had also included some that enhanced breathing. "You may think you have a good pair of lungs," she told Karie, "but just wait till you try my new *prānāyāma*—you'll be like the bellows in a furnace."

Karie was surprised at how taut her body became.

"Consider this, my pupil," Julie said, "if a man can eat a fried egg off your stomach without losing any of the yolk, you have arrived."

In the second month of Lou's program, he followed up with another trick. He wanted Karie to mix bounding—taking large strides—into her schedule. They spent one afternoon watching video clips of Kenyan runners and a film of their training camp at Thompson Falls, near the Great Rift Valley.

"Look how they do climbs at over 8,000 feet—they call it Agony Hill. You'd think that with the Kenyans cleaning up everywhere, we'd pay more attention to them," Lou said. "Watch this segment. I call the technique Overdrive."

They sat on the floor, using freeze-frame replays and slo-mos to study the entire sequence.

"See. They shoot out like pinballs, then they ease off their cadence and yet cruise along at the same speed—as if they're in a fifth gear."

Karie said, "It must be that they slightly lengthen their stride."

He nodded. "Believe it. I counted the steps."

"Overdrive—that's neat." *Sort of like gliding*, she thought.

"Like going upstairs three steps at a time."

She watched the segment several times—the runners seemed so effortless. "I think you're onto something, Coach." To be able to maintain speed at a more relaxed pace was every runner's dream.

"Maybe I could sell it to Andy?" he said.

"He spoke of you often—he called you 'that cockamamie Lou Gertz.'"

"And you stood up for me."

"Of course. I said, 'Lou who?'"

"Well, your cockamamie coach wants you to mix some 200 meter bounding stretches into your altitude routine."

Karie had never trained at over 7,000 feet before. She felt she was sucking in twice her normal intake of the thin mountain air. When she first tried out the Overdrive, it set off the alarm on her heart monitor, which registered anaerobic periods of 190 plus beats per minute. Lou wanted her to be cautious; he thought the bounding might jar her body or affect her style. But she persisted. To be able to blast out at the start of the race, then throttle back while your competitors had their tongues hanging out was almost obscenely unfair. Karie found it very appealing.

Once a week she did their version of Agony Hill when she took the Webb Peak trail up to well over 8,000 feet. It left her feeling like road kill. On these occasions, she would lapse into visualization and summon the strength that had protected her since Goodland. It was beginning to come together. She imagined little guys cruising her bloodstream in fast PT boats with red crosses on the sides, and silently, she gave them their instructions. *Zap the lactic in my left quad. Check out the lats, they seem bundled today. I'm feeling a buzz in my right knee and we're about to turn on the after-burner.* On the real high altitude stuff, when her lungs were catching fire, she willed her bone marrow to churn out fresh batches of red blood cells faster than Carl Lewis could dash the straight. For the first time in over two years, she began to enjoy watching and listening to her body.

She soon found out how serious Lou really was about preventive medicine. "This is it, Karie," he would say, "we're on final approach and we can't afford any injuries." So when they took the truck up to the Coronado Forest training site, he would pick up two bags of ice and fill two five-gallon buckets with water. When she finished training, he made her strip off her boots and stand in a plastic garbage can of ice water up to her crotch, a heavy blanket over her shoulders, for precisely 10 minutes. "Horses do it," he said. And when Murray trained with her, Coach dunked him too.

* * *

On her third week of mixing some Overdrive training into her running schedule, Karie began to feel twinges of pain in her right hamstring. Her first instinct was to ignore it—she couldn't bear to stop training again—but then she decided to tell Lou.

"That's it—no more bounding," said Lou.

"I was just beginning to get the feel of it."

"I could tell."

It was his innovation, and Lou sometimes ran with her to perfect the Overdrive technique. He looked so dejected now.

"Maybe that's not the cause," she offered.

"We can't risk it." He shook his head. "Look, four months from now, mid-way to Mount SAC, in November—we're all going to the brand new Olympic Training Center in San Diego. After that, we'll see."

"Time trials?" she asked.

He nodded. "You'd better tell the Earth Mother about the hamstring."

Julie dosed her up with homeopathics, and as an added precaution she insisted on taking Karie to see Dr. Wu Pei, the acupuncturist Murray had called Dr. Prick.

Dr. Wu and his young assistant, Shin Yu-Ling, greeted them graciously. Dr. Wu smiled and nodded as Julie explained their visit, until Yu-Ling returned with small cups of tea and said that she would act as interpreter.

Dr. Wu wore tan slacks and a white short-sleeved shirt as if he had been playing cards in the back of the house when guests arrived. He had a young and open face, and Karie found herself relaxing as Yu-Ling started speaking quietly in the background. Karie let Dr. Wu take her left hand in his while he felt her pulse with his right hand. He wasn't looking at a watch—he seemed just to be listening. Yu-Ling explained that the simplest way for a Westerner to understand acupuncture was to forget about the needles and to think in terms of precise access points on the surface of the body. By locating and treating the blocked access points, the practitioner could act on the vital energy flows to prevent injury or relieve pain.

Dr. Wu now reversed positions so that he was feeling the pulse of Karie's right hand with his left. As he did so, he spoke briefly to Yu-Ling. "He wants you to know that he is listening to music," she said, smiling. "He is reading your pulse in three different positions on each wrist and at two levels, so that he discerns twelve different flows of blood. This is what he calls your life-song. Each pulse is like an instrument of an orchestra."

Karie looked at Dr. Wu, who had now closed his eyes—perhaps something was out of tune. "Can you do this?" she asked Yu-Ling.

"Oh, no," Yu-Ling replied. "I can begin to notice some differences, but it takes years of practice before one can interpret the music." Yu-Ling had graduated from Berkeley in Internal Medicine and was now seeking to integrate her formal training and the practice of medical acupuncture. She said the Chinese teach that energy continuously circulates along 12 pathways known as meridians. An obstruction in any channel of energy acts as a dam. The energy then backs up in one part of the body and is restricted in others. Once the problem has been diagnosed, applying the right stimulus at the acupuncture point gets the energy flowing again and restores balance.

"In my mind," said Yu-Ling, "I try to think of these rivers of vital energy—the meridians—as an electrical flow through the body. And in this way, I see the acupuncture locations as points where you can plug in, like outlets."

Julie said, "I know that when you massage you emit radio waves—" She looked around and saw Dr. Wu had finished listening to Karie's music and sat back smiling.

"He wants to know if you feel any pain—any discomfort?" said Yu-Ling.

"Well, yes," said Karie, not looking at Julie. "Occasionally I feel pain in my right shoulder. It's from an injury I had about three years ago. It's fine now, but sometimes it bothers me."

Yu-Ling and the doctor spoke. Then Yu-Ling turned to Karie and asked her to stand. "My uncle says he thinks your shoulder is okay now, but he hears a discord in your bladder meridian."

Dr. Wu was now looking up at her nodding and smiling. "My bladder is fine," said Karie, taking a step back.

"No, he means the meridian—the pathway," said Yu-Ling. "Let him show you." Dr. Wu lightly touched Karie above the inside of right eye and then gently traced a path over her head to the back of her head. "He is showing you where the bladder meridian goes." Now the doctor used both index fingers to trace down her back, along her thighs and legs to her feet. *What has this got to do with my bladder?* Karie wondered. Yet she felt completely at ease with the doctor, who was squatting at her feet and talking to Yu-Ling.

"He says that the meridian ends at the root of the little toenail on each foot, and it has many acupuncture points along its way."

"How many?" Karie asked.

Yu-Ling turned back to Karie. "He says 67, more than any other meridian. He also says that you need some treatment for your right leg and that maybe you have suffered some trauma?"

This guy's no prick after all, thought Karie, feeling foolish about trying to deceive him by feigning a shoulder problem. "Tell him that I had this injury here at the back of my right knee," she turned sideways to feel the spot, "and I'm worried that it might flare up again." Her reticence gone, the words poured out as if making up for lost time.

"Dr. Wu says he will treat you with a little massage so that you feel comfortable. He will use a little bone instrument on certain acupuncture points. Don't worry, he won't use any needles this time."

As they drove back, Karie said, "Now I understand how over a billion Chinese live just fine without the benefit of Western medicine."

"Don't let Lou introduce you to any more stuff from his bag of tricks," said Julie.

Karie nodded—but she still liked Lou's Overdrive concept and was tempted to keep trying it.

Chapter Nineteen

When Karie saw the track at the Olympic Training Center just south of San Diego, she hoped it was not a mirage. The center perched on a promontory overlooking the Otay Reservoir, as if resting briefly before migrating to some concrete conch elsewhere in California. She rushed down to the brick red tartan and whirled giddily down the 12-lane stretch. From this vaulted platform, she could imagine herself gathering speed down the straight and then wafting out over the water to the golden hills beyond. Excited, she sat in the infield and laced up her shoes.

First she needed to make sure her spikes were right for the track. Then she wanted to keep walking around the oval until she felt comfortable with her plan for tomorrow's time trial. They had driven most of the night before checking into a motel, and it was now early Saturday afternoon. She had agreed with Lou that she'd do a very light workout this afternoon, have the medical tests later and then start visualizing for their big check point on Sunday. If she wasn't within reach of her 4:15 qualifying time for the trials, she would be in deep trouble. They would leave early on Monday so that Murray would not miss too many classes.

After more than three years in Arizona, she was overwhelmed by the contrast in landscapes. Gone were the stark desert lighting and the harsh crenelations of the distant mountains. Here everything looked soft and rounded and nestling—as if the surroundings had tripped out on Ecstasy. The November rays beamed down from an azure sky, a steady shore breeze fanned her face and caressed her legs and arms, and a pair of sculls dipped over the chromatic blues of the lake. Julie beckoned her over to the grass.

"It's time to unify the body, mind and soul," Julie intoned. "High Priestess Julie brings a new *āsana* to her lowly pupil—so watch carefully now."

"This is known as *Nakrāsana*," said Julie, "and as any pupil should know, the name comes from *Nakra*, meaning crocodile. I have chosen the Crocodile pose because it rejuvenates the entire body and makes one feel lively and vigorous—horny too." She lay flat on the ground, head up, and pushed up on her palms so that the rest of her body seemed to levitate in the air. "To tell you the truth," she flopped down on the grass, "it's a real bitch, but the strain is on the wrists, which won't hurt your running." She sat up, rubbing her palms together. "You do a couple of those before the 1500 trials in Atlanta and then throw in the Camel or the Serpent, and your competitors will pucker up tight."

Karie tried a couple of times, without much success. But she had found that any new *āsana* required a huge amount of discipline before she could do it. It was as if the position would not happen unless you committed yourself to it completely in mind, body and soul.

Lou walked up. "Murray has never seen a place like this. Right now," he pointed to the lake, "he's trying out for single sculls." He turned to Karie. "Has the Priestess schooled you in Tantric Yoga yet?"

Julie said, "Not yet, Master."

Lou smiled. "I think my instructor was merely trying to get my attention when I was told about it. All about awakening the coiled snake within, if I remember."

"The *kundalini*," said Julie.

"I remember something about an awareness of the body and a heightened level of feeling," he said.

"The path to enlightenment," murmured Julie.

"And moving energy up and down and between couples. The summit of erotic connection, right?"

Julie bowed. "Just so."

They watched him go. Julie said, "Our peerless coach seems to know plenty. What else is in his bag of tricks?"

Karie stood and stretched. Lou was full of surprises. "Who would've guessed?" she murmured.

Around six they all gathered in the motel lobby.

"I figured we'd head to the Gas Lamp District for food," Lou said. "I haven't seen it since I was in the Marines. Then it was a seedy little area with strip joints and tattoo parlors where sailors hung out. Apparently it's been cleaned up and is quite hip."

"Bummer," Julie said, "I was longing for adventure."

"Do they still have the tattoo parlors?" Murray asked, perking up.

"I dunno," Lou said pulling down on the brim of Murray's ball cap. "Like I said, haven't been there in ages."

Team LunaSi drove to the Gas Lamp District and parked in Horton Plaza Garage. They walked down the block, past a few bars where live music and young kids poured out onto the streets.

"Let's go in there," Murray said.

"It's a bar, you have to be 21. Sorry," Julie said.

"I never get to do anything," Murray moaned.

"Hey look," Karie said pointing across the street at a neon tattoo sign, "they've got something for you."

They headed across the street and spent a few moments looking at the tattoo designs pasted up in the window.

"Hey they do piercings, too!" Murray said.

"Would you get a tattoo?" Karie asked Lou.

"Not my style," he said.

"Then what's this?" Karie asked, pulling lightly on his goatee.

Lou smiled. "What about you? Would you get one?"

Karie shook her head. "I don't want any more needles."

They settled for a Japanese bar and grill called Takasumi's. At eight they were just finishing up their miso soup and chicken teriyaki rice bowls.

Just then a voice crackled over a speaker near the bar section. They could hear the first bars of Madonna's "Like a Prayer" and a man's falsetto matching lyrics to the music.

"Oh my God, karaoke!" Julie cried, "Hurry, let's sit up front."

Julie and Karie looked through the song book. Would-be performers were called to the stage, where they were given a microphone and followed the words printed on a TV monitor. Most of the performers rated "As" for effort, but "Cs" for ability. The two surprises were a tiny woman, all of five feet, who belted out the Aretha Franklin version of "Respect" as if she had made a bet with the devil, and a heavyset black man who sang "Disco Inferno."

Karie was thinking of leaving when the emcee called, "Lou Gertz."

Julie, on her third Red Tail beer, shrieked, "Oh my God," again as Lou walked confidently to the microphone. The music came up and at first Karie didn't recognize the song.

"What song is this?" Karie asked.

"Bobby Darin, 'Beyond the Sea,'" Julie replied, not missing a beat.

On a table off to the side, two girls were making eyes at Lou. Karie watched him. He had a great voice and was really getting into the song, even singing the "hahs" and the "whoa, baby I knows" with a sense of cheeky bravado. She had to admit he was cute the way he smiled around the notes and cocked his head to one side to the beat.

Karie caught Julie looking at her. "What?" she asked.

"Oh, nothing," Julie smiled.

At the end of the song, the entire place clapped, and there were some very shrill cries from the table off to the side. Paul, the emcee, said a very emphatic, "Thank you, Lou!" and went on to his next performer. Lou sat down with a big grin. "Didn't know I had it in me," he said.

"Are you sure you haven't been here before?" Julie asked.

"Yeah, you're just full of surprises," Karie said.

"Where's Murray?" Lou asked.

"Oh-oh, I forgot about Murray," Julie said, "He went to the bathroom before you got up."

Lou went and came back quickly. "He's not there."

"Do you think he left?" Julie asked.

"Must've," Lou said, "Let's go."

Luckily they didn't have to go far. Outside the restaurant they saw a lanky figure heading their way.

"Murray," Lou yelled. He sounded cross.

Murray grinned sheepishly.

"What were you doing? We were worried sick," Julie said.

Murray pulled off his baseball cap and revealed a pierced eyebrow. "Wait, that's not all," he said. He pulled up his right jean leg and revealed the LunaSi logo tattoo—the one-armed cactus with Chino sitting underneath.

"Are you okay?" Julie asked.

"Yeah, the guy gave me some Jack to ease the pain."

"How much is 'some'?" Lou asked.

"A couple of shots."

Lou sighed and Julie laughed. Karie asked, "You don't think you're gonna regret that?"

Murray stopped smiling. "No way," he said seriously, "you guys are in here." He pointed to his chest, "I want that feeling with me for life."

*   *   *

The next morning, Karie felt ready to show her stuff. She was planning to start strong on her first 300-meter lap, ease into a high cruise mode for the next two laps, and hammer home on the bell lap. Murray had become an experienced partner, and she knew he would pace her well, certainly through the first three laps. If he had recovered from last night, he would probably hang in to the finish for his own time trial. He was state champion for two years now in both the 800 and 1500 meters, and took third in the 1500 meters in the July junior nationals. It had done wonders for the stature of his high school coach.

Karie thought about her own high school coach and what he'd done for her. She hadn't clocked herself since her last time trial in Luna—her disappointing 4:42—because she had kept faith with Lou, training without regard to time. Every month she had gone back to the track for a workout, but always it was for pace and feel only. Karie had been under Lou's Halfway Program the entire time and, by the second month, she felt that Lou had gotten it right.

She had repaid him by training with such fervor that her legs were really smoking each time she climbed into the dunk tub of freezing water. Now as she put her left foot to the line and Lou said, "Set," she felt as primed as she ever had.

She went out a little too fast, and then throttled back a bit too much. *Story of my life*, she thought and smiled, pleased at her own relaxed attitude. Perhaps it was the panorama of the lake and distant hills. By the time Lou called, "Bell lap," she felt like a rocket that had jettisoned its tanks, and she flew home.

Lou shouted, "4:14—qualifying time." They locked arms and danced around the infield, and Karie kept saying, "Thanks, guys," and tearily embracing each one, until they lay down on the grass facing each other.

In one brief moment, she caught Lou beaming at her and she wanted to hug him out of gratitude. Instead she said, "It's the strangest thing, here I am feeling like I could do another three repeats—last time I did 4:42 I could hardly stand up."

"It was worse than that," said Lou.

"What?"

"Coach's call," Lou said, turning to Julie. "So I took a few seconds off."

"Just as well," said Karie, smiling up at the sky. "I was ready to quit."

"Well, Murray, the old prairie dog, despite his hangover, finished in 4:26," said Julie. "I do believe that's a PR and a modern miracle besides, all things considered."

Lou said he wanted Karie to run another 1500 and to try mixing in some stretches of slower cadence with a longer stride. Then he wanted to videotape a series of timed 200 sets in which she would alternate between the two cadences, so he could review the slo-mos later.

"OK with you?" he asked, looking at Julie. "We're not going to try any bounding training, this is just research."

"Then why're you doing it?"

"I'll publish and be famous. Even Andy Nagy will beat a path to my door. And if you're nice," he patted Julie on the shoulder, "I'll mention you in the credits."

*   *   *

Later, Lou Gertz pulled another trick from his bag. As soon as they returned to the motel, he told everyone to meet at 7:30 for dinner. He met them in the lobby, clean shaven and goatee free.

"Is that the surprise?" Karie asked as she touched his face.

"Just the first," he said.

They drove up to a little Mexican restaurant in Ocean Beach. As they sat with their menus, two men walked up. One said, "How you doing, buddy?" and gave Lou a big hug. Lou turned to Team LunaSi and introduced his friend Bill Toomey.

"The Bill Toomey from the '68 Olympics photo? Wow!" Karie deadpanned. "You look as if you've just stepped out of the frame."

"A lady of acute perception," said Bill with an impish grin that would put Puck to shame. "Sorry to interrupt, but we'll have to do this quick. I'd like to introduce my friend, Dr. Stefan Berd, from the Karolinska Institute in Stockholm."

Dr. Berd nodded at them and was about to speak when Bill continued. "His research focuses on the free radicals that we read so much about—the rogue molecules in the metabolic process."

"Yes, yes," said Dr. Berd eagerly. He lowered his head as if seeking inspiration. "Picture this. The good molecule is like a beautiful girl walking down a street—while the free radical lurks in a dark alley, intent on doing her serious harm. But a good guy—the antioxidant in the blood—rushes to the rescue and grapples with the radical, so that they both die." He looked questioningly from under his bushy eyebrows. "That is happening inside of you all the time."

"No kidding," said Murray.

"Trouble is, when you exercise very hard, the good guys can't catch all the radicals and," Dr. Berd paused, "your muscle suffers pain, even trauma."

Satisfied that he had their attention, the doctor took off on a lengthy explanation of his work with the Swedish soccer team and the search for products to assist elite athletes in controlling the free radicals. Just when Karie thought that the doctor was about finished, he seemed to get a second wind and began taking them through the detailed results of the tests—introducing a new bogeyman, plasma creatine kinase, which, he assured them, was a ringer for cell trauma, poor integrity and protein leakage. She looked across at Julie, who was rolling her eyes and stifling a smile.

But Bill Toomey interrupted and said, "Look guys, I know how interested you are, but I find I'm responsible for Stefan on this visit, and I don't want to take up too much of his time."

He picked up a shoulder bag and put some bottles out on the table. "Exhibit number one is what the doctor has been talking about—we'll call it Berd's Best. It's what he used so successfully with the Swedish soccer team." He passed a supply of capsules to each of them. A label listed the composition.

Vitamin Q (Co-enzyme Q10): 200 mg.
Vitamin F (Omega-3 Fatty Acids - 60% concentration): 3 g.
Vitamin E: 1,000 I.U.

"Omega-3?" said Julie.

"Yes, I'm glad you asked," said Doctor Berd, beaming. "It's a triglyceride obtained from pure fish oil. Only in Sweden can you get this fatty acid concentration—"

"Trust me," said Bill, "the fish volunteered." Then he turned to Karie, "We've used this combo of ingredients with some serious athletes—decathletes, water-polo players—it works. Protects you against injury, so it permits you to go harder and recover faster."

Karie said, "These are all okay substances?"

"They're vitamin supplements," said Bill. "Ask Lou."

"When I was at Arizona University, we participated in the clinical testing," said Lou. "They work, and they're okay."

"Most of these products are brand new because we weren't aware of their properties or we didn't know how to extract them," said Bill. "Which brings me, " he passed out another set of bottles, "to what we call Vitamin P, for phytochemicals, because they come from plants.

"In the event that you don't wish to incorporate a couple of glasses of red wine in your daily routine, this does the trick. The principal ingredient is from grape seeds. Now I can lecture you on the endocrinology of the phytos, or I can tell you they'll shave seconds off your time and make your hair curl. Trust me."

That sounds like something Andy would say, thought Karie apprehensively, but looking at Bill and Dr. Berd, she decided she wanted to trust them. The products were legal. Lou said they were okay. Whether the effects would be mostly physiological or psychological or both—she really didn't care. They were another trick in the bag. Maybe someday they would rival the popularity of steroids, without the side effects. *A better choice than most athletes face now*, she thought.

On the way back to the motel, Murray kept saying, "I can't believe I met Bill Toomey."

"Did you notice his hands?" Julie asked.

"You mean the ring?" Murray asked.

"No," she said, though he did wear a beautiful aquamarine ring that looked custom made. "I mean his actual hands. They were gracious hands, magnanimous. Too bad I didn't have a chance to read his palm. "

*   *   *

They drove back to Luna at 4:30 the next morning. Julie and Murray dozed in the back while Karie and Lou settled into some strategizing.

Mount San Antonio College was the first hurdle in April '96, said Lou, but it was not a drop-dead date. He had chosen it early in the season so that there would be plenty of other races at which she could qualify for the trials. Realistically she should not expect any dramatic improvement from her 4:14 time at the Olympic Training Center. He wanted her to focus on grooving—she would continue her conditioning over the winter months so she maintained a platform that her body could easily return to without stress. If things progressed, she could drop to a 4:10, and not go higher than 4:15 under normal conditions. Then by March they would work on a program that would have her peak at the trials in June.

"What's it going to take?" said Karie.

"Look at what happened in Barcelona," he said. "Boulmerka from Algeria won the World Championship in '91 *and* the Olympics in '92. It's unusual. She did 4:05 in the World and 3:55 in Barcelona. That's a huge difference."

Lou drank some Powerade and passed her the bottle. "That's why I'm convinced that the trick is to build the platform and lock it in—say it's 4:15. If we can ratchet it down by the day of the trials to below 4:10, then we're really cooking because everything's in reach. What every world-class athlete seeks is consistency."

"So we need to groove 4:15 for now," she paused. "Yeah, we can do that." Karie looked ahead at the first uncertain blush of dawn. "So, Coach, assuming no screw-ups, how will it go?"

"At the trials?"

She nodded.

"No BS, you should make the team." Lou ran a hand through his thick black hair. "When you started out last year, I was just happy to see you back—no great expectations. But now—no problem." He looked at her. "You tell me."

"I'm thinking about it." She reached into her bag for a notepad where last night she had started making notes. Now she went over them again, occasionally looking up at the sky. "I kind of did an inventory—so I could compare with the summer of '92. Here," she tore the sheet off.

Lou put the notepaper on the steering wheel. She had written:

> *Strength - Weights*
> *Endurance - Altitude*
> *Flex - Yoga*

"As regards strength," said Karie, "I can't lift what I was doing by New Orleans—no way. That's what steroids do for you. But I feel I have more resilience now, more snap, like the muscles are smarter."

Lou nodded.

"On endurance, I'm ahead because of the altitude training, I guess. But in '92 I was only doing 800 meters."

"Your hematocrit is now 50," said Lou.

"Is that all?" She wrinkled her nose.

"Don't worry, it's okay. The guy at the training center told me that when you're fit, the blood takes on more plasma and gets thinner. But your total count of red cells is up, and thin blood is good because it pumps faster. You've got hi-test, 95 octane, no-knock in your veins."

"Yeah, I know, I've got the lead out," she said.

Lou laughed.

"Okay, on flex, I'm good. Yoga is a real trick." She looked at him. "Of course, I don't know any Tantric stuff yet."

Lou reached over with one hand and patted her arm. "Tell me about it when you do." He looked back at her list.

Training
- *Halfway Program*
- *Aquatics*
- *Technique*

"On training, what can I say?"

"Yeah," said Lou, "even a blind hog gets an acorn now and then."

"Then on the technique—what about the Overdrive stuff?"

"Look, I don't want you to forget it," he said. "Do some minimum bounding, but don't try to incorporate it into any track practice."

Lou returned to the final part of the list.

Preventive Medicine
  - *Massage*
  - *Homeopathy*
  - *Acupuncture*
Nutrition - Berd's Best

"It's all there," said Karie. "Julie's doing great and Dr. Wu really knows his stuff."

Lou handed back the list. "So what's the bottom line?"

Karie thought back to the Can Do Kid coming into New Orleans, the take-no-prisoners attitude and the overall kick-ass confidence that was then. "I think we stack up pretty good with our bag of tricks—and we don't have the risks." She paused. "But I've got to tell you, if you had people cycling successfully on steroids, GH and EPO—whatever—and doing this list, then they'd have the edge."

He nodded. "But they wouldn't do the list, huh?" He looked at her.

Karie shook her head slowly, "No. They'd figure they already had all they needed."

*   *   *

In April '96, they made the journey to the Mount SAC Relays. Karie had always liked to run there. It was where the Can Do Kid thing had started. Perhaps that was why she felt relaxed, but she also knew there would be other opportunities to qualify.

"I want you to focus on the pace," said Lou. "Watch out if the bell-lap time is over 3:10."

She nodded. Andy would have coached her to win—because every race mattered to him. She had not seen him around, but she hadn't been looking for him either.

"So how does it feel?" said Lou. "The outfit—"

"Oh, it feels fast," she said admiring the blue and gold uniform of Team LunaSi that Julie had designed. "It's the first time I've raced in a one-piece tight."

"It's our first race in 10 years," he said.
"It feels right," she said. "Like I'm back home."

The gun sounded and the athletes jostled for position. Karie realized that competition was even tougher now. Elbows were flying and one woman was DQed for stepping into the infield. Karie's third lap was slow, and she had to pick it up at the bell. But she finished third in 4:12.65, less than two seconds off the lead, and qualified for the trials. She gathered her track bag and wondered whether Peter Bernier would look to interview the winner.

That night Lou treated the team to dinner and gave them each a silver statuette of a runner that bore the inscription:

> *Team LunaSi*
> *April 14, 1996*
> *Mount San Antonio College Relays*

"It's Atlanta in June," he said, and they toasted.

Chapter Twenty

Lou Gertz prided himself on covering all the angles, but now it seemed the red blood cell thing was going to bite him in the ass. Up till now Karie's high altitude training had worked just as nature had intended. With a hematocrit of around 50, she felt turbocharged whenever they swooped down from their mountain training aerie to compete with lowlanders. But that was it—they swooped down and competed a couple of days later. For the trials he had planned to come down some two weeks earlier—for heat and humidity acclimatizing—and he had heard that the red cell count could drop dramatically in a week.

And, of course, it wouldn't it be a level playing field. Any athlete who was doping by taking EPO could time everything just right, without having to climb a mountain to train. Lou had studied the latest report of the IOC Medical Commission which piously noted that while Erythropoietin had been banned since 1990, they were only now getting around to some serious debate on how they might detect violations. The Department of Biochemistry and Molecular Biology at the University of Ferrara had been working on the problem since 1992, but there was still no agreement on methodology. In fact, one stumbling block was how to establish maximal values for athletes who train at altitudes because such training was known to stimulate endogenous EPO production, and no lab test had been able to tell which was faked and which was not.

Lou also contacted two triathletes who trained all summer in Boulder, Colorado, because he knew that they would be on the Kona coast, in Hawaii, well over a week in advance of competing in the Ironman Triathlon. He quickly got the impression that they thought the science was bullshit. Lou thought of their reactions as a little of the steroid saga revisited. When steroids first hit the scene, the scientists had started off by proclaiming that steroids didn't work. But the athletes knew better, and when science belatedly warned of the consequences, nobody was listening. An athletic version of the boy who cried wolf.

In the end, Lou decided to keep his concerns to himself. Even if Karie's blood count dropped, her belief in her added strength could be enough to propel her through to a strong finish. As he watched Karie powering up Agony Hill, at 7,500 feet and 80-plus degrees, he couldn't imagine that her gloriously athletic body would be so fickle as to immediately filter off some of those precious red cells, just because she dropped down to Atlanta's altitude. And now that she was packing some seven million red blood cells per cubic millimeter of blood, he could surely count on every last one of them to do their bounden duty and keep her firing on all cylinders for the full 1500 meters.

Everything else was being fine-tuned just right. They had chosen to focus on speed while maintaining all other aspects of her workout. Now she was doing at least ten 200-meter intervals at her run sessions—although still only three times a week in keeping with the Halfway Program. Karie had mastered the technique of running hard while treading water in the pool, so when she hit the track, she felt as if she were pawing great strips off the tarmac as she accelerated into a sprint. Murray would bring his friends to the track on Friday evenings, and they cheered them both with an intuitive understanding of what they were witnessing.

Julie became more of a mother hen as the time drew near. She had arranged for acupuncture on a bi-monthly basis and had Karie doing the *Ardha Chandrāsana* or Half Moon so she could spook her competitors. Julie also carried enough homeopathic remedies to control a minor epidemic.

*   *   *

Karie got home from her errands and checked the mail. There was another letter from Bonnie. *Probably more photos of Timothy and Gregory*, Karie thought. Bonnie's sons were getting big so fast, and Karie loved the thought that when she ran in the Olympics, her nephews would be watching. Bonnie's letter was sweet. Everything was pretty much the same, according to her. She wrote that

Mom and Dad were well and that Annie would soon be graduating from law school and had gone to New York to interview for a position in a firm. Towards the end of her letter Bonnie mentioned that Annie had run into Rafael on a subway platform. Annie said he looked good and was happy to hear Karie was training again.

Karie hadn't heard from Rafael in over two years. He had written after the Bernier article and again six months later, telling her about a gallery show where his work had been featured. He always sent the letters through Kansas and Karie's mother. Karie looked through the box where she kept her letters and found his number.

Karie rung and hoped for an answering machine. She just wanted to say hi and leave it at that. Rafael answered.

"Hey, it's Karie."

"Karie, chica. How are you?" Rafael sounded very happy to hear from her.

"I'm fine. Actually, I'm really great. How are you?"

Rafael told her about the designs he'd been doing under the Darson Small label and about the gallery on the east side that represented his sketches and paintings. He was at a crossroads and didn't know if he should pursue painting or design. He said he missed the open space of Kansas, but that New York was cool and here he wasn't an exotic, just another Mexican.

Karie told him that she finally made it to the trials, and he was thrilled.

"And then what?" Rafael asked.

"What do you mean?" The question threw her off.

"You used to talk about going to Mexico after the Olympics."

"But that was with you."

"That doesn't mean you shouldn't still go."

Karie was silent.

"Look, Karie, I'm sorry. I don't mean to dredge up the past. I just meant what are you going to do next?"

"I haven't thought about that yet." Karie answered.

"How's your family?" Rafael asked.

They talked for a while longer and then hung up. Karie guessed it might be another two years before she spoke to him again.

*　*　*

On her last rest day before traveling to Atlanta, Karie took another strategy walk with Lou.

"What are you going to do when it's over?" asked Karie.

"You mean when the applause has died and the interviews are finished?"

Karie laughed. "When every piece of confetti has been swept away," she said.

"That's easy," he said. "Whenever I need to chill, as Murray says, I head for the sea."

Karie smiled and then caught herself. She hadn't considered the fact that he might leave. "Where?" she asked.

"Anywhere. But it has to be the right kind of sea with waves that crash and pound—not some tepid little pond. There's something hypnotic about a restless sea." He stopped on the path and held out his hands, with fingers splayed. "By the second day I can feel the tension leaving through the tips of my fingers—it's a renewal sort of a thing."

"The years in Kansas must have been tough."

He laughed. "Actually, sailing brought me to Goodland. In a round-about way, of course."

"Now this I've got to hear," she said.

"When I got out of the hospital in 1976—I think it was May—I threw myself into sailing with a vengeance. I had known how to sail since I was a kid. It was my catharsis. I had failed to make the Olympics, but by God I was going to pit myself against the elements in my other sport, where my injury would not hobble me."

He turned to her. "I haven't talked about this before?"

She shook her head, and they continued along the foothills trail back towards town.

"I signed on to take boats up the coast to Newport, or Maine, or wherever the owners might want them for the summer. Sometimes with a skeleton crew or even on my own—the hairier, the better."

"This was therapy?"

"Yes—I had a lot of demons. And Astrid was never far from my mind. Then I went with a guy who had a 30-foot sloop up to Nova Scotia and I got this crazy idea."

"A sloop?"

"Sorry. That's a single mast with a jib and a mainsail. But she was beautifully fitted out, Marconi rigged and quite fast. So I chartered the boat for a month to sail over to Montreal for the Olympics. I decided I would go across the Cabot Straights to Newfoundland and then do the long haul up the St. Lawrence to Quebec City. Piece of cake, I thought. I could say I made it to the Games."

Lou shook his head. "I've never seen seas like that before. It wasn't just the size of the waves, it was their fierce intensity. On the third day out the wind veered, and I was caught by a Force 8 gale against the current. By next morning, trying to ride out the storm, I caught sight of a ship when I was jacked up on the crest of a huge Atlantic roller. I fired off all my flares and then panicked, thinking maybe my eyes had deceived me."

They walked in silence. Karie remembered old movies with the hero-captain lashed to the wheel as giant seas raged over the deck.

"Luckily, the ship was heading my way. Back at home, life suddenly seemed pretty good. I realized that when somehow, somebody saves your life like that, you'd better put it to good use. I figured I'd been lucky to survive my kamikaze wishes and, quite suddenly, I wanted to share my experiences. So I started teaching and decided to pick somewhere far away from the sea."

"Then I take it back. Kansas was probably perfect." Karie thought of the times she'd sat with Lou in his cramped little office without any idea of how he'd washed up there. *It's funny*, she thought, *I may not have cared that much if he told me then. Now it means everything.*

"I really believed in coaching. We had an instructor in the Marines who used to say something like, 'You cannot help others to be better without becoming a better man yourself.' And all went well, until this final saga at AU, when I quit coaching without a whimper."

"What do you call all the work you do with me?"

"Karie," he said closing his eyes and tilting his head back to the sky, "Like I said, you're a natural. I'm just a technician. You've had all this ability, this stuff inside you, all along." He turned to face her. "I've just shown you the door."

Karie grabbed his arm. "Lou, don't sell yourself short. You have no idea what you've done for me or—"

Lou reached for Karie's hands and held them both in his. Then he placed them flat against his chest. He leaned forward, "It won't be long now," he said.

*   *   *

The track at the Olympic Stadium in Atlanta was brick-red rubber, supplied by Mondo of Italy. At a special press conference, Mondo claimed that the Sportflex Super-X track was identical to surfaces that had allowed over 130 world records. It was considered very elastic and very appropriate for the heat. To Karie it was hard and fast, and it had carried her through the prelims and into the finals of the 1500 meter trials.

Now it was late afternoon on Saturday, June 22, as she looked around again at the brand new stadium. So far, she had not had any surprises from the competition, and her times were consistently under 4:15. Lou said this was fine. Still, she could hardly suppress the desire to let go and bang one out, just to show them her stuff. She was at least four years older than any of the 11 others who now waited for the "Set" call and the chance to make the U.S. Olympic Team.

Lou's only caution had been to watch out for the unintentional rabbit who would go out too fast from sheer adrenalin—until Karie reminded him of her :55 first lap at Indi in '88.

"Of course—you're a three-peat at these trials," he said.

"This is it for me. I'm a no-show in 2000."

320

He looked closely at her.

"Yeah, I'm still a bit nervous," she said.

"Anyone who isn't will test positive." He'd hugged her and gone to join the team in the stands.

Karie sprinted out at the gun to get clear of the pack and then held back from two rookies who were going out way too fast. She had hoped that the pace would be slow, as it had been for her in the prelims, because then she could smoke them in the sprint, but it wasn't. Early on, Suzy Hall, the runner from Oregon that Andy was coaching, established a strong pace and Karie fell in just off her shoulder.

In the stands, Lou felt so wired he folded his arms and hugged himself despite the intense heat. Julie looked sick with apprehension and hadn't said a word. Murray was on his feet, yelling encouragement. Karie had started well and was running smart. She could win, Lou knew, but the unexpected always hovered. After this, he promised himself again, he would quit coaching. By the end of the second lap she was keeping step with Suzy and they seemed to be heading for something under 4:10, which was within Karie's range.

As they came down the front stretch of the third lap, Karie felt that Suzy was easing off a little—perhaps she would overtake her, although Karie would have preferred to hang on her shoulder. Just then she felt her left ankle catch something and she was bumped so hard that she staggered wide, instinctively bringing both arms forward to break her fall. Stabbing the track with her left hand, she yanked her body upright and kept on running as she heard the bell ringing on her left.

Lou leaped up, willing Karie to keep going and regain her pace as a sign that she was not injured. Running wide now and at about fifth, she might still have a chance to qualify. The woman who had tripped her was totally disoriented and didn't seem to know whether she should continue—it would be small consolation even if she were DQed.

Son of a bitch. Karie felt a wave of anger wash over her as she went up the back straight. This was her race. She had been ready to move into the lead, and now there were four women in front. *Please, please, let's get back into that high-stepping rhythm, don't break too soon, and stay wide. I can do it*, she thought.

By the final curve, she was fourth and closing on number three. She kept to the outside running wide, and hit Lane 3 on the final straight. *Yes, that's it*, she thought. She passed into second place. With her head high and arms pumping, she could hear the crowd responding to her furious pace as she bore down on Suzy, who glanced apprehensively to her right as they both crossed the line.

Lou and Murray were shouting and embracing. Julie sank back in her seat.

* * *

"Coach Gertz, congratulations."

Lou had noticed the man watching him at one of the concession areas at the stadium.

"Peter Bernier, from *Inside Track*. I spoke to you on the phone a couple of years ago."

Well, it had to happen, thought Lou. It would be some time before Karie got through with the testing, and he had bet that this little jerk counted on that lull to swoop in. "I remember."

"So Karie Johnson has made it to the Olympics. Thought I'd do a piece on her."

"You already did, remember?"

Bernier looked away.

"Check your files," said Lou. "Let's see, there was, 'A Great American Failure,' and before that something on the 'Can Do Kid'—plus a few others."

"We just do the record."

"Who's we?"

"The editorial staff."

"The staff did a real hatchet job."

"We raised a question."

"That was just to cover your ass," said Lou easily. "What was that about 'a talent so squandered as to make the Baron thrash in his grave'?"

"I think you're taking it out of context."

"I don't give a flying fuck what you think. But you seem to be missing something here—why would I want to talk to you? Why would she?"

"To tell her side of the story."

"To you?" Lou looked puzzled.

"Look, Coach, we both know that Karie would have won if she hadn't been bumped—"

"Tripped."

"Which makes Karie the leading U.S. contender. Plus, I figure she did a bell lap of :58, which is world class if she can get it together."

So the little fuck caught that. "Like I said, I'll talk to her," said Lou. He turned to go and then remembered something. "What's the story on Andy Nagy—I heard he was under investigation?"

"The word is, they've got him. But it won't happen until way after the Olympics."

"Who's telling?"

Bernier looked at him. "CeeCee Thomas. A sprinter who was at Pace. Karie must know her."

*   *   *

Julie insisted on a compression bandage for Karie's ankle and made her sit and rest her foot on the couch in Lou's room. They had already finished a bottle of champagne and were now onto the red wine —"to keep up the phytochemicals," Lou said.

"Coach," said Karie raising her glass, "I vote we go for it."

"Way to go," said Murray, "you had her beat." Suzy Hall had been declared the winner, but their times were identical at 4:11:28.

"All right, let's have it—go for what?" said Julie.

Karie said, "Look, I did 4:11—what would it have been?"

"With the stumble and running wide, I figure you lost two to three seconds," said Lou.

"That's it. I'm doing about 4:08, and I might do a 4:05. I say we go for it."

Lou smiled and said to Julie, "We've talked about this before. World competition is very tough in the 1500 meters—about five to 10 seconds faster—it's a big gap."

"So?" said Julie.

"Thanks to Team LunaSi," said Karie as they clinked glasses, "I've done what I wanted to do. So now I'm thinking, why not give Lou's Overdrive a shot? You know, where I lengthen my stride and ease off the pace? Maybe I can narrow the gap and have a chance—otherwise I'm dead meat." She leaned across the table to Julie, "What the hell, we've got nothing to lose."

Julie shrugged, "Just as long as we don't have to go through another race like today."

"So where do we go from here, Coach?" said Murray

"I've had enough of track," said Julie. "The Gold Club."

"What's that?"

"It's a tittie club, Murray, like the Top Hat in Luna—but nude. Or as they say here, 'nekked as jay birds.'"

"Cool."

"Think he'll get carded? We can always say he's legal in Arizona."

Karie motioned to Lou. "Look." She handed him a card.

It was Andy's. He had written,

Breakfast 9 a.m. Ritz Carlton Buckhead.

Lou looked up, "Did you see him?"

Karie shook her head. "It was given to me by one of his girls."

"You going? It's just up the street."

"No way."

"Maybe he wants to beg forgiveness," said Lou. Then he caught her look, and gave her a hug. "Just kidding."

* * *

Maybe this is a mistake, Karie thought. Then she saw Andy striding towards her in white slacks, a safari jacket and Vuarnet shades. It looked as incongruous as grits in California. She felt much more at ease.

"Thank you for coming," he said.

She smiled. It was good to see him looking apprehensive.

They sat at a table that he had reserved.

"You ran well, Karie."

That was what he had said in Wichita. "I had a good coach."

"Ha. It is good that you remember. I heard that you were training in Arizona and about your change to the 1500—that was smart of you."

She made a note to tell Lou that it was her idea.

"And Gertz—does he use the new techniques? Because we always move on, you know."

"We train, we work hard."

He shook his head. "But now there is new equipment for analysis—"

I bet he still uses the caliper, she thought.

"— and for the women on the Star Program we now use the UCLA facility. We have come a long way."

Perhaps I should tell him that Team LunaSi has the very latest, including a greyhound called Chino. Karie looked perplexed and said, "Really?"

"A lot of new things. They could help you."

"Well, you know, I'm happy to have made it to the Olympics." She shrugged, "I'm just going to try and do my best."

"Do my best—cockamamie stuff." He took off his glasses. "This is not my Karie. You can medal. Even win it all. But not with Gertz."

She looked at him. *He's incredible,* she thought. *It's as if nothing happened—he's ready to pick up where we left off. Go back to his place and watch some tapes.*

325

"He's a good trainer. Not a coach."

"He always said you were the best, Andy." *In a way, of course.*

"Gold, Karie. Gold." He looked around and lowered his voice. "I can get you there. Think. When did an American woman last win the 1500?"

She shrugged. "I haven't really been paying much attention to statistics."

"That's it—it's a total breakthrough. The great comeback. You'll be front page around the world. D'you know what Jackie Joyner gets for appearance fees?"

He sat back as the waiter poured more coffee. "And the modeling. Look at Christy, or Linda, or Elle." He shook his head dismissively, "They don't have gold legs. Tanya would offer you a piece of the action."

What does Jackie get for an appearance—say for the Mobil Indoors? she wondered.

"Movies, Karie. Remember *Personal Best* and *Golden Girl?* Neither of them was worth a shit because the actresses couldn't run." He spread his arms in annoyance.

"Of course, there's a detail you're forgetting," she said.

"Gertz? He can be your trainer."

"I mean you're assuming I can win."

"With me—yes." He paused. "A race is part training, part mental prep. You need me to see your way through the race."

And part is doping, she thought. *He's still at it.* "How are Dr. John and Brad Barnes?"

"I don't know any Brad Barnes," he said impatiently. "Karie, this can be really big time. You'll be set for life. I can make it happen—because we're a team."

She looked at him sadly. "So you want me to go back and tell Coach Gertz goodbye."

"What has he done for you that Andy wouldn't?"

Everything, she thought. She rose abruptly. "I have to go."

"Karie. Karie, wait," he said, "Remember I know you. I know your weaknesses and your strengths. If you want to win, you need me."

"You don't think I can win with Coach Gertz?" Karie smiled inwardly. She could remember Andy telling her to run back to Lou.

"Gertz, what kind of man is Gertz? He's a cardboard coach—no smarts."

Karie bit her tongue.

"You need me," Andy said "It's like that song. You got me under your skin."

Karie suddenly flashed on Brad and the bi-weekly shots. She moved to leave. "I'll think about it." *Right.*

He followed her out. "We're a team. We always have been."

*   *   *

Team LunaSi drove back from the Phoenix airport in Lou's car. The drive was almost as long as the flight. They stopped at a Mexican place in Globe for dinner and it was dark when they got back to Luna. Lou dropped off Murray and then Julie.

"It's late," he said, "d'you want to leave it for tomorrow?"

"I've got some beer," she said.

"Two's the limit."

She laughed. Lou had cut his RDA to two beers as a gesture of solidarity with Karie and as a subtle hint to Murray, on whom he'd been keeping an eye ever since San Diego.

"How was the super coach?"

"He wants me back."

"He spoke highly of me?"

"That too, of course." She paused. "He said we're a team, he and I. That got to me." Karie sat with her head bowed and scratched distractedly at a crack on the kitchen table.

"Lou." She grabbed both his hands impulsively, "Just bear with me. All the way home I've been trying to figure it out. When he said a team, something clicked." Karie got up and started pacing around the table. "I've been trying to remember things. And I can see my own complicity in the doping—"

327

"Karie, you can't—"

"Please, Lou, stay with me on this." She stood behind him and began to rub his shoulders. "I've been playing the role of the innocent little dupe who was tricked by a switch to testosterone. Now something inside me says that I must deliberately have switched off. Denial, pure and simple. I should've known that I was way too strong to train the way I did. I just didn't want to know. That's probably why I didn't take his ass to court."

"You think Andy knows that?"

"Knows? It's what he believes. To him, we are accomplices," Karie said. "That's probably why I went to see him today. Here I am, finally winning," she continued, "and I still have to deal with this shit." She sank down across from him, and they sat in silence.

Finally he said, "You feel like an accomplice?"

She nodded.

"Well, don't stop there—go with it. There's a purpose. It's what I came to believe in."

She searched his face. "I don't follow."

"You may have blocked it out—or not—but you've been given another chance." He stood up excitedly. "Don't you see? You're clean now. You have a chance to do it right."

Karie stood up slowly and put her arms around him. "Keep telling me that."

*　　*　　*

Lou had forced himself to leave Karie's place last night. The cot in the room over Oscar's garage was always pretty dank, but last night it had seemed especially uninviting. He couldn't remember when he'd wanted a woman that bad. Not even Astrid made him feel like Karie did, but Astrid was his reason for holding back. Karie was going for the big time. Even with all her experience, the Games were a pretty heady event. Lou knew all that pressure could throw people together for a spell, only to leave someone in the lurch when it was all over. No way was that going to happen to him again, and he cared too much for Karie to do that to her. *No*, he thought, *this is going to be done right*. Besides, there was work to do.

Lou picked up the phone and dialed Karie's old Marina del Rey number. It had been disconnected, but there was a forwarding number and Lou quickly scratched it down on a pad of paper. He dialed. A woman's voice answered.

"CeeCee Thomas?" he asked.

The woman hesitated. " Who's calling?"

"This is Lou Gertz, I'm a friend and coach, actually, of Karie Johnson."

"Karie? Oh, I know who you are. Karie used to talk about you a lot. How is she?"

"Good."

"Tell her I said hi and congratulations," CeeCee said. Lou could hear a smile behind her voice.

"CeeCee, this may seem out of the blue, but I heard you were bringing charges against Andy Nagy."

"Where did you hear that?"

"Let's just say a little Peter Bernier Bird told me."

"Ugh, him. Did you see that piece he did on Karie?"

"I think too many people saw that piece," Lou replied.

"I don't want Karie to get involved," CeeCee began. "I know she's had it rough, and I don't really need her testimony. I've talked with other runners. A girl named Trish Edelman agreed to testify with me. Andy had Trish wrapped around his thumb. She thought she was going to marry him."

"So you and Karie were on the stuff together?"

"No, we never even talked about it. Except for the times I tried to warn her," CeeCee said.

"She's stubborn." Lou chuckled.

"No shit," said CeeCee, laughing a bit as well. Her tone became serious again. "I was on the stuff before L.A. in '84. I had to tank my Olympic preliminaries. Do you have any idea what it feels like to lose a race on purpose?"

"No, I don't. I'm sorry." *That's worse than not being able to show*, he thought.

"That's okay. I figured Karie was on the juice by the way she was acting, but I was positive when I taped her and Andy talking."

"You taped her? Does she know?"

"No. Yeah. I know, not a very cool thing to do. But I just knew something was up. Andy came to our place. He hardly ever hung out at the girls' apartments. He always wanted them at his place. He came over when he knew I'd be gone, and he looked pissed when I was there. On a hunch, I went back in and set the answering machine to record externally. Turned out I was right. I still have the tape."

"You do?" Lou asked, "What are you going to do with it?"

"Actually, I was going to mail it to her after the Olympics. I figured the last thing she needed now was to be reminded of that scumbag. I don't need it anymore. For years I kept it just to remind me. It kept me angry and on my toes. Anyway, now we've got Andy on our testimony alone."

"Well, believe it or not, after the trials the scumbag offered to coach her again," said Lou.

"I believe it." CeeCee sounded disgusted.

"I'm curious. Why now? Why not in 1984?"

CeeCee sighed. "Man, a lot of reasons. I'm married now. It's actually CeeCee Thomas-Fierson. Robert and I want kids, but we are having trouble and the doctor thinks it may be the steroids. Who knows? But it's not so much that. It's the mother thing in general. If I have a daughter, I can say 'Mommy almost went to the Olympics, and here's why she didn't.' I will have no problem telling her Mommy made some mistakes. But I couldn't bear to look into my child's face and tell her I didn't do a thing about it. I knew what I was screwing around with. I don't think Trish and Karie did. Andy used them. I can stop him from doing it again."

"CeeCee, I think you are the one who deserves to be congratulated."

"Hey, something's got to give somewhere," she said.

Lou figured they had 30 days to work on technique. He started by asking himself what the physical limitations were. Was it that the muscles lacked strength or was it that the body couldn't deliver oxygen and sugar fast enough? It sounded like a chicken-and-egg thing. But then why should a slightly lengthened stride in the middle reaches of a race allow you to save stamina without sacrificing speed? Maybe the longer cruising stride was more efficient. Perhaps it used a different balance between the hamstrings and the quads. Either way, they didn't have a place to do biomechanical testing, so it would have to be trial and error.

"You realize we might screw up?" he said. "Your times could get worse."

"So?"

"If you can get down to 4:05 without the Overdrive training, maybe a little lower, you could medal."

"Sure—as long as a couple of the front-runners trip and others test positive."

"Okay, just checking," said Lou.

Everything on the training schedule stayed the same, except that for the first two weeks he wanted her to mix in the lengthened stride. For the final two weeks, Karie would try it on the track. Lou advise her to take the first lap, or lap and a half, at a strong pace, then shift into Overdrive and cruise. "You may drop back a little. Just do it as long as you can hold it through the third lap, and then on the bell lap shift back into top gear and go for it." The trick was being able to move back to her normal rhythm, because that's where her kick speed came from. "Just like when you floor the accelerator in a car," he said. They agreed to heavy up on the preventive medicine to accommodate the increased level of stress.

Karie knew that what they were trying to do was right. The energy saved more than made up for any lost ground. She could make it pay off on the last lap. Lou said it was like feathering the propeller on a plane. The only problem was that it would normally take a season of racing to get comfortable with the technique, and they only had a month.

By the end of the third week she knew it was going to be hit or miss. "I've only got two problems," she said. "First I have difficulty changing into Overdrive. Then I can't get back out." She was surprised to see Lou look so worried.

"Maybe I'm just messing you up," he said.

"Lou—"

"At this stage, maybe it's like buying a ticket halfway to Europe."

"Lou, don't say that." She gripped both his arms. "This is my only chance. Stay with me."

"I'm worried, Karie," he said quietly. "I'm worried that it's just a theory that won't work. You deserve better from me."

"It's all or nothing for me, Lou. I don't want to come in fifth or fifteenth." She smiled and stepped back. "We're going for it, okay?"

"Okay," he said. "We'll know pretty soon."

"And you'll be down to the sea again."

"There you go," he said enthusiastically. "It's the same principle as setting a sail on a boat," he angled the plane of his hand in demonstration. "All other things being equal, one boat goes faster. That's the technique."

She could see him in a pair of cut-offs, trimming the sails, or whatever sailors did. "Will you take me sailing? Way out—like out of land-sight?"

"You've never done that?"

She laughed. "Once I went from Marina del Rey to Catalina Island on a motor yacht with a crew. People shot skeet off the stern."

Lou was silent. "You've never heard the sound of the rope beating against the mast at night, when you're at anchor?" He looked up and closed his eyes. "Sometimes, when I can't sleep, I think of that."

Chapter Twenty One

"ATLANTA IS READY. Y'ALL COME." The waggish head-line caught the mood. The city had finally decided to kick back, celebrate its southern heritage and enjoy the Summer Games.

In the beginning, Atlanta had looked for love everywhere. Awed by the success of Barcelona, the city had agonized over how to create its own Rambla among the jumble of downtown and how to rival the cathedral of the Sagrada Familia with landmarks like the Big Chicken, a weird metal construction over a fast-food out-let. But few foreign visitors were impressed by the city's efforts to spiff up and attempt an international panache. The press viewed Hotlanta as a plump target and had a great time ridiculing "Bubba" and the "Redneck Games."

As time passed, Atlanta got fed up with self-analysis and apolo-gizing for the weather, and the city simply decided to be its friendly self. After all, it was the home of the Centennial Olympics, the greatest peacetime event in history. Why worry about journalists anyway? They were normal, biased folks, with small spaces to fill and deadlines to meet. So the city boosters hoped everyone would be of good cheer, something along the lines of, "We hope y'all have a high old time, but if you don't despite all we have to offer, then come back when the leaves begin to turn."

The official blessing was, of course, never in doubt. Juan Anto-nio Samaranch, President of the International Olympic Commit-tee expressed, as was his custom, the belief that the 26th Olympiad would be the "best games ever."

Atlanta *was* ready. Some things had to be made secure. The uranium core was removed from the nuclear reactor at Georgia Tech and placed out of harm's way. And for the first time in a hundred years, doves would not fly at the Opening Ceremonies. Their high mortality rate, due to poor night vision and the pres-ence of the Olympic cauldron, had been deemed too high a price for the symbol of peace.

Some things that weren't there, now were. The Olympic Sta-dium would live only for the Games, and then be sliced up to become a new baseball park. A new aquatic center, horse park, tennis complex and shooting range now stood ready for the champions. So much earth moved, and so many new facilities built. More people from more countries than ever before, and more enterprises to feed on them. Even the taxi drivers had spruced up their cabs and could be relied on to ferry visitors to the better-known locations.

Other things were less visible. Security had received the attention of the best and the brightest, and access to restricted areas was protected by a new system that read the geometry of the palm of your hand. It was further rumored that sample analysis for drug control had been tightened and that new testing equipment was on hand. Yes, Atlanta was ready.

Now, a week before the opening ceremony, rising up over the drowsy magnolias and the urban press was the fever and excitement of the event. A druidic gathering of the world family, drawn together by an obscure symbol of five rings that traced back to ancient Greece. And in all the bright faces of the hosts was the hope that the South would do itself proud.

As they drove in from the airport, Lou said, "I came to Fort Benning for a meet once, and a couple of times we snuck off to Atlanta in the evening."

"Well?" said Julie.

"It was a fun place."

"Is that all?" She persisted, "No lurid details? No telling of your heroic deeds on the field, followed by nights of even sturdier prowess?"

Lou laughed. "The early '70s was the time of the great debate in athletic circles about sex or abstinence before your race."

"Or sitting on the side of the bed," said Julie.

"How about sex instead of?" said Murray.

"So what's the word, Coach?" said Karie.

"Jury's still out." He turned and looked at her, "We need more research."

Karie smiled and looked out at the Atlanta skyline. It would not be long now.

* * *

When Andy got back to his room, the message light was on.

"Nagy, old fellow," said Dr. John. "Hope you've tucked all your talent in for the night. Anyway, a spot of news for your ear only."

Andy kicked off his shoes and stretched out—the doctor always took his time.

"Have you heard of a high-resolution mass spectrometer?"

"No."

"Well, Atlanta has it now."

He makes it sound like a disease, thought Andy.

"It's a much better mousetrap, you see. My fellow tells me they can detect some steroids as far back as four months."

"Now wait a damn minute." Andy jerked upright. "What the hell has that got to do with us?"

"Nothing really—but it might."

"For Chrissake, will it or won't it?"

"Look, dear chap, I don't like you barking at me like that," said Dr. John irritably. "Now just calm down, old cock."

Andy mouthed, Fuck you. *Goddamn Brit was lecturing him again*.

"As I was saying, Mr. Nagy, this new equipment can pick up a trace of *exogenous* steroids from way back." He paused deliberately because he knew Andy would be trying to decipher that one. "*Exogenous*, as in outside the body—unlike testosterone. And of course, it has no effect on GH or EPO."

"So we're all right then," said Andy testily.

"Not so fast, Coach. Are you sure your charges have not popped any extra pills of late?"

"What d'you mean?"

The doctor shook his head—Andy was falling into denial these days. It was not a good sign.

"What I mean is that some of your athletes might have strayed from the straight and narrow when they were at the gym, say, and gobbled a pill or two. Maybe some D-bol or Anavar, when they

335

were on an off-cycle." He paused. "Does that ring a bell, Coach?"

Andy was silent.

"They've been told it would clear the body in two weeks. But now this high-resolution process can catch it."

"Nobody would be that stupid," said Andy.

"Well then, you have nothing to worry about, do you? You can sleep well."

"Why are you telling me this now, when we're three days away—"

"Forewarned is forearmed," said Dr. John and hung up. He sat for a moment, thinking. Nagy didn't seem to understand the consequences.

*   *   *

On Wednesday, July 31, at 10:15 a.m., the Olympic Stadium looked like a three-ring circus. There was the qualifying round of men's pole vault and the men's long jump—part of three decathlete morning events—and the first round of the women's 1500 meters, all taking place at the same time. Karie Johnson ran in the first heat and placed third in a slow race.

"I couldn't get the fricking thing in gear," she told Lou as they were walking through the tunnel under the stadium. Patches of sweat were dampening the blue and white uniform with the spray of red stars. "It's just tough to get the rhythm." She stopped and shook her head. "Then you've got to watch out, because all those arms and legs were really flying."

"It looked pretty good," Lou said softly.

She looked up, eagerly. "You think?"

He put an arm around her. "We'll wait for you outside."

Lou watched her go. So calm and beautiful in repose—she had just been one explosive figure of action, as her body did what it had been trained to do. First, her ATP matches ignited for a three-second flash off the pad. Creatine phosphate burned for another seven seconds before passing off to the lactate system for the duration. In the meantime, a five-bell fire alarm was sounding as electric impulses flashed through the system, and the heart thumped it out at 200 beats per minute.

Now here we are, he thought, *just talking it over as calmly as if we were choosing an entree for lunch.* Tomorrow it would be the same. He walked off to round up the others.

* * *

On Thursday, August 1, at 7:30 p.m., Karie ran the second semi-final and qualified for the finals. Tenth position in a field of 12.

"Jesus, I panicked," she said.

Lou hugged her. "Two down, one to go."

"Re-entry's a bitch." They walked together. "Here I'm grooving along in Overdrive, and I can see they're hurting and suddenly the bell's going. And I'm trying to snap out of it and work the change up; otherwise, there's no after-burn."

She stopped and turned. "The only reason I made it was because I was so pissed with myself that I wanted one more shot."

He smiled.

"It's been great, Lou—but now I want more. I want the gold."

"I think you've got the hang of it now. The bugs are out."

"Goddamn, I'm ready to show them some stuff. But I need to know that you're there. It's all or nothing, because if I'm heading for gold that means you are too. You can't sit on the side of the bed on this one." She was really worked up by now and held his hand in a tight grip.

"Karie, I'm with you, all the way."

* * *

Lou had agreed to meet Peter Bernier in the bar of the Tongue and Groove Club in Buckhead. It was early, and they found a table in a corner, away from the band.

"Congratulations, Coach. Now for the finals."

"She ran well," said Lou. Even this little jerk seemed agreeable to him now.

"Tell me about this cruising thing that Karie is doing."

"You caught that, did you?" Lou was pleased.

"Everyone's talking about it, Coach."

Lou sat back and smiled.

"Some coaches are saying it's a key breakthrough in training. Others say the opposite, that she's doing well in spite of it."

"What d'you think?"

"I think she's cut about five seconds off her time in a month, so she must be doing something." Bernier leaned forward. "I think this is big, and I'd like to do an exclusive on it."

"Karie just likes to mix it up a bit," said Lou. *Let him dig.*

"Andy Nagy doesn't go for it," said Bernier. "He said I could quote him." He pulled out his notebook, " 'Anyone who cruises, loses.' But Andy's not having a good Olympics."

"Really," said Lou. "I know Suzy Hall didn't make it today in the 1500"—Karie had beaten her easily in the same semis race— "but I thought he had some other women?"

"Coach Gertz," Bernier chided gently, "you're not in the buzz. Sure he's got one Pace woman who made it to the long jump finals tomorrow and someone in the 400 meter relay, but the big deal is Andy's stealth athlete—a young 100 meter hurdler straight out of Pomona State."

Lou shook his head. "What in the world is a stealth athlete?"

"He's had her under wraps all season. She would only show in some remote meets, and he never allowed any interviews. Well, turns out she's one explosive kid. She makes it to the finals and gets a bronze. Just like that—out of nowhere, to world class." Bernier looked around and said, "The word tonight is that she tested positive—for Anavar or some simple shit like that."

"So she's DQed?" Lou didn't bother to suppress his smile.

"Not exactly." said Bernier. "Do you know how this works?"

Lou shrugged.

"First, the lab issues a finding on Sample A and it goes to the Medical Commission of the IOC. The commission reviews the data and contacts the athlete, the coach, the Federation, the NOC, whatever, and then the offender is given the option of witnessing an identical procedure on Sample B."

"So Andy has been notified?"

"Takes the shine off the celebration for sure. It'll take a day or two still if they test the B, but it's pretty certain. And it won't help Andy." Bernier was relishing the story. "Now, Coach, what about Karie Johnson?"

Lou took his time. "I could talk to her. I think she deserves a good story after your last job."

Bernier put away his notebook.

"A very positive article," Lou persisted.

"Of course, Coach."

Lou stared at him. "Fuck with me and I'll come after you."

"I'll let you read it before we print."

"As long as we all understand the program," said Lou easily. "You can talk to her after the finals. Ask her about Overdrive."

"Overdrive." Bernier got his notebook.

"Karie will tell you the key is discipline. The athlete has to believe..." *Handling the press can be fun*, thought Lou. "You know, Bernier, you could have Andy's comments on the technique and Karie's response."

"Yeah. Coach and athlete. Point and counter-point."

"There you go." Lou stood up.

"Coach—what can I say?"

Unctuous bastard. But Lou couldn't wait to read the story.

*   *   *

Saturday, August 3, was the big ticket day for track and field with prime-time finals starting at 6:30 p.m. for high jump, javelin, relays, 1500 meters and 5,000 meters. There had been a thunderstorm in the late afternoon, and the air was heavy as the crowds moved into the Olympic Stadium.

Eigel Johnson looked uncertainly at Lou and Karie as they stood outside the Cheney warm-up track. He asked Coach Gertz, "Don't you two need to talk? I don't want to be in the way." All he wanted was to accompany his daughter to the point where she would check in for her race.

"It's okay, Mr. J," said Lou. "Karie knows what to do." There was no longer any need to talk plans or competition or cautions— she was ready. "The latest heat index is 93—it's more in there," he nodded toward the stadium, some six blocks away.

"Home country advantage," Karie said. She was the only American in the finals.

"The early predictions were for a 3:55 time," he said. "But I think anything under 4:00 will be tough."

"Here." Lou took his badge, put it around Eigel's neck and handed him Karie's bag. "You're in charge now." He hugged Karie and walked off towards the stadium.

Eigel looked at the entrance to the Cheney facility and the two uniformed security guards. "Do you have to check in soon?"

"I can go in two hours and 20 minutes before race time for warm-up and treatment, but I don't have to be in the call room until one hour before," she said. "We've got plenty of time."

"Let's walk a little."

"Sure, Coach." The pavement was still damp from the storm and occasional raindrops fell from the dogwood trees that lined the street.

"Remember the other day when you lined up for the semi-finals," he said, "before you were called forward to your mark?"

"Yes." She smiled at the technical detail. "We stand on the dotted line, three meters back."

"Right. Well maybe it was the tension or something but I had this thought. It suddenly occurred to me that we had to have two wonderful daughters before you came along."

Karie stopped walking and looked at him.

"As if it had been so ordained beforehand, you see." He glanced quickly at her. "So you could not have been born had Bonnie and Annie not come before you."

"Yes," she said uncertainly.

"So we are all linked. And when you run, we all run, as a family." He turned to her. "I guess that's why I've been so hard on you, because you carry us all."

"Dad—"

"That's why I demanded so much of you, because you had to do it for all of us."

Karie said, "There were times when I thought you were being way too harsh. But now I'm grateful in a way. It's like...what's the word you said...pre-ordained?"

"You think?"

"You have to be hard to handle this stuff, Dad. If you weren't the tough guy, I would've never made it."

"I always hated that son-of-a-bitch Nagy. I'm glad you're rid of him." He smiled and put his arm around her. "Is it going to be tough? I mean, will it—?"

"Hurt? You bet. That's what I do best—a high pain threshold."

"What that asshole Bernier called 'heart.'"

"You got it."

They stopped close to the security gate. "I'll be running with you."

"Dad." She put her arms round him. "Now I'm getting nervous. Race jitters are always a bitch. One minute you're fine, the next...I'm scared."

"Don't be."

"I really want to show you guys my stuff."

He held her shoulders. "You've already done more than we could ever hope for. I don't care if you walk it."

"You really mean that." She smiled happily at him. "Don't tell anyone, Coach, but I'm going to pop the cork on this one."

"You'll have 80 thousand people going bananas."

Karie passed through the gate into Cheney Field. Now she was ready to focus.

           *   *   *

At 6:50 p.m. Karie went to the call room and was issued her race bib, as well as her hip number for the line-up order. Shortly after that the runners boarded the bus for the short ride to the stadium, where they were told to be ready for final call at precisely 7:20 p.m. Karie felt as if she were in the bowels of a huge ship. The movement in the stands echoed down into the concrete corridors above the constant drumming of the crowd. Then she heard the strains of the German national anthem. *Probably for the javelin,* she thought. She was suddenly eager to emerge onto the field in the vast amphitheatre of people. This is what it was all about, a celebration had its beginnings on a plain in ancient Greece. Now she was part of it.

Calm down, she told herself, as they were ushered into the stadium call room. As she waited her turn, she glanced at the time sheet for Athletics Day 8 that was pinned to the wall and found the schedule for W 1500m Final:

Check-in Call Room	19:20	Minus Time 0:30
Depart Call Room	19:35	Minus Time 0:15
Arrive FOP	19:40	Minus Time 0:10

I suppose FOP means field of play, she thought. *How quaint.*

Race	19:50	Minus Time 0:00
End Event	20:10	Plus Time 0:20
Post TV/Enter Mixed Zone	20:15	Plus Time 0:25
Awards Ceremony	20:35	Plus Time 0:45

And who will that be, she wondered? After her semis on Thursday, she had seen the winner and finalists in the Women's 100 hurdles paraded before the barricade of the world press. How would the ancient Greeks have handled it?

                           342

| *Media Interview* | 20:50 | Plus time 1:00 |
| *Report to Doping Control* | 21:50 | Plus time 1:20 |

So one hour and 20 minutes for the urine sample. She had been tested after her prelim, but not after the semis. Maybe they'd lost interest in her. Now she came to the check-in table where it was all business: spikes, not more than 11 per shoe and a maximum length of nine millimeters; uniform in accordance with the photos submitted by each National Olympic Committee; and, finally, they put tape over the Team LunaSi emblem on her gym bag.

They lined up and were led out into the tunnel by two marshals and followed by the kids who carried the baskets with their belongings back from the line-up. As they emerged from the air conditioning, Karie felt the heavy evening air wrap around her. *Lou's right, people are going to get real tired. There's really no point in trying to psych these women with a Half Moon āsana—not now, anyway.*

As they came onto the field of play, Karie felt like breaking ranks and whirling around the stadium to dispel her sudden surge of energy. This was the ultimate platform. She had stepped through a door. Nothing could corrupt the purity of the moment, and she felt like racing down the straight and up into the enfolding crowd. Karie turned to wave toward where she knew Team LunaSi was sitting in the stands—was that Lou?

Come on Karie, don't lose it, don't get hyped like you did at Indi. Focus, get in the zone, start visualizing the race, you're going to need every last bit of this energy for the track.

What was it Lou said? "You've been given another chance to do it right." *This is your home turf, so look at these women, and remember how you're going to handle each of them. Hold them off or haul them in, and let them drop behind you.*

Now the official countdown was on. Officials signaled that the track was clear. Timers checked their instruments. The special high-speed video equipment was already rolling, and reporters from almost 200 countries were priming their audiences. The crowd hushed as the starter ordered, "On your mark." Karie was number 9 in the line-up, and she intended to get ahead of the main group even if she had to sprint.

As the smoke puffed from the starter's gun and the sound barreled through the stadium, Tanya Likovna from Russia raced to the lead with Karie tucking in behind her. *Keep strong into the second lap*, she thought, *and then increase stride and ease the cadence.*

Lou could see a tight knot of runners behind Karie, and then the field strung out. He knew she was going to be aggressive. He just hoped she'd save enough for a strong kick. There were three women who had PRs of under four minutes, and Karie's best chance was to bag them with her kick. Murray was already up and yelling. Julie was in a rabbit-in-the-headlights trance. Nancy and Eigel Johnson, having reminded themselves once again that at least Karie made it to the finals and they shouldn't expect too much, now huddled together for support.

As the runners came down the front stretch at the end of the second lap, Karie had already eased into the slower cadence, hoping she wouldn't lose ground. But she was hurting more that she should at this stage. Maybe she'd gone out too fast? Or the Overdrive wasn't giving her much relief? Or maybe the heat was making it an even more painful race. She was already breathing pretty heavy. *Try and keep above the pain, Karie*, she told herself.

She was still running a couples of paces behind Likovna but, as they rounded the curve into the back stretch of the third lap, two women jumped past her—Bourgiba of Morocco, the world record holder, and Alessandri, the Italian. At the top of the next curve she could see that Bourgiba was right on Likovna's shoulder with Alessandri in step behind, and they seemed to be pulling away. *I've got to stay with the plan*, thought Karie—*if I try to snap out and chase them, I'm dead meat for the kick.* She remembered Lou saying, "All athletes make mistakes…every race is different…they've never done Atlanta."

The bell rang for the lead group, just as Karie heard someone else coming up behind her.

Jesus, thought Eigel Johnson, seeing Karie drop to fifth at the start of the bell lap, *she must be hurting bad*. He wished he could be running on the track beside her, to shout out that he loved her and that all he wanted for her was to have a good race.

Murray was saying, "She's going for the change-up now. She's going for it." He had run with her so many times he knew the routine, but he could see that she was leaving it late.

Lou watched Karie going into the curve and gauged that Bourgiba, who had passed the tiring Likovna, was now about 10 meters ahead. Karie was now barely holding fifth. *If she's going to pop the cork, it'll have to be now.*

Andy had seen the moment when Karie eased off her cadence in the second lap; now he shook his head. *That two-time cockamamie stuff wasn't worth it.* Gertz was expecting too much from his athlete—even for Karie. Well, she was learning now what bad coaching does to you, when she could have had it all. Even if she did come back knocking at his door, it was time to move on. But it would be fun to give her a good spanking, set her straight—that's what she had always needed.

Karie sensed that whoever was just behind her would keep the draft and then slingshot past her onto the final back straight. *Enough,* she decided angrily, *this is it.* She snapped her arms into a faster rhythm and felt her legs jump into the cadence. *I'm gonna spook somebody even if I crash and burn.* As she drew level with Likovna she heard her breathing and saw how ragged she was. *Maybe everybody's really hurting. Let's see how they handle the pain.* For the first time she felt the spark of opportunity, and it deadened her own screaming voices. *This is my country, so let them puke,* she thought. Just ahead, she could see Alessandri's shoulders had dropped and her arms were looser. Karie tore into the last curve with her head high and her legs pumping.

Lou jumped up the moment she snapped into high gear on the back stretch. Suddenly he remembered her at Indi. *That's it. It's the pepper kicking in. She won't quit. Pepper in the blood.* He felt his own blood raging through his veins.

"Coach, Coach." Murray had his arms around him and was shouting, "She's cutting loose. Son of a bitch, look at her go."

Lou felt a painful grip on his right arm and realized it was Julie digging in with her nails and leaning into him like a dead weight. He knew Karie would keep hammering until she dropped. *Please, don't let anything happen to her.*

Nancy Johnson leaped up with clenched fists and started yelling, "Come on, Karie. Go, baby, go."

The crowd sensed the same spark of opportunity and were now roaring for the red-white-and-blue Karie Johnson who was high-stepping past Alessandri, as if their collective voices could sweep her round the curve and blow aside her challengers.

Karie swung onto the home stretch and saw Bourgiba twist her head around. *It's just you and me now, and I ain't backing off. Focus on the finish. Keep the rhythm and keep driving.* She pulled even and, for one mad moment, out of the corner of her eye, she glimpsed Bourgiba's clenched face and her desperate stride. Then Karie moved ahead. There were the last, final lunging steps as she crossed the finish, and the screen flashed 3:56.81. She tried to raise her arms and almost blacked out. She felt an arm around her as she gasped for breath.

Karie felt the noise from the crowd revive her, and she reached for the Stars and Stripes as the waves of sound washed over her. She jogged back around with her arm high and the flag billowing out behind her. *It's finally over for me now*, she thought. *I can move on.*

She looked up at the stands. Her eyes searched for her parents and Lou but couldn't make them out. The wind whipped the American flag with a snapping sound and she heard the rope beat against the pole. Karie smiled. *I'm going sailing.*

About the Author

Brian Dyson is perhaps best known for his 35-year career with The Coca-Cola Company where he served successively as President of Coca-Cola USA, then as President of Coca-Cola North America, and finally as President and CEO of Coca-Cola Enterprises. Throughout his life he has competed in athletics, achieving national ranking in triathlon and squash racquets events.

After retiring from Coca-Cola in 1992, Dyson founded Chatham International Corporation, a consulting and investment firm, and pursued an erstwhile dream of writing fiction. *Pepper in the Blood*, Dyson's first novel, deals with the competitive world of international track and field and draws on his organizational knowledge of the sport, as well as his involvement in the Olympic Games as an attaché for Argentina.

A native of Argentina, Dyson grew up on a 4,500 acre ranch in the pampas. He studied economics at the Facultad de Ciencias Economicas in Buenos Aires, and later at the Harvard Business School. Dyson lives in Atlanta, Georgia, with his wife Penny. They have two daughters, Tania Louise and Susana Carolina.